That which the deep heart knows

To Lisa
Wishing you all the best for an enjoyable read!

RJ/xx

RJ Wheldrake

Copyright © 2022 RJ Wheldrake. All rights reserved

No part of this publication may be reproduced, distributed, ortransmitted in any form or by any means, including photocopying, recording, or other electronic or mechanical methods, without the prior written permission of the publisher, except in the case of brief quotations embodied in reviews and certain other non-commercial uses permitted by copyright law.

ISBN: 9798836558253

For Linda

Erenor in 3972AN

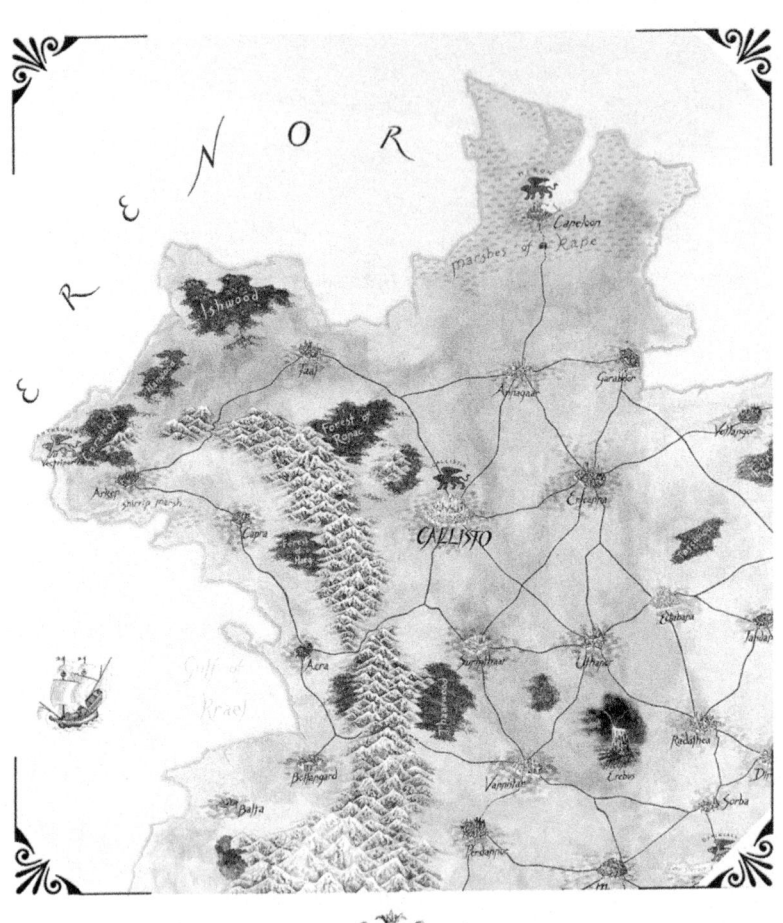

The song of Ohbrid-Part (trans. Eudokios)

Amid star-burnished reeds by heavens limned
The Mother bows her heavy-tressèd head
Her eyes deep-sunken and with sorrow rimmed
With backward glance she walks the halls of dread
Deep shadowed where Tamarin's sceptre looms
O'er all the echoed vaults, high-columned deeps
Death's massy legions dreaming in their tombs
She stands before the dark lord and she weeps,
Her voice rings out, entreating to that ear
Her earnest reservations to his suit
That she might make her protestations clear.
Tamarin now inclines his pond'rous brow
And turns his leaden gaze upon her face
'Our two worlds do adjoin, you must allow,'
He then declares. 'I urge you to embrace
The darkness and the depth that lies beneath
The tangled roots and waters of this earth
For mountain, moor and forest, pool and heath
Oppress my soul with anguish at my dearth
And if you were to place your hand in mine
I'd walk the earth beside you as my wife
Turn countenance upon the stars divine
And draw into my lungs the breath of life.'
'And taint the wells and stain the rivers broad,
O'er reach your shadow on my verdant land,'
She sayest then, 'My great and noble lord.
Dark is the world when you extend your hand
And dark the chambers that are your domain
The dryads and the naiads in their streams
Do tremble at the mention of your name
And word of your soft wooing haunts their dreams.'

Prelude

Prata - December 3993an

The island was bleak in December, although there was something grim about it even at the height of summer, when the naked sun baked its rocky shores and the scrub-covered hills inland. In the grip of winter now, the narrow windows of the monastery of the transfiguration, beneath the lee of one such hill, looked out upon the meagre fields and olive groves of its lands from beneath leaden roofs and domes hunched against a leaden sky, like the sightless eyes of a skull. So, it had always appeared, to one of the dwellers within, who looked up from the path on the slopes beneath, pulling her cloak more closely about her. It had snowed a little and the wind had blown thin drifts of it into the corners of the stone-walled fields and the little cemetery she now approached.

'The exercise is surely good for you', said the younger woman at her side. 'Notwithstanding your condition. Although, I wonder that you should choose the cemetery for your destination. I believe the other side of the hill offers a gentler, more cheerful prospect and, today at least, a little shelter from the wind'.

'I always come here', said Adala with a shrug, pushing at the little iron gate that gave entry. 'It suits my mood and my circumstances'. Once therein, with the other at her heels, she stooped to scrape a thin scatter of snow from one of the grave stones that dotted the little enclosure, regarding the inscription pensively.

'"Marielo"', the younger woman read, standing at her shoulder. 'Just that. One of the monks, I suppose'.

'Then you suppose wrong', corrected Adala, straightening up, stretching her back carefully. 'Here lies the mighty Emperor Teradore, who departed this earth more than a hundred years ago. His sons are here – just yonder – and there are others, too, who wore the purple and paid the price of it. See, there is the great Timon Drakarenos in the corner beneath that slender stone, exiled here by his own sons, much good it did them. Look you now and ponder on the great equality of death. Humble monks and emperors moulder side by side. Look how the great are brought low. This is the graveyard of hope and ambition, the price at once of aspiration and of failure'.

Her broad gesture encompassed the dismal plot with its stones like broken teeth.

'I see', said the younger woman, whose name was Ureni, and who was newly arrived as a maidservant and companion. She glanced about surreptitiously for evidence of a newly dug grave that might mark the resting place of her predecessor.

'Over there, by the far wall', said Adala with a gesture, divining her companion's thoughts.

'And perhaps I shall be next', she added, adjusting her cloak once more, turning to look out across the iron-grey sea towards the vague horizon and far beyond to where The City lay.

'Surely not, my lady', said Ureni brightly. 'Your physician was most encouraging, was he not?'

Adala said nothing. Ureni, regarding her thoughtfully from beneath her own cloak's hood, could see that she had once been as very beautiful as everyone had said. Even now her face retained the shadow of that beauty, although the skin had shrunk back upon the bone. That little hair disclosed by her headdress was shot with grey now, and the eyes that turned upon her were grey, too. It was the prevailing colour of Prata, like the hue of the fabled underworld or of purgatory, perhaps.

'And you believe him, do you, in all your wisdom and your knowledge? You believe I shall live to see The City once more?'

'Of course'.

Ureni was about to add something encouraging about hope springing eternal, but the words died on her tongue. The wind whipped their clothes around them and the monastery bell began to toll. Long seconds passed, became minutes, or so it seemed. The cold wind gnawed at her bones, and it was all she could do to stop the tremor in her jaw.

'Tell me how you came to be here', said Ureni at last, to break the silence between them, although all the world knew at least the bare outline of that story.

Adala's mouth twitched vaguely with the rumour of a smile.

'If you wish', she said.

Chapter One

August 3970 AN

'I shall never go again', she said as she hurried down the hillside path.

She said it again as twigs clawed at her hair and she squeezed between the two great rocks where an old tree clung to the sun-baked cliff, the limestone seared brilliant white at midday.

'Never', she said once more, this time between clenched teeth, sparing a backward glance at the shoulder of Cape Lucatis and the blue sea beyond. Beyond even this, at the furthest extent of shimmering vision, the coast of the sea's far edge loomed sweltering through the haze.

'Never, never, never', she repeated, as though to chime with the cicadas in the olive groves and with the hot blood that pulsed at her temple. 'May I be damned to Hell if ever I do. So help me God and all the saints'.

A glance now heavenwards at the perfect blue bowl of the August sky, as the path came out between the scrubbiest of the uppermost olives and the terracotta roofs of her distant village showed at last above the trees. Distracted by the briefest pang of pious scruple in a brain still seething with outrage, she missed her step and stumbled, jarring her ankle, cursing, muttering oaths and the hurried appeals for divine pardon that must inevitably follow.

'There, you see? Your foul actions condemn me even from my own mouth', she muttered, striding out now amongst the larger olives, past the broken wall and down the rough flags that made an uneven stair between the two steep levels of the grove. 'But you shall not lay eyes on me again; eyes or... or...', a nod of acknowledgement

to old Mardianos, framed in the low door of his tumbledown house as she passed. He raised a hand. She hurried on, brow-knitted, before his mouth could fall open and his slow wits evolve some laboured greeting.
'Yuzanid at your heels, would he be?' came the words at last but too late, his voice already lost in the voice of the cicadas. 'And that cloud upon your brow now? That dark cloud, hah!'
Mardianos watched her long white frock and her dark hair vanish among the branches, and he grinned, scratching the back of his head.
'Adala', he said, and the name was enough, bringing to mind a slow surge of familiar thoughts that he could chew over like the blank-eyed goats in the yard behind. 'Adala'.
And now she was through the yard behind her father's inn and the linen was white on the washing line. The chickens scattered raucously before her as she strode into the kitchen, slamming the half-door behind her.
'Adala!'
Marta's face, emerging from the shadows within, was pale with sudden concern. Her eyes met her sister's, which smouldered with an unexpected heat. 'What is it?'
'Where is Father?' she asked, ignoring this enquiry and glancing around urgently, as though she thought Marta might be concealing him in the log store or in the privy under the stairs.
'Adala', said her sister once more, taking her by the arm but finding her hand shrugged away.
'Where is he?'
'With Andronis, the smith', said Marta, conceding defeat while making a few faltering steps in pursuit of her younger sibling as she strode out through the bar. Finally, hands on hips, she watched Adala's receding form in the street beyond. A few passers-by turned their heads, but it

was beyond noon and the village slumbered on in the stifling heat of summer.

'Father?'
Corasto, the innkeeper, looked up from where he was applying salve to the smith's arm. His wife, now long-parted from him, had been a physician's daughter, and he, even at this remove, had gleaned some meagre understanding of her father's profession. Certainly, he was better qualified than anyone else in the village to tend to the medical needs of its inhabitants, and so he found himself called out from time to time to set broken limbs or to bring the slight weight of his knowledge to bear on the dropsical, the sore of eye or the fever-stricken. On this occasion, he had been summoned to tend to one of Andronis's frequent burns. He was a careless smith, with hands and arms to show for it – a network of ancient scars traversing his grizzled forearms. Now there would be a new one.
'Adala?'
A grunt of invitation from Andronis immediately preceded the girl's entry into the room, a room where flies circled lazily beneath the rafters, the air blissfully cool after the smithy beyond. Adala felt her frock cling sweat wet to her back.
'I must speak with you', she said to her father in a low voice, after the barest glance of acknowledgement for his patient.
Corasto raised an eyebrow, reaching for the strip of moderately clean cloth that was to serve as a bandage, exchanging a private wry smile with the smith.
'You must, child? You *must*? Perhaps I shall be the judge of that necessity'.
The girl, conscious that she may have overreached herself, bit her lip and stepped back. Her eyes, however, continued to blaze with a fierce sincerity, and this argued

her case more insistently than any form of words. The innkeeper sighed, tied off the knot, slapped his patient affectionately on the cheek and wiped his hands on his breeches.

'And your fee?' called Andronis as Corasto followed his daughter from the room.

Corasto waved dismissively. Although money was amongst his guiding passions, Andronis was an old friend.

'You can fix the hinges on that old outhouse door of mine', he said.

There was no conversation between them as father and daughter made their way back to the inn and up the little stair to her room, past the wondering faces of her sister and two of the house girls. With the door shut behind them at last, Adala turned upon her father and opened her mouth to speak. Then, closing her mouth again, she returned to the door and glared out across the little landing. A giggle and a scuffle of withdrawing feet betrayed the interest of her household.

'Go away!' she called petulantly, stamping a foot for emphasis.

Closing the door now, she found Corasto, arms folded, sitting on the edge of her bed.

'Well?' he said. 'What is it?'

Theodolis was a monk. The elder brother of Corasto, he had dwelt once in the monastery of Saint Stelgios on the far shore of the Gulf of Marmo. Then, when the monastery burned down, he came with two other brothers to find refuge in this place. One of the brothers soon died, and Theodolis quarrelled with the other. Within the space of six months, he was alone, withdrawing from the world to live in a cave beneath the headland of Cape Lucatis. But he was never quite alone; not really, so long as he had his books. And he had many books, saved from the library of Saint Stilgios when the fire took hold and carried away to safety across the sea. So Theodolis cultivated solitude here, content with the company of Miron, Cantanoro, Vilmo and the other ancient writers. These precious works he kept in the furthest recesses of his cave, preserving them from the damp of the sea air. Their quiet voices consoled him when his long contemplation of the holy truths faltered at last and prayer withered on his tongue.

Every day, Corasto's daughters would bring him food and drink, making their way along the dusty track through the olives and up to the cape. To begin with, the girls would take their turn but, as the years passed, it was more often Adala that made that journey. Theodolis' eyes began to fail, and he taught the girl her letters, watching with indulgent satisfaction as her finger crept across the faint lines of cursive script and her small mouth formed the words. Marta learned the same skills, too, but it was Adala who found joy in unlocking the voices of the ancients. It was Adala who read aloud to Theodolis, day after day when, as he had known they would, his eyes failed him and the words of his old friends swam vaguely before his despairing gaze.
'And so you prefer Miron to Tsando?' he asked her one afternoon while they sat together in the shade of the bowed oak that stood at the threshold of his cave.
'I do', she admitted, looking out to where an eagle soared lazily above the shoulder of the cape, riding easily on the air that rose shimmering from the sun-baked slopes.
'Why so?' asked Theodolis, taking the book carefully from her hands and glancing sidelong at the perfection of her profile. She was no more than eleven years old then, but already the promise of an exquisite flowering was

rising in her form. He bit his lip, casting down his eyes, intoning a silent prayer as she turned to him.

'Because Tsando tells of us Tsando's deeds – and Tsando is at the centre of it all. Miron glorifies Callisto, and all the Callistenes are celebrated there, all who won glory in the war against the Perdiani'.

'Except the infamous Dardoni', pointed out Theodolis. 'And those others who preferred the ignominy of the Perdiate yoke to the uncertain fortune of war'.

'As you say', agreed Adala with a wry half-smile. 'And I love him because he tells of the deeds of the Radagari; those whose blood is ours'.

'You believe the blood of Leandrines and Genstrinor runs in your veins, then?' asked Theodolis, doing his best to supress the importunate smile that tugged at the corners of his mouth.

'Father has assured me of it', she replied, her eyes holding an iron certainty that defied contradiction.

'Because he is from Radagar'.

'Of course. As are you'.

'Indeed, although we came with our father to The City before Corasto was yet weaned. Even I have no recollection of it, and I am four years his senior'.

'The blood does not forget'.

'Perhaps', he conceded.

They sat in companionable silence for a time whilst Theodolis placed the book with the others at his side and Adala shaded her eyes to watch a distant ship, its sail bright white against the deepening blue of the sea. It came into Theodolis' mind to mention that the vast majority of those who dwelt in Dromantos in ancient times had been helots, hundreds of thousands of them, whose cruel servitude had sustained the privilege of a few thousand Radagari. Constant vigilance, lives devoted entirely to the perfection of the arts of war, were at once the cost and the reward of their dominion.

'Do you imagine our forebears were slaves?' she asked, as though perceiving his thoughts.
'I have no way of knowing', he shrugged. 'Nor indeed does your father. And neither do you'.
'The blood of kings runs in my veins', she said. 'I know it'.
The flash of pride in her eyes, the thrust of her small chin, caused Theodolis' answer to wither on his tongue. He nodded slowly, gathered up his books and stood, wincing with the ache of old bones, stretching himself cautiously.
'Well', he said at last. 'Perhaps you do. I suppose there are none who could prove to the contrary'.

Three years had passed since then, and as Adala had grown towards womanhood, so had Theodolis come to find her presence troubling to his peace of mind. Long hours he had prayed for salvation from the shackles of his mortal frame and from the temptations of the flesh that came with it. And yet still he had watched her tread the path along the cliff's edge to his abode and felt a leap of joy in his heart – that and the clutch of guilt in his belly. At last, those dark animal instincts at the core of his being had surpassed the command of his rational being.

'He placed his hand upon my thigh', she said in a low voice, sparing a sidelong glance at the door, leaning closer to her father.
Corasto bit his lip but said nothing, although a furrowing of his brow, a wondering consideration in his eyes, spoke of some internal dialogue.
'I know what was in his mind, Father. I saw it there'.
Her eyes met his now, and there was a blazing sincerity there.
'I have seen it before – seen it often', she wanted to say, but the words caught in her throat and her lips fell open.
'He wanted me', she said at last.

Corasto nodded slowly. All males in the vicinity between the ages of puberty and dotage, and not minded to sodomy, shared Theodolis' inclination with varying degrees of fervency. She was, by common agreement, the most beautiful girl in the region, and many a potential suitor dreamed of possessing her. Likewise, many a jealous father would have kept her close-guarded in the house until some desirable match could be made. However, Corasto was not of that mind. He knew his daughter well, her virtues and her frailties. Besides, Adala could look after herself. The perfection of her form was matched by a fiercely independent spirit and a rapier tongue. This instrument had already skewered a good number of those who sought to establish themselves in her favour, or whose hands had unwisely trespassed upon her person.
'He will be in Hell, then', he said. 'Roasting in a Hell of his own making before he passes to any higher judgment'.
'And I shall never go to my uncle again', Adala told him, her mouth set in a firm line now. 'He is dead to me'.
'I would not require it of you', Corasto frowned, scratching the back of his head. 'And neither shall Marta. Timo shall take him food and drink now'.
Adala nodded. Timo, the pot-boy, a hulking youth of sixteen, had a countenance and a physique such as to dispel all fleshly temptation. Besides, he was a dullard. Theodolis' books would be closed to him now.
'He will have more leisure to reflect upon the nature of sin', said Corasto, bringing to utterance what was in both of their minds, 'and so approach nearer to our lord'.

Interlude

The two gods stood and gazed upon a representation of the world, spinning in the void, its oceans and continents streaked and coiled with cloud.

'A hurricane', observed the one that was called Tio, pointing this out.

'Or a typhoon, depending on the circumstances', said Yuzanid, his identical twin.

'Then a hurricane', said Tio, 'looking at its location – and a large one, too. I imagine a large number of our creatures will be carried off to their graves'.

'Rather more of yours than mine, I think', smiled Yuzanid. 'Judging from the continent it afflicts'.

'I trust you have no hand in this', frowned Tio.

'I do not', said his brother. 'Although you may be certain I should bitterly afflict your subjects with storms and tempests of all kinds, if the rules allowed it'.

'Always the rules', mused Tio, accepting this assurance.

'Always the rules', agreed Yuzanid. 'And how do things fare in your favourite part of Toxandria? I trust your interests prosper there?'

'If they do not, then I'm sure you can take credit for it'.

'I shall, dear Brother, I shall', said Yuzanid smoothly. 'I sense that affairs there approach a fortunate conjunction of circumstances, where each of us may play our hand a little more overtly than we usually can'.

'Perhaps', agreed Tio with a nod.

Yuzanid laughed. 'The empire that you set such great store in, and whose inhabitants fawn upon you so, appears to be in for another period of stormy weather, if I may continue the initial theme of our discussion. You must have been so delighted to see that recent period of stability. How disappointing it must be to see another paroxysm of turmoil and bloodletting on its way. Unless you have some scheme to avert that. Do you, Brother? Do you have some great plan by which your empire might be conducted safely through the coming squalls and brought once more into calm water?'

'Do you believe in love, Brother?' asked Tio, turning upon him.

'It is a concept that is familiar to me', agreed Yuzanid.

'As an abstract, no doubt', observed Tio with a smile. 'But perhaps my question was ill-formed. I should have asked you, *do you believe in love at first sight?*'

May 3972AN

Rain lashed the tumbled black rocks and poured from the streaming cliff face as the men urged their horses onwards. Hunched under dripping cloaks, they were at last obliged to dismount, as the path narrowed where it hugged the mountainside. At least here, close to the treeline, there were some glimpses of the looming low hills and of the forested ridges that lay between.

'"It'll be fine", you said', observed one of the three as he tugged at his mount's reins. '"It'll pass in a few minutes," you said. Just you see'.

A grunted obscenity from the figure ahead, a momentary flash of a pale face as he turned to scowl, was his friend's only response.

'I only mention it in passing', muttered Jory, his words quite obliterated by a sudden rumble of thunder. 'I intended no criticism'.

Looking down at the mud-churned path to spare his face from the downpour, he came within inches of colliding with the hindquarters of the horse in front.

'Oh! You...!'

'Wait!' called Taian, at the front of the file, holding out a hand to his side, standing stock still as he listened. 'Was that the dogs?'

The others listened, too, but a brilliant flash of lightning and another great reverberating roll of thunder drowned out all other sounds.

Rayo, moving up beside Taian, shook his head bleakly, shifting his grip on the sturdy hunting spear that had served him more as a staff than as a weapon these last few hours.

'Don't say it', warned Taian, raising a finger and wagging it from side to side.

'Because you are my prince, my lord?' muttered Rayo.

'Because you have no need', said Taian with a laugh, raising his voice over the wind. 'Because I am glad to admit the fault is mine. An excess of zeal...'
Zeal indeed. The Prince's hunting party had set out in high spirits earlier that day, eleven noble youths with as many servants and a score or so hounds. But the party had become divided in pursuit of the celebrated white boar that was said to frequent the woods. Then, even as the prince and his friends had pursued a sudden sighting with heedless abandon, the gathering clouds had burst with sudden violence upon the land. Within minutes, day was turned to night and the woods were a strange pouring wilderness in which all waymarks, all indications of location, were suddenly obliterated. There was no way to tell which way lay north or south, no hint of the presence of the sea.
'I suppose we shall come upon a road in due course', finished Taian with a glint of optimism in his eye that found no encouragement from his companions.

It was almost dark when they filed from the edge of the dripping woods and out into the muddy lane at the edge of the village. Mounting their horses, blinking the rain from their eyes, they followed the track down through the first rough dwellings to where the road widened and met another that meandered down through fields and orchards towards the sea. Here, where the roads met, stood The Grapes, its broad dripping eaves dark against the pouring sky. A few chinks of light showed behind tight-closed shutters, and the sign swayed creaking with the north wind's fitful gusts.
Taian glanced up, wiped his wet face with the back of a wet hand and rapped on the door. 'Any port in a storm', he shouted to the others, glancing over his shoulder to where they were dismounting, huddled under their soaking cloaks.

'I suppose we shall find our way back to the lodge tomorrow'.
The door opened a crack, revealing a narrow strip of Timo's wondering face, surmounted by a mop of dark hair. After a moment, the door was pulled fully open, and warm yellow light spilled out over the rain-thrashed black puddles beyond.
'Get these horses stabled, if you will', Taian told the boy, thrusting the reins of his own mount at him. 'And get us some mulled wine, for God's sake. We're half drowned out here!'
'Come in, gentlemen', said Corasto appearing behind, pushing at Timo's back. 'And do stop gawping, boy. Take those there spears, now. I'll send a couple of the other lads out to help you rub the horses down. Go. Go now!'
Stepping back, Corasto beckoned Taian across the threshold and took the sodden cloak that his guest soon shrugged from his shoulders. The innkeeper's eyes gleamed with sudden interest as they fell upon the newcomer's coat. The broad embroidered borders, the glint of gold thread, spoke eloquently of high status.
'Do take a place by the fire, you and your fine friends, sir', said Corasto, beckoning them in, keeping up a stream of observation and complaint about the appalling weather. A couple of elderly regulars were playing dice at the broad table closest to the fire, at the far end of the room. These were old acquaintances of Corasto. Looking up, taking in the developing situation and reading the look of savage command in his eye, they quickly shuffled aside.
'Hunting, is it?' asked Corasto, having called for mulled wine. 'I daresay the pickings are good enough in the woods out east. Have you come far, my lords?'
'Far enough in this tempest', answered Taian, pulling out a bench for his friends. 'There is a lodge between the cape and Garabdor. We became separated from the rest of our party and lost our way'.

'I am not surprised to hear it', said Corasto, wiping the bench with the cloth from his belt. 'A filthy night indeed. And I suppose you are hungry, too?'

'You suppose right', laughed the gangling youth at Taian's side, brushing lank wet locks from his eyes. 'Our spears have found no marks'.

'I'm afraid I can't offer you venison, but I'm sure we have something hot and filling that will answer'.

Corasto hurried off to the kitchen, hardly able to supress the wild grin that threatened to burst out upon his countenance. Could it be that the stars were moving towards some unlooked-for and highly beneficial conjunction?

'We have quality amongst us', he hissed, closing the kitchen door behind him. 'You have only to look at them'.

Marta and the cook looked up from where they were preparing vegetables.

'Hmm?' said Marta.

'Young noblemen', said Corasto, jerking his thumb over his shoulder. 'Noblemen, d'you hear? With gold jingling in their purses, I don't doubt. They'll be from that imperial hunting lodge along the coast up towards Garabdor. Lost, see. How's that rabbit dish coming on?'

'Good, good, nearly done, I should think', replied the cook, wiping her hands on her apron. 'I suppose I'll be fetching out the best silver plate?' she added with an ironic smile.

'They'll have to manage with earthenware, like the rest of us', grunted Corasto, picking up a spoon and stirring the greasy surface, raising it to his lips. 'Hmm. Not bad. Not your best, but not half bad'.

Turning to Adala, who was getting out plates, he snapped, 'Go up to Temestrios at the harbour and ask him if we may borrow his glass goblets. Our guests are not used to drinking from clay cups, I suppose'.

'I shall be soaked!' objected Adala with a glance to where a few drips made their way through the smoke-dark thatch above them.

'So you shall!' snapped Corasto, his dark eyes daring her to make further objection.

With a shrug, she was gone.

Returning to their table from the privy, some minutes later, Taian passed by the threshold of the kitchen. Glancing within, he found Adala, shrugging off her soaking cloak, headdress cast aside. For a moment, as she turned, shaking out her damp curls, the pale oval of her face was framed in dark ringlets. Their eyes met, a spark of lamplight in her own, and then the door was pushed shut. There had been a flash of consternation in her eyes but other things, too, and these Taian pondered as he made his way through the crowd at the bar. What else had he seen? Certainly, a startling beauty, one that caused his heart to skip a beat, but there was pride there, too, and the suggestion of some inner strength, inner serenity, that he found more intriguing than any other aspect of that instant of revelation.

'What is it?' asked Jory, pulling in his chair to let him past. 'You look like you've seen a ghost'.

'Not a ghost...' started Taian, but whatever else he might have added to this was cut short by Marta's attendance at the table as she lay plates and a basket of bread.

A ghost... an unquiet spirit, denied the peace of the grave or the prospect of communion with the lord. Taian could only reply with a grunt of assent as the stew was ladled onto his plate. The voices of his friends and the clamour of the tavern seemed distant, strangely muted. Rather, he was conscious of having glimpsed something illicit, as though he had seen her unrobed in all her glorious nakedness. And then, she was standing before him, her hair now concealed beneath her headdress, with a single loose curl to prompt his vivid recollection of that enchanting revelation.

'Honeyed wine, sir?' she asked, offering a steaming jug to the fine glass goblet she had brought. 'Good and hot'.

Their eyes met once more, and she did not cast hers down in the manner that her status demanded. She was a servant girl, a tavernkeeper's daughter, and he was second son of the emperor, amongst the most exalted lords of the empire. But she did not know. How could she? And the cool grey eyes that held his glance searched his in return. He smiled, a delightful coincidence of ideas and circumstances occurring to him in that moment.

'*Nul tini mir possino volonares si maricoli ne paret ani volonari te!*' ('Now you may tell, if you dare tell a soul, that you have seen me naked!'), he murmured in Cantrophene, quoting Viridon.

'I fancy you will not be too shy to tell your friends that you saw me with my hair shook down', she said, wiping the rim of the jug, a flush rising in her cheeks. 'But if you claim more than that, and if you cast me as Saint Cataria, you had best recall the fate of he whose role you take unto yourself'.

And then she was gone, although not before the beginning of a wry smile had tugged at the corners of her lips.

'What was that all about?' asked Jory, chewing a mouthful of tender rabbit and nodding with approval.

'Meditations, Book Four, as I recall', said Rayo, whose knowledge of Middle Kingdom literature was rather more extensive than Jory's. 'Where the wandering sculptor, Arcteaon, chances upon Cataria naked and she dares him to tell anyone'.

'And did you? See her in the raw, I mean?' asked Jory, eyes wide.

'No, of course not', laughed Taian, waving this notion aside with a crust of bread. 'She's a rare beauty, though, isn't she?'
'And what does she mean about fate, though?' asked Jory.
'She turned Arcteaon into a pillar of marble', said Rayo. 'And his own son sculpted a statue of her from it'.
'Ha!' said Jory with a grin and a nudge in the ribs for Taian. 'And is any part of you turning to stone, friend?'

Adala had her own cause to reflect on this encounter as she went about her duties. The tavern was crowded, as those whose own dwellings were not wholly impervious to such torrential rain had taken refuge there, enjoying the conviviality and drinking as little mulled wine as was consistent with their admittance. Most of those faces had been familiar to her since her infancy, but the three young men at the table in the corner intrigued her. They intrigued her neighbours, too, as many a sidelong glance and a muted enquiry indicated, since scions of the nobility were infrequently to be found beneath The Grapes' smoke-stained rafters. And yet the villagers had not caught the eye of the tallest of the strangers in the way that Adala had, had not looked full into his face and seen an answering spark of interest there. Sure, she was used to the frank stares and the leers of those whose admiration of her form could not be contained, but somehow this was different – as the flush in her cheeks confirmed. Now she regretted her bold response to the young man's Cantrophene quotation. It had been pure instinct, triggered by a recollection of that author's words, long dormant within her but suddenly rekindled. In retrospect it seemed bold, even insolent, given the circumstances. Had she given offence? Corasto would be furious with her. She ran her hands down her face now, wiped her hands on her apron, as her father appeared from the bar.

'The quality', he grunted with a jab of his thumb towards their unexpected guests. 'See to it they want for nothing'.
'I intend to', said Adala, looking past him anxiously. 'I suppose they will pay well. Did they mention their names, perchance?'
'They did not. I wonder if they know Count Artemios?' he asked, naming the nobleman who owned much of the property thereabouts.
'Don't much look like him', observed Marta, squeezing past them with a basket of bread.
'And what's that got to do with it, or with you for that matter?' called Corasto after her receding back. His attention turned once more to Adala. 'And what about you? I don't suppose you're going to stand their gawping when there are all those pots to be cleared back there'.

But Adala had hardly set to work when Corasto was back, an expression of barely contained delight competing with mystification for the mastery of his features.
'The young lord has asked for you', he said. 'So, let's set aside that apron, shall we, and turn your sleeve a little to hide that there stain'. He tugged at her garment briefly, looked at her critically, pursed his lips. 'There. You'll do. Get you in there now and see what you can find out'.

'And may I know *your* names, sirs?' asked Adala, after she had seated herself awkwardly at their table, when required to do so, and answered that question for herself. 'If you will pardon my impertinence'.
'No impertinence at all', said the tall young man who had quoted Viridon. 'This is Jory, this Rayo... and my own name is... Bardilis', he added in a manner that certainly marked it as a falsehood. 'Your father may have mentioned that we were hunting in yonder woods and became lost in this tempest'.

'Indeed', she nodded, her eyes cast down in her lap now. 'And how may I serve you, sir?'

'Well', said Taian, leaning a little closer to her. 'You may certainly begin by telling me how you come to be acquainted with my friend Gaion Viridonios Naso'.

'Viridon?' said Adala, looking up. 'Well, my uncle has many Cantrophene books and his eyes were failing. I used to read them to him'.

She told him about her Uncle Theodolis, his hermit's abode in the lee of Cape Lucatis and his precious collection of books. Not that she had cast eyes upon him or those volumes since that day, more than a year ago, when he had trespassed upon her person. Perhaps her face betrayed something of her reluctance to discuss Theodolis, who was almost completely blind now, according to her father.

Taian, detecting this, nevertheless pressed on, his curiosity aroused.

'He sounds a man of culture, your uncle', he said, 'and possessed of a potential treasure trove of literature, if what you say is true. My own father is a passionate student of the ancient authors, a keen collector of their works. I wonder if your uncle appreciates the true monetary value of such items, quite apart from their literary worth? Do you think I might have sight of them? We shall certainly be lodging beneath this roof tonight, supposing that you have a room available. Perhaps tomorrow you would conduct me to your uncle's dwelling, presuming that this storm has passed by then?

'It would be my pleasure', said Adala, regarding him cautiously and realising that this declaration was more than mere formality. There was something very engaging about the young man that faced her, something that went beyond the smooth regularity of his features, the soft curls of his beard. Certainly, there was a directness in his gaze that would have provoked resentment under normal circumstances. But these circumstances were far from normal. She told herself her ready acceptance of this was no mere ignoble deference to a social status made evident by the gold rings on his fingers and the fine embroidered silk of his jacket.

'Rayo here is likewise familiar with Viridon', the man who introduced himself as Bardilis was saying.

'But I do not regard him as a friend', laughed Rayo, whose face was well suited to the expression of humour, a broad brow and a mouth that fell readily into a grin. 'We are reluctant acquaintances, he and I, brought together by necessity and the rod of my tutor'.

'And to me he is entirely a stranger', added Jory, whose own bearded face betrayed a more serious disposition as he set down his goblet. 'Nor do I regret it. I prefer my friends to be amongst the living'.

'And did your father likewise bring *you* to a reluctant acquaintance with the ancients?' asked Adala of 'Bardilis'.

The momentary amused look shared between the three young guests suggested also a shared secret that contributed further to her interest.

The arrival of Corasto at their table, ostensibly to clear their plates, but actually to gather some sense of the nature of their conversation, curtailed further discussion of this.

'I hope that was alright for you, gentlemen?' he asked with a sidelong glance of enquiry for Adala that promised an extensive interrogation in the near future. 'And can I be offering you anything in the nature of dessert? My cook has a very good honied pastry on the way'.

'Certainly you can', said Taian, settling back in his chair. 'That sounds most appetising. Your delightful daughter is evidently sprung from a very cultured family. She tells me your brother has a rare collection of books. I wonder if I might beg you to allow her to conduct me to him tomorrow? I should certainly like to meet him and look upon his library'.

Adala found herself blushing furiously during this, since Corasto was entirely a stranger to culture and as unlike Theodolis as chalk and cheese, a circumstance he betrayed with a perceptible stiffening of his back. Nevertheless, he nodded, declared his joy to be of any assistance to such fine young gentlemen and placed a hand on Adala's shoulder that signalled the end of her encounter with them.

'And now you must excuse Adala', he said with a passable attempt at a courtly bow. 'Doubtless she has trespassed enough on your indulgence, and there are a hundred and one domestic tasks demanding of her attention'.

Chapter Two

The next day dawned bright and clear with curls of mist rising damply in the olive groves above the inn as the resurgent sun warmed the earth. Jory stayed behind to see to the horses, but Taian and Rayo accompanied Adala as they made their way up the familiar path towards the cape. Corasto was there, too, of course, as convention demanded, and he kept up a stream of inconsequential chatter that derived partly from a desire to find out more about his guests and partly from a gladness of heart inspired by the handsome payment they had made for their food and lodgings.

Adala, from her place at the rear of the file, found herself separated from the young man who had occupied her thoughts throughout the night, so that she had lain awake even as the last few drops of the departing storm pattered on her shutters. Glancing back from his place behind Corasto, the young man smiled at her from time to time, a face even more handsome than the memory she had dwelt upon, now that the full sun of morning shone upon it. And then Rayo had detained her father with some enquiry about the inn, and the young man was suddenly at her side as they came out on the short grass beneath the cape.

'Your name is not Bardilis, is it?' she asked bluntly, after hearing out his observations about the weather.

'It is not, I confess', he laughed. 'You have pierced through my subterfuge'.

'And why would you seek to deceive me?'

'Because the truth may be still harder for you to believe'.

'Why so?'

'Because my father is Gelon Starcorides, that is called Leogenitos, he who is our lord and Emperor', said Taian with a glance over his shoulder to where Corasto and

Rayo were now discussing wine. 'And my elder brother is Cato, Duke of Ericanna'.

'Then you presume to tell me that you are Prince Taian, his son', gasped Adala, stopping so suddenly that he almost collided with her. 'And you expect me to believe that?'

'Yes', agreed Taian, smiling but with a look that enjoined secrecy upon her. 'It is no more than the simple truth. But I see we are almost here, if I understand your description. Is that your uncle I spy?'

Theodolis, thin to the point of emaciation and with a wispy beard blown about him by the morning breeze, was sunning himself upon the convenient rock at the mouth of his cave. He turned his pale, sightless eyes upon them as the party approached and hawked noisily, spitting over the edge.

'Is that you, Timo? he asked. 'And who's that you've got with you?'

It was the work of some moments to bring Theodolis to understand that he had distinguished visitors, that breakfast was not immediately forthcoming and that the visitors were interested in his books. Adala, mindful of her vow, stood back and settled herself some way away on a grassy slope as her companions conversed and then passed within the cave. She wove a circlet of wild flowers for her head as she waited, and she watched as an eagle soared distantly over the point of the cape, the warm wind tugging gently at the stunted trees behind her. If her nimble fingers were busily engaged, her mind was no less active, as it laboured to confront the circumstances that had been presented to it. A prince! Could it be true? Could it really be that this handsome young was amongst the most powerful in the whole of the realm, son and anointed colleague of Gelon himself? Truly, that would explain the richness of his clothing, the urbane sophistication of his manners and his speech. And it was well known that the court hunted in those woods. Andronis' cousin had had a chastening encounter with their gamekeepers whilst trespassing there some weeks ago, coming home without his bow and with an ugly set of weals on his back that Corasto had been required to dress.

'He likes me', she said to herself out loud. 'I saw it in his eyes. He likes me, so he does'.

What did it matter? Doubtless he was engaged to some heiress of the noble clans, one of the proud ladies of the court. Doubtless he was more than used to breaking the hearts of girls of the common sort, who he could take up and cast aside as he fancied, crushed beneath the chariot wheels of vanity and pride. Perhaps he was accustomed to the indiscriminate satisfaction of his carnal desires, and he had already marked her down as one such brief diversion. A flush rose into her cheeks at this prospect, one that derived from shame but also from a curious flare of heat within her loins – one that mere dismay had no power to dispel. She was reflecting on this and on other connected matters when the object of her thoughts emerged blinking from the cave with his companions. Before his eye had settled upon her, she had plucked the circlet from her brow and cast it aside into a bush.

'I have never seen such a good copy of "The Onopaneion"', Taian was saying to Corasto as they made their way down the path towards her. 'And I'm quite sure my father's agents would be interested in cataloguing the collection'.

Theodolis remained at the threshold of his dwelling, regarding his departing guests pensively, no doubt wondering whether to rejoice in or to regret this visit. His eyes seemed to meet Adala's for a moment, and although it was likely enough that he saw nothing, she nevertheless turned her gaze aside.

'So here you are', said Taian, extending a hand as she rose, the firm pressure of his flesh on hers for one electric moment that she would afterwards recall with pleasure and with wonder. 'I suppose the dark and gloom of your uncle's inner dwelling is oppressive to your mind'.
Corasto's face fleetingly disclosed his understanding of the true nature of her reluctance, but he was soon caught up with telling Taian how glad he would be to entertain their party once more, should they choose to return. More suitable guest accommodation would be prepared, paint applied, floors brushed and washed with superhuman exertion; so it appeared. Adala barely heard their conversation as they retraced their path to the tavern. She was conscious of exchanging pleasantries with Rayo as they walked, murmuring the polite responses society required from her, but her mind was elsewhere, focused entirely on the tall young man who strode ahead of her, taking in every aspect of his carriage and deportment, the tilt of his chin, the engaging way he had of stroking his beard when listening.

And then he was gone, his departure marked by the snorting of horses in the yard, the jingle of harness and cheery cries of farewell as the little party made its way along the muddy track that led back to the forest. Silence descended on the yard, marred only by Timo's cursing as he laboured to close a stable door swollen by the damp.

'Well', declared Corasto at Adala's side, rubbing his hands together with satisfaction. 'What do we make of that, eh?' He placed a rough finger beneath her chin and turned her face to his. 'Struck on you, he was, chief of those there lordlings, so he was. Don't tell me you didn't mark it'.

'And what of it?' she asked, moving his finger aside, annoyed by this flawless summation of her own private thoughts.

'Aye, that's the question', he observed. 'What of it, indeed? And I don't suppose his name was Bardilis, either'.

His searching look into her eyes probed for the secret that was hidden there, and for a moment she stood on the brink of yielding up his name. But then her father looked aside, scratching the back of his head, and the danger passed. She breathed once more, unclenching her fists and lifting up her face in relief to the midday sun.

There was much talk in the inn in the subsequent days of the noblemen's visitation, with much speculation as to their identity, particularly since none had conceded more than their first names, politely batting aside all queries as to their house, clan or parentage. Roie, one of the house girls, had a sister who worked in the kitchens of Count Artemios in the big house over the hill. This sister had heard talk that some of the Katacalon clan had taken property away to the west, where they were building a lodge. Adala, very evidently the focus of the visitors' attention, was inevitably much interrogated by her household, until her smouldering impatience forbade further enquiry. In truth, Adala felt inclined to hide herself away, as much as the demands of her duties allowed, where she could lie on her bed, stare at the rafters and obsessively ruminate on the events of those few hours.

'I hope this furious itch across my side isn't what I think it is', observed Jory, who suspected he may not have been the only living inhabitant in his bed the previous night.

'I think you're not alone in having acquired an itch that needs scratching', observed Rayo with a grin. 'Isn't that right, Taian?'

The little party was making its way down through the woods towards the sea, sure of their direction now, certain that they would soon strike one of the broad green rides that traversed the forest, closer to the lodge.

'I don't doubt the inn could have supplied a few willing local girls to keep us company in bed', laughed Jory, 'and help us scratch our itches'.

'I didn't go there for the whoring', said Taian a little prissily, causing his friends to exchange a private glance of amusement, and to privately supply '*on this occasion*' to complete their prince's statement. 'And besides, my father will be pleased to hear of those books'.

'So, our providential visit was a success, you would allow?' suggested Rayo. 'And the increase of our learning is a result to be applauded, no doubt. The only result, would you say?'

'Is that Altherion and the others down there yonder?' cried Taian, glad of this distraction, naming the Lodgemaster at the head of a file of servants and their own companions. 'Altherion!' he called, waving his arm, spurring his mount down the mossed and narrow path that lay that way.

'We have been concerned, my lord', said Altherion a few minutes later when the parties were reunited and there was a fine cheerful reunion. He shook his grey head gravely. 'To lose a prince may be considered a serious error. We have been out all night looking for you'.

The truth of this was unmistakeable in the filthy and bedraggled appearance of the party, but relief drove out exhaustion, and soon flasks of wine were being passed round, the prospect of a good breakfast doing much to revive spirits.

'Well, now you have found me', laughed Taian. 'And I thank you for your solicitudes, needless as they were. We found refuge in an inn and spent the night enjoying the boundless hospitality of our subjects'.

'I trust the white boar eluded you, after all?' proffered Altherion, riding at Taian's side.

'It did', agreed Taian. 'Although we found other consolations'.

'And hunting may be judged to have a wide variety of definitions', added Rayo, who was one of the few amongst the court whose longstanding friendship justified such boldness.

Taian suppressed a private smile but turned severely upon him, his glance enjoining circumspection and the closure of that subject, at least for now, at least in public.

'Marta?' whispered Adala from the threshold of her sister's room a few days later. It was after midnight, so far as could be told, and Adala's face was weirdly uplit by the oil lamp in her hand.

The rustling of blankets, a faint creaking of bed boards, preceded Marta's sigh and her enquiry.

'What?'

She sat up in bed now, suppressing a yawn. There was a pause as Adala looked down and seemed to struggle to find speech. There was a strange uncertainty in her features, one that Marta saw infrequently there and caused concern to drive out irritation.

'Come, sit', she offered, patting the bed beside her. 'What is it that couldn't wait until tomorrow?'

Adala had slept hardly at all since Taian's visit. The events of that day seemed like a dream to her, ones that she endlessly revisited. They were there when she washed the dishes or swept the floor, but most of all they were there, vividly replaying themselves before her mind's eye whenever her head lay upon the pillow and

darkness settled around her. At last, the secrecy enjoined upon her, in that dream became a burden too great to bear alone. Now Marta's face was close to hers, her soft hand on her cheek.
'You can tell me', she said. 'You know you can'.
'You will think me mad', murmured Adala.
'Let me be the judge of that'.
Adala bit her lip. 'Those young men who were here on Tuesday', she began.
'Yes'.
'I was talking to one of them. I think he liked me'.
'It did not escape our notice. I suppose you liked him in return'.
'I cannot deny it. At least, I think I did. I felt something, something that I struggle to explain or describe, even to myself. And... he told me something... I would share this with you, but I must swear you to secrecy. Do you so swear, sister?'
'Why, yes', agreed Marta, her eyes perceptibly wider now. 'Of course'.
There was a pause as Adala strove to bring to utterance the truth that she had held within her during these last days and that could be contained no longer.
'He told me that he is Taian, our prince and second son of the emperor', she said at last. 'There, I have said it, and now you may judge me as you will'.
There was a further lengthy silence, during which the wind sighed faintly in the eaves above them. Marta swallowed hard.
'He did?'
'He did'.
'And you believed him?'
'I don't know what I believe', admitted Adala with a rueful glance. She set down the lamp on the floor and climbed into bed with Marta to embrace her. For a while

she found comfort there, her cheek united with her sister's, Marta's warm hand in her hair.

'I suppose it could be true', conceded Marta at last, drawing away a little. 'The imperial lodge is at hand, and the prince is known to love hunting. It seems remarkable, though'.

'You don't think me mad, then?'

'Why, no. But why do you trouble yourself so?'

'I don't know', sighed Adala. 'Perhaps because I don't know whether it were at best a dream. Perhaps because I fear to embrace such reality'.

Marta held Adala away from her now, looked into her eyes, smiled.

'You, Adala? Afraid? Now you *do* stretch my credulity'.

Within two weeks came assurance that the dream had been no dream. A ship arrived at the harbour, bearing with it a thoroughly seasick and elderly official from the university, together with his equally elderly servant. These gentlemen sought out Corasto and begged to be directed to Theodolis, whose collection of books they proposed to catalogue. They brought with them a letter of introduction from one Rayo Kerkuoas, who thanked Corasto once more for the hospitality extended to him on the occasion of his visit there.

'Of course, I'm sure my brother would be glad to accommodate you', said Corasto, holding the letter up to the light, reading it through a second time.

'Would you be offended if I did not accompany you on this occasion?', he gestured around him in a manner designed to convey the great burden of work that a tavernkeeper must endure. 'Perhaps my stable boy might take you there. He knows the path very well'.

'Pray do not trouble Timo. I should be glad to conduct these gentlemen', said Adala, appearing behind Corasto, her features carefully arranged into a semblance of neutrality. 'It being a fine afternoon. Perhaps Marta shall accompany me', she added to dispel any conceivable notion of impropriety. 'And I believe I have finished with the washing'.

'Very well', nodded Corasto to his visitors. 'Happy to oblige, I'm sure. May I offer you food or refreshment first? Perhaps you are fatigued by your journey?'

'Fatigued, indeed', conceded the official. 'But I am unused to ocean travel. The restless motion of the waters, the relentless turmoil of that briny element has quite destroyed my appetite. Perhaps upon our return. For now, I would rather engage with my mission without delay, if you will forgive me'.

'Of course', agreed Corasto, and then in a mighty bellow that caused his guests to wince, 'Marta, get you down here now, will you!'

In truth, there was no need for him to raise his voice, since Marta was already standing listening outside the door – and had been doing so since her sister's first excited discovery of their visitors' arrival.

'I had hoped that he would come in person', said Adala to Marta as they led their guests towards the cape. 'But I wonder if they have some message for me, that they may disclose when we arrive'.

'Dear sister', frowned Marta. 'I do wonder whether you have not built some vast edifice of fancy upon a very insubstantial foundation. You can barely have spoken for five minutes with this notional prince of yours, and princes are wont to be swayed by momentary urges and impulses in their journeys through their realm, no doubt. I implore you not to set too much store in this and disappoint yourself unnecessarily'.

'I suppose we are almost arrived there now', came the breathless voice of the official from some way down the path behind them. 'I had not anticipated that I should be required to traverse such a precipice'.

'Indeed, a few more minutes shall bring us there', called Marta, turning back, and then to Adala once more, her eyes filled with concern. 'And if I hear no more of this strangeness after today, I shall be pleased, both for my sake and for yours. You have been a stranger to me these last few weeks, a stranger I say. Even our father has remarked upon it, and his powers of perception are hardly to be marvelled at. Adala!'

This last yelp of alarm was occasioned by Adala's sudden clutching of her arm, the faltering of her step.

'He is there!' she gasped.

She had barely dared to hope for this, but there he was, the tall figure she recalled so vividly, in conversation with Theodolis at the entrance to his cave. Hearing their step upon the loose stones, he turned, raised a hand and bowed as the party approached.

'My good Mecrodios', he said, grasping the sweating official by both hands. 'I have watched your vessel approach these last few hours, and now you are here at last. The way is steep in places, is it not? I trust you will recover your breath in due course. Certainly, you will need all your faculties to wonder at the stored-up treasure of literature my friend Theodolis here is about to reveal to you. I trust you have brought writing materials, yes?

'Dear ladies', he then said, turning his beaming face to them. 'It is good to see you once more, and I thank you for your indulgence in assisting us. As you may have gathered', he waved to where a fine horse was tethered to an ancient, stunted tree, some way away, 'I was hunting away yonder and came this way independently. My friends await me just beyond'.

After some necessary pleasantries, Theodolis withdrew within, taking with him his visitors and leaving Taian with Marta and Adala outside. Taian and Adala exchanged glances. Adala turned to Marta.
'I daresay Theodolis may appreciate your attendance, too', she said. 'His vision is very poor, of course, and he may wish you to assure him that these gentlemen make a proper record of what they find and that nothing is missed'.
'Of course', said Marta with a knowing smile. 'It would be a shame to see anything missed'.

And then they were alone, in defiance of all convention and propriety, a circumstance that added a strange and delicious savour to the moment.
'I have thought of you', he said, patting Theodolis' convenient flat stone, inviting her to sit next to him. 'If I may be direct with you'.
'And I, you', she said, settling herself within what might be considered a respectable distance. 'And what you told me. It seemed a dream'.
'Because I am Taian Starcorides, and because an emperor's blood runs in my veins? There are times when it seems a dream to me, too. And other times when it seems a nightmare', he added with a chuckle.
'Surely not', she said, eyes wide. 'How many hundreds have spent their lives in fighting for that throne. How many have poured out their gold and their life's blood to win that diadem?'
Taian shrugged and glanced at her sidelong.
'I do not seek to justify my sensations, only to present them to you unadorned. I was born as my father was, in that same chamber beneath Niall's porphyry lion. Leogenitos, that makes me, as it has made my ancestors. I do not *seek* dominion over others. I was born to it'.

'I suppose you will concede your birth was more fortunate than mine', replied Adala. 'And my destiny, like yours, is as Tio wills it'.

'But may we not exercise free will in our unknowing pursuit of his plan for us?' asked Taian. 'If free will it is, indeed. I know my father has a very clear notion of my future, notwithstanding the lord's designs'.

He spoke of his family, of his illustrious father, his stepmother and his elder brother, whilst Adala listened with her head bowed. In truth, it seemed like a dream once more to hear the flesh of homely detail placed on the bare bones of the names that all Erenori knew.

'My father wishes to make of my brother an emperor in his own image', said Taian, 'and should my brother be unexpectedly embraced to the lord, he would wish to do likewise with me'.

He looked out wistfully across the sea and stroked his short beard pensively in the way that was already becoming dear to Adala. 'He wishes to live a second life through me when he has been gathered unto Tio. He has written a vast great volume for me in which he describes the manner in which I should rule, enumerating all the nations of the earth and how the Erenori should address them'.

'How very thoughtful of him', said Adala. 'You will be saddened to hear that Corasto has penned me no such volume for the management of The Grapes. Your father must love you very much'.

'Certainly, he loves the idea of me,' said Taian, moving a little closer to her now, 'and he loves the idea of what I might be if I shared his aspirations for me. But I do not share them. And I fear I am a disappointment to him. We could not be more different, he and I'.

'It is extraordinary that you should tell me these things', said Adala, looking up into eyes that were suddenly clouded with sadness, the humour fleeing from his cheerful face. 'My status hardly merits the sharing of such confidences'.

'Status, pah!' said Taian with sudden vehemence. 'We are not in the palace now. What do I care of status? I care for this'.

Placing a finger beneath her chin he turned her face towards his.

'What do you want from me?' she asked after a long moment in which they gazed into each other's eyes. 'We are of different worlds, you and I. Two worlds that may barely touch'.

Taian opened his mouth to speak, seemed to consider, but before he could answer, the sound of echoing conversation from within the cave heralded the return of Theodolis and his visitors to daylight.

'I will come again', whispered Taian. 'At noon tomorrow. Meet me there'.

He indicated the path below the cape, where his horse cropped the short grass amongst bent trees sculpted by the winds.

She nodded, squeezed the hand he placed in hers and drew it away as Marta and the others emerged blinking in the bright afternoon light.

'I trust your mission was attended by success', said Adala. 'And yours, too', said Marta sotto voce with a grin, bringing a fine flush to her sister's cheeks.

'She was there, then, my lord', observed Rayo upon Taian's return to where his friends lounged on a grassy bank. 'If I read your expression right'.

'She was and you do', answered Taian, dismounting and hitching his horse to the branch of a convenient tree next to the others. 'I suppose you have some of that wine left?' Jory threw a leather flask to him. Taian drank deeply, replaced the cork and wiped his mouth with the back of his hand.

'Well, I suppose you will wish to share with us what transpired?' supposed Jory.

'We talked, that is all', said Taian distantly, his eyes unfocused.

'But why did you talk? That is the question', said Rayo. 'Why did you have us come up here? As your friends we are bound to fall in with your desires, however far removed from decency or logic they may be. Nevertheless, it would be interesting to hear your motives for requiring this of us'.

'It surely cannot be that you are smitten by a common servant girl?' said Jory. 'Can it? What is this new game you play, this sudden affectation?'

'She is not a servant girl', said Taian, turning to them.

Rayo and Jory shared a private glance of wry amusement.

'Nor is she the Empress of Honshiang!' laughed Rayo.

'I'm not sure I take your point', said Taian stiffly.

'I think you do', said Jory. 'This strange subterfuge of yours, this private excursion by the three of us from amongst the bosom of our friends and servants, cannot infinitely be repeated unless questions are to be asked. How should we respond to such enquiries? Should we offer falsehoods on your behalf?'

'I have not asked it of you', replied Taian, regarding them suspiciously.

'Yet', supplied Jory.

'Be not concerned, Jory and I would lie for you from dawn to dusk if you required it of us', said Rayo, placing a hand on his shoulder now. 'But what purpose would that serve? What are your intentions with this girl? Sure, she is pretty, but the empire can offer a thousand such beauties, and there are those even amongst the ladies of the palace who are not entirely repulsive to the eye. Surely this is a distraction, and if you court her, you court controversy in equal measure'.

'There would be a storm of it', observed Jory. 'A veritable tempest that would shake the foundations of the palace, no doubt. And everyone would laugh at you', he added.

'It would not be the first time such a thing has occurred', said Taian in a plaintive tone that showed that he nevertheless recognised the truth of their objections. 'Although I speak in generalities, as I trust you will understand. Did not my ancestor, the exalted Emperor Myriado, marry an actress, a whore by any other name?'

'Four hundred years ago!' scoffed Jory. 'And so marriage is already in your mind. You have already advanced beyond mere consideration of the pleasures of the flesh'.

'There have been other, more recent examples', offered Taian, ignoring this. 'Why, I could...'

'My prince', interrupted Rayo, shaking his shoulder gently now. 'Clearly, you toy with us. Clearly you wish it to be thought that you have entirely taken leave of your senses. Naturally, as our prince, we shall indulge you in this, so I must say it is our duty as your subjects and your friends to lay our concerns before you. And besides, what can you possibly have in common to unite your interests and your sensibilities?'

'I suppose you have told her you were already married?' asked Jory.

'Princess Cortha? That was no more than a formality; we were betrothed, that is all. We were children. The poor child died when she was barely nine, and I scarcely knew her. I certainly never *knew* her in...'

'Of course', said Rayo, raising a hand.

'And anyway, I have told her, told Adala', Taian added, as though he thought their conversation should be dignified by the presence of her name at last.

'And I suppose we will be required to bend our steps this way again?' asked Jory after a period of silence during which each busied themselves with their private thoughts.

'We will', said Taian firmly. 'Tomorrow'.

A new day, but one that brought with it pouring rain. Adala, amidst her household tasks, looked out upon the puddled yard and the orchard despondently, quite sure that her tryst must be abandoned. But as the sun rose somewhere amongst grey-clouded skies, so the rain eased and eventually stopped. By a time that she judged approached midday, it had ceased altogether, and a watery sun pierced scudding clouds.

'I am going for a walk', she told her father at last, pulling her shawl around her.

A grunt from Corasto, mending a chair, signalled no objection, and before he could summon one up, she was gone, the wet grass dampening her long frock as she made her way towards the cape. This time she would take the lower path, one that found its way beneath the great limestone outcrop where Theodolis had his abode. At length, treading in the footsteps only of the goats that dwelt thereabout, she emerged onto the narrow grassy slope that Taian had indicated the previous day. For a moment, as she approached, the place seemed empty, but then, as she made her way past an ancient stray olive tree, she found him, perched on a rock, swinging his legs easily.

'Ahoy', he cried, waving an arm in a broad movement that encompassed most of his body. 'That is what the mariners say. And here comes a stately vessel to carry me away'.

She smiled, hands on hips as he climbed down from his perch and crossed to her, making a stately bow. A momentary hesitation and she made her dip in response.

'I trust I find you well', she said, resorting to convention for momentary want of anything more inventive.

'You do', replied Taian earnestly, laying down his thick hunter's cloak for them to sit on. 'And all the better for the sight of you, I may assure you. How you have occupied my thoughts, I can tell you, barely an hour of quiet sleep. Not that I complain, far from it...'

There was more of this, an irregular procession of connected thoughts that Adala recognised as substitute for considered speech.

'What do you want from me?' she asked bluntly, at length supplying considered speech of her own, speech long considered, in fact. 'I asked you that question on the occasion of our last meeting, and you did not answer me then. Will you answer me now?'

Marta had had plenty to say about her own suspicions, namely that he would simply seduce her and move on to pastures new when he was tired of her. It was quite contrary to Marta's firmly stated wishes that she sat beside him now.

Nevertheless, her enquiry silenced Taian abruptly, and for a long moment he seemed incapable of response to it, unless gazing into her face, eyes apparently unfocused, could be considered a response. At length he frowned and seemed to summon resolution.

'I want you to throw back your headdress, so that I may see your hair again', he said. 'Countless times have I revisited that hazy recollection from the first time I set eyes on you'.

Slowly, after a moment's hesitation, she pushed back that strip of linen, shook her hair loose and regarded him solemnly, feeling as though she were indeed naked before him.

'There', she said. 'Is it as you remembered?'

Taian sighed, passed a hand across his mouth.

'More than I remembered with the sun shining upon you now. You are perfection, you know, a goddess'.

'Let us not revisit Cataria', she smiled, taking the hand that he extended to her now. 'You know the story does not end well, at least for you'.

'I almost think it would have been worth it'.
'What, to be turned into a pillar of marble?! You jest with me'.
'I do not'.
His hand was now warm around hers and his face was close.
'I ask again', she sighed. 'What do you want from me? For I cannot believe that the sight of my hair is sufficient to satisfy your desires'.
'Not what you fear, perhaps', he said, drawing away a little, his face suddenly serious.
Why should you think I fear it? came unspoken to her mind, but she only cast her glance down, pushing at a stone pensively with her toe.
'But in truth I do not know what I want, not in its entirety', continued Taian. 'I only know I want to see you. Is that enough? Is the moment not sufficient unto itself? Besides, I could ask you the same question. You have consented to meet me here today, when you could easily have busied yourself about your domestic duties and set me from your mind. What do *you* desire?'
She could not answer this, not in that moment, and when his lips approached hers, her own moved upward – smoothly – to that blissful union.

Chapter Three

Corasto retired to bed with a head cold that same evening, and his immobility, his boundless self-pity, his ceaseless demands for sympathy and hot possets immeasurably tried the patience of his household. Nevertheless, the necessary relaxation of his vigilance made it possible for Adala to attend her daily tryst with Taian in that private place beneath the cape over the course of a whole week. There was one occasion when a wandering goatherd came in search of some of his charges and they were required to hide amongst the scrub, but in general they were free to talk and to hold hands and to approach an understanding of each other that went beyond the merely superficial. There were kisses, too, although Adala made plain a quiet resistance to any more robust advances upon her person, and Taian, for his part, had not pursued them. It was enough that they were together, at least for these few blessed hours.

Nor was there any further talk of intentions. It was as though neither of them wished to bring to mind the future path that each of them must walk. And then suddenly that continual and apparently limitless 'present' found its end. This became brutally apparent to Adala when, upon approaching their habitual tryst, she found Jory **Marinaris** in Taian's place, sitting upon a cloak with two leather bags at his side.

'Greetings, Adala', he said without rising, a wry smile acknowledging her ill-concealed dismay. 'I'm afraid our lord may not be with us today. His father, the emperor, is about to set forth on campaign, and he has been summoned in haste to take counsel with him in The City'. Adala swallowed hard as the implications of this circumstance occurred to her.

'No more than his duty, I suppose', she managed to say over her confusion. 'Our prayers must be with the emperor and his army'.

'Indeed', nodded Jory. 'And our lord sends his apologies for his necessary and urgent withdrawal'.

'Of course. I thank you for conveying that message', said Adala.

'I don't doubt he will return here in due course', said Jory in answer to her unspoken question. 'If he is offered encouragement'.

'Encouragement? A curious choice of words, if I may observe it so, my lord. Pray, what do you mean by it?' asked Adala, feeling the small hairs stand up at the back of her neck.

'I think you know exactly what I mean', said Jory, regarding her seriously now.

'Supposing I don't...' said Adala with a stirring of anger in her breast now.

'Well, if I must spell it out', said Jory. 'Your lord's friends are concerned that he places himself in danger through these liaisons with you. It would be no betrayal of friendship to disclose that despite his many virtues he is an impetuous prince, much given to brief dalliances and sudden infatuations. They do not last. He is perhaps less jealous of his reputation than he should be. I speak plainly with you. As I say, we see danger here'.

'What danger?'

Her eyes flashed cold fire now and Jory climbed to his feet, approaching to look down upon her in a manner that she could only regard as threatening.

'I think we are the best judges of that – and you, my dear girl, should be mindful of your humble station', he said coldly.

'Never mind my station', she snapped, all consciousness of rank and social convention suddenly forgotten. 'I ask you again. What danger? Spell it out for me'.

'The danger of ridicule, for one', said Jory with a harsh laugh. 'Do you not think all the palace will think it a great joke if the emperor's second son is known to be mooning over some ignorant peasant girl?'

'Ignorant', scoffed Adala, clenching her fists. 'And how is *your* grasp of Miron or Vilmo, or Antrophon? If knowledge of carousing and hunting and other idle pleasures is the learning you value, well yes, I am ignorant indeed'.

'I have never been one of those who equate spouting ancient literature with actual wisdom or intelligence', said Jory abashed. 'And certainly, the state's future should be amongst considerations when a marriage is considered', he continued. 'There are high politics at stake, and marriage amongst the great is universally acknowledged to be an indispensable tool of such politics...'

'Who is talking of marriage?' interrupted Adala, eyes suddenly wide.

'Why no one', admitted Jory. 'But certainly, you must accept that such foolish dalliance might tend that way, if allowed to proceed to its natural conclusion, I mean'.

'So, you think your lord a fool?'

'I do not, certainly I do not!' protested Jory, reddening once more. 'I only fear his vulnerability to one whose undoubted charms might seduce him from the path of duty and plunge his future into confusion'.

'I have not seduced him, I assure you', she said, shaking her head. 'And your friendship evidently does not extend to a full understanding of his character, if you consider him so vulnerable to mere feminine wiles, so ignorant and neglectful of the responsibility that his status imposes on him'.

'Enough of this', said Jory, the blood draining from his face now. 'Enough, I say! I have not come here to debate with you. I have come to instruct you that you must desist

from this, must confine yourself to your little tavern and decline in future to attend such meetings with my lord'.
'I will make no such undertaking', she said, her mouth held in a hard line. 'Nor will I ever'.
Jory glared at her.
'I could simply snap your silly neck and bury you in yonder woods. No one would ever find you', he growled stepping forward, looming over her.
'But you will not', she said defiantly, raising a finger. 'You will not, Jory, because I believe you to be a true friend to our lord and I trust his judgement in his choice of you. He speaks of you in the most cordial of terms. I know that he would never think so highly of anyone capable of wounding him so deeply'.
The momentary anger and the associated resolve seemed to drain from Jory's person as he stood back from her, rubbing his chin ruefully.
'You are right', he admitted. 'Of course, you are'.
After a moment, he reached down to the cloak at his side and brought up one of the two leather bags, which gave a familiar metallic rustle, like the chainmail of soldiers.
'Very well, if your ears are deaf to my arguments, I wonder if this will more eloquently argue my case', he said, opening the neck to pour a stream of heavy gold coins into his hand.
'This and that other bag should be enough for your father to set himself up very comfortably in any city in the empire, saving the one City, of course, which must forever be denied to you'.
For a moment, her mind touched upon the wealth poured out before her – the fine house, the fine clothes and the respectable status it would buy – but only for a moment.
'Nor do I set a monetary value on my honour', she said. 'You cannot buy me. Nor will you ever, even if you set all

the wealth of the world before me. Our business here is done, I think'.

Jory regarded her thoughtfully, replacing the coins in their bag.

'Perhaps it is', he said. 'And perhaps we have misjudged you, Rayo and I'.

'I am certain of it', said Adala as Jory bowed and withdrew, crossing to where his horse was tethered.

'Be sure to tell our lord of this encounter', called Adala as he rode away through the trees. 'Because we have no secrets, he and I'.

Walking down from the cape, reflecting upon that curious meeting, Adala had wondered at her resort to such a statement. In truth, their acquaintance was yet so slight it was impossible that each could know more than a fragment of the other's private mind. And yet the truth of that statement remained, impervious to acknowledged fact. She knew that she would conceal no secret from Taian, and she felt quite certain that this would be reciprocated in the object of her affection. Was this what "love" was like, she asked herself, and for more than the first time. Or, more than that, was this *actually* love itself that painted the image of his face before her mind's eye, like the icon adored at the altar.

Visitors to the inn coming along the road from Garabdor reported no news of the emperor's campaign against the Zanyari in the south, or of any significant event likely to have detained Taian there. Could it be that the emperor had obliged the prince to accompany him? It seemed unlikely, if Taian's character and interests had been accurately described to her. The weather took a turn for the worse, however, and the rain-lashed forests seemed also unlikely to entice noble huntsmen from their lodges or from The City. Adala began to despair of seeing Taian again. She could be sure now that his friends sought to discourage him from it, and there were doubtless myriad distractions in the palace that might diminish the ardour of the passion he had expressed for her. With Corasto restored to his full watchful vigour, his full attentiveness to the duty of others, the inn returned to its usual round of purposeful activity. Days passed, became weeks, and with the approach of summer it seemed as though she must abandon hope of seeing him once more.

But then, one day, a mud-splashed courier dismounted wearily in the yard, crossing to knock on the door. By the time Adala had hurried through from the kitchen, Corasto had already opened the letter and was holding it up to the light, his lips moving slowly as he struggled to decipher it.
'Cantrophene', he grunted, passing it to Adala. 'All in Cantrophene. List of books by the looks of it, but I can't make heads nor tails of it. Why do these library people persist with such anachronisms?'
'That'll be the catalogue they promised us from the library', said Adala, picking up the enclosure, her heart pounding in her chest. 'Addressed to my uncle'.
'Well, he wasn't going to read it for himself', said Corasto, detecting criticism. 'Was he?'
'No, of course. Let me read it', said Adala, sitting down, smoothing its two leaves out on a table.
The first sheet consisted of no more than the expected list with notes underneath in neat palace script and values written next to them. The second sheet, however, was laid out in the same way, but the notes underneath contained a message from Taian, spread across several lines. It was all she could do to master herself, to read those lines without evident agitation, to read them as though dutifully perusing some dull academic detail.

'My dear', she read. 'I beg that you will excuse my lamentable absence. My father's campaign is well under way and my brother accompanies him. Accordingly, I must remain here in The City, and my waking hours are much taken up with palace business. Your understanding of my character will lead you to conclude that this is oppressive to my soul. Do not imagine that you are absent from my thoughts, however. On the contrary, you are never far from them, and I live for the time when we may meet again. If you wish to reply to this message, you may place a letter in the hollow of that ancient tree we once sat beneath at the cape. I shall send a servant to look there. Yours affectionately, Taian'.

Corasto had a small supply of paper which he used mostly for his infrequent correspondence with their aunt in The City. Years ago, when Adala was very young, Corasto had quarrelled with their mother and she had withdrawn there, scandalously living with the pork butcher whose charms and importunings had been the source of their dispute. Since then, she had suffered a stroke, brought about by God's judgement, if Corasto were to believed, and now she dwelt with her sister: deaf, blind and largely paralysed. The box he kept the paper in was kept locked in his own room, and Adala dared not ask him to spare her any of it in order to write love letters to the prince. Accordingly, her reply to Taian was written on a narrow strip torn from the bottom of his own letter, consisting of the simple message.
'Dearest T, please send paper. A'.
This, sealed in a much larger waxed fabric enclosure, was dispatched in the manner prescribed, with much anxiety for its safe collection. However, before any further reply was received, wholly unanticipated new circumstances threatened to set her life on another path altogether. This much became apparent when Corasto's conversation

with her and her sister began to be frequently interspersed with references to Phodios, a gentleman of previously moderate means who had now inherited a considerable estate in the neighbouring village. Phodios had always been on cordial terms with Corasto and an occasional customer at The Grapes. Now that Phodios' improved income added lustre to his name, Corasto was keen to befriend him, calling at his new residence to pay compliments and offering him preferential terms at the inn. Accordingly, Phodios became a frequent visitor, bringing with him his three sons, one of whom was impossibly dull – and besides betrothed already to the miller's daughter. The younger two, it had to be admitted, were handsome young men, attractive enough to catch any girl's eye, even without the additional allure that broad acres supplied. Marta was evidently rather smitten with Lenzhios, the elder of the two, and Gridorias might be expected to be the recipient of Adala's approval, at least so far as her father's own desires were concerned. In fact, both young men were wholly in awe of her, Gridorias barely able to utter a coherent sentence in her presence. Nevertheless, Corasto's intentions were transparently clear to both his daughters: these young men, fine fellows with such good prospects, were the shining stars of his aspiration, and so their marriage to his daughters would bring with it the consummation of his desires for self-aggrandizement. Marta, already past her sixteenth year, was delighted to acquiesce in this, charmed by this potential coincidence of inclination with fortune. Adala, on the other hand, was filled with a sense of foreboding. Corasto had yet to spell out his plans for them, but that day must surely be at hand – and how then might she refuse? She could hardly say that she preferred to await a proposal from an imperial prince in the far-distant City.

She had, on several occasions, asked Taian what his intentions were with regard to her, and he had declined to answer her. Content to disassociate his person from his status, to see him simply as a person like her, she had been glad to persist in their liaison, but such a disassociation was ultimately dishonest and she must now admit to herself the nature of her ultimate desire. She wished that she might marry him. That desire, once made plain and acknowledged, could be scrutinised for legitimacy and for purity of intention. With regard to legitimacy, she must certainly be thought mad, if she declared her intention of securing the prince's hand in marriage, and she questioned her own sanity for daring even to picture it in her mind's eye. It was like a children's story that even the dullest ten-year-old might think far-fetched. A girl from her background might as well dream of journeying to the moon. On the other hand, she flattered herself that she passed the test she had set for herself with regard to avarice or ambition. The notion of boundless riches, matchless jewellery, the adoration of thousands and silk next to her skin was not an unattractive one, she was bound to admit. However, she told herself, Taian was Taian, whether a prince or a poor man, and she would marry him regardless, should the question be put to her. But would it? Besides, could she refuse the certainty of reasonable prosperity for the more than uncertain prospect of a prince's hand, the insubstantial fancy of a maiden's mind? For that was surely what it was, and knowledge of this was a conviction that grew upon her each time she visited the letter tree and came away empty-handed.

And then present reality was brought brutally face-to-face with whimsy and a choice forced upon her. Corasto came in beaming one afternoon, announcing that he was the bearer of good news, carrying a letter in his hand, in fact, which he held up for them to inspect with great complacency. Marta's light anticipatory step was already on the stair as Adala came in from feeding the chickens, foreboding in her heart.

'Girls', he said, his face alight with an unrestrained joy such as Adala had rarely seen there. 'Fortune has smiled upon us. Why? You may ask', he continued, looking into Marta's excited face, too full of his own exuberance to recognise reserve in Adala's. 'Well, I shall tell you what this glad missive contains. My good friend Phodios and I have arrived at an understanding. An understanding of very great significance in all our lives. An understanding that relates to those fine young men that are his sons and to my fine young daughters, too. An engagement is proposed, no less! An engagement! You are to be married! What say you to that?!'

Marta clapped her hands, jumped up and down and embraced her father with many exclamations of delight, for this is what she had long hoped for, and the pair danced a little step together in the passageway. At length their faces turned to Adala, who abruptly burst into tears and ran from the room.

'Hush, leave her be, there are more ways than one of expressing delight', she heard vaguely from her place by the hen house.

'That did not strike me as delight in any form', Corasto said, his voice muffled, suspicion driving out the joy from his voice. 'Does she have another? Does she deceive me?'

Before Corasto could even attempt to satisfy himself on this point, Adala was away, skirts hitched up, running along the familiar path as fast as her legs would carry her. Panting, sobbing, mopping at streaming eyes and nose with her sleeve, she ran from the fate marked out for her.

The tree, when she reached it, yielded at last a blessed letter that brought a leap of hope to her labouring heart.

Tearing off the enclosure impatiently, she sat down amongst the twisted roots as her eyes drank up the words of her love, as a parched man laps at a clear, cool stream. There were eight leaves of closely written script, with as many for her reply. Delightfully, there were also two pens for her use and a small bottle of ink. Calming her breathing, stifling her sobs, Adala read the letter through for a second time, clasped it to her breast, looked up to praise the heavens and read a third time and a fourth. Much of the letter was entirely conventional in nature: enquiries for her family's health, descriptions of the wearisome palace duties he must submit to, assurances of his continued affection for her, but there was also a passage relating to her encounter with Jory that she read with particular interest.

'It is true to say that my most intimate confidantes were initially opposed to my meetings with you, made their objections clear in a direct and earnest manner made more eloquent still by their transparent affection and loyalty to my person. Naturally, as you may imagine, I was entirely deaf to their entreaties, armoured as I am by the ardour of my feelings for you. They tell me that they had brought their reservations to your attention, too, importuning you with their false accusations of venal interest, calling into question the purity of your motivation for consenting to our association. I am told that you held fast to that blissful association and refused to forgo it, even under threat of violence or when offered monies of the most persuasive kind. It was not enough for them to accept my assurances of your stainless character. They must establish it for themselves. I trust you will forgive them, as have I. I trust and believe their motivations to be of the noblest kind, and doubtless you will grow in their affections as they come to know you better. I may assure you that you have already kindled a new respect in their hearts by your steadfast resistance to their approach'.

At last, Adala set down the letter, took up the pen and drew the stopper from the little bottle, finding a smooth patch of earth to serve as her writing desk.

'My dearest Taian', she wrote. 'This note must be of the briefest, because I fear a decision of a most momentous nature is forced upon us. I have allowed myself to conceive of a future in which we are together, and I trust you will excuse me if my imaginings have outstripped the bounds of reality. However, I should tell you that marriage to another rushes up towards me with indecent haste. My father has entered into an agreement with a neighbour, and there is no legitimate reason for my refusal to wed his son, a young man of fair countenance and good prospects. I shall do what I can to delay what must be my inevitable submission to my father's will, but I cannot say how long I may resist. If, as I hope and pray, your unspoken intention has been to make me your wife, I urge you to take necessary action with all possible dispatch'.

The sound of voices from above made it impossible to bring this letter to its affectionate formal conclusion. Adala hurriedly did her best to restore the torn enclosure around it and thrust it into the tree once more. She concealed the remaining paper within her clothing, cast pen and ink aside and turned to the steep path that led up to Theodolis' cave. Marta was questioning her uncle, receiving from him assurances that he had not seen her, not now, nor for some days since the letter from the library had arrived.

'Sister!' she exclaimed, seizing Adala by the arm, hurrying her away from a wondering Theodolis. 'What can you mean by this? Corasto is beside himself, wavering between fury and mystification. His triumph hangs by a thread, and you, that thread personified, must urgently assure him that all is well. Phodios will certainly be insulted, will abandon this match forthwith. We will be rightly condemned abroad for passing up such a promising alliance. I trust that you are not still entertaining foolish pretensions with regard to the prince. Set those aside, dear sister', she demanded with a glance that held steely resolution. 'For I will not have your idle fantasies destroy my own chance of felicity'.

'I will not', muttered Adala, nevertheless allowing Marta to impel her along the olive grove path. 'I cannot'.

'Why not?' her sister demanded angrily. 'Why would you not consent to such a match? Gridorias is such a fine young man, is he not?'

'I do not deny it', admitted Adala, 'but I cannot – and will not – commit myself to him'.

'But you must', said Marta, stopping suddenly beside Marcianos' house and wagging a censorious finger. 'You absolutely must, for I will not have you stand in the way of my happiness for the sake of your own folly. And besides, our father will insist on it'.

'How so? I will never willingly submit. Will he connive at the rape of his own daughter?'

'You are mad! Quite mad!' cried Marta, throwing up her arms in despair. 'Will you not see reason?'

Chapter Four

Perdannor 22-6-72

Four legions and their associated light troops made for an impressive spectacle when on parade or arrayed for battle, but now they were strung out over miles of rutted track, beneath lowering clouds, lashed by rain, hunched beneath coats and waterproofs that were the dark, dun colours of the mud that clung to their boots. At intervals, on either side of the line of march, scouts stood vigilant on the ridge tops or urged their horses back and forth along the line. At the head of the vanguard rode the emperor himself, Gelon Starcorides, Dawnstar of the Bright Host, as he was officially styled in this role, Hammer of the Heathen. Beneath his sodden grey surcoat, he was clad from throat to toe in steel armour, since they were deep within enemy territory, and contact with his forces might be expected at any moment. The armour was light and marvellously articulated, but Gelon was in his sixtieth year and it was not light enough. The armour was twice as old as its wearer and was a holy relic, blessed by St Eustadios, and so impervious to edged weapons and even to musket balls, as a number of slight dents proved. Various other holy relics were at hand, including the lance of St Moalin and the holy standard of the Eternal Sun, which raised the martial spirit of the righteous and spread gloom amongst the wicked. This last-named rode upon a carriage at the centre of the column a mile or so behind, attended by bishops and a troop of the warrior monks, whose sacred duty was to protect it.
Gelon's ornate plumed helmet hung at his saddle in a leather bag, but a broad-rimmed hat kept the rain from

his thin grey locks, dripping and sagging at the rim. Now, two scouts came cantering towards his party, splashing through puddles, hunched under soaking cloaks.

Raising his hand, plucking at the reins, Gelon urged his mount aside so that the column could continue its march and he could confer with them. Daval, his aide-de-camp, Triado, his leading general and a score or so of officials and personal retainers came after him, forming up in a loose group to his rear. One of the scouts dismounted, passing reins to his companion and advancing to genuflect before the emperor, casting back his hood. Rain trickled down his sallow face and he cast his eyes down as protocol demanded.

'Go on, man', said Gelon brusquely. 'Do you bring word of the other column?'

A further two legions and as many foreign mercenaries marched in parallel with this one, a mile or so distant, separated from them by woods and higher ground.

'No, my lord', said the scout, using the simpler, more practical form of address permissible in military contexts rather than the elaborate formal address of the court. 'I come from the head of the column. We approach a stream up yonder, beneath the rise by that there single oak. Do you see it?'

'Yes, yes', grunted Gelon. 'I may be old but I'm not yet blind. Is the bridge broken down?'

The rutted track they rode on was the handiwork of his ancestors, built by the toil of skilled engineers in the distant past. Since this part of the world had fallen into the hands of barbarians a hundred years previously, such roads had fallen into disrepair, and even some of the more lightly constructed bridges had collapsed.

'Never was a bridge there, my lord', said the scout, blinking rain from his eyes. 'It were always a ford. May struggle with the wagons, though. The stream's fair swollen with all this', he announced, gesturing in the air around him for emphasis. 'No sign of the enemy, though', he added, anticipating the emperor's next question.

Gelon nodded and turned in his saddle.

'Opinions please, gentlemen,' he said, looking from face to face.

'How wide is the ford?' asked General Triado Melanthros of the scout, who remained kneeling. 'And how deep at its shallowest point?'

'Fifty paces, maybe more', announced the scout. 'And knee deep at most, but a stony and uneven bed'.

Gelon stroked his chin. History had proved the folly of being caught with half an army across a watercourse on occasions too numerous to recount. But fifty paces was a manageable constriction in case the army should need to form up for defence.

'Well, gentlemen?' he barked. 'We must judge whether there is sufficient daylight to get us through or whether we should encamp hereabouts and await the morrow. I think we shall ride ahead and see for ourselves. Please do lead on , sir', he added, addressing the scout. A few moments later and the party was cantering past the head of the column, spurring their mounts up the low rise where the lone oak stood. Beyond was a low valley with stone-walled fields, woods and the occasional dwelling, long burnt out by the advance parties, showing the ruined thatch and charred roof timbers that were typical of their passage. Scouts were posted up- and downstream. A further party could be seen on the distant southern horizon.

'Good', grunted Gelon. 'Petrocles knows his business'.

'He should do', laughed Triado at his side. 'He's been engaged in it long enough'.

Gelon felt too uncomfortable and out of sorts to respond in like measure, although the image of the veteran chief of reconnaissance, with his white beard tucked in his belt, was certainly one to cherish. The man had served his father before him. Gelon spared a glance for Triado as the two men rode abreast now, slowing their mounts to a trot. The general was looking downstream, stroking his own black goatee beard pensively. He was undoubtedly a successful and experienced practitioner of his craft. He was also Gelon's second cousin. But he did not trust him. An emperor was forever beset with rumours and reports of disloyalty amongst his entourage or court, and a wide variety of plots had been investigated during the sixteen years of his reign. As was the way of such things, most such suspicions had been found to be baseless, but a few successfully exposed plots had resulted in the imprisonment, exile or even death of their participants. Still, the reports that reached him from his intelligencers struck him as particularly credible, and Gelon's own understanding of human character lent further credence to this. There was certainly no problem with ambition per se, a perfectly admirable quality, the emperor was bound to concede, but the occasional venal glint in Triado's eye hinted at an ambition that knew no bounds, reaching even to the throne itself, perhaps. It was for this reason that Triado rode at Gelon's side. Keep your friends close but your enemies closer was a well-worn but sensible adage.

'You are too old for this', his eldest son had told him, before the outset of the expedition.

'I am not yet in my dotage', the emperor had retorted as they stood pondering over the map table. 'And besides, you have no experience of this country. I have campaigned there twice in the fifties, and I don't suppose much has changed since them'.

'I can lead the army', Cato assured him, placing a hand on his father's forearm for emphasis, his cool grey eyes earnest now. 'I have led before. I hoped I had won your trust'.

Gelon bit his lip. Cato's campaign against the men of Vhanakhor had been inconclusive, resulting in a stalemate after three months of fruitless march and counter-march.

'We forced the Vhanakori to the negotiating table, did we not?' Cato added, as though sensing his father's reservation.

The Vhanakori had certainly sought to break off the war, although a revolt on the island of Eudora was the likeliest source of their sudden urgent desire for peace. Cato had proved to be a cautious general, excessively cautious in his father's view. An opportunity had occurred when the enemy's host had been taken unawares, halfway through striking camp. It was not impossible that another fully readied force lurked nearby, but Gelon would certainly have taken that chance in order to seize the opportunity to destroy what was likely to be the foe's main field army before it even had the chance to form. Good generalship required that risk, and reward should be weighed in the balance, and it was often the case that the greater the risk, the greater was the reward to be garnered. Sometimes, it was necessary to trust to one's god and to pray for good fortune. Good generals were lucky generals, god-fearing generals, but Prince Cato had placed his trust in neither.

'Shall we cross and take a look at the ground on the other side, my lord?' asked Triado now as the scout galloped off to his station to their distant flank. He indicated the turbulent grey waters of the stream ahead of them.

'Certainly', grunted Gelon with the brief movement of the heels and the tug of the reins that was all that was necessary to urge his mount down the gentle slope before them.

Nor was Cato a leader of men, mused Gelon, returning to his reverie. He was deemed by those he commanded to be haughty and aloof, qualities unlikely to win the affection of his troops. A few miles from there, Cato led the second column, but his father had ensured that his own trusted lieutenants were charged with interpreting his commands, conveying them to subordinate officers in the manner that all true leaders instinctively employ. In addition, his neglect of the commissariat during that campaign had led to a shortage of supplies – and this, in its turn, to hardship amongst the soldiers. The regular troops had behaved themselves well, by and large, but there had been deplorable outbreaks of rapine and plunder amongst the mercenaries, even in imperial territory. In essence, the war had been a failure, a pointless effusion of blood and treasure, leaving frontier provinces on both sides of the border wasted and depopulated. It was impossible not to blame Cato.

Even as these thoughts were traversing the emperor's mind, his narrowed eyes were surveying the folds and the contours of the land ahead. A well-sited camp required a moderately elevated and well-drained position with clear terrain and unobstructed views on all sides. The low rise beyond the stream showed promise, but it was always imprudent to camp with any significant obstacle blocking a likely line of retreat.

Gelon turned and beckoned to Dailon Euscathion, his chief engineer, who was some way behind, hunched under his soaking cloak.

'Go back to the column and organise camp on the last best site you noted on this side of the stream. I'm going ahead with the others to reconnoitre the ground on the far side'.

Dailon bowed in the saddle, touched his brow and was gone, his two lieutenants galloping after him. Gelon spurred his own mount forward once more, to where Triado and other officers awaited him.

Gelon sniffed, missing the characteristic smell of slow match in the air that inevitably accompanied the march of an imperial host. It was the familiar whiff of soldiering, as much as excrement and spilt blood. The matchlock muskets of a large proportion of his infantry depended on the slow-burning match they all must carry. This cursed rain effectively neutered those regiments. Even if the muskets could be charged with dry powder, and dry powder then placed in the pan, the absence of smouldering match rendered them useless, unless as clubs. Armies had been defeated before through the baleful intervention of a sudden downpour. Their enemy barely used firearms, but in these circumstances the empire's technical advantage became instead a vulnerability. He must hope that the rain would cease during the coming night. Hope. Gelon found it hard to conjure that precious commodity in his breast. His mind was oppressed by a sense of impending doom, by a consciousness of his own mortality and the uncertainty that lay beyond. He was well aware that his body was growing old, that the deep ache in his bones owed more to encroaching decay than to the rain and the damp and the chill. And who would continue his work when he was gone? It was certain that the church and senate would confirm Cato in his place; precedent was clear enough, and the prestige of his father would undoubtedly carry his endorsement through the senate. Besides, the man had – as yet – demonstrated no incapacity so troubling as to prompt his disqualification. The empire might survive his rule, provided that he chose his ministers well. But what if Cato should, by some bleak stroke of fate, predecease him? Then, in all likelihood, the throne would pass to Taian, his second son. Gelon shuddered at that prospect, shook his head so that the heavy drops that fringed his hat cascaded around him like crystal. He clenched his lips in a hard line. That was certainly not a prospect to be countenanced. The boy could not be more different from his severe, serious-minded brother. All Gaian cared about was hunting, chasing girls and carousing with his friends. At some point it would be necessary to take him in hand, to bring him to a proper sense of the duties and responsibilities that his privileges enjoined upon him. Perhaps a position in the church, governorship of one of the more remote outlying provinces...

His mind was toying with such possibilities as he urged his mount through the stony shallows of the ford. Here and there, sizeable rocks thrust like cutwaters from the rushing torrent, each girded with a tangle of broken branches from the woods upstream. Suddenly, his mount missed its footing, lurched, panicked and rose up on its rear legs. The emperor, lost in thought, was fatally slow to react. Amongst cries of alarm from his companions, he toppled backwards from the saddle. The armour that Saint Eustadios had blessed offered no protection from the swift clutch of gravity, nor did it save him from dashing his brains out against a slick black rock. In a moment his steel-clad body was borne down, half submerged, buffeted by the waters, a thin red stream of the imperial blood mingling with the torrent. In another moment his subjects were dragging him to the pebbled shore, regarding the shattered skull in horror. It was clear that he was quite dead. Murmuring prayers, Brodon Radigores, Duke of Taal, gently closed the emperor's blank, staring eyes. As second in command, it fell to Triado to manage the situation from this point on. The dismounted officers around the emperor's sodden corpse, and those troopers of the bodyguard who remained mounted further back, regarded the general anxiously as he remained kneeling at Gelon's side. Everyone seemed stunned. Triado appeared lost in thought, lost in grief, and long moments passed in which the only sounds were the rushing of waters, the snorting of horses and the jingle of harnesses.

Let me think, let me think, let me think, Triado urged himself privately, whilst the river of time, the stream of his own life, flowed inexorably on. He shook his head, ran his own hands down over his own eyes and face, in a passable semblance of grief. In truth, he felt no regret at all for the passing of his venerable sovereign. His own heart raced within him as the emperor's ceased to beat. He was well aware that Gelon neither liked nor trusted him, had observed his actions closely for signs of incompetence or disloyalty by which his disgrace or demotion might be encompassed. But now the emperor was removed from the game, and all things were possible. First, to demonstrate firm leadership, take control. He straightened himself, stood and eyed the gathered soldiers, amongst whom a low murmuring had begun.

'Silence! Listen to me now. Daval, Radigores, take four men and go back to the column. Speak to no one until you find Bishop Ainscoth. Bid him bring a wagon hither with four of his monks and an altar cloth that they may pray for the emperor's soul and array him in some dignity. If they should seek explanation,

say that we have encountered a wounded holy man who craves audience with him'.

He turned to two of the bedraggled imperial guard, who sat their mounts wide-eyed.

'You two. Take off your cloaks and drape them over the body. We don't want any prying eyes to see what has happened here. Form up in a loose group so that the body is less visible, should any of our own scouts come sticking their noses in, until the bishop arrives. None must know of this...', Triado stuttered, simulating gaining mastery over a trembling voice, '... this terrible, terrible tragedy until arrangements have been set in place. When the body is taken up on the wagon, you must re-join the column and make camp as the emperor ordered. If his

absence is noted, you must say that he has ridden to the other column to confer with the prince. Is that clear?'
There were nods and grunts of agreement.
'Good. There will be time for grieving later, but first I must notify the prince. Your discretion, your silence, is absolutely imperative until then. I trust I can rely on you'.
Triado was perfectly sincere in declaring that arrangements must be set in place, although his understanding of this may have differed from that of most of his listeners. Now he beckoned to Gendrian and Tustin, two of his personal retainers.
'You two, come with me. If we strike out along the stream bank we should make good time'.
And then the three were gone, leaving the small party of horsemen disconsolate around the corpse of their fallen emperor, lashed by a new intensity of driving rain as afternoon moved towards dusk.

Triado had not ridden far out of sight of the party when he drew his men off the path and into the shelter of a wood. For some time, he had been aware of a pair of what were surely Zanyari scouts shadowing them on the further bank of the stream.
'We will wait here awhile', he told them, noting the puzzlement in their eyes. 'I would rather the prince learned of the emperor's death in more dignified circumstances than a conversation on horseback. We shall wait here until it is certain that his column will have made camp for the night. But first I shall see if those are our own scouts out yonder'.
'You two stay here', he hissed, raising a cautioning hand.
The two men exchanged glances, aware that their general was taking a risk in so doing but bound by their oath of obedience.

There was no real way of telling how long had passed, but it seemed to them that more than an hour had elapsed before Triado returned, by which time both were on the verge of concluding that he had been killed or captured. At last, though, he threw himself down at their side, brushing aside their enquiries and their protestations of concern.

Loitering in this manner in enemy territory in such small numbers was undoubtedly dangerous, but this was a risk that Triado was prepared to take. The wood offered good protection from prying eyes and some from the rain. Now they pushed further between the close-set trees, tethering their horses and settling themselves amongst dried leaves where the canopy above was densest, as the daylight drained from the weeping heavens and a growing darkness settled around them.

At last, when it seemed certain that the prince's column would by now be entrenched and beneath canvas, the party moved on, following the stream bed eastward with barely enough light to find their way. It was not long before they came upon the scouts and outposts of the prince's column, who recognised Triado and led him to the force's encampment. As convention dictated, this had been sited on a low rise facing the stream, already fortified with bank and ditch by the infantry, already set up with neat rows of tents and orderly lines for the cavalry mounts in a manner that was straight from the military manuals of old. Greeting the sentries at the west gate smartly, Triado led his little party along the mud-trampled main throughfare to the centre, where the commander's tent had already been raised. The rain was beginning to ease now, and the smoke of skilfully but effortlessly kindled cooking fires was acrid in his nostrils.

Once admitted by the sentries at the threshold of the prince's tent, Triado found himself in a broad space, inadequately lit by oil lamps hung from the poles and stretchers. A group of officers had been consulting a map laid out on a trestle table, but now they turned to greet the newcomer, their faces registering varying degrees of pleasure or calculated neutrality. All faces were suddenly drained of any form of levity as they read the expression in Triado's grim countenance. The prince, on the further side of the table, looked up. His long face, with its broad mouth and small grey eyes, was unsuited to the expression of joy, and it held only a wary puzzlement as Triado approached to genuflect and to make his salute.

'You have news from the emperor's column?' asked Cato. 'And news that must be carried by such a distinguished messenger as yourself? There has been no engagement with the enemy, I trust? My outposts have not brought me word of it'.

'I bear grim, grim tidings', said Triado, rising at the prince's gesture. 'News that I must bring myself. The emperor is dead'.

As Triado had anticipated, had already thoroughly rehearsed in his mind, the gathering beneath the sagging canvas was immediately stunned into silence and immobility. After a moment, eyes and heads began to turn to Prince Cato, from whose reaction they must take their cue. Cato swallowed hard, his eyes suddenly wide, and placed his hands on the table as though to steady himself. For a long moment he bowed his head, his eyes fixed on the ink horn and the papers with which the table was scattered. Then, at last, he straightened himself, conscious perhaps that a great mantle of responsibility had now fallen upon his narrow shoulders, and regarded his subjects steadily.

'May Tio embrace his soul', he said, using the more formal name for God appropriate in these circumstances. 'And may we all rise to follow the example he has set us. I know that I can rely on your loyalty and support'.

There were a great many declarations of shocked grief, a great many fervent declarations of loyalty as the significance of the moment settled upon the gathering. The senate would be required to endorse it, but the likelihood was that Cato stood before them now as emperor. Men began to make the sign of Tio in the air before them and sink to their knees. Cato listened to their protestations with solemn good grace, inviting all to stand at last.

Triado, who had stood with the appearance of humility during this, adding his own expressions of loyalty to the clamour, was required now to describe the circumstances of Gelon's death. Pledging allegiance to Cato brought him some vague anxiety for the integrity of his immortal soul, but his conscience was perfectly clear with regard to the manner of the emperor's demise, at least, and he made a clear, brusque account of it, received in respectful silence. More detail was requested and supplied, followed by a breakdown of the orders that Triado had issued to those present at that fateful moment.

'So the column is unaware of my father's death, with the exception of those you have enjoined silence upon?' observed Cato, stroking his chin thoughtfully.

'Indeed, my lord', nodded Triado.

'Then my duty is clear', announced Cato. 'I must ride to the main column and confer with my officers there. Surely, the campaign must be abandoned for now. My place is in The City'.

With an army at my back to reinforce the strength of my claim, was the unspoken rider to this, which all present understood perfectly well.

'I trust the route you took is the most direct', he continued, addressing Triado. 'You shall lead me back that way now'.

He rolled up the map on the table with a finality that perfectly symbolised the termination of this campaign, handing it to an aide-de-camp at his side.

'Shake out a troop of my bodyguard', he added. 'We leave at once'.

'But lord!' protested one of Cato's more seasoned officers, a man with a grizzled beard and a puckered scar across his brow. 'It would be safer to wait until daybreak. Your duty...'

'Do not presume to teach me my duty, Scordas', snapped Cato, causing Triado a leap of joy within his heart. 'We go right now. News such as this has a way of leaking out and must be conveyed in the proper fashion with the utmost celerity. I must take a firm grip on both parts of the army. You will plan an orderly retreat to the frontier, and officers of senior command rank will join me at dawn for conference with the main body. I trust that is clear. Now, General Melanthros, let us waste no further time', commanded Cato, buckling on his sword belt whilst an officer stood ready with his coat and cloak.

Destiny awaits, a more imaginative man might have added, thought Triado, but he had his own plans for Cato's destiny – ones that must not be permitted to rise into his face. So he bowed deep and strode from the tent to retrieve his own companions and his mount.

With thirty of the imperial bodyguard at their backs, they retraced the trail westward along the stream bank. The rain had stopped by now, and the moon, riding high between ragged scudding clouds, made the path more easy to trace. They saw no signs of life other than a ghost owl on the wing until they came within the outskirts of the same wood that Triado had sought shelter in earlier that night. Here, though, there was a great deal of life to be found, and of death in equal measure. A large force of Zanyari tribesmen lay in ambush there amongst the trees. As the horsemen urged their mounts through, all too conscious of the heightened danger in such terrain, the enemy rushed out with sudden fury, hurling their spears and uttering their ululating war cries. There were several hundreds of them, and the riders were unhorsed or overwhelmed in minutes. Triado hacked around himself desperately, his sword biting into screaming flesh or turning aside the questing blows of his assailants. It was useless, as he had known it would be. Impressions raced across his consciousness, almost too rapidly for his brain to interpret and comprehend: the clash of steel, a confused din of voices, horsemen dragged from their rearing mounts, Cato's holy sword Esteldir snatched from his faltering grasp, that pale anguished face, falling amongst the dark silhouettes of the surging crowd around him. Triado's horse took a spear in the chest and toppled, taking its rider with her. He crunched to the ground with a bone-jarring impact that expelled every vestige of breath from his body, struggled to scramble to his feet, was thrust down once more and felt a searing pang of agony as a well-directed blade was thrust into the unarmoured space beneath his arm. He lurched away, whirled, was thrust down once more and fell gasping on his back, stunned, helpless as his helmet was wrenched from his head. A blade glinted above him, and then, even as it plunged downward at his throat, a mailed hand pushed it aside.

'Not this one', said an authoritative voice in Zanyari, a tongue he knew well.

The battle was over, although the night was still filled with harsh voices, the screams and pleas of the wounded, each abruptly curtailed by the inevitable coup de grace that must follow. Triado felt dizzy, lightheaded, and the searing agony in his armpit told him that he had sustained a significant wound. Perhaps he had already exsanguinated a fatal quantity of his lifeblood. Despite this, he lifted his eyes to the heavens, where branches stirred across the face of the moon and the first outriders of dawn drove back the night. He had gambled everything for the highest prize of all, and now he awaited the verdict of fate. He laughed, tried to sit up, slumped back once more, conscious that the enemy were melting away into the woods now, leaving behind the corpses of Cato Starcorides and his men. Time passed, the pain faded to numbness and the light grew in the sky above, but Triado felt the darkness settle upon him.

'There is one yet alive!' an urgent voice cut through the cloying fog that drowsed his conscience. 'He smiles', the voice added, vaguely puzzled.
And well he might. An imperial patrol had stumbled upon the scene of what could only be termed a "massacre," and yet Triado still lived. He praised God, his lips moving wordlessly as strong men stripped his armour, investigated the wound and sent for the medics. In his heart he knew now that he would survive. In his heart he knew that God himself had destroyed the emperor and bestowed on him the strength and guile to bring about the destruction of his son. In his mind he envisaged himself following in the path of a great golden lion as it led him through a high hall to a high dais where stood the highest throne of all.
'Thank you', he breathed. 'Thank you. Give me strength now'.

Chapter Five

Callisto

'I have grave news for you, Taian', said the empress, standing at the foot of his bed. 'And you must prepare yourself to face it'.
'Huh?'
Taian, whose head ached as though a team of hammer-wielding demons was at work within, turned his head cautiously towards his stepmother. On most occasions, such headaches derived from excessive consumption of wine and spirits, but this one derived from flu, so his physician had advised him, although the man had also mentioned the possibility of malaria.
'Huh?' he said again, wincing at the light that silhouetted the empress from the tall window behind her.
'Your father is dead, and so is your brother', she said after a deep inhalation and a perceptible stiffening of her pose. 'There is no way of mitigating such news'.
Taian, who had spent days treading the path between waking and sleeping, and whose brow was beaded with sweat now, struggled to focus his mind, conscious that a matter of importance had arisen that required that he should summon his mental resources.
'How?' he asked, having considered this information. A small part of him, one deeply buried beneath fever, struggled to make its voice heard, to urge him to recognise that a crisis of the first order was at hand.
'Well, your father fell off his horse, and your brother had the misfortune to be slain by the Zanyari savages rather more than a week ago', said the empress, hands on hips. 'I would have told you before, if it hadn't been for this fever. You have been insensible for days'.

'Huh! Does that mean I'm emperor?' asked Taian woozily, attempting feebly to sit up before slumping back on his pillow.

'Don't be ridiculous!' snorted the empress derisively. 'No one in their right mind would accept *you* as steersman of the state, and the senate would certainly laugh at such pretension. No, the Duke of Uthanor has declared himself emperor and approaches The City with an army at his back, even as we speak. The senate meets tomorrow, and unless there is a compelling alternative claim to consider, I daresay they will endorse him. Starcorid blood flows in his veins, of course, although muddied with less exalted gore, and it is almost certain that the army will follow him.

'What about us?' asked Taian weakly, after these astonishing circumstances had come within his understanding. Triado Melanthros, Duke of Uthanor, was a powerful and ruthless man. He knew that his father had distrusted him. The small internal voice warned him that inconvenient potential aspirants to the throne rarely made old bones. If what his stepmother said was so, he would surely be categorised as such.

'He has written to me, proposing marriage', said the empress matter-of-factly. 'I am minded to accept. I am a widow now, of course, and the duke's own wife died some years ago. It would be a convenient match'.

'It is a convenient match', observed Rayo Kerkuoas a week later. 'The senate will certainly endorse Triado as emperor tomorrow, and each of them is free to re-marry. It would help to cement Triado's legitimacy, and I don't suppose Cresara would wish to be ejected from the palace'.

'Indeed', agreed Jory solemnly. 'I suppose a period of mourning must first be observed for the sake of propriety.'

'A month will suffice, no doubt!' snorted Rayo. 'Expedience trumps propriety. Cresara is not one to be cowed by the disapproval of the court, and Triado has thirty thousand troops to stiffen his resolve.

'And what of Taian?' asked Jory, voicing the concern that had loomed large in their minds since news had first reached The City of Triado's coup.

The two young men drank wine together, in a chamber in Jory's family house, in the grounds of the Great Palace. Jory's father was a senator and held an important post in the navy, a circumstance that Rayo was fond of making humorous reference to, given that The City stood eight days' march from the sea. Jory leaned forward to the table that stood between their chairs now and poured more wine, heavily watered as circumstance dictated. Cool heads and clear thinking were required.

'Cresara has no blood ties to him', observed Rayo. 'Nor does she feel much affection for him, it appears'.

'Ha!' scoffed Jory. 'She despises him. You know this. Everyone knows it'.

'Well, yes', conceded Rayo. 'And this illness could hardly have come at a worse time. He can barely speak, let alone see to his own interests, fight his own corner'.

'So, we must fight his battles for him, as best we can', said Jory, setting down the ornate silver pitcher. 'But I fear his first and most vital battle will be the one he fights against this malady'.

'Are we to trust Mordanios?' asked Rayo, mentioning the imperial physician.

'Gelon trusted him', answered Jory with a gesture of his glass. 'But he was Cresara's appointment in the first place, was Cresara's own physician before her marriage to Gelon'.

'And therefore tainted by that association, to my mind', replied Rayo. 'I trust him as much as I trust Cresara. And there are rumours that he dabbled in the dark arts when he was in the East'.

Jory frowned, sat back in his chair and stroked his bearded chin.

'A thousand monks, or so, daily raise their prayers to the heavens in order that the Lord may be induced to spare him', he observed.

'And yet one well-placed and unscrupulous physician may undo all their good work', noted Rayo. 'And who are we to anticipate Tio's intentions?'

Jory laughed.

'I had hardly expected to see such fatalism on your lips, my friend. Tio's will is as *we* exert it, as I believe I have heard you say on more than one occasion. And so, I ask again: what of Taian?'

'He is very weak', admitted Rayo. 'I was shocked when I saw him yesterday. It as though the flesh has shrunk back from his bones. I was not allowed to approach close, as the fear of infection is very real, of course, and Mordanios was there present, so I was not able to exchange more than the most formal of pleasantries. I tell you, I don't trust that man'.

'I am convinced of it', laughed Jory grimly, 'since you can barely utter a sentence without mentioning it. Still, I daresay it would be well within Mordanios' compass to poison our prince, should he show signs of an inconvenient recovery'.

Rayo bit his lip.

'But would Cresara really wish him dead? It is not as though anyone thought Taian capable of aspiring to the throne, even should he desire it'.

Jory's cheeks reddened.

'I fear he would not be a conscientious sovereign. To rule and govern others was never amongst his aspirations'.

'His skills lie elsewhere', agreed Rayo loyally. 'But so long as he lives and breathes, others more ambitious, less

scrupulous than he might choose to employ him as a figurehead by which to advance their own cause. I have heard that the Duke of Vollangor is less than fulsome in his congratulations to our new emperor. Whatever his public pronouncements, he cannot be other than resentful of Triado's elevation. He, too, has Starcorid blood in his veins on his mother's side, and he is very well connected in the North and East.
'Not that blood means a jot when swords are counted', said Jory.
'And yet it cannot be discounted', observed Rayo, shaking his head. 'The legitimacy that blood confers carries great weight with the populace, as you well know. In that respect, the duke is at least as well qualified as Triado. So long as Taian lives, our new emperor will not feel secure, I tell you. From his perspective, there will never be a better chance than now to remove this last threat to his position, and Cresara cannot be relied upon to prevent it. You know this'.
'I don't disagree', sighed Jory. 'But where does that leave us?'
Rayo met his friend's cool grey eyes and drummed his fingers absently on the table top. Long moments passed, marked by the elegant brass clock on the mantelpiece.
'Well, I suppose we must look for an opportunity to steal him away', he said at last.

'How fares the prince?' asked Cresara Rhovanion, Empress of Erenor, the next morning as Mordanios emerged from Taian's bedchamber.
Mordanios, a tall, gaunt man with high cheekbones and deep-sunk eyes, turned his face upon her, washing his hands at the basin that stood outside the chamber.
He bowed, dried his hands upon a small white towel and indicated the uniformed guards on either side of the door with the smallest twitch of his head.

'Leave us', instructed the empress, divining his intention. 'Join the others in the corridor beyond'.
'Well?' she asked, when the guards had withdrawn.
'The crisis is past, I think, and the fever has broken', said the physician. 'He should recover, unless...'
'Unless?' prompted the empress, placing hands on hips.
The physician's thin lips twitched into a tight smile.
'Unless some other contingency should occur. I trust that the prince's recovery is your heart's foremost desire'.
'We have known each other a long time, Mordanios', observed the empress, approaching closer and placing her hand on the man's shoulder. 'In my employment you have become wealthy, enjoyed every privilege and honour it has been in my power to bestow upon you'.
'Indeed, and I am most grateful', replied Mordanios cautiously.
'So, I feel sure that I may discuss matters of the most confidential nature with you, trusting to your loyalty, your complete discretion and, I may add, a compelling conjunction of interest'.
'Of course', agreed Mordanios, his face set in a severe mask of wary neutrality.
'The Empire faces a crisis', continued the empress. 'As you are aware. Gelon's death and that of Cato so shortly afterwards dealt a devastating blow to us. I have it on good authority that the senate will acclaim the Duke of Uthanor in his place, but our enemies would like nothing more than to take advantage of disunion and uncertainty in the Empire. They sense weakness... vulnerability. That is why it is imperative that we present a united front and ruthlessly exclude all potential for internal conflict. It is incumbent on all of us to place the interests of Tio's earthly realm above our own personal inclinations. You do understand me, do you not? It is our holy duty, those of us in high office, those of us with the fate of the Empire in our hands'.

Mordanios nodded, wondering whether the empress was ever going to come to the point. There could be no doubt as to where her argument tended, no matter how garnished with noble sentiments it might be.

'Do you wish me to ensure that the prince does *not* recover?' he asked after first having instinctively glanced around the chamber.

Merely to bring that sentence to utterance implied a crime of the gravest kind. If the empress wished to encompass that end, he would oblige her to make it plain to him.

There was a lengthy silence, during which the empress appeared to deliberate, casting her eyes down, running her hand through her dark tresses. At length she met Mordanios' gaze.

'The death of all three of them within so short a time might incur suspicion', she said. 'Those who oppose unity might point fingers, spread rumours or accusations injurious to the interests of the state'.

'Perhaps something might be accomplished short of death', suggested Mordanios. 'How would it be if the prince were to lose his memory, his mind and the whole of his rational being, were to become an empty husk, in fact? A living corpse incapable of speech and movement quite disqualified by those disabilities from holding power or position of any kind'.

'Indeed', agreed the empress, her gaze distant now. 'Murder is a terrible thing. I should not wish to have Taian's blood on my hands, or on my conscience. If he were to be reduced to this level of incapacity, that would surely be sufficient. He could be no one's puppet then, no figurehead for any rival claim. And you could bring this about?' she added, looking Mordanios full in the face once more.

'I can', he confirmed with a slight inclination of his head. 'There are drugs that I know of. None shall suspect'.

'Then do it', she said. 'The Empire demands it'.

'I don't like it, Master Jory', said Ilda in tremulous tones. 'He's fading away before my eyes'.

Jory and Rayo had sought out Taian's old nurse, in her own quarters, in one of the narrow streets to the north of the palace. Now they sat in her plainly furnished parlour whilst she paced in front of the window. A vase of flowers stood on the mantelpiece. Leaning against the wall next to it was a silver-framed miniature of the infant Taian that she had once received as a birthday present from his mother. Now she crossed to pick it up, kissing it reverently and clutching it in both hands.

'I can't understand it', she said. 'I could have sworn he was getting better. There was something of his natural colour blooming in his cheeks once more, and we even had a little conversation from time to time. His brow is cool now, where once it was ferocious hot, and he seems less restless in his movements', she frowned. 'But to tell you the truth, there haven't been much in the way of movements to recount. There is no tautness in his limbs, no life in his eyes. It's so strange. It's like he's withdrawing within himself. Doctor Mordanios assures me it's quite usual in these cases, of course. Sometimes, it is necessary for the body to withdraw and gather its internal resources before blossoming once more into the fullness of health. That's what he tells me'.

She turned upon her guests anxiously, seeking confirmation or reassurance in their eyes but finding none.

'I mean, I'm sure he knows what he's doing, an eminent man like him', she continued, brow furrowed.

She spent her nights with the prince, sitting at his bedside, attending to his bodily needs, passing water beneath his lips whenever it seemed possible. Jory and Rayo's visit had found her just returned, about to retire to her own bed as the day nurse, one of Mordanios' nominees, began her shift.

'And does he eat?' asked Rayo, pushing absently at the beaker of small beer the nurse had set before him, lamenting her lack of wine for such fine gentlemen.

'He does not, has not for some nights under my care. He can no longer sit up to do so. Floppy as a flounder he is, pardon my disrespect in so describing him. The day nurse and Doctor Mordanios assure me that he takes his meals with them, you see, not that I've seen any evidence of it, and his stools have been right meagre'.

Rayo and Jory exchanged a glance.

'And have you been present when Doctor Mordanios has attended our prince or administered his medicines?'

'That I haven't, sir. He always insists that I withdraw'.

'And do you know what medicines he has prescribed?' asked Jory.

'I do not. I hardly think he would share such knowledge with the likes of me, proud and dignified gentleman that he is. He brings it in a leather bag, so he does. He sets it down on the table next to the prince's bed and then he bids me to leave the chamber until he has done his work'.

'I'm sure he does', said Rayo with a bitter smile.

'And what am I to take from that, sirs?' asked Ilda, approaching them now and pulling out a chair. Her brow was creased with suspicion and her eyes darted from face to face. 'If I may make so bold'.

'We think that Mordanios is poisoning our prince', confided Jory at last. 'He is the empress's creature, and she sees him as a threat to her own position'.

'Why, he never!' cried Ilda in outraged tones. 'I never knew a soul less likely to crave power of any kind'.

Or to merit it, she might have added, but she sat back in her chair, mouth working silently as she struggled to digest this intelligence.

'Can it really be?' she asked at last. 'Is she really so wicked?'
'You know her as we do', observed Jory. 'Do you think it beyond her compass?'
'I do not', she admitted. 'Certainly I do not, though it is surely evil to contemplate. Then what is to be done?'
'Will you help us to get him from that chamber and to a place of safety?' asked Rayo earnestly.
'Before it is too late', added Jory.
'I will with every breath in this old body, every pulse of this here heart', she cried, pressing the little painting to her breast. 'Just tell me what I must do'.

There had been no opposition in the senate worthy of the name. The Duke of Vollangor, seeing the way the wind was going, added his vote to the motion that endorsed Triado's candidacy for the throne. There was no point in declaring his hostility to the Duke of Uthanor, not unless that hostility could be demonstrated to command broad support. With an unsubdued enemy and an unfinished war on the southern frontier, all could see that national unity was imperative. Strong and uncontested leadership was essential. Triado could offer such leadership, and in the immediate crisis there were many who set aside their private anxieties that the new emperor's dramatic elevation might portend their own oppression, that strong leadership and tyranny are close neighbours, in fact.

The emperor's coronation took place in Sancto Imridion, of course, the great cathedral of The Trinity in the highest circle of The City that had witnessed such spectacles scores of times over the thousand years since its construction. Tisilat, the High Patriarch of the Empire, presided, and the ceremony was attended by hundreds of the bishops, abbots, monks and assorted clergy representing all regions of the empire. The cavernous gloom of the cathedral was redolent of drifting incense, shadows pierced through and through with slanting beams of coloured light from the glorious stained-glass windows that relieved the severe stone walls. The chant of monk-song and the murmur of prayers reverberated beneath the high gilded ceilings of naves, choir and chapels, and the ascending heat of ten thousand beeswax candles stirred the dusty banners high above.

'It has begun', whispered Jory to his aged, blind grandmother. 'The procession has entered now'.

'I know', she murmured. 'I can tell from the hymns. I have lived long enough to have witnessed six of these, you know'.

Triado, having processed through the south doors, at the head of the long column of civil and ecclesiastical magnates, knelt before his own throne and felt the weight of the imperial diadem settle upon his brow, placed there by the High Patriarch, robed in all his glittering finery. Triado made the holy signs in the air before him as the jewelled purple mantle was draped around his shoulders. The cathedral was dedicated to the trinity, and ceremonies reflected this. Triado stood now, careful to ensure that no unlucky stumble could cast a premonitory shadow across his reign, and turned to face the west.

'He is crowned. He bows before the moon', whispered Jory, amongst the murmured prayers of the hundreds in that space.

At the west side, a great rose window held at its centre an image of the crescent moon. Having bowed, Triado removed his new crown and held it out towards that window, signalling his submission to Earthmother, whose symbol this was. Next he turned to the east and repeated this gesture towards the image of the sun that dominated the rose window on that side.

'And now he holds his crown up towards Skyfather', said Jory, conscious of a disapproving glance from the woman seated to the left of him.

At last, Triado turned to the south and held his crown aloft in the direction of the rose window above the doors there, where a huge image of Tio, the Son of Heaven, in his incarnation as a winged lion, frowned down upon the congregation, encircled by stars, enthroned amongst saints and sages.

'That's it, then', muttered the old woman. 'I suppose we have the loyal addresses to endure and his Holiness's sermon, God give us patience'.

'Not at all', said Jory, leaning close to her ear. 'The empress's own procession approaches now. You forget that they are to be wed'.

'Of course', she sniffed. 'Our empress. And our dear Gelon barely cold in his grave. That impious bitch!'

'She is attired all in black', explained Jory, having looked round to see if any in the surrounding pews had heard this grave indiscretion. 'And I beg that you may speak more softly. They are to be separated immediately after the marriage, in order that she may observe the period of mourning'.

'Ha!' said Jory's grandmother. 'In which world does re-marriage precede mourning?'

'Indeed', mumbled Jory as the empress walked past with her ladies and attendants, at the head of a column of nuns and abbesses.

I imagine her support was conditional upon this indecently hasty union. She may have feared that Triado's gratitude and his ardour to win her hand might prove less enduring than the minimum period of mourning required by convention.

These last words were unspoken, could certainly not be uttered in this context, but continued a train of thought that had already cost him several nights' sleep and left him hollow-eyed and haggard, attracting the anxiety of friends and family alike. Where was Rayo now? Oh, there he was, some way distant in the adjacent nave, seated amongst his clan with his father at his side. Jory tried to catch his eye, but the bowed heads of the singing procession came between them and he returned at least a part of his attention to the ceremony instead.

Chapter Six

Garabdor

Adala had not shared with her sister the secret of her meetings with the prince during the period of Corasto's illness, although she might have wondered at Adala's prolonged absence from the house when her own turn came to minster to their father's very considerable needs. Nor did Adala share that secret now. There was little chance of persuading her of the legitimacy of her feelings for Taian, no chance at all of convincing her that the imperial prince might suddenly descend upon the inn and make a proposal of his own. Even for herself, she hardly dared hope that such a miraculous intervention might spare her from her plight. Fleeing from the society of her perplexed and enraged family, Adala hurried to her room and lay face down on her bed, refusing to speak to Corasto, closing her ears to his furious threats and entreaties. Even the prospect of a thrashing, even her sister's tears and beseechings, could not stir her from her un-responding torpor, and as the hours passed, so did her father's agitation mount.

'He is away in Garabdor at present, but I must certainly give my answer by the time he returns', she heard him say outside her door in exasperated tones. 'And he will be wondering why my grateful acceptance of his proposal is not already on its way. What on earth is wrong with her?' It was the question of the moment, one that had been posed to her with varying degrees of urgency, varying tones and volumes, since her return from the cape. Until now, her sister had not yielded up the secret of her deranged and hopeless affection for the son of their emperor, but surely that forbearance would not endure –

could not – as the hours and the days passed. Outside, a cold west wind scoured rooftops and rattled shutters. Within, Adala clung to her pillow and wept bitter tears as the long hours of the night crept by. Tomorrow must bring with it her acquiescence to her father's will, and the prospect of this was more than she could bear.

It was long before sleep could be induced to enfold her in its quiet embrace and her mind to cease from its desolate maunderings, and when she awoke, it was in the knowledge that another shared her room with her. Her eyes sprang open to find that the narrow space was filled with an unearthly radiance. Sitting up, drawing a sudden deep breath of alarm, she saw that a radiant winged lion stood beyond the foot of her bed. His mane was a tousled mass of gleaming gold, and great white wings were at his back. He was enormous; towering over her, seeming to extend through the walls and timbered ceiling of her room and yet be fully visible to her. He smelled of honey and incense and mountain thyme, a delicious scent that entered through her nostrils and permeated the whole of her body.

Adala blinked, drew her legs under her and clasped her knees in a tight embrace. After a while, though, her initial agitation at this soft assault upon her senses began to dissipate, and her soul opened like a flower in the warm air to exult in the beauty of him. There was no sound, none at all, and the golden honey of the lion's great eyes poured upon her like liquid joy. His noble head dipped towards her own, and his dove-soft wings unfurled wide above her so that the high stars glinted bright beyond the spectral tiles and rafters of the tavern.

'Tio', she breathed ecstatically, finding her voice at last, and she reached for the lion's muzzle. As her fingers moved through the star-bright air, the lion's image shimmered, the vision shifting and shimmering before her eyes to be replaced by one of Taian, lying abed, his pale face, limned by the same leonic gleam that lit her own. Her body was suddenly radiant with a bliss such as she had never known before. It was as though she were a crystal vessel, filled with the warm nectar of Tio's love. Her eyes closed, her soul soared upward and darkness enveloped her.

When dawn came and her eyes eased wide to find her humble room as dull and as plain as ever, a tiny remnant of that glorious vision remained before her inner eye. It warmed the soul within her, like a sip of spirits, and tingled in her fingertips.
'It was not a dream', she said out loud, casting aside her sheet. 'It was not'.
But what did it mean?

For long moments after her vision, Adala lay in bed and searched the dusty rafters above her for some answer. It had been a vision, surely it had. She was not a particularly pious person, rarely troubled herself over the fate of her immortal soul and found no compelling inspiration in the words of the sages, saints and luminaries. Her friend Doria, whose speech was heavily leavened with quotations from scripture, had devoted her life to the faith, had entered a convent, in fact. But she, for all her piety and devotion, had been offered no glimpse of the divine, had prayed in vain long hours before the altar and found the heavens mute. And yet, Adala, unworthy as she was, had been granted this glorious vision of the divine. Tio had shown her the prince, lying asleep. She swung her legs out of bed whilst her mind once more calculated the time that must be taken to cover the sixty leagues or so to The City by a servant carrying her letter, the time it would take for that letter to reach its intended recipient and for him to learn that she was to be married. She had reluctantly concluded that their strange dalliance must then be at an end, that she must dwell in the real world. Surely, she must set aside fancy, accept this undeniably attractive match and accede to the wishes of her parent. So, her mind had moved, even as her letter, retrieved by Taian's servant, had embarked on its long southward journey. But now all that had changed. Her vision had changed everything.

'Daughter, I suppose you have recovered your senses now', growled Corasto as she descended the staircase to the ground floor corridor, pulling her shawl about her. 'Doubtless you have reflected upon your strange obduracy as you slept, for I will not force you in this matter. I expect that Phodios will be insulted and that he will withdraw his offer to Marta, too. I expect that by so doing, your sister's dreams of future happiness and prosperity will be utterly destroyed. May Tio forgive you for your selfish and foolish intransigence, if you choose to adopt that course'.

'I suppose I have a little time to consider', she told him, hurrying past him into the kitchen, feeling the weight of his scowl upon her back.

'She will come to her senses in due course', Marta assured him, looking up from where she cleared the hearth. 'Surely she will, for she is not a fool'.

Her own eyes, when they met Adala's, carried no spark of conviction, nor did they hold any sisterly affection.

'Well, when Phodios returns from Garabdor, then he must have his answer, and he is rarely there longer than a week. Think well, daughter'.

Eyes cast upward, an expression of weary indignation in his long face, Corasto turned on his heel and went through to the bar, where presently he could be heard rolling a new beer barrel up from the cellar.

Marta seemed disinclined to converse with her sister, and Adala, for her part, was still taken up with the awed

consideration of her vision, so it was an oddly quiet kitchen into which Kreo the cook walked, some minutes later, bearing a basket of vegetables.
'Tio's breath', she muttered, 'there's a storm a-brewing here'.

That storm did not break as the days passed. Corasto made no further mention of the match, and Marta, for her part, barely uttered a word to her sister, unless it was necessary for the plainest and most functional of communication. The house held its breath and waited for Adala to recover her senses. Adala wondered whether she should tell her sister of her vision. There were few secrets between them, and the weight of this enormous one burdened her soul. There were many occasions when it almost burst from her – when they were sweeping the bar together or working at the washing – and it rose in her breast like a great tide. But then Marta's closed face and her elusive eye obliged her sister to seal her lips and let that tide wash over her, unspoken. At length, when the burden became too great to bear, she went to see Father Maric.

She found him attending to his geese, in the small plot that adjoined his dwelling by the church. Wiping his hands on his robe, he led her into the cool gloom inside, and there he sat on one of the rough pews and beckoned her to sit beside him.
'I am pleased to see you on an occasion other than a high or holy day', he said, looking quizzically at her from beneath his mop of tangled grey hair. The tall hat that lent dignity to his role had been partly eaten by an impious goat and awaited mending before the next high day. 'Your devotions are evidently largely of a private nature', he added.

'You may be sure that I offer my prayers at the proper times', she said ruefully. 'But it is another issue that brings me to your door today'.

'I see', murmured the priest with a slow nod.

He was not a learned man, stumbled terribly over his Cantrophene, when such literary embellishment was needed in his services, and, in terms of his personal hygiene and manner of dress, often presented a spectacle inconsistent with the dignity of the church. And yet he was loved by the villagers; a simple, humble, pious man, who attended conscientiously to his duties, preached a readily comprehensible sermon and faithfully administered the holy sacraments that conducted his flock from the cradle to the grave.

He tilted his head to one side now, in lieu of further enquiry, and waited patiently whilst Adala gathered her thoughts.

'What does it mean when people see visions?' she asked haltingly at last.

'It can mean many things', answered the priest, regarding her with those kindly brown eyes. 'I cannot answer for myself, more's the pity, but saints, sages and seers are all said to be subject to such occasional manifestations of the holy spirit. We read that Tio is apt to appear to those he considers worthy to be the vessels of his will. Moonmother and Skyfather, the other aspects of the Trinity that we call God, may also manifest themselves thus. We must interpret each vision in its proper context'.

Everyone knew that their great, broad world was the arena in which Tio and his dark-hearted twin Yuzanid contested for the souls of humanity, that each found agency in the unwitting deeds of mortal men. More rarely, Tio's will found expression through the actions of those whose souls were nearer to their lord, more readily touched by the hand divine. The Six Sages of the Faith conveyed his word along the ages, written in the holy scriptures that all revered, although, of course, much fervent blood had been spilt over their interpretation. And then there were the luminaries, the seven holy men and women who embodied a spark of his spirit and his power, choosing their successors from generation unto generation.

'Does your question tend to the general or to the specific?' asked Father Maric whilst Adala pondered his words, her brow clouded.

'And how are they regarded, those who experience such visions?' she asked, ignoring his question. 'Are they dismissed as fools or dreamers? Are they suspected of pretending a special piety or holy privilege, something that sets them above lesser mortals?'

'They may be', agreed the priest mildly. 'And yet also they may be acclaimed a saint, as you know. Circumstances dictate, do they not? Am I to assume, then, that you have experienced such a vision, dear child?'

'You may', admitted Adala with a sigh. 'And I submit to your judgement'.

Outside the little church, the world got on with its business: children ran laughing in the sun-baked street, a manure cart trundled past, a tinker with his heavy-laden mule called out his wares. Within, the pool of light cast by the south window moved slowly across the cool nave as her story emerged. The window was said to have the finest stained glass in the region, a bequest from a grateful noble donor many years previously. From there, in artfully arranged coloured glass, Tio's winged lion looked down solemnly upon the description of his vision as motes danced in the broad shafts of afternoon light.

'Remarkable', breathed Father Maric when her story was complete, glancing up reverently at that window, making Tio's sign before his breast.

'You believe me, then?' asked Adala earnestly, leaning towards him.

'I do not *disbelieve* you', agreed the priest. 'I have known you since your birthrite, and I do not know you for a dreamer or a liar'.

'Then how should I interpret it?' she continued, pressing his gnarled old hand in hers. 'Since I think it fair to assume I am not a saint'.

'I do not know the content of your heart', answered the priest. 'But Tio does, and he has spoken to you there. Your heart will tell you'.

Hardly had Father Maric spoken these words when the sound of hoofbeats could be heard and the cry of 'Tidings!', both of which were growing progressively louder.

The news courier came by from Garabdor every week or so to spread news of the empire and beyond. Those with a thirst for such knowledge could pay a penny and be admitted to the public bar of The Grapes, where they could hear his news first hand. Payment of a further penny entitled those literate members of his audience to a printed broadsheet for later perusal. There was something in the tone of his cry and the pace of those hoofbeats that suggested news more compelling than the usual run of trade missions from abroad, or relief funds for harvest failures.

Father Maric's eyebrows twitched upward. Adala, after murmured thanks and a last squeeze of his hand, hurried out into the street, where Timo was already advancing to secure the courier's horse.

'Tidings of great import!' bellowed the courier even as he dismounted, plucking a sheaf of broadsheets from a saddlebag. 'Come pay your penny and hear the news!'

Villagers began issuing from their houses, fields or gardens, talking excitedly amongst themselves whilst the courier established himself before the bar and Corasto gathered in the pennies, carefully setting aside the agreed portion for himself. Beyond the crowd of interested paying customers, the faces of those less fortunate, or more parsimonious, could be seen pressed to the windows. They would hear soon enough from their more fortunate neighbours, but an overheard snippet was always to be valued until then, and all the signs indicated that significant news was to be imparted.

'When you are quite ready', announced the courier, enjoining an expectant silence on his audience, a smile of smug complacence traversing his perspiring face.

'Our Emperor, Gelon Starcorides, Dawnstar of the Bright Host, Hammer of the Heathen... is dead!' he proclaimed, glancing around triumphantly to see the impact of his words.

He was not disappointed. There was an audible collective intake of breath, a few gasps of shock or grief – the emperor had been widely loved and admired. A low murmuring began, together with cries of 'How so?' or 'When?' abruptly stilled as the courier raised his hand.

'We grieve, we grieve', he said, having licked his lips. 'The nation grieves our great beloved sovereign, but there is more'.

Silence settled once more upon the room, disturbed only by a low speculative muttering from outside.

'Prince Cato is dead, too!'

There was more shock, more anxious calls for further information. Adala, standing at the man's shoulder behind the bar, was as shocked as anyone. Her mouth was abruptly dry, and a thin buzzing began in her ears that sometimes preceded a faint. Her legs were suddenly weak beneath her, so she clutched at the bar for support.

'What of Prince Taian?' she blurted.

The courier swivelled in his place, drank in the sudden pallor of her face, her wide dark eyes, and smiled a sad smile.

'Mortally ill, they say'.

'Something I said?' asked the courier in the general clamour as Adala turned and ran from the bar. Marta snatched at her sleeve, but she pulled herself free and was gone. Marta looked after her for a moment, her eyes wide with concern, biting her lip as the courier gleefully fleshed out the bare bones of his story.

Adala lay face down on her bed and wept into her pillow. 'Mortally ill,' the man had said, and the terror of that simple term clutched at her heart. The vision that Tio had shown her came into her mind once more. Had he lain there mortally stricken in that vision? Certainly, his dear face had been uncommonly pale. Is that what the vision had meant? Was it intended to show her that the prince was in mortal danger? Surely, she must pray that Tio might spare him. Her face started up from the pillow, and wiping aside her tears, she knelt at her bedside, making the sign of Tio and crossing her hands on her breast. Tio was rarely troubled by her importunings, despite her earlier protestations to the priest, but now she earnestly beseeched his care and his indulgence, murmuring the bidding prayers she had known since childhood and adding fresh inventions of her own.

Tio did not respond.

No further visions came to her mind, no reassuring glow warmed her heart to indicate that her prayers may have been answered. There was nothing to do but enshrine Taian in her thoughts and continue with the daily round of activity that was her life, until Tio came to her once more, so she concluded.

Marta sought her out when the news courier had departed, pushing open Adala's door and finding her still on her knees, slumped forward over her bed, dark tresses fanned out across the coarse, dun blanket.

'Sister, you must abandon this', she said firmly, closing the door behind her. 'It is idle to pin your hopes upon a chimera, a will-o-the-wisp. It is said that Triado Melanthros will be our new emperor. He leads the army back from Zanyawe, and everyone says the senate will acclaim him. I fear to tell you that your prince may be put away, or even... disposed of. His survival is an inconvenience, and none would support his candidacy for the throne, even were he well. He is a good-for-nothing wastrel and idler, this prince that you adore. Everyone says so'.

'You fear to tell me!' snapped Adala, raising her head and turning upon her sister, her face flushed with anger. 'And well you have conquered that fear to pour your venom upon me. Truly you rise above that trepidation with magnificent success. Taunt me, if you will, but I tell you that Taian never sought that throne. He is a simple, gentle soul – and I love him for it'.

'How can you?' scoffed Marta, folding her arms. 'I say again, it is time for you to climb down from your cloud castle and dwell with us once more. When Phodios returns from Garabdor, our betrothal must be agreed. You know that. Despite all your ludicrous pretensions, you know that. Tell me that you do not'.

But Adala could not. Nor could she tell her sister of her vision. A distance had come between them, and the thread of trust was broken. Adala could only clench her fists and glare as Marta spared her a cold smile and turned on her heel.

It so happened that Corasto and Marta's hopes were dashed on the same reef that a trading ship of the Travontine fleet was dashed. Phodios had sought to increase his fortune by investing in a cargo of spices from the West, lured by the subtle tongue of a Garabdori speculator, well-practised in parting incautious gentry from their gold. The cargo had been insured, but the insurance agent defaulted and fled, so that Phodios was ruined. He had been induced to mortgage much of his land to invest in what he had been assured was a certain success, sure to increase his wealth by a remarkable degree, to enable him set up his coach, indeed. But now he was brought low once more, lower even than before that fortunate legacy had raised him from the humble. Accordingly, his sons had lost all the allure, all the charm that broad acres had brought them, and Corasto, learning of this, was relieved to reflect that he had made no written agreement, that a verbal undertaking may handily be repudiated. Now it was Marta's turn to weep and Adala's to regard her with a supercilious air, reflecting that Marta's dreams had been cast down as thoroughly as her own.

'Adala was in the right of it, so she was', said Corasto that day, brandishing a letter like a judge's gavel. 'I don't know how you knew it, daughter, but you were a better judge of folly and improvidence than myself. Who would saddle his daughters with such a sap for a father-in-law? Not I, on Tio's fist', he added with a shudder, as though having narrowly averted some violent physical injury.

Marta, whose head had been bowed as she sobbed, looked up and caught Adala's eye with her own. The glint of Adala's unspoken secret showed there for a moment, and Adala felt a prickle across her scalp. Marta's mouth opened, as though her sister's illicit dalliance with the prince sat poised on her tongue. She shrank before Adala's indignant glare, however, and her handkerchief rose to conceal her mouth. Adala, her own heart softening, extended her hand to comfort her sister. The love and the trust between them may falter, on occasion, but it never failed.

Days passed. Each day, Adala made her hopeful journey to the hollow tree at the cape and then her dejected progress homeward, her hands empty of any further correspondence from the prince, whose destiny, she had persuaded herself, was entwined with her own. She had conceived the attractive notion that the prince, freed from the burdens of public life, might be sent away to the provinces to live in comfortable obscurity. After all, his desire to claim power was slight indeed, and his suitability for wielding it slighter still. Surely the new regime could hardly regard him as a serious threat. Perhaps, then, stripped of all rank and status, he might marry a tavern girl without invoking censure and ridicule. So, she assured herself, but Triado Melanthros carried with him a reputation for ruthless efficiency and a hard-hearted realism that left little room for sentiment. When this assessment rose to the surface of her mind, she paced gloomily or thrust her knuckle to her mouth, chewing at it savagely, leaving great red marks on her pale skin.

Matters came to a head one morning, when Adala was lying on her bed, watching flies circle lazily in the stifling air amongst the ceiling joists. Her mind had set aside its usual preoccupations and lay quiet within her, so that her consciousness could expand wide beyond the confines of her frame. Distantly, dogs barked and a cottage door slammed. Cicadas thrummed amongst the olives on the cape. Surf beat languorously on the pebbles of the shore… and there were hoofbeats and horse breath in the lane, the jingle of harness.
And there was Marta's voice out in the yard.
'Father! Quick! Come and look. There are soldiers!'

Adala's broad-cast spirit poured back and her eyes sprang open. She gasped, drew on a cloak and rushed out to the end of the landing where a narrow window gave out onto the front yard. Even as she opened her door, she could hear the whinny of those horses, the creak of leather and the clink of mail. An officer barked commands as six riders trotted into the yard. Already, villagers were out in the street to observe this unlooked-for event, chattering excitedly at their doors or fences. All this brushed only briefly across the surface of Adala's mind. What seized her immediate attention, what sent her pulse racing and a prickle of anticipatory horror across her brow, was the dark uniform of the investigators worn by the leader of the file. He dismounted in one easy movement and strode to greet Corasto, who had emerged to meet him and was already issuing instructions for Timo and his daughters.

'Greetings, good sir', she heard him say with a respectful bob that fell somewhere short of a bow, his voice laden with unspoken enquiry.

'What is this, now?' she cried, turning for the stairs.

'Aye, she is here', said Corasto, glancing over his shoulder as Adala emerged from the front door. His face was filled with concern. 'May I ask...?'

'You may not', snapped the investigator who stood at the door, his cloak's hood thrown back now to reveal long, sallow features. 'My name is Chief Investigator Drael Trimestrion. The emperor's business is lawfully mine to transact, and I shall ask any questions that are necessary. Your duty, sir, is simply to assist as required or suffer the consequences. I would speak with your daughter, Adala'. His cool blue eyes flicked from Corasto's to her own, eyes so cold as to chill her to the core.

'You are she?' he demanded. 'Then step with me, please', he added upon her cautious nod of confirmation, drawing her inside and through the door into the bar. 'I must speak with you privately'.

'You, stay there', he ordered Corasto, who had made to follow, shutting the door in his wide-eyed face and now turning to Adala. 'I have it on good authority that Prince Taian Starcorides has been a visitor in this house'.

'Yes', answered Adala anxiously, once they were in the bar and various servants had been driven out, 'he has'.

She found herself trembling. The investigators had an evil reputation for pursuing their enquiries through terror and torture.

'We have correspondence suggesting that there might have been *conversations* between the prince and yourself, before his death, ones that a person of youth and naivety might have fancied amounted to a relationship, although, of course, such a liaison would have been absurd. *Is* absurd'.

The man was not heavily built but had an air of easy confidence about him and those pale blue, unblinking eyes beneath close-cropped black hair, shot with grey.

The latter parts of his discourse had fallen upon deaf ears, because the single word "death" had caused Adala to gasp, to clutch at her breast as an icy pang of horror pierced her heart.

'Dead!' she murmured. 'It can't be true', she choked as tears sprang to her eyes.

'I'm afraid it is', the officer told her, the official tone in his voice softening a little. 'Five days ago. I trust word of recent events in The City has yet to reach these remote parts. Emperor Triado has taken the Lion Throne, Heaven be praised. He celebrated his coronation two days since and has taken the Empress Cresara as his own wife, in order to ensure continuity of rule and the security of the realm'.

Adala barely listened, casting her head down, holding back the sobs that threatened to convulse her, fighting to master herself.

'Prince Taian, dead?' she said once more, looking up at last. 'How so?'

'He died of a fever, Miss', said the officer, briskly. 'So they say. And I am tasked to investigate this dalliance of his before the onset of his final malady. You must give me any correspondence you received from him. If I suspect that you have failed to disclose any items that may assist in my investigation, my men will conduct their own search, in a manner highly disruptive to the order of these premises. It may, in fact, be necessary to burn the building to the ground in order to ensure the destruction of any evidence we suspect remains within but find ourselves unable to recover. I trust your father is unaware of the circumstances of your correspondence. I trust he would resent the destruction of his livelihood, should his daughter, having deceived him, seek to deceive us, too. Do I make my meaning plain?'

'You do', murmured Adala bleakly. 'You absolutely do. I shall surrender them to you, of course I shall. But why? Why does it matter now?'

'I'll thank you to contain your curiosity, lest it be taken for impertinence', snapped the investigator. 'I have my duty to perform, that is all you need to know. Now, perhaps you would care to furnish me with the items of correspondence in question'.

Chapter Seven

Callisto

Tyverios Ohk, in his narrow bed, in his attic bedroom, opened his eyes, summoned abruptly from a dream of sun-kissed shores and waving palms, framing an azure ocean that reached away as far as the eye could see. He blinked, knuckling away sleep, striving to penetrate the inky blackness that enfolded him. What was that tiny sound he had heard? As his eyes became accustomed to the darkness, he could make out the dim contours of furniture, the paler shape of the window behind its threadbare curtains. There were no further sounds, but Ohk, with a deep sigh, roused himself to investigate, swinging his legs out of bed and reaching for a robe. It would not be the first time this house had been burgled, and it would not do if his mistress were placed in danger. For a moment, he stood listening. Were those voices he could hear downstairs? Yes, and drawing aside the curtain, he could see that there was activity in the garden behind the house. There was no moon but enough light from the sky to show two figures in conversation behind the sundial. Ohk pulled the robe about him and reached for the sturdy stave that leaned in a corner behind the door.

Outside, a cool breeze stirred the leaves in the tall trees around the ornamental fishponds. Earlier that night, the city had been vibrant with the celebrations of the imperial coronation, and later with the clamour of bells from the palace, but now all was quiet and a gentle breeze stirred the branches through which the waning moon could be discerned. Ohk frowned and stepped out from the scullery door, glancing warily around him, taking a firmer grip on his stave. The intruders were at first nowhere to be seen, but after a moment two figures stepped out from the shadows cast by the high garden wall.

'You! Stop right there!' barked the larger of the two, reaching for a sword. There was a faint glimmer of naked steel as they approached Ohk. For his part, Ohk relaxed; the broad sashes they wore and their air of easy, not to say *swaggering*, authority marked them down as members of the City Watch.

'Not a move', said the taller figure, menacing Ohk with his blade.

'Set that down, steady now', instructed the other, indicating Ohk's stave. 'Black fellow', he added. 'Black as shadow, look'.

'What is your business here?' asked the first, after a brusque nod for his companion. 'Quickly now, unless you want my boot up your arse'.

Ohk, having set down the stave, straightened himself to his full height and folded his arms, looking down severely upon both of the watchmen. The one with the sword, fully aware of Ohk's stature now, took a wary step backward, although his sword point continued to hover at Ohk's throat.

'Come on!' he said, more sharply now. 'Your business here, sir! Do you not have a tongue in your head?'

'Jared, Jared', came another voice as a third man came up behind them. 'Leave him be. Put down your sword'.

Ohk turned his gaze that way, remarking another member of the Watch, this time wearing the broad-brimmed hat of a captain. He placed his hand on the swordsman's shoulder and the tension evaporated, the blade dropping to his side. Ohk nodded, recognising Tuke Mercurios, an old acquaintance of his.

'This is Ohk', laughed Tuke. 'He lives here. And you'll wait 'til doomsday for an answer from him, because he does not, in fact, have a tongue in his head. Isn't that so, Ohk?'

Ohk inclined his head, continuing to fix Jared with a steely glare.

'He's a freed slave, servant of Cortesia Tyverios', continued Tuke. 'You must have heard of her'.

'The court lady? The one who got...?'

'That one', agreed Tuke.

'But that's years ago'.

'Twelve years, yes, maybe more,' Tuke confirmed, straightening himself before turning to Ohk once more.

'We're in search of some fugitives, Ohk. One of my men thought he saw someone enter these grounds a while ago. Have you seen anyone?'

The words *only you people* formed in Ohk's head, and, as ever, the frustration of his condition tugged at the fringes of his consciousness. What little remained of his tongue twitched on the floor of his mouth. Only unformed sound and bestial incoherence would issue from his lips, were he to open them. Instead, he shook his head and shrugged.

'No? Well, you'll drop by and let us know on the morrow, if you come across any evidence of someone hiding here, won't you, Ohk? There's a good fellow'.

And then they were gone, talking in low voices amongst themselves, passing through the side gate they had apparently forced, dragging its ruins half-closed behind them.

Returning to the house, Ohk mounted the stairs two at a time and found his mistress on the landing outside her chamber, a flickering candle in her hand. Even in these circumstances she had swathed her head in dark cloth so that only a section of pale cheek and her single good eye were revealed. Candlelight glinted there as Ohk bowed before her.

'What is it, Ohk? Do we have burglars again? I trust you have dealt with them'.

Ohk shook his head once more and made a sign indicating a sash and a broad hat.

'The Watch? What do *they* want?'

Ohk's two inverted fingers and a moving hand mimed running.

'Chasing someone. Did they catch them? No? Are we all locked up downstairs? Good'.

She shuddered, drawing her shawl more closely around her.

'Still, I'd be happier if you slept here outside my room until daylight. Go get a blanket now and stir your damned idle legs to it. I'm not standing here all night'.

Later, with a pile of his clothes for a pillow and a blanket clutched around him, Ohk resigned himself to sleeplessness as the hours passed and the first hint of dawn crept along the corridors. The boards were hard beneath him where once, years ago, there had been carpet. Like many things in this house, they had been sold.

The house was hollow, dark and empty now, where once it had been filled with light and life. Windows were draped or shuttered, and only those rooms frequented by Ohk enjoyed the benefit of daylight. He remembered the day when one state of being had abruptly transitioned to the other, or at least to the genesis of that transition, and he would never forget so long as he breathed. How beautiful she had been, and it had seemed that the house and the garden had reflected that beauty, too. When Ohk closed his eyes he could see her there, her lovely image enshrined in perpetuity, refreshed, burnished anew whenever he revisited it. It was like standing before a holy icon in the scented gloom of a chapel whilst incense and candlelight disclosed to him a glimpse of Heaven. Ohk summoned her name into his mind now as he shifted his weight on the hard boards. Cortesia Tyverios. To utter those syllables would have been pleasure indeed, but his tongueless mouth lacked the skill. Instead, his lips moved wordlessly in an approximation of that homage.

Cortesia's house had been host to a famous "salon" where the great and the clever and the beautiful of The City came together to converse, to flirt, to enjoy the company of their peers and to discuss the great issues of their day. Some came to importune the wealthy for their influence or to add to the allure of their own name through association with citizens or courtiers more illustrious than themselves. Some came in pursuit of romance, but there was no hint of scandal or even debauchery such as attached to other less distinguished salons. A few were little better than brothels, it was said. Some sought Cortesia's company simply to observe the theatre of humanity, to amuse and be amused. Over all these frequent visitors, these elegantly attired denizens of court and mansion, presided the young woman who was, by common agreement, the most beautiful woman in The City, if not the Empire, if not the world. Blessed by wealthy, indulgent and obligingly short-lived parents, this only child of a noble house had entered upon her glittering inheritance at the age of twenty.

Ohk's eyes sprang open. He pulled his blanket more closely about him. The eye of his mind turned to that fateful morning, in another age, when he accompanied his mistress to the flower market in the second circle, beneath the mighty grey shoulder of St. Serdinos' Church, brilliantly lit on that May morning. He shuddered, feeling his fists and his jaw clench as those fateful moments unfolded in his mind once more. It was too late now to turn his thoughts elsewhere, too late! Impressions began to pour into his mind: the scent of roses, cheerful chatter, an unfamiliar face, a challenge, a sudden splash of liquid. Acid. In slow motion, the stream of liquid writhed across the sunlit air, amidst a sparkling constellation of spreading droplets. He felt its lethal spatter on his sleeve, turned his head, saw swift shock wide in her eyes and heard her scream. He heard it now, reverberating in the deep marrow of his bones, and he closed his eyes tight shut, drawing himself abruptly into a rigid foetal ball. He rocked, he moaned, he clutched his knees to his chest, but that terrible scream continued to echo across the years, an agonising spectre of sound. That was the moment, the watershed in time, that cleaved the old world from the new, the light from the dark. And the dark clutched at his soul.

'Get up!'
The nudging of a toe in his back summoned him once more to the waking world.
He rolled onto his back, saw her figure limned with vague daylight now, scrambled to his feet, stepped back, made his bow.
'Am I to have breakfast or must I starve?' she demanded, her one eye regarding him critically.
Ohk's internal clock told him that it was not yet seven, but he supposed her own judgement of these matters was impaired by her disturbed night. He nodded, touched his hand to his brow, collected his makeshift bedding and made his way to the kitchen, stifling yawns as her door slammed shut behind him. The spectre of his dreams walked with him still as he prepared her breakfast, cut fruit and a little bread with butter, the shadow of it undismissed by his awakening. He savagely drove the

knife down through an apple as the aftermath of that assault continued to play out in his mind. His mistress had sunk to the ground, screaming, clutching at her face. In the panic, her assailant had melted into the crowd that soon gathered. Her maid servants were screaming, too. He remembered witnessing her flesh begin to redden where the acid had splashed, a vivid trail across her face, one eye already closed as she knuckled it, her mouth wide, saliva strung between her lips. *Acid*. Now it became clear. *Water*. They must have water! More than ever now, he cursed his useless mouth. The screaming continued, searing through his soul like a hot knife. He heard himself roaring, a vast, formless incoherence of sound that meant nothing to anyone despite his desperate gestures. At last, shoving aside her panicked companions, lifting her bodily from the cobbles, heaving a way through the milling crowd, he had dumped her writhing form into the fountain. He could see her there now as he looked up from buttering bread, her head twisting frantically beneath his hand as he held it beneath the splashing streams and her beauty ebbed before his eyes. Too late. It had been too late, and consciousness of this rose up in him like a dark tide as strong hands had plucked him away. There was a roar of indignation, of fury and condemnation as the uncomprehending mass bore him down.

'Black bastard! Tried to drown her, he did!'

He had tried to cover his head with his arms, as the kicks and the blows came in, but the pain seemed distant, irrelevant. He wept bitter tears, but those tears were not for him.

Ohk stood back from the table now, set down the knife and closed his eyes. He took a deep breath, exhaled slowly, tried to slow his racing heart. The Watch had saved him from the insensate fury of the mob. Her maids soon realised what had happened, how Ohk's actions had almost certainly saved their mistress's life, if not the perfection of her face. The crowd had stood back, melted away. His mistress had been hurried away to a convent infirmary, where the holy sisters would do their best to treat her for her injuries. Statements were taken, an investigation set in motion and at length Ohk had limped home alone to contemplate the shattering of his world.

He knocked on the door of her chamber and left her plate on the table that stood beside it, as was her requirement. She would eat alone, as she always did. An ornate brass-framed mirror had once hung above the table, but it had been removed long since. There were no mirrors in Cortesia's house, except the meagre shard that Ohk used when shaving, and that was kept in the chest at the foot of his bed. Rubbing his stubbled chin at the thought, Ohk walked away, taking the stairs down to the ground floor, making his way out through the scullery to survey the ruins of the garden gate. It was certainly beyond his powers to repair.

Bardo, once resident handyman to the great house, now dwelt along the narrow lane that passed behind, only a few moments away.
'Oh, it's you, Ohk', he said, drawing open his door, blinking away sleep. 'You caught me still abed'.
A glimpse behind him into a room strewn with bottles suggested the reason for this indolence.
'A few of the lads came round last night', he said, by way of explanation. 'The coronation, see? Raised a few glasses, so we did'.
Bardo stroked the back of his head, cautiously, perhaps locating the source of a headache. At the same time, he attentively observed Ohk's gestures, the nods and tilts of his head.
'Got a job for me, have you? Give me a minute'.

A short while later, and Bardo, assisted by Ohk, was pulling away broken timber, sucking air in over his teeth in a considering manner and scratching his head.

'Only the paint holding that together, there was', he announced. 'All them timbers rotten to the core, rusty nails, hinges an' all. Knackered'.

Ohk stretched wide his arms, rolled them and then made a gesture with the fingers and thumb of one hand, universally suggestive of money.

''Course it'll cost', chuckled Bardo. 'And I know there ain't no money in this old place, not any more. So, what's to be done, then?' he asked as he began turning over a few planks. 'I suppose this 'un'll do, and maybe this 'un at a pinch. You still need plenty more, though, not to mention new hinges and a latch. Who did this anyway? Burglars was it? Oh, the Watch... the Watch, you're saying. I suppose you'll be droppin' them the invoice, then, them being keen to recompense honest citizens for their heavy-handed way with property an' all?'

Ohk regarded Bardo uncomprehendingly as the man straightened up. He was a small man in his early forties, with close-cropped iron-grey hair and an untidy beard. His eyes held a sparkle of lively intelligence, and his mouth bent itself into a grin now.

'Joke, Ohk. Joke', he assured, shaking his head and chuckling. 'Ne'er mind. You don't really do jokes, do you?'

Ohk sighed and nudged a broken plank with his toe.

'Another anniversary it is today', observed Bardo, drawing a tape measure from his pocket and running it across the opening in the wall. 'A baleful one, too. I suppose you know what I mean'.

Ohk nodded and made a splashing gesture towards his face.

'That'll be the one, my friend. Our poor mistress. That's where it all went wrong, wasn't it? Do you think they'll ever pin it on *her*? You know, *that* bitch?'
Ohk bent one of his fingers to form a letter C and shook his head sadly.
'Cresara. Yes, evil cow', grunted Bardo, turning the tape over in his hand pensively. 'Hell awaits that one'.

Ohk supposed that jealously was a common enough determinant in human relationships, that the rival aspirations of two beautiful women to secure the affections of one man was frequently the source of rancour or even mischief. So it had been with Cortesia Tyverios and Cresara Rhovanion. Each had fallen in love with the dashing Lexo Tricopolos, successful general in the latest border wars against Zanyawe and a rising star at court. He had been a frequent guest in each of their houses, and he was said to be equally enamoured of both. Cresara's raven-haired beauty was of a fine-boned sculptural style with slanting dark eyes framed by high cheekbones. For all her elegance of carriage, for all her quick wit and her carefully calculated flirtation, there was something of a hard edge to her. She was of the extensive Rhovanion clan, a group that had fallen from prominence at court in recent years, proud and vain in equal measure. Her parents were keen that Cresara should wed the young lion and so restore their own fortunes, bring them once more into the full glory of the emperor's closest circle.
Ohk nodded, his mouth clenching in a firm line.
'Still, untouchable by the likes of us in this life', said Bardo glumly. 'Ain't that the truth of it!'
Cortesia's beauty had been of a different kind. There was a wide-eyed innocence about her, a readiness to engage with the world and to like what she saw there, that people found entrancing, whether they were nobles or the

humblest of the humble. There was a delicacy in her features, a fragility that seemed ethereal, other-worldly, as though she were a momentary vision of the divine, a sudden conjunction of the planets that might be witnessed only once in a lifetime and must be treasured ever after in the mind of those blessed to have seen it. Ohk held that treasure deep in his heart, and he would never let it go until his dying day. There had been an unconscious grace in her movements that entranced male and female alike and that all must inevitably compare with the more performative poise and elegance of her rival.

'Not that they're ever going to prove it, anyways', added Bardo, pulling out a small slate and making a few marks on it with a stub of chalk. 'That ship sailed many a long year ago, sure as sure is sure'.

There had been rumours that the young hero's inclinations had tended in Cortesia's favour. His friends whispered that a proposal might be forthcoming, that he meant to make his intentions clear before the onset of the new year's campaigning season. So Cresara, or her parents, or both, had decided that Cortesia's challenge to their ambition must be neutralised. An assassin had been engaged to direct, with fearful effect, the acid of their spite. That brief glimpse of a turning face, as the assailant faded into the crowd, festered darkly on the surface of Ohk's mind. He was grimly certain that he would know it if he saw it again, even after the passage of these twelve years, and he nurtured within his heart the spark of vengeance that would flare into fury if he ever did.

'Are things any better with… her?' asked Bardo, looking up from his slate.

It was as though he hesitated to pronounce her name, as though the Cortesia of *then* was not the same person as the Cortesia of *now*, a reasonable enough assessment, as everybody knew.

Ohk shook his great head sadly. Twelve years ago, to that day, the house had been filled with servants, ranging from footmen to scullery maids, from dressers to grooms and liverymen for the stables. Now there was only Ohk. Cortesia was brutally disfigured by the acid. One eye was entirely destroyed, her nose and more than half of her face melted and distorted into a livid ruin of red flesh. A few strands of thin hair clung to one half of her scalp where once golden tresses had swept to her shoulder. For months she had hovered on the brink of death, sustained only by devotion of her servants and the skill of her doctors. For weeks, all had refused her demands to be brought a mirror, and when at last her demands could be refused no more, she had sunk back on her pillow and asked to be allowed to die. This release had been denied to her. Instead, her body had regained its strength, even as her spirit died within her. What remained was a bitter and vindictive woman. Those of her closest servants and companions had known only the gentlest of dispositions, but now they came to endure blows and insults from a creature that raged at the world around her and was consumed by hatred. Within a short time, most were driven away. Cortesia did not wish to see daylight or to face the cruel agony of her reflection. Windows were shuttered and rooms plunged into gloom, lit only by candles or the feeblest of lamps. Mirrors were taken down. Sunk in apathy, abandoned by those who once had managed her household, Cortesia was an easy victim to sharps and speculators. Under the pretence of relieving her of the burden of management, a succession of these took the opportunity to empty her bank accounts, leaving her with nothing. Soon the house was empty and neglected. The bulk of its fine paintings and furnishings were carried away to satisfy the rapacious needs of her creditors, leaving echoing rooms and corridors. Ohk often stood a while in the ballroom, remembering the life and light and colour of the balls she had held there. The movement and the music, the whirl of elegantly dressed dancers, the clink of glasses and the hubbub of cheerful chatter. Now that great space was empty, except for the harpsichord at the far end, draped in black velvet now as though in mourning, too. The whole of the house was grieving for the spirit that had once dwelt there. Now plaster crumbled from the ornate ceiling and rain dripped eerily into various buckets set about the floor.

'Don't suppose you can pay me, then?' supposed Bardo, placing the chalk behind his ear. 'No, thought not. Well, you know what, on this anniversary I'll see what I can do for free, in respect for your mistress. Loved her dearly, didn't we? All of us who lived here?'

He had once been charged with the maintenance of this place. Now he jerked a head at the house that loomed behind them, its empty shuttered windows choked in places with the ivy and with the wisteria that scaled the walls on this side.

Ohk nodded, felt moistness grow in his eyes and passed a hand across them.

'Why doesn't she sell it?' asked Bardo, stroking his chin. 'Prime spot this is. Someone with a mote of cash could fix the place up right fine again. You and she could move to a nice cottage somewhere quiet, set yourself up quite well, I don't doubt. Do you want me to broach it with her again?'

Ohk shook his head glumly. There was an inescapable logic in what Bardo proposed, but it was a logic that quite failed in face of his mistress's obstinance. She had heard such proposals year after year, and year after year she had turned them down.

'I was born here, I have lived here and I shall die here', she would retort.

'But it is dark and cold and falling into disrepair', her friends would argue.

Still, she had shook her head and fixed them defiantly with her one eye, and at length her friends had ceased to call. Even her few living relatives stayed away, certain of a frosty and ungracious welcome whenever they should set foot on the premises. Only Ohk remained, and it was he who supplied her simple needs, he who cooked, he who washed her linen, he who did what little he could to stave off the gradual ruination of the place.

'At least you don't answer back, Ohk', she had told him once. 'At least you don't try me with your insolence like all those others'.

Ohk, whose capacity for answering back was exactly nil, had embraced this as a compliment, had glowed with this meagre acknowledgement of his service and his duty. In truth, no heedless cruelty, no vindictiveness or harsh words, no kicks or blows could have driven him away. Because he loved her. He loved the person she had been and the person she had become in equal measure, and his love knew no bounds. It asked no questions, made no criticisms and required nothing in return. It was sufficient unto itself. It burned in his heart like a candle in a shrine.

'What's going on there?' asked Bardo as they passed the cellar entrance. Here, almost concealed by weeds and undergrowth, the cracked and split wooden horizontal doors to the cellar gave access to steep steps. Although drawn shut once more, one of the doors had clearly been forced open, and yellow splinters of wood lay around it. The undergrowth was trodden down, too.

'Got intruders, have we?' asked Bardo, stooping and placing a finger to the edge of the door. He held the finger up for Ohk to inspect. Their eyes met.

'Blood', said Bardo quietly. 'Quite fresh. I wonder if this has something to do with the Watch being here?' He

frowned. 'Is the cellar door locked? I mean, is there any other way out of there for an intruder?'
Ohk shook his head and made a gesture of a key turning in a lock.
Bending down, he pulled back one side of the damaged door and then the other. Together, they peered down the brick steps and into the gloomy void. Morning light painted a bright trapezoid on the floor there. Into the corner of this shape encroached a pale bare foot.
'Hey!' called Bardo. 'You there. You'd better come out. We've got weapons'.
Ohk cast his eyes upward. Bardo spared him a thin smile. In truth, Ohk's impressive stature was security enough. There was no reply.
'Hello?' called Bardo, and then louder. 'Hey there!'
Was that the faintest of groans? The two men exchanged puzzled glances and descended the steps cautiously, Bardo peering out wide-eyed from behind Ohk's massive bulk. As their eyes became used to the dark, they could see that a young man was slumped between two barrels, wearing nothing but a grubby night-shirt. The tops of his feet and toes were bloodied and raw, as though they had dragged on the ground. His hair and his short beard seemed a light chestnut colour, and his eyes were tight-closed. The slight rise and fall of his chest was the only sign that he still lived.
'Go get a lantern', said Bardo softly.

A few minutes later, they had the intruder turned onto his back. No amount of shaking, no shouting, no slapping of his cheeks could induce him to stir or even to open his eyes. Bardo placed his nose close to the young man's mouth to see if his breath reeked of alcohol and this insensibility stemmed from consumption of strong spirits. It did not. He scratched his head and then exchanged a puzzled glance with Ohk.

'And how did his feet get like that?' he asked.
Ohk shrugged and spread his arms wide.
'Stay with him', said Bardo, placing a hand on Ohk's shoulder. 'I'm going to get Sister Mora'.

Sister Mora was not, strictly speaking, entitled to that title, since she had been expelled from the convent of the Blessed Birch, on account of her illicit sexual relations with a painter who had been engaged there to decorate the refectory. However, since then, she had placed her considerable medical skills at the service of the wider community and consequently enjoyed a large measure of respect in that quarter of the city.
'He has certainly been drugged', she concluded somewhat later, having conducted a cursory examination. 'His pulse and his respiration seem sound enough. And you had best bring me some clean water and bandages for his feet. I assume he is a fugitive of some kind, although I think we can conclude that he did not reach this place unassisted'.
She turned her cool grey eyes upon Ohk.
'I suppose you had better consult with your mistress'.
Ohk's eyes clouded as the complexity of describing the circumstances by gesture alone oppressed his mind.
'I'll come with you', announced Bardo with a sympathetic hand on his shoulder.

'So why haven't you summoned the Watch?' demanded Cortesia, when Bardo had made his account of their injured invader. 'I suppose we're not responsible for the tender care of every thief and vagabond who chooses to break into my house. I suppose...'
Cortesia's further suppositions ceased as Ohk held up a ring. He had taken this from the unconscious young man's finger whilst Bardo went in search of Sister Mora.

It glinted bright in a shaft of sunlight that crept past the edge of the shutters at the window behind her.

Cortesia took the ring from his outstretched hand and held it up before her eye. Light sparked from the tiny jewelled winged lion that surmounted the gold band. For a moment, she bowed her head, clenching the ring tight in her fist.

'Do you know what this is?'

Ohk shook his head, although a glint in his eye showed that a shrewd suspicion was nurtured there.

'Make a bed up for him', she said with a sigh. 'And do not mention this to anyone'.

Chapter Eight

The imperial coronation was celebrated in great style on the evening after the ceremony. The great hall, known as the Parakoumenion, was crowded with nobles, courtiers and functionaries of every kind, bathed in the light of thousands of candles in the vast chandeliers that descended from the high-vaulted ceiling. Even those with private misgivings about the new reign were able to set this aside for a while, in order to enjoy the company of their peers and the seemingly endless succession of rich delicacies that proceeded from the palace kitchens. Wine and conversation flowed freely, the latter increasing in volume and decreasing in restraint, in equal measure, as the evening proceeded. Outside, in the three walled circles of The City, festivities were also in progress, prompted by a lavish distribution of beer and wine, in order that the populace might share in the joy of the occasion. An astute observer might have noted that Rayo Kerkuoas and Jory Marinaris were not partaking of the wine in their accustomed full-hearted manner, and instead they were in fact watering their goblets generously. When desserts had been served and the company began to rise from their places in order to circulate and seek others in their acquaintance, Rayo and Jory took the opportunity to slip from the hall, all but certain that their withdrawal would pass unremarked.
Moving quickly, they made their way to the imperial quarters, through corridors and covered passages quite empty at this hour. At length, having passed through the Aulophagynt, the emperor's audience hall, with its great gilded lion throne, they found themselves in the corridor that led to the prince's chamber. Oil lamps hung at intervals along the walls, but it remained dark there and the long shadows of columns barred the mosaic-tiled

floors. Two guards stood outside the chamber, privately cursing the cruel logic of the roster that had enforced this duty on them this night of all nights. Rayo and Jory approached from a narrower intersecting corridor that formed a T junction with the main one, so that the prince's door stood at the intersection. They carried their shoes in their hands, hardly daring to breathe, advancing stealthily on stockinged feet, ducking behind columns wherever these occurred. Even at this distance the faint sound of music and singing found its way along the passageways. At last, when they were fifty paces away and apparently unobserved, they took refuge behind a column and waited. The palace clock struck the hour, and a few moments later they heard Taian's door open, and a conversation begin. Ilda had emerged to tell the guards that she had saved a little wine and cake for them, that they may wish to step inside a moment to gather up a tray. The guards, grateful for this diversion, nevertheless explained that they were duty-bound to remain in place and would be found sorely wanting if they were to be found drinking at such a time. Nonetheless, the distraction was sufficient.

'Now', hissed Rayo, emerging from the shadows and advancing to try the handle of the chamber adjoining the prince's, no more than twenty paces from the guards. It was unlocked, as arranged, and the two young men passed through into the inky darkness within, closing the door softly behind them.

'We were unobserved?' breathed Jory.

For a moment both focused simply on listening, on controlling their own breath and heartbeats.

'I believe so', said Rayo at last with a sigh of relief.

They found themselves in the servants' quarters that adjoined Taian's chamber. This was usually to be found locked at this hour, but on this occasion, Ilda had unlocked it for them. A single oil lamp burned at the far end of the space, and a little moonlight penetrated through the curtains at the window.

'Where's the stretcher?' asked Jory, peering around.

'Here', replied Rayo, reaching behind a cupboard. Two curtain poles and a strip of canvas, roughly sewn into sleeves at each side, had been brought in earlier that day. 'Decent stitching', grunted Rayo, holding this up to the light whilst Jory slid the poles into place.

'Well, when your father is in the navy, you get used to working with canvas', observed Jory, provoking a snort of laughter from his friend, quickly stifled.

'I'm sure it's the same with rope and tackle', observed Rayo, hefting the completed stretcher.

'Let us hope so', murmured Jory, reaching inside a cupboard, holding the lamp closer to inspect its contents. 'And here we are. More than sufficient rope to rig a galley. The blessed Ilda has served us well. Although getting our friend down over that balcony may prove to be a challenge'.

Burdened with their equipment, the friends cautiously pushed open the door that gave access to Taian's chamber. Here it was a little lighter, with various oil lamps standing about on tables and another, turned well down, hanging from the ceiling. Rayo and Jory were well used to visiting the prince in this room, so their attention was drawn immediately to the grand canopied bed at the far side, where their friend now lay. It had been more than a week since last they had seen him. Mordanios had forbidden all visits, warning that the prince's affliction was infectious, that his recovery depended upon his remaining quite undisturbed.

'How fares he?' asked Jory softly as Ilda rose from her seat at the prince's bedside.

'You may judge for yourselves', she said as the two young men approached.

'Pale as death', murmured Rayo. 'Does he not open his eyes?'

'He does, sir', said Ilda, turning up his bedside lamp, 'but it is as though he sees nothing – and he barely speaks. When he does, it seems that he voices only disconnected thoughts. He barely responds to me, or to Doctor Mordanios, it seems'.

'Taian', said Rayo, leaning over the prince whilst , together with Jory, placing a hand to his shoulder. 'It is Rayo and Jory. Can you hear me?'

After a moment, Taian's eyes opened slowly. His pupils were wide and directed sightlessly at the soft dark folds of the embroidered canopy above. His lips moved but no sound emerged.

'Can he sit up? Can he support his weight at all?' asked Jory, straightening.

'I think not,' Ilda answered, shaking her head regretfully. 'Although you may try it, if you will'.

Rayo stroked his chin, glancing about. His eye fell upon the bedside cabinet where there stood a jug of water, a glass, a folded towel and a small spoon.

'That spoon,' remarked Rayo with a nod in its direction, 'is that the one Mordanios uses to administer the prince's medicine?'

'That it is, sir', agreed Ilda.

Taking a handkerchief from his pocket, Rayo folded it within and tucked it away with a grim smile.

'Then it may have its own story to tell, in due course', he observed.

Jory pushed open the double doors that led out onto a broad balcony, one where they were accustomed to sit together drinking in happier days, since it enjoyed a wonderful prospect of the palace gardens, the city and the landscape beyond. Jory advanced to lean against the balustrade and peer down into the small arm of the palace grounds that was called the Cherry Garden. It had been a hot day, and the scent of flowers continued to unfold in the warm night air. He sniffed, frowned and assessed the options for securing the long rope.

'Now I'm actually here, I can't see how we're going to manage with the stretcher', he said at length, pensively rubbing the back of his head.

'I think you're right', agreed Rayo, having joined him. 'I suppose it will be easier once we have quit the palace and have him in the streets outside'.

'Indeed. Perhaps you would drop it down to us', he said, addressing Ilda, who stood in the threshold, her small face pale with anxiety.

'Then how do you propose to get the prince down there?' she asked with a glance that encompassed the edge of the balcony.

'We must make a sling and tie it under his arms', said Rayo. 'Then we may lower him gently to the garden. I trust you are also good with knots', he added with a nod for Jory.

'None better', agreed Jory, paying out a loop of the rope. 'It is in my blood, you know'.

Taian proved to be as flaccid as his nurse had feared, but he made no sign of objection, and it was easy enough to secure him with a length of blanket-padded rope, passed under his arms in a loop and made fast above his head.

'So sorry, my friend', murmured Jory as, supporting his weight between them, he and Rayo brought the insensible prince to the edge of the balustrade.

Jory glanced from side to side to see if there was any sign that their activity might be observed from the other wings of the palace. Here and there a light showed at a window, but the hour was late, and it was a fair assumption that all the palace's attention remained focused on the celebrations in the Parakoumenion. He told himself that he was not afraid, that the vague trembling in his hands and the dryness in his mouth were solely induced by anxiety for his friend and pity for his situation. In truth, their rescue plan had evolved so rapidly there had barely been time to ponder the consequences of failure, or even the ramifications of success. If they should be successful in stealing the prince away, what then were they to do? A house in the suburbs had been secured as a temporary refuge, but it was as though the two rescuers hardly dared to consider a future more remote than the next few days. It was as though the whole of their being, the concentrated power of their minds, had been poured into these last few days of preparation. In truth, they had had little choice, as Mordanios' *treatments* hastened Taian's journey into imbecility. The prince hung between them now, like so much dead meat, as they eased his weight over the balustrade.

'Careful, now!' warned Rayo, readjusting his grip on their friend's legs. 'Steady as we go'.

Even in the darkness, Jory noted the unfamiliar gleam of fear in his friend's eye, and this from one whose whole persona exuded easy confidence and bravado. He considered his friend incautious to the point of rashness, a little too free with his tongue, particularly when in drink. These opinions he was glad to share with Rayo, whenever circumstances prompted such disclosure. A longstanding friendship such as theirs could readily withstand plain speaking. Rayo, for his part, thought Jory excessively timid and slow to act, views that he was likewise more than ready to make plain. Now, though, there was no time for disharmony. Success relied upon swift, decisive action.

'Take a hold here, madam', said Jory to Ilda as she emerged onto the balcony, wrapping her shawl more closely about her. She took the proffered rope's end and added her slight weight to their own, as the two men set about lowering the prince into the cherry garden below.

'It will be a fine thing if any honest courtier or guard comes past and finds their prince dangling like some strange fruit amongst the branches', muttered Rayo, darkly.

'Tio send that they do not!' gasped Ilda as a sudden slackness in the rope indicated that the prince was earthbound once more. 'Moonmother, too', she added, making the sign about her brow and sparing a glance to where a yellow moon shone above the world, casting her reflection back from the broad curves of the river Canto in the plain beneath.

'I shall await you below', said Rayo to his friend, grasping the rope and disappearing below with much muffled grunting and cursing, which rapidly diminished with distance. The stretcher was let down, too, twisting and turning as it vanished into the darkness.

'And now I'm afraid I must bind you', said Jory, turning to Ilda, rubbing raw hands together. 'I pray that you will forgive this indignity'.

'Not at all, sir', said Ilda, withdrawing into the prince's chamber. 'Make it good and tight, too, if you please. A little discomfort will add to the verisimilitude of my situation. I should not wish to be judged complicit in your conspiracy, and a few moments of inconvenience is nothing to compare with the risks that you young gentlemen are taking on behalf of our dear prince. Here, bind away, and bless you, sir', she said, holding her thin wrists before her. 'My heart goes with you in your bold endeavour, and may damnation fall upon the wicked queen and all her cohorts!'

'You are a good soul, mistress Ilda', grinned Jory, reaching for more rope. 'And you may be sure that we shall give of our very best for him'.

When Jory joined Rayo beside Taian's pale, slumped figure in the garden below, it was time to make their way to a part of the palace's outer wall that overlooked a maze of narrow lanes. The place chosen was well shaded by trees, a dead end barely frequented at this hour. Here, Rayo's servant was meant to await them in a covered cart. An elderly watchman in a turret was assigned to keep watch over this section of the wall, his uncertain and intermittent vigilance deemed sufficient in time of peace, and overlooking a section of the palace outer wall that was particularly sheer and lofty. Jory, pretending drunken disorientation, had brought him a flask of spirits earlier with which to toast the new emperor's health, and this, containing a powerful sleeping draught, had quickly rendered the man insensible. Even so, lowering a nightgown-clad prince down sixty feet of naked, unadorned masonry was sure to be the most perilous part of the proceedings. Nor did it seem that things were proceeding according to their plan, as became apparent when Rayo peered over the wall into the narrow street below.

'Damnation!' exclaimed Rayo.

'What ails you?' asked Jory, appearing at his side.

'That', grunted Rayo, indicating the empty street with a flick of his hand.

'Where's Meric and the cart?' demanded Jory, dismayed.

'I don't know', admitted Rayo, passing his hands through his hair.

'Well, we can't carry him across half the city on a stretcher'.

'I know, I know! Let me think!' Rayo demanded, his eyes glinting wild as the moon showed herself behind a bank of slow-drifting cloud before disappearing once more. A cool breeze whispered in the branches of the cherry trees behind them.

'We'll have to pretend he's drunk and carry him between us', said Jory grimly. 'Unless you have a better suggestion'.

'No. You're right', nodded Rayo, glancing at the sky. 'And that is an auspicious cloud up yonder to close the eye of lady moon. Let us do it now and pray that Tio is with us'. The street remained empty down below, but how long would it remain so? There was no time for debate or hesitation. Once more, the prince was rolled over the top of the wall, thankfully, free from crenelation in this section, and lowered away as swiftly as was consistent with not breaking his legs upon arrival. For one horrible moment, his nightshirt snagged on a projecting ridge and rose up around his neck. Anyone turning down the street and chancing to look up would have seen a pale, naked prince suspended eerily overhead. Fortunately, a firm upward tug and gentle release was all that was necessary to clear the obstruction. Within a few minutes it was done; Rayo and Jory had the prince between them, and they were lurching away towards the end of the street, making a very passable pretence of drunkenness. The street made a junction with a wider way, this one lit by lamps on tall standards. Here, singing could be heard from taverns, and a man was pissing copiously against a wall, supporting himself with one arm. The familiar stench of stale beer, sweat and inadequately covered sewers assaulted their nostrils.

'I trust you know your way', muttered Jory.

'Meric knows the way, curse him', said Rayo, raising a hand of acknowledgement to two passers-by who called out, gesturing with a bottle. 'We're fine, I thank you!' he called to them, and then to Jory, 'We was born and raised in this quarter. But Meric is not here present, as you have observed, and we can hardly carry the prince between us all the way to Sanderelm', he added, mentioning the name of the suburb that was to be their refuge. 'It must be more than a mile'.

'Well, we shall steal a cart', grunted Jory, already feeling the fatigue gather in his legs.

'Indeed, we must certainly steal one of the many conveniently unattended horse-drawn vehicles with which this street is furnished'.

With his free hand, Rayo gestured about at the empty street as they hurried down the winding hill, past boarded up shops and warehouses, past the substantial houses of merchants and nobles.

'I suppose you have a better idea?', muttered Jory bleakly.

Rayo might have been pondering further sarcasm, but at that moment a fearful clanging of bells began from the palace behind them. Almost simultaneously, a patrol of mounted guards issued from the mouth of an intersecting street, some way further down the hill, and crossed their path at a canter.

'What!? How so? How is the alarm sounded already?' cried Rayo. 'It is barely half an hour since we descended the wall'.

Now a patrol of foot guards was advancing up the street towards them, still distant but closing the distance with alarming speed.

'Quick! Down here!' gasped Jory, drawing Rayo and the dead weight of the prince into a narrow alley between two houses.

'Hey! You there!' they heard from one of the still-distant guards.

'Run!' barked Jory, unnecessarily.

It was dark in the alley, but the dim radiance from the clouded sky was sufficient to disclose the path before them, cluttered with abandoned refuse or plants in pots. The buildings loomed high on either side of them, and their own laboured breathing, their own heavy footfalls, echoed from the walls. Behind them a whistle blew and pursuing footsteps could vaguely be heard. They turned a corner and sensed – more than saw – the end of the enclosing buildings, the opening of a broad space behind the high wall to the left of them. Ahead was another turning, this time to the right. Jory's blood sang in his ears, his heart pounding heavily in his chest, his arms and legs leaden.

'Here!' gasped Rayo, groping for the handle of a door that came suddenly to hand in this wall.

The handle resisted, but the door was half rotten and burst open noisily when they both set their shoulders to it. Scooping Taian up once more, they dragged him through the door and pressed its shattered timbers shut within its frame, even as the guards lumbered gasping past beyond. Their footsteps diminished. Rayo and Jory stood calming their breathing, half bent, hands pressed to thighs. At length they turned to find themselves in the grounds of a large house, one that showed no lights and carried with it the air of emptiness, of abandonment. The spaces on either side of the path were choked with rank grass and with the gently rustling dried husks of last summer's taller wild flowers. The house was black against the scudding clouded sky as mother moon showed her bright face once more.

'Come on!' urged Jory. 'Perhaps we can...'

He had no need to complete his sentence. Already Rayo was stooping to shoulder their burden once more, and within a moment they were in the shadows around the base of the house, seeking a point of entry. There were only narrow windows on this level, but at last, beneath their feet, they found the creaking boards of a cellar access hatch. Setting down their prince, Rayo groped for an edge and, finding one, hauled upwards. The door eased upward with a resounding creak that caused each of them to pause and listen in silence for a moment. In the distance a dog barked, replied to by another, and the faint voices of their pursuers could still be heard. There was no sound from the palace, high above them now. The tolling of bells had ceased. Jory made his way cautiously down the steps that were now revealed, sensed rather than saw the space beyond, hemmed about with boxes and barrels. In unspoken agreement the two friends manhandled Taian to the bottom and laid him down gently at the foot of the steps.

'What now?' asked Jory as they cautiously re-emerged, setting down the doors with infinite care before peering about them into the gloom of what had once been an elegant formal garden.

'You stay here', suggested Rayo after a moment's thought. 'I'm going to try to find Meric, or at least make my way to Uncle's house in the lower ward. I can borrow a cart from there'.

'It'll be dawn before long', murmured Jory with a glance toward the eastern sky.

'Well, if you have a better suggestion, I shall be interested to hear it', hissed Rayo, his eyes narrowing.

Further discussion was curtailed by the sound of men's voices and the garden door being forced open once more.

'Run!' gasped Jory a second time.

Chapter Nine

'I gather The City drank its fill last night', noted Cortesia. 'And I suppose the new emperor will be pleased with his reception.'
She looked up from the days-old newssheet that Ohk had found for her in the street and pushed her breakfast bowl aside. He never saw her eat.
'And now that bitch has made her second imperial match', she continued. 'She wears the purple well, no doubt, and nothing short of death will induce her to set it aside. How happy she must be'.
The sour note in Cortesia's voice was one that habitually accompanied any discussion of her erstwhile rival. Even so, Ohk felt a sharp twinge of pity for her, swathed in the cloth that concealed the ruin of her looks.
'With two husbands in the grave and a stepson, too, she must surely yearn for a child of her own to ascend the throne in due course, although she approaches her thirty-seventh year. Old Gelon was dry as a stick, of course, but Triado... she must have concluded that our virile and energetic general would have the verve and vigour to put a child in her. Would you not agree, Ohk?'
Ohk inclined his head.
'And what of Prince Taian? An inconvenient prince he would be, think you not, with that legitimate Starcorid blood a-swim in all his veins'.
Ohk's brow furrowed.
'A useless wastrel that no one would entrust a whelk stall to, leave alone a throne, you may say, Ohk, and you would be correct. Of course, you would. But there are plenty who would advance him as a figurehead to cast a mantle of legitimacy over their own ambitions. Do you see? Do you see, Ohk? Hmm?'
Ohk nodded, pursing his lips.

'And inconvenient princes do not make old bones, that's what history teaches us, does it not?' Cortesia frowned. 'I thought I heard the tolling of the palace bells in amongst the general clamour last night. I put it down as a contribution to the celebrations, but...'

She looked up as Bardo's arrival, cap in hand, followed from a soft knock on the door to her chamber.

'Ah, Bardo. I trust you have looked in already on our guest. How fares he? Sister Mora should be with us soon enough'.

'He still sleeps, Ma'am', said Bardo, having made his bow. 'Although he opened his eyes for a moment, 'is pupils were wide, unfocused, like. He didn't respond when I spoke to 'im, neither'.

'Exactly as last night, then', said Cortesia, leaning back in her chair, steepling her black-gloved fingers on the table before her. 'And have you any idea who our unexpected guest might be?'

'None, Ma'am', answered Bardo with a glance to Ohk, who made the slightest of shrugs.

'I believe the palace alarm bells rang out across the city last night, amongst the general hubbub, the fireworks and the general ringing of bells in churches. Even through the fug of my sleeping draught I marked it. Ohk sleeps like the dead, or he would surely have stirred. Isn't that so, Ohk?'

Ohk cast his eyes down, conscious that his vigilance had been found wanting.

'How else could an unconscious man be introduced to my property? Nor did he manage this feat alone. Undoubtedly, he was dragged or carried by others. The damage to his feet is testimony enough of that. So here we have a palace alarm and intruders in my house. Is it possible that the two are connected? Hmm?'

Her single eye roved piercingly from Bardo to Ohk and back.

'I suppose, Ma'am', agreed Bardo at last. 'But what connection have you in mind?'

'This connection', said Cortesia, reaching into a drawer and bringing out the ring that Ohk had given to her. Bardo had glimpsed it the night before, but then it had been dark and Ohk had removed it whilst his thoughts, and his person, were elsewhere. In daylight it could be seen that it was of gold, surmounted by a winged lion with his forepaw upon the Book of Ages. His eyes glinted with rubies, and tiny diamonds encircled his form. She held it up before them, so the jewels caught the light from the edges of the draped window, reflecting it around the dark walls of her chamber. Bardo drew in his breath with a low whistle. Ohk nodded thoughtfully.

'This is a prince's ring', she said. 'For none but the Leonogenetii, none but those born in the great lion chamber of the palace are entitled to wear it'.

'So, we've got Prince Taian under this roof', breathed Bardo, the blood draining from his swarthy features. 'Mother's eye!'

'We do', agreed Cortesia with a nod. 'Which rather begs the question of what we should do with him'.

Ohk made a gesture that suggested picking up the prince and moving him upward towards the palace. Bardo raised his eyebrows.

'Have you not been listening, you dolt?!' snapped Cortesia, causing a heat to rise in Ohk's dark cheeks. 'Some person – or persons – chose to steal our recumbent prince from the palace. Why would they do so, at great risk to their lives, no doubt, unless they feared for *his* life? As I have suggested, the mark of death is upon Taian Starcorides, so long as he dwells under that roof. Someone has removed him to a place of safety', she deduced, piercing Bardo and Ohk with that fierce eye once more. 'And they will be back'.

The two servants digested this information whilst Cortesia turned the ring in her hand, studying the subtleties of its form.

'That would put us in danger, then', warned Bardo, glancing from face to face. 'Surely it would. The palace will be scouring the city for him. If they find him here, they'll think we're in on it...'

The glint of anticipated torture and imprisonment showed in his eye.

'The empress wants him dead', said Cortesia. 'Perhaps this *condition* of his represents a form of poisoning. If Cresara Rhovanion wills it, then I shall oppose it with all my breath and all my strength. You may be sure of it! Bardo Komnestrian, may I count on your support?'

'Always', said Bardo after a moment's hesitation, clutching at the brim of his hat before him. As with Ohk, the shadow of her beauty haunted his dreams.

'Then may I beg you to take up residence within these premises once more?' she asked, removing a small bag of coins from the drawer where the ring had been and pulling open the draw strings.

'Please, don't', began Bardo, meaning to say something about Cortesia's straightened circumstances but unable to find the words to convey this handsomely. A vague gesture of one hand made his meaning clear, however, and, after a moment, she set down the bag.

'I thank you', she said, and somewhere behind those dark folds of fabric Bardo imagined her ruined lips twitch into the semblance of a smile.

Rayo and Jory had evaded their pursuers. Joining a party of revellers passing from tavern to tavern, pretending drunkenness, they had faded into the streets. Besides, the Watch had been instructed that they were looking for several men carrying the prince who might, on account of his malady, appear drowsy or unconscious. It was the

Watch's misfortune that groups of men bearing with them comrades suffering various degrees of incapacity were all too commonplace amongst the celebrating citizens in the streets that night.

'I would not normally call on the prince at that hour', said Doctor Mordanios, but I was returning to my quarters and the idea came unbidden to my mind. Call it instinct, if you will'.

'It is unfortunate that the idea did not present itself a little earlier', chided the empress amidst her pacing. 'I suppose the guards and the nurse have been thoroughly interrogated'.

The horizon beyond the tall windows of the empress's chamber was already rosy, and the towers, domes and spires of The City were limned by the first touch of the resurgent sun. The emperor slept deep in the adjoining chamber, having launched his reign on a sea of wine. The City stirred uneasily, the hundreds of thousands of its inhabitants rising to nurse sore heads and sour mouths. The empress had not slept, nor had she drunk deeply. Neither had Mordanios, who forswore such entertainments, although a decoction of silphrion swam in his veins. It was this that enabled him to stand tall and clear-headed as the empress paced before him, this that enabled him to temporarily shrug aside the vexatious accretions of age.

'The guards will be disciplined, I am told. It seems that they were not drunk, but their vigilance was certainly found wanting. The nurse was discovered bound hand and foot, although it appears she suffered no violence. She maintains that there were two men, masked and hooded, who entered through the servants' apartments and made their escape with the prince, over the balcony. It is likely that more were involved, however. The ropes remain there, still, and on a section of wall in the cherry garden to show the route of their escape'.

'It was well planned, then', observed the empress, pausing in her pacing.

'It was, and I asked the guards to sound the alarm straight away. In a few hours from now, the whole city will know that the prince has been abducted. His face is well known, and it would be an accomplishment to spirit him away with a quarter of a million of your subjects alerted to his plight'.

'I see, and the nurse? She is sure she did not recognise the assailants, did not remark their voices or their mannerisms?'

'She did not. As you are aware, she has attended to the prince since birth and was greatly stricken by the... crime'.

The empress nodded, pursed her lips and crossed to the window, from where she looked out pensively across the awakening city. She had been summoned urgently from her bed but wore her silken robe with the conscious elegance that was ingrained in her. She could have worn a wool sack and made of it a marriage robe, Mordanios reflected. Far down below, vessels were already moving on the broad current of the Canto, plying amongst the mile-long river wharfs that furnished the bulk of The City's wealth, or conveying early passengers between those landings and the suburbs of Missendil on the far side of the river.

Mordanios regarded his empress thoughtfully, admiring the easy pride of her carriage, the glossy mane of her uncombed black hair, magnificent against the scarlet silk. One part of him, one that on the whole he disapproved of, was momentarily seized with the desire to seduce her, to strip away that robe and know the smooth, pale flesh that it concealed. Another, his more rational being, reasoned that her beauty was that of the serpent, that it was no more than the lure for her venom.

'I am told that you have remarkable powers', she noted with a glance over her shoulder.

'I believe that people speak highly of my medical skills', conceded Mordanios, cautiously.

'I'm sure they do', agreed the empress. 'But it is not those skills to which I refer'.

She turned to him now, approaching to raise a hand and place a slender finger to his lower lip. 'There are some that say that your powers are those of a luminary, that you are touched by the divine'.

'But there are only seven luminaries', said Mordanios, conscious that a delicious warmth was enveloping his frame. 'And their names are widely known'.

'Six are acknowledged', she agreed. 'But the seventh, one Balian Drumarion, is the subject of some dispute, I believe, having so far demonstrated neither piety nor potency. Regardless, I have been told that you are in possession of powers that fall beyond the regular compass of human accomplishment. I am also aware that you have travelled widely in the east, a region where other deities hold sway…'

The finger fell away and the empress fixed him with a piercing look, one that seemed to strip away any barriers of private thought or secrecy that he might have set in place.

'The infidels revere Yuzanid, of course – he whose name is poison to pious Erenori lips, he whose divine brother Tio commands our unwavering love and our loyalty in this realm', she continued.

'Indeed', nodded Mordanios, his mouth suddenly dry.

'That is their error, those infidels, their fatal error and the reason that they shall be damned in due course. Those who burn their own children and pour out the blood of their compatriots to prove their devotion to their false god deserve nothing but the fires of eternal hell. And so shall they be condemned to it'.

'Your fervour commends you', said the empress smoothly. 'But is it not also true that their false god pours out his essence into some of his followers, in the same manner that Tio inspires our holy luminaries?'

'As you say', agreed Mordanios urbanely, his eyes fixed on the empress with unwavering attention. 'And they are called "Arcani," although I believe there are no fixed numbers in their case, the quantity of such creatures and the powers they possess varying with the ebb and flow of faith and fortune'.

'So I understand', said the empress, continuing to fix him with that hypnotic gaze. 'And I also believe that such agents of the dark lord are wont to travel in the realms of his enemies, whether to do his will or to use the powers he has bestowed upon them for their own selfish ends. A thousand pyres, a thousand inscriptions in the legal record, testify to the exposure of those whose malice has been uncovered over the centuries'.

Mordanios found that his flesh was afflicted by a cold prickling sensation, one that caused a disquieting twitch in his bladder.

'To what does this consideration tend, may I ask?' he asked, exerting careful mastery of throat, lips and tongue.

'Oh, nothing in particular', laughed the empress with a careless flick of her wrist. 'I was merely thinking aloud. Another thought that occurs to me is that the present *situation* may be turned to our advantage'.

'In what way, my lady?' asked Mordanios, much relieved at this sudden turn in the conversation.

'Well, if it could be proved that the prince were dead, that his abduction had immediately preceded his death, none could accuse us of complicity in that death. You are aware that there are those whose hatred of us compels them to interpret every circumstance in the least favourable light.

He was known to be seriously ill. Let us say that his friends, in some misguided concern for his wellbeing under our new regime, stole him away, but their actions, their ignorance of the prince's frailty, the mortal severity of his condition unwittingly brought about his death through the rigours of their escape'.

'He was *very* ill', conceded Mordanios. 'Although, as you are only too well aware, the condition of his mind had deteriorated even as his physical frame had recovered'.

'I know this', agreed the empress, her eyes flashing fire now. 'Because that is what *you* have brought about...'

As you required of me, hovered on Mordanios' tongue but it refused to come to utterance. Instead, he merely inclined his head and maintained a watchful silence.

'But no one else knows this', continued the empress after a moment. 'Nor should they ever – and there is our advantage. What we need now is the prince's body, and our ends will be accomplished'.

'The prince's body, repeated Mordanios slowly. 'But nobody knows...'

'Of course no one knows where the prince is now', snapped the empress. 'I'm not a fool. What we need to do is to present the court with a body who *appears* to be the prince. I am well aware that you conduct illegal, and possibly heretical, anatomical investigations on corpses in that prison down by the river. There must be hundreds of fresh corpses in this city every day. It is my judgement that it lies within your power to find a suitable corpse and present it in a manner that will convince the court that it is that of my stepson. If that lies beyond your powers, I would be glad if you would tell me now'.

Mordanios brought his two hands to his face and stroked them slowly down over his sallow cheeks and mouth whilst he considered this alarming proposition. How the empress knew that he had some limited ability to mould flesh, that he had long ago pledged secret allegiance to the Dark Lord, was beyond his power to ascertain. Certainly, it might be possible to find a corpse matching the prince in terms of size and stature from amongst the many who ended their mortal existence in the streets of the less salubrious regions of the city, or who were found floating in the slow current of the Canto. There were contacts who would assist him in this. To find a corpse whose face resembled that of the prince represented more of a challenge, but the empress had somehow suspected his ability to intervene in that area.

'I shall bring this to pass', he said at length.

'Excellent', said the empress, placing that elegant digit on his chest now. 'Let us hope that our investigators can bring these fools to justice, but if they do not, then they will be encumbered by a person resembling the dead prince with neither control of his limbs nor knowledge of his identity, nor indeed any knowledge of anything at all. Am I correct, Doctor Mordanios?'

'Indeed you are, my lady', agreed Mordanios as the finger was withdrawn, making a low bow. 'And I congratulate you on your sagacity'.

After Mordanios had withdrawn, Cresara Rhovanion settled herself in a chair and watched the new day's sun paint its brilliance on the streets below or spark flame from the gilded roofs and high windows of churches and basilicas. She stroked her belly thoughtfully and spared a glance for the door that gave access to her new husband's great bedchamber. The marriage had been consummated, although the groom had been thoroughly drunk, and the coupling had been an awkward one. It had taken all her feminine wiles to coax the imperial member to the performance of its duty, and the ensuing brief period of heaving and grunting had brought her little pleasure. Still, it was done, and there would be other opportunities to explore the possibilities for mutual satisfaction. Besides, she could entertain the prospect that a tiny spark of life may now be incarnate in her womb. Her first husband had proved unable to get her with child, and his death in battle, all those years ago, had left her a childless widow, albeit a fabulously wealthy one. Her second, the late emperor, had demonstrated his fertility quite amply through the siring of three sons. The first, Gelian, the bright star of his hopes, had drowned when his ship had been sunk in a tempest, full fifteen years previous. The second and the third had been disappointments to him, and those couplings with his new empress had resulted in no further issue. So much for Gelon and his line. She frowned, shook out her hair and stood to summon the servants who would bathe her. But now her years of fertility were drawing to a close. Perhaps she was barren. It was that dark thought which had occasioned her frown and now caused her to press her full lips into a hard line. She looked to the window once more, so that the first warmth of the sun caressed her face. How she longed to bring into the world a child of her own, that she might transmit her immortal essence into the dawn of days to come.

It did not take Mordanios long to find a fresh corpse that answered the empress's description. His friends at the prison and in the hospital could be relied upon for their discretion, and soon they furnished him with a number of promising candidates from amongst which he could choose. Having made his selection, he had the body brought to his own house in a closed cart and laid out upon a table there. His servants were used to his ways, used to the discreet disposal of bodies, once the doctor had conducted his anatomical investigations. On this occasion, the more perceptive amongst them might have noted the unusual irascibility of their master, the palpable tension in his frame when the shrouded body was brought in. Any resentment this prompted was soon assuaged when he dismissed them all from the premises, urging them to enjoy the well-earned day of leisure that he had been intending to allow them since Yearturn. So they were told. At last, when the cook had finished expressing her anxiety about the preparation of his luncheon, he waved her away with a weary smile, returned to his study and found himself alone with the cadaver that was to become a prince.

He pulled the shroud aside to reveal the corpse of a young man of approximately the prince's age, bearing a fatal stab wound to the back. Unusual in not being visibly ill or malnourished, he had likely enough met his maker following a street robbery or a violent disagreement during the festivities of the previous night. His hair was curly and a light brown colour, most unlike the prince's, but this could easily be altered in due course. More problematically, his nose was far too long and his face generally rounder. Even the most myopic and undiscriminating observer, even one kept at a significant distance through fear of "contagion," could not fail to spot the substitution. Mordanios sighed and stroked his chin, and then he drew the drapes and ensured that the study door was securely locked before extinguishing the lamps.

It was almost completely dark now. Only the vaguest radiance crept from behind the drapes. At length, he positioned himself in the centre of the room, extended his arms on either side of him and threw his head back, closing his eyes. Fools and charlatans pretended that opening the door between the worlds required the drawing of arcane symbols on the floor, the lighting of candles and the chanting of mumbo jumbo. Mordanios knew better. He had pushed at that door more times than he could count, and what had once required hours of intense concentration could now be accomplished in a few minutes of focused attention. Mordanios was old. He had lived one hundred and sixty-eight years, dwelling in various places within Toxandria during this time, always moving on before any acquaintance could remark his apparent immunity to the indignities of age. His body presented the appearance of a forty-eight year old man and had done so since his agreement with his divine patron, Yuzanid. In a bargain that many others had made before him, he had promised his eternal soul to the fiery embrace of the Dark Lord in exchange for a further two hundred years of earthly existence. The diseases that the common run of humanity was subject to left him untouched, although he was no less vulnerable to a well-directed blade or bullet. For many of these hard-won years, the bargain had seemed a good one, but now, year by year, there was a growing ache in his bones, a growing palsy in his limbs and an oppressive weariness in his soul, very much at variance with the apparent healthy vigour of his frame. He had lived too long. It was as though his substance had been stretched thin across the years.

Now, however, it was necessary to set these considerations aside and open his soul to his master. As ever, a whiff of sulphur preceded the arrival of that being, together with a strange tingling at his fingertips.

'Well?' said a soft voice that existed inside his head, rather than within the room. A writhing area of total blackness, like swirling ink in water, began to manifest itself in the dark air before him.

'My lord', breathed Mordanios. 'Lord of Darkness. Master of my soul. I wish to draw upon your strength'.

'To what end?' enquired the voice. 'And how might this increase the power of my kingdom?'

'I believe it would serve to increase the power of Cresara Rhovanion and strengthen a regime all too likely to provoke civil discord in this realm. I have seen the signs before. Rhovanion is ambitious and unscrupulous. Her husband, the new emperor, is a simple general with no understanding of politics and a conscience no less robust than hers. I predict that she will dominate the state in his name, that she will continue to add to the burgeoning ranks of her enemies and that the state will tear itself apart in due course'.

'Persuasive arguments', mused the voice in his head. 'And you may be sure that I am well aware of the two you mention, prize them as unwitting agents of my will, indeed. Any increase of chaos in this realm increments my strength, as you know'.

'I am sure of it', murmured Mordanios, allowing his muscles to relax now that the channel was secure, before opening his eyes.

'So how may I assist you?' asked the voice after a moment. 'You are aware that the wall between the worlds is a sturdy one, that any breach of it costs me dear'.

'I am, and I do not require flaming swords or thunderbolts, only the power to mould flesh. In particular, I wish to conceal a stab wound and to remodel the face of yonder cadaver so that it resembles that of Prince Taian'.

The voice laughed. 'It shall be done, but it will cost you. My price is ten years of your life'.

Mordanios sighed. Once he would have demurred at such a bargain, but now he only inclined his head. Seventy remained to him – the same span that ordinary mortals may aspire to at birth. And yet life was becoming a burden, one that might become intolerable at last. There would come a time when the eternal damnation of his soul might seem an acceptable alternative. And that time drew near, he feared.

'I accept', he said.

'Then let us begin', instructed the voice. 'Place your hands upon the corpse's face and I shall direct you'.

A faint red glow now disclosed the corpse on its table, the shroud drawn back to its waist. Mordanios crossed to it and placed his hands on the cold, dead flesh. Within a moment, he found that his fingers were pushing and tugging at nose, cheeks and forehead. The light became stronger, whiter, and the scent of death rose in his nostrils. He gasped as the eyelids of the corpse sprang open, but it was only to see the irises fade smoothly from brown to blue. Now his fingers were kneading the flesh and bone of the chin, squaring it off, drawing it gently forward. Finally, he turned the corpse on its side and smoothed the dark slit of the wound on its back until it entirely disappeared. With this final task complete, the corpse slumped back and Mordanios breathed a deep sigh. His hands became limp, as though a firm handshake had been released, and he allowed them to fall to his side as he gazed wonderingly upon the face of Prince Taian Starcorides.

'The likeness is convincing?' asked the voice.

'It is exact', muttered Mordanios. 'None shall doubt it'.

He turned as the light faded to the dimmest of reds once more.

'Do you know where the original now resides?' he asked. 'His death would be to our advantage'.

'I don't doubt it', laughed the voice. 'But the way between the worlds is dark and I may only see through the eyes of mortals in my service, like yourself. I know not where he lies. Are you content?'

'I am', agreed Mordanios. 'And I thank you, lord'.

'Then I shall leave you'.

Chapter Ten

Callisto

'I'm sure it was here', said Rayo looking along the passage, active now with an elderly woman bearing washing in a basket, two dogs and a child with a runny nose that regarded them balefully from a doorway.

'You were equally sure an hour since', grumbled Jory. 'In another wretched shithole altogether'.

'I was less than wholly sure then', laughed Rayo, edging past the laundress and tousling the child's hair in passing. 'Now my confidence knows no bounds'.

'Which should be engraved on your tombstone in due course', observed Jory caustically, nevertheless following after his friend. Both were feeling tired and out of sorts after a few hours' uneasy sleep in the attic room of a riverside inn. Their clothing, chosen for its age and anonymity, was even more rumpled and stained than it had been when they had embarked on their adventure. Both were intensely conscious that they must be the subject of an investigation by now, that the whole of the Watch might be searching for them. Jory's body cried out for a bath and a decent breakfast, but his mind mourned for the life he had once led. It was certain that he was an outlaw now, certain that he would be constantly looking over his shoulder throughout the remainder of his mortal existence. His family connections might spare him from the more grisly and imaginative forms of execution, but torture would undoubtedly ensue from capture, as sure as night followed day, and Jory did not feel confident that he would behave well under such circumstances. Still, he had made his choice, as had Rayo, and they must live with the consequences. Their friendship with Taian was a bond that could not be unmade, and he felt sure that were the situation otherwise, the prince would act in like fashion. Nevertheless, he shuddered, sparing one more glance behind him as he hurried in pursuit of Rayo.

'I told you, this is it!' cried Rayo from further along the passage, prompting Jory to place an anxious finger to his own lips.

The previous night, the door had been semi-ruinous. Now it had been restored, after a fashion, and resisted the cautious pressure that Rayo exerted on it, turning the door handle vigorously the while. To his surprise, after a moment, the door sprang open and a short, bearded man appeared in the gap.

'Can I help you, gentlemen?' he asked, regarding them suspiciously.

'I, er...' began Rayo hesitantly.

After a moment for thought, the man opened the door a little wider and thrust his head out to look along the passage in both directions. Apparently satisfied, he returned his gaze to the two young noblemen.

'You'd better come in', he said, opening the door wide now. 'If you two are who I think you are'.

There were various ways in which this might be interpreted, but neither Rayo nor Jory sensed immediate danger. After a moment's hesitation, a momentary shared glance, they passed through the door and turned to see it carefully locked behind them. It was clear that they had found the right place. What had been a dark silhouette a few hours previously now resolved itself into the form of an elegant house, albeit one that showed clear signs of neglect. Tiles had slipped here and there on the roof, and several windows were boarded up on the ground floor. What had once been a formal garden now presented a strikingly informal appearance, and a silent fountain stood forlorn in a weed-choked pool.

'Seen better days', agreed the small man, reading their thoughts as he led the way along the path towards the house. 'I'm guessing you'll be wanting your friend back, then. May I enquire as to your names? Mine's Bardo, by the way, and it seems you were trespassing on my mistress Cortesia Tyverios' hospitality last night, so you were, this here being her house'.

Hesitantly, Rayo and Jory gave their names, the first that occurred to them, whilst Bardo paused at the end of the overgrown rose arbour to consider them, eyes narrowed. 'So, Misters *Danec* and *Lostian*', he began, his voice heavy with scepticism. 'A couple of fine noblemen, to judge by your speech, if not your clothing. And who might your sleepy friend be, hmm?'

'That would be Dromo', said Rayo cheerfully, whilst the different name that Jory had invented died on his lips. 'I trust he fares well?'

'Dromo', laughed Bardo with a wry glance for Jory's flushed cheeks. 'Well, we all know that's not true, don't we? And if your names are Danec and Lostian, I'm the Emperor of Honshiang. Still, no matter. My mistress will be wanting to have words with you, if you'd care to step this way'.

Having passed their point of entry from the previous night, the doors standing open now, Rayo and Jory followed Bardo warily around the side of the house and to a kitchen entrance. Any notions they might have entertained of overpowering their diminutive guide were of necessity abandoned as a tall and powerfully built black man met them here, regarding them curiously.

'These will be the ones', Bardo announced with a nod. 'A couple of the quality. Palace written all over 'em. In the green drawing room, is she?'

With the black man following behind, the party made their way through various gloomy corridors, before being shown into a large room with a high ceiling. The drapes were shut so that it was dimly lit, the size of the room emphasised by the removal of most of its furniture. Only a table remained with a scatter of plain kitchen chairs. Behind the table sat a woman wearing black. Her head was swathed in a veil so that only a single eye and a section of pale cheek was revealed. That eye regarded them dispassionately, as they settled on the chairs that Bardo indicated. The black man remained standing, arms folded, like a looming dark cliff behind them.

'I take it you are Prince Taian's friends', said Cortesia after Bardo had made introductions. 'You may be assured that he is well, if we may refer to his curious physical condition as such. You may be reunited with him presently and judge for yourself. Whatever lies you told Bardo here can be set aside now. You are amongst friends, since whomever opposes the empress is a friend of mine. I would know your names, your real names...'

'I am Rayo Kerkuoas', said Rayo after a moment in which he reflected that his instincts were as good a guide as any in addressing such a situation.

'And I Jory Marinaris', added his friend, thankful that Rayo had taken the initiative. 'And we thank you for your... hospitality, on behalf of the prince. The empress wishes him dead, or at least permanently incapacitated, so we felt bound to act. Now we have openly placed ourselves amongst her enemies. I suppose it will not be long before we are identified as his abductors'.

'May I ask wherein lies your own enmity for the empress?' asked Rayo, head tilted to one side.

After a moment, Cortesia pulled aside the black veil to reveal the distorted red ruin of her face, the puckered emptiness of her right eye socket. Rayo and Jory gasped, flinched, cast down their eyes. Even Bardo blinked and swallowed hard. Only Ohk appeared unmoved. He knew this horror full well, and pity had no power to shock.

'Is this reason enough?' she asked.

Cortesia had spent the last few hours in a state of mental ferment. It was as though twelve years of self-imposed mourning had fallen away, as though she had shouldered away the darkness and awoken to greet a new dawn. Cresara Rhovanion had defeated and diminished her all those summers and winters ago, but her triumph had fallen short of destruction, and now the notion of retribution, an ember that she had nourished over the dark years, flared bright once more. Tio had brought her a prince and a cause to fight for. She had resolved that she should rise to that challenge.

'More than enough', Rayo forced himself to say through a mouth rendered sandpaper-dry. 'But how...?'

Cortesia told her story. It was a strange thing to hear it from her own mouth, to clothe in words the dread visions of that day that had haunted her all these years. Rayo supplied detail when Cortesia's voice failed, and even Ohk nodded or shook his head vehemently whenever circumstances dictated.

'My mother has spoken of this often', said Jory when the story was complete. 'But the world barely knows what became of you'.

'And you had no recourse to the law?' asked Rayo.

'The investigators did their business', said Cortesia, 'but my enemy covered her tracks well. The finger of suspicion pointed at Cresara Rhovanion, but there was no proof, and so without clear proof the investigation withered on vine. I received no justice'.

Rising from her seat, Cortesia crossed to the drapes at the window behind her and pulled them firmly aside, flooding the austere chamber with bright afternoon light.

'And so, at last, I shall make my own', she said.

Prince Taian was much as he had been when Rayo and Jory had left him, eight hours or so earlier. His feet were bandaged and he had been dressed in a new nightshirt, but his pale face remained impassive, his ears deaf to his friends' greetings or enquiries. When nudged, his blank, unfocussed eyes eased open for a moment before closing once more, giving no indication of having seen.

'We should have taken the time to have dressed him', observed Jory regretfully, regarding Taian's feet. 'But we were in great haste and we believed we had a closed cart wating for us, ready to stow him in once the walls were passed'.

'He has evidently been drugged', said Cortesia, who had replaced her head coverings now, felt naked without them, in fact.

'Perhaps with whatever is on this spoon', said Rayo, drawing it out from an inner pocket in his coat. He sniffed it and passed it to Bardo to do likewise.

'It smells of cherries', he said after a moment. 'But with a musky undertone'.

'I suppose Doctor Mordanios would be able to tell us exactly what it is', observed Jory with a frown. 'Not that he ever will. Who else may we ask?'

'Perhaps you would take this to Sister Mora', suggested Cortesia with a nod to Bardo. 'She may be able to assist us'.

Ohk was finding food for Cortesia's new guests, and the three were discussing their options for the next few days, when a clamour of distant bells began. Rayo crossed to open a window. Louder than all was the palace bell of Saint Ramuold, quite close at hand, but the booming voice of the great cathedral of Saint Trichinos could be heard from further away as well as, in a growing chorus, the hundreds of bells of all the other churches, abbeys, priories, convents and basilicas in the city. The tolling was slow and measured.

'Passing bells', said Rayo, turning back to the room, his brow wrinkled. 'But who...?'

'They say the prince has been found', said Bardo, throwing open the doors, bursting in like a thunderclap, eyes wide. 'And he is dead!'

There was a long moment of silence between them as each looked from face to face, each striving to reconcile this information with the knowledge that the prince lived and breathed in the adjacent room.

'They lie, of course', said Cortesia at last as the discordant tolling continued from outside. 'But it is a useful lie'.

'How so?' asked Jory. 'There will be many who will wish to see his body, many who are entitled. No conveniently available corpse will suit their purpose, I should think. What can they be thinking?'

'Perhaps they will bundle some cadaver into a tomb and say risk of infection makes it too dangerous that any should gaze upon it', suggested Rayo.

'I doubt it', said Cortesia. 'That would be a most suspicious ploy. Too many would doubt their honesty. It would cast an exceptionally dark shadow over the new reign'.

'Well, how do you explain it?' asked Jory.

'I do not', admitted Cortesia, raising her gloved hands to her chin. 'I cannot'.

'And another thing, begging your pardon, Ma'am', said Bardo, drawing the cloth-wrapped spoon from his pocket. 'On Sister Mora's direction I took this here spoon down to Doctor Ardail, in the second circle. He is reputed to be the best pharmacist in the city, so she tells me. Whatever was on there, he can't name it, not even when I outlined the symptoms of our prince for him. Quite at a loss he was, and there's barely a smell of it left now, either, what with it being...'

'Thank you, Bardo', said Cortesia, raising a hand. 'I believe whatever they are contriving in the palace makes no difference to our own situation. They will continue to seek out the prince and his abductors, and if they find him', she said, regarding Jory and Rayo, grimly, 'you may be sure that they will bring fact fully in line with fiction'.

'So what are we to do?' asked Rayo.

'Well, certainly our first step must be to secure the prince's safety', replied Cortesia. 'And that surely means getting him away from this city. Once secure, you should put out feelers to those powerful enough to confront the empress and our new emperor, insist that he is left undisturbed. I say *you*, because whatever wealth or influence I once wielded are long gone. I will assist you in any way I can'.

Rayo uttered a hollow laugh.

'It is one thing to contemplate a journey, quite another to travel it', he said.

'Although, of course, we thank you for your support and for the kindness you have shown us', added Jory with a critical glance for his friend. 'And besides, our first priority is to find out what ails the prince and to seek whatever may restore his wits. Who is the foremost physician in the empire?'

'We can hardly approach the Sisters of Mercy', observed Cortesia. 'Word would certainly reach the empress's ears. And besides, Reena is said to be at death's door'.

The Sisters of Mercy dwelt in a convent a few miles south of The City. Within the walls dwelt Sister Reena Ducatirina, the living saint, one of the six acknowledged Luminaries of the Faith. Sister Reena had the God-given power to heal and had used this ability to spectacular effect over many years. A pious and independent person, she had refused to place her abilities at the service of the rich and the powerful, considering all deserving causes brought before her, regardless of their wealth or status.

Naturally, the early years of her life had seen vast crowds of the afflicted throng the walls of the convent. It was found that curing the sick depleted the life-force of the saint, rendering her increasingly frail, increasingly elderly in her appearance. She was not yet fifty years old but presented the appearance of great age. Accordingly, the Sisters of Mercy had, for many years, screened all applications for her services with the greatest of care. It had been some time since a successful application had been made, and the saint was said to be close to death, close to nominating her successor in the traditional way. It was most unlikely they would sanction a cure that might prove fatal for their saint, and certainly not until a successor had been identified.

'Perhaps you should go back to Doctor Ardail', said Rayo with a glance at Bardo. 'It is the opinion of physicians and learned men that we require'.

'If I were in search of a sick prince, I should have all the leading physicians in The City carefully watched to see if their advice is solicited', observed Cortesia. 'The palace has all the resources of the state to command, and they can be patient'.

'But that is a counsel of despair', objected Jory. 'On that basis...'

'Ohk?' interjected Cortesia, cutting Jory short with a gesture of her finger.

Ohk, when all turned to him, had his hand in the air like a child in the school room.

'What is it, man?'

Ohk made a symbol in the air before him.

'Hmm? What's that, Ohk?' asked Cortesia, narrowing her eye. 'Is that a *seven*?'

'It is, Ma'am', said Bardo. 'And I think I know what he means by it'.

'Go on', said Cortesia, leaning back in her chair, steepling her fingers.

'I believe he's referring to the seventh luminary, Ma'am, a fellow by the name of Balian Drumarion'.

'We all know who you're talking about, Bardo', sniffed Cortesia. 'But his nomination is widely considered to have been a mistake on the part of his predecessor, as you well know'.

'You're in the right of it there, but despite that he's a very learned fellow, so they say', continued Bardo.

'And he lives up in the mountains to the west', added Rayo. 'He's a neighbour to one of my uncle's estates. I heard him grumbling about Drumarion's tenants illegally hunting game on his land and saying he's so wrapped up in his books, he barely cares or pays attention to anything that goes on in the world beyond'.

'That sounds all too likely', agreed Cortesia. 'He was a visitor in this house on more than one occasion back in the fifties but spent most of his time in the library. That was before he was nominated, of course. I believe he took that very ill'.

Balian Drumarion, Professor of Anatomy at The City's university, was widely suspected of being an atheist despite his outward conformity with the tenets of the Faith. Accordingly, when the most recent High Luminary, Perico Aspenthios had, on his death bed, announced Balian as his successor, it was universally regarded as an aberration. Perico had been greatly admired and revered, a man whose God-given powers had been more considerable than any of the other luminaries of his generation. He had eradicated a devastating sheep murrain in the West, conjured rains when drought afflicted the South and summoned a violent tempest to wreck a fleet of pirates that had been raiding the northern coasts. His nominated successor, dismayed at his utterly unexpected elevation, appalled by the stream of pious pilgrims to his door, withdrew from society and presently from The City itself. He had dwelt in truculent and unresponsive isolation for many years, ignoring all advances from church authorities or representatives of the secular state.

'Well, I suppose we must run and hide somewhere, at least in the short term', murmured Jory. 'It may as well be out west. Perhaps Drumarian has been awaiting this opportunity to unleash his powers'.

'Perhaps', conceded Rayo doubtfully. 'But I shall await the *prince*'s funeral with interest. Half the nobility of the realm will be attending. It would be surprising if those gazing upon the dead face of whichever corpse they have enlisted don't notice that something is amiss'.

'Unless they cremate him straight away', suggested Rayo.

'In defiance of a thousand years of royal and then imperial tradition?', scoffed Cortesia. 'I think not. I rather think their precipitate action in declaring the prince dead is the result of hurried, muddled thinking – and one they will regret'.

The next day, having conveyed a message secretly to his cousin, Rayo met with him at the polo fields by the river meadows and received a sum of money from his family, together with assurances that his blood relatives would stand by him. A few years older than Rayo, Lando Kerkuoas had graduated from the military academy and was awaiting posting to a regiment. He was an earnest, plain-living young man who rather disapproved of Rayo's manners and habits. Nevertheless, there was a common feeling between them that transcended such differences at a time like this.

'Your mother sends her greetings and best wishes', he began as they walked under the poplars below the last of the pitches. 'Although she deplores the manner of your leaving'.

'Well, I could hardly have announced it at dinner', scoffed Rayo, casting one of many anxious glances over his shoulder to see if they were being followed. 'An element of secrecy was essential, she must allow'.

'And you are charged with the prince's murder through neglect', continued Lando. 'Evidently you abandoned his body in the street when it became clear that the rigours of your escape, the severity of his condition, had occasioned his death. You are outlaws. The Watch has been alerted to look out for you in every province of the realm, the investigators are charged with hunting you down',

he said, now laughing at Rayo's pained expression, 'and I should add, whoever you have stolen away is not the prince. I have gazed upon the body in its casket, as have half the court, and it is most certainly Prince Taian. Even his own nurse acknowledges this. She is said to be distraught beyond consolation'.

'How can this be?' demanded Rayo, throwing his arms wide in exasperation. 'I know Taian's face as well as I know my own, and I assure you it is he who lies insensible in our safe house'.

'Then what are you suggesting?' asked Lando, his serious features assuming even deeper gravity. 'Are you suggesting some manner of sorcery?'

'I don't know what I'm suggesting', moaned Rayo. 'Nothing makes sense'.

'But you have *your* prince', said Lando, placing a hand on his cousin's shoulder, alarmed by Rayo's uncharacteristic despondency. 'And in your custody, he is surely safer than he was just a little time ago'.

'He is', agreed Rayo, covering Lando's hand with his own. 'But what the future holds I do not know'.

'It is God's to know', observed Lando. 'And ours to approach it day by day'.

Chapter Eleven

Garabdor

It began to appear to Adala that the world around her, the world of The Grapes, the village, the cape and all that it contained, was an irrelevance, that the true focus of her being lay elsewhere. It lay in The City, where Prince Taian Starcorides lay ill. 'Mortally ill' the news courier had said. Dead, claimed the investigator, Trimestrion. Her head had reeled at these revelations, but her heart denied the truth of them, knew with unbreakable certainty that her love still lived.

The period immediately following from the investigator's departure had not been a happy one. Trimestrion had pronounced himself satisfied with the letters that she had given him, leaving Adala to explain the circumstances of this visit to an exceedingly curious and suspicious parent – a parent ready, willing and poised to unleash a tempest of rage once Adala's liaison had been explained to him.

'So this is why you refused to bend to my will in the case of the marriage I proposed!' he roared. 'You foolish, foolish girl! Did you really imagine that an imperial prince ever wanted you for anything other than the momentary enjoyment of your flesh?'

There was no defence that could be made of her conduct, no basis in logic with which she could refute his arguments. She must bow her head and weather the storm, conscious that this one would blow out in due course. At length it would do so, but for now, Corasto strode disgusted from the inn, slamming the door behind him, trudging across the street to take refuge with Andronis and a jug of apple spirits.

Marta, who had stood quietly during her sister's chastisement, came forward to wipe a tear from her eye.

'It will pass', she assured softly, tilting Adala's chin upward with a finger. 'Perhaps the prince's death has saved you from the consequences of your folly. We can put it behind us now, move on. Soon it will be just a distant memory'.

Adala nodded and agreed that this was so, but the practice of deception had become a habit to her, and her inward self looked outward to the wider realm and to The City on the far horizon of her imagination.

Marta, who could read the content of her mind as well as anyone, could see that her sister was distracted, that her mind lay elsewhere now, and the tavern had become a profoundly unhappy household. Corasto's fury and disgust with Adala overspilled into his attitude to Marta, where a peevish irritation at those around him had evidently been occasioned by his disappointment with regard to the abandoned marriage match. Nor was his mood improved by Marta's spirited defence of her sister, a circumstance that led him to conclude that the two of them were in league against him. Certainly, he was quick to find fault with even the slightest deficiency in their housekeeping, even the slightest disrespect to be detected in the tone or the content of their speech. He had, in fact, become quite intolerable to live with.

Three days later, the sisters left home with the expressed intention of visiting their aunt and their mother in The City, a journey that Corasto himself regularly made twice a year. A note explaining this was left on the table in Corasto's office. The reasons for their departure at this time were not stated, but Marta and Adala hoped that he would look to his own conduct and find the explanation there. Perhaps he might seek to mend his ways accordingly, they thought, although with no great depth of conviction. They took the pony and trap with Timo as companion, in order to present to the world at large the impression that they travelled with an adult male companion. Any conversation with Timo would correct this view, of course, would assure any questioner that they were in the presence of a simpleton. However, such circumstances could be managed, and they felt safer to have him with them. Fortunately, Corasto was engaged in visiting a friend in a neighbouring village when the trap rattled out of the stable-yard and set out on the road for Garabdor. As the last outlying houses of the village vanished around a bend in the road, Adala set her lips in a firm line and resolved that she would never return, that to set out on this road was to embrace her fate, whatever Tio willed for her.

'I trust Father will manage without us', murmured Marta with a backward glance.

'He will doubtless take on Mando and Erida again', noted Adala, naming two of the villagers who periodically worked for them. 'I suppose they will welcome it'.

A minor subterfuge had been to tell Timo that they were visiting another aunt who lived a few miles away, in order to disarm any objections he might have conceived of when setting out.

'Do carry straight on, Timo', instructed Marta when Timo made to turn into the lane that led to this aunt's house.

'But, Miss...' started Timo with a sideways glance, in his thick, slurring voice. 'Your aunt...'

'I think you are mistaken', said Adala. 'We go to The City to see my mother and Aunt Callie. You have been with us before, have you not?'

'Yes', agreed Timo with a smile, seemingly accepting this surprising change of destination with equanimity. 'Your mother... I likes The City'.

It would have been less arduous, less hazardous indeed, to have travelled to Garabdor and secured passage on one of the larger sailing barges that plied the broad course of the lower Canto between the coast and The City. This journey might take two or three weeks, however, depending on the caprices of the wind and the number of halts enroute. The road journey, on the other hand, should take no more than eight days on the broad-paved imperial way, and there were many inns where a traveller could stay. The City stood at the edge of her mental horizon in more ways than one. She remembered her first visit there as a seven-year-old, the furthest extent of her travel in the realm. But it was a conceptual horizon, too. Adala could not conceive of what she might do once arrived there, nor would she trouble herself to puzzle over it. Only a few days previously, her relationship with the divine had been a distant one, one marked by indifference on her side and apparent disinterest from that of the heavens, but her glorious vision had changed everything. Tio had spoken in her heart and she entrusted herself to *his* guidance now. When she arrived in The City *he* would show her what she must do. She was sure of it.

They made good progress on that first day, not only feeling a great sense of relief and of shared adventure at having escaped from their father's custody, but also sharing some anxiety when they considered the apoplectic rage that must certainly ensue from his reading their letter. The grim prospect that he might saddle up his grey mare and ride straight after them was one that neither of them liked to dwell on. However, they consoled themselves with the thought that The Grapes was to host the annual dinner for the local landowners' guild in two days' time. Given that this required a great deal of preparation and was by far the most lucrative event of the year, they surmised that the desire to secure that most handsome payment must drive out any parental concerns, at least for the present.

The weather was fine, and the first day passed quickly after joining the wide and well-maintained Margantine Way that led towards Annagaar, having skirted the suburbs of Garabdor itself. They spent the night in the cheapest room available, in a roadside inn, and ate frugally in order to eke out the slender funds that were required to endure as long as their journey. Timo made no objection to sleeping on the floor, swathed in blankets, but he took whatever vengeance might have informed his private mind through a persistent snoring that provoked occasional peevish hammering from the neighbouring room. Accordingly, the sisters slept poorly and peered blearily at the surrounding landscape next morning as the pony drew them clattering briskly towards Annagaar. The milestones came and went, as did a succession of country towns and villages. They approached the bleak waste of Skellig Moor towards dusk of their second day, rising shoulders of barren land dotted with windblown stunted trees and scattered copses. The steady stream of farm traffic, itinerant merchants, post coaches and other private travellers thinned out, and at times it appeared that they had the road to themselves from one horizon to another. They passed an inn with a swinging sign in the shape of a kettle as the red rim of the sun crept beneath the western heights of the moor, and Adala would have been content to have ended their day's journey there, but Marta, judging it to be of a dark and disreputable appearance, thought another quarter of an hour or so might bring them to a better place. They soon had cause to regret this. As they passed the summit of the moor and began their descent, a group of men strode out from the shade of a shallow spinney that drew near to the edge of the road. It was almost dark by now, and a half-moon had emerged from amongst the clouds in the northern sky.

'Mother preserve us', whispered Adala, making her sign with a sidelong glance at her sister's anxious face. A sickening lump came into her throat as the men approached with an air of easy confidence.

'I suppose we shall have to give them our money', murmured Marta, although the unspoken fear of what else they may require of them hung heavy in the air between them.

'I told 'ee we should have stayed in that-there last place', muttered Timo resentfully, letting the reins drop. The trap drew to a halt. One of the five men came forward to take the pony's bridle, while another, with a laugh and curse, hauled Timo down from his perch, urging him away with a kick. Adala, whose impulse to protest withered on her tongue, felt fear clutch at her heart. How could she have been so foolish?

'Evening, young misses', said a long-faced fellow, whose air of easy authority marked him down as their leader. Enough light remained to show his broad grin, punctuated by the dark gaps of missing teeth. He tipped his cap with mock respect, reaching forward to push back the hood of Adala's cloak and then sucking in breath with a low whistle when her pale face was revealed.

'Well look what we have here, lads', he laughed. 'A pair of rare beauties, rare beauties indeed, such as we don't come across in these parts every day'.

'Ain't that the truth', chuckled another, pressing forward and being held off by the first man's extended arm.

'Steady on, Chally', warned the first man, drawing a knife from his belt. 'These fine young ladies might think we lack breeding, if we lay hands on 'em without first wooing 'em, without pressing our suit, as you might say'.

Marta seemed dumbstruck, her eyes wide, gripping her sister's hand with a vice-like intensity.

'Please...' began Adala, finding her voice at last. 'I, er...'
'Shhhh', said the first man, pressing a big finger suddenly to her lips so that she gasped, and the words she had intended emerged as a strangled yelp. 'It is folly for travellers to venture onto this here moor after dusk' he said. 'Have you not heard? A stranger in these parts, are you? Don't you know that this region is frequented by lawless, wicked men with theft, murder and rapine in their dark hearts? I should know. It would be a shame if you were to fall in with them, would it not?'
'Surely', she heard herself croak. 'I have money'.
Marta nodded, her lips moving wordlessly.
The greasy finger returned to her lips.
'No doubt you have, my sweet, no doubt you have, and we shall part you from it in due course, but I wager that what's beneath that frock is a greater prize by far'. He nodded to where Timo could be seen cowering at the edge of the road. 'I suppose this here bold knight is your protector. Is that right, son?' he barked so that Timo recoiled from the force of his words. 'Are you going to fight us to preserve the honour of these ladies?'
Timo could say nothing but could only stammer, regarding Marta with eyes that were wide pools of terror.
'Come on then', said a short bulky man, giving Timo a shove. 'Show us what a brave lad you are'.
Another provided a kick to Timo's seat that span him round, in time to receive a brutal fist to the jaw that toppled him like a tree. Timo, on hands and knees, whimpered, tried to regain his feet but received a further succession of kicks and blows.
'No!' screamed Marta, finding her voice at last. 'Run, Timo!'
At the same time, she rose from her seat and tried to leap from the trap but was secured in a tall man's strong arms, another of their assailants grasping her around the thighs. Screaming, struggling, weeping, she was slapped,

punched and dragged briefly to the ground, lifted to her feet once more and hauled roughly to the damp and hummocky grass at the roadside.

The same fate befell Adala. Yelping, gasping, she was pulled roughly from her seat and to the ground at the side of the trap. The one called Chally pinioned her arms whilst she writhed and begged and screamed. Chally placed his hand over her mouth. She bit it so that he swore and whipped it away.

'She bites, Danno', he grunted.

He struck her hard on the left side of her face, so hard that her vision was momentarily shrouded in swirling blackness with a million pinpricks of dancing light. There was blood in her mouth.

'Listen missy', barked Danno, who loomed over her, unbuckling his belt. 'We can do this easy or we can do it hard. We don't much care if you're live or dead, so long as you're warm, so lie still there, won't you!'

Suddenly there was the cold edge of a knife against her throat. She gasped, closed her eyes tight shut and lay motionless now, still moaning, still begging, still crying 'No! Please don't, please! No!' as her dress and her underclothes were pulled up.

'Go on', grunted Danno. 'You take this one. I'll take the other now that the lads have stopped her squirming'.

Chally laughed, and then the weight and the stench of him were upon her, another man at her side, pinning her wrists to the earth. She wriggled and twisted with sudden desperation, turning her side to him. There was a curse, a roar of anger and another blow to the head that caused a fierce jet of pain across her brow. She felt herself losing consciousness, her legs being forced apart. Despair and a great tide of darkness welled up within her.

Before Chally could complete her humiliation, before his flesh was within hers, there came the sound of hoofbeats and the attendant vibration in the cold earth beneath her naked flesh. Chally and his friend released their grip on her and swivelled to face whoever was galloping down the road towards them.

'Get out of here!' she heard above the sound of jingling harness and horse breath. 'Or you'll taste this steel, so help me God!'

Rolling groggily onto her side, struggling to focus her eyes, she could see the dark silhouette of a rider on a rearing horse, the blade of a sword glinting suddenly in moonlight. The men turned and ran, laughing raucously amongst themselves, before darting up the grassy bank, seeking the refuge of the trees. Adala pushed herself upright, pulling her dress down about her as the newcomer dismounted and approached.

'Marta!' she cried, hearing her sister's anguished moans from the far side of the trap.

'Damn their eyes!' the newcomer cried. 'Are you alright, ladies? Have they... used you ill?'

Above the vast tide of relief and shame in Adala's breast there was a note of recognition. That voice was familiar. He turned his head now and beneath his broad-brimmed hat the moon picked out the smooth features of Drael Trimestrion, Imperial Investigator.

'I am assaulted, sir', sobbed Adala. 'But they did not... they did not...'

The wild glint in her eye, her anguished expression, supplied the end to her sentence, and the disarray of her clothing further underlined the reality of the plight that his arrival had spared her from, causing Drael to cast down his own eyes awkwardly. He bit his lip, recognition dawning now.

'Is that you, Adala Radagarion?'

'It is, sir', gasped Adala. Marta's plight drove out all other thoughts now and she gasped, calling her name.

Murmuring curses, Trimestrion dismounted and strode to her sister, where she lay slumped, weeping at the roadside beyond. Adala, pulling herself to her feet, followed him, a hard lump in her throat. It soon became apparent that the fate she had so narrowly averted had been visited upon Marta. Trimestrion, awkward in these circumstances, assured himself of her immediate survival and turned aside to seek Timo, who could be heard whimpering in the gloom, as soon as Adala had tenderly embraced her distraught sister.

'Your servant is here, miss', reported Drael, helping him from the wet roadside ditch where he had lain, his head buried in his hands. 'And no bones broken, I think'.

He gestured to Adala, turning his head aside to respect what remained of Marta's modesty as Adala helped her to arrange her clothing. 'Do please... I trust you are...'

It became quite clear that Marta had been brutally raped. Even in the growing dark he could see the misery in her tear-streaked face as Adala cradled her head. Trimestrion's eyes met Adala's, and the sympathy she saw there was accompanied by the helplessness of a creature that could only begin to imagine the pain and the suffering that Marta had endured. Adala's head already ached furiously, and she knew full well that the new day would reveal a great deal of bruising, besides. Her legs felt as they might buckle beneath her and she recognised the thin buzzing sounded in her ears that usually preceded a faint. She staggered to the trap and clung to the wheel, where Drael Trimestrion gently handed her in, returning to lift Marta gently to her position. A fierce fire burned in Adala's heart now, one that she knew would continue to smoulder until she put the man that was called Danno in the ground for the crime he had committed. This yearning for vengeance gradually shouldered aside the many other considerations that whirled in her brain, driving the fog of shock and anguish from her mind, giving her the strength to compose herself and to take her seat in the trap. Timo, bleeding profusely from the nose, soon climbed up to sit beside her, regarding the two girls with wide-eyed horror as Drael passed him the reins.

'See them hung... heath infested with scoundrels... must find a doctor...' Drael spat, keeping up a ceaseless stream of disconnected thought throughout his work to re-establish Adala, Marta and Timo in their places, as though he did not dare to let grim silence envelop them, as though he thought the sound of his voice a comfort. Vaguely, part of Adala's mind wondered that this was a very different presentation of the man who had personified hard-faced officialdom only a few days previously.

'There is an inn no more than a mile from here', he said at last, mounting to the saddle of his horse with one easy motion. 'The pity of it is that you had almost reached its sanctuary'.

His eyes clouded, as if mention of her folly in travelling this road at such an hour had occurred to him, but he only nodded and set off at an easy pace that Timo could urge their pony to match.

'And then I shall summon a doctor', he called over his shoulder.

Before long, beneath a bright moon, the road curved around the last incline of the heath and an inn stood at the side of a wide mere, where there was a crossroads with an intersecting lane. The landlord proved to be very hospitable, and his soft-spoken wife, all anxious sympathy, conducted Adala and Marta to a fine, clean room where their grazes and bruises could be dressed or salved and their persons washed, before they were placed together in bed. However, no quantity of cool water, no soap ever contrived by the hand of man, could wash away the anger and regret that brought Adala to the brink of screaming. She was indeed a fool, as Marta and Corasto had declared, and now her folly had led to her dear sister's rape and come within moments of bringing about her own. At length, the kindly woman withdrew, Marta's bloodied clothing in her arms, and Adala could hear her low conversation with Drael from beyond the door.

'No doctor for twenty mile or so', she heard, and 'Fear you not, sir, it's a truly dreadful thing but she'll mend, poor dear, provided they haven't put a child in her, that is. And things could have been a lot worse, as I'm sure you will allow. They might have cut her throat, as many do, when they had done with her. She may have cracked a couple of ribs but the bruises will pass. She's had a terrible, terrible violation and a mote of trauma. How she mends from this will depend on her nature, that's for sure. She may go into a decline. She may rise above it. She may weep and mope for a month or more. You'll know better than me as to her character'.

'I assure you I do not', said Drael, his voice muffled. 'She and her sister are known to me only in a professional capacity and then hardly at all. I chanced upon her and that band of rogues quite unexpectedly as I rode this way tonight'.

'The other has a great bruise to her head, I see', he added. 'She has that, but her wits are not astray. She should mend soon enough, although I daresay this night will long live with her'.

The latter parts of this continuing exchange were lost to Adala as she succumbed to a shallow, restless sleep, finding Marta's hand beneath the clean white sheets.

'I have the blood of the kings of Radagar in my veins', she murmured to herself. 'Tio send that I may live to exact vengeance from he who stole Marta's maidenhead'.

A tremor rose in her body and a wave of white-hot fury prickled across her brow, and then she slept.

'Surely we must return home now', said Adala the next morning, when it became apparent that Marta was awake. Her sister's face was pale but her eyes red and puffy after a night when neither of them had known proper sleep. She squeezed Marta's hand.
'It was my folly that brought us here and...'
'Nonsense', said Marta, squeezing back. 'I was glad enough to come with you, and we share equally in whatever culpability may be attached to us. Surely, they will call us fools, as you know'.
'And you have suffered for it', said Adala softly. 'You have suffered so much'.
Marta's lip trembled momentarily and her eyes filled with tears once more. She bit her lip, however, and continued with a voice that was evidently not hers to command.
'I have. But I will not have you come with me', she said. 'You have this dream and you must pursue it'.
'No, but I...' protested Adala, before Marta's finger on her lip stilled her voice.
'I will not hear of it. Tio knows how foolish your errand is, but I will not have you forever resenting that I prevented you from pursuing it'.
'I should not, I certainly should not', protested Adala, eyes wide.
'You lie, and you know it', sighed Marta. 'Don't you? Answer me!'
Now it was Adala's turn to bite her lip and to cast down her eyes. It was true and she could not deny it. Nothing must come between her and the completion of the quest that Tio had set for her.
'You will write. Of course, you must write', said Marta, seeing that Adala had submitted to this truth.
'Of course I will. You know I will. As soon as I arrive there. But dear sister, are you sure? I shall feel so wretched to leave you here'.

'Don't be silly. I shall send to The Grapes and father will surely come for me. I shall have to face down his petulant rage, of course, but surely even his stony heart must, must...'

A soft knock on the door and the mistress of the house came in to attend to them, curtailing any further discussion. The good lady withdrew at last with a reassuring look for Drael, who passed her in the doorway and advanced to stand at the end of the girls' bed, hat in hand.
'I trust your condition... is improved', he said awkwardly after conventional greetings had been exchanged, looking from face to face.
'We are as well as you might expect, under the circumstances, and we are truly grateful to you for saving our lives', Adala answered, and then with a sympathetic glance for her sister. 'I thank you for saving me from further indignity or injury. Your arrival was indeed a timely one. You must forgive me for not making my gratitude plain last night. I was...'
'No, not at all', protested Drael with a dismissive wave of his hand. 'I only regret that I did not run at least one of them onto my steel'. He patted the hilt of his sword for emphasis. 'May I?' he asked tentatively, indicating the chair at Adala's bedside.
'Do please', offered both Adala and Marta, raising themselves a little on their pillows.
'And may I ask how you came to be travelling that road at such an hour, in defiance of all good sense?' he asked, when he was established there.
Adala saw that the smooth contours of his face were marred in two places by fine scars, paler than the surrounding flesh, one across the brow and another beneath his left eye. A rough, grey-flecked stubble

darkened his jaw, but his features were generally fine and well-proportioned. Those cool grey eyes regarded her curiously now, but there was none of the inflexible official arrogance of the person that had first interrogated her. Adala found herself blushing at this wholly accurate description of her conduct, found herself spilling out the story of her journey from her village. Nor was she able to stop there. An imperial investigator, whether on duty or at leisure, was inevitably a person of insatiable curiosity, and this one possessed the skills, the acuity and the inclination to tease out the whole of the story that preceded and explained her journey. When she faltered or showed reluctance, he sat patiently in silence, before renewing his enquiry once it seemed that any agitation had subsided. Marta remained largely silent, only nodding at intervals or making noises indicative of support or agreement. Her own intention had been to state simply that they journeyed together to visit their aunt and their mother, so it was surprising to her to see Adala disclose the content of her mind in this way. Adala found that it was easy to be entirely open with this man. He passed no judgement, offered no frowns or wondering stares at the more outlandish imaginings that she shared with him and listened attentively until she had finished.

'There', she said when her story was complete. 'You have me, and you may judge for yourself what a wicked and stupid girl I am'.

For a long while, Drael said nothing, merely regarding her with apparent neutrality as he pondered what he had learned from her. There seemed to have grown a strange intimacy between them by this time. Having poured out her story to him, she felt doubly exposed to his gaze and yet undisturbed by it. She felt quite secure with him, very much at rest, as though a burden had been lifted from her.

'As you know', he said at last, 'the prince is dead and your errand futile'.

'He is not', she said with quiet conviction. 'Tio has shown me'.

Drael stroked his chin pensively but said nothing to contradict her.

'May I enquire as to your own errand on this road', she asked into the resultant silence.

'You may', he agreed. 'You are aware of my work, of course, since my duty has already caused our paths to cross. I have heard that my mother is ill, and I ride to The City to visit her. I have taken a month's leave, the first for two years, so I challenge any superior of mine to criticise it.

'And what would you do now?' he asked when Adala likewise raised no objection. 'Do you propose still to pursue this dream of yours until the evidence of your prince's death is too overwhelming to deny?'

'I do', she said simply, her mouth held in a firm line.

'Your sister', he said, now turning his gaze to Marta, 'is she always like this?'

'If you mean by that, *is she always impossibly headstrong and stubborn as a mule?* Then I must answer in the affirmative', she answered. 'She must do as she must do. We have already discussed this. I shall return to our home in due course. Adala must continue on this road'.

Drael sighed, stood and walked to the window, where he regarded the sunlit mere pensively.

'Well, may I ask if I may accompany you, at least as far as The City?' he said when it began to seem inevitable that he had frozen into a statue.

Adala felt tears of relief and gratitude rim her eyes.

'I would be honoured', she said. 'Most grateful'.

'And I, too', added Marta. 'To know that she has a fine, strong companion on the road would be a great comfort to me. Thank you, kind sir!'

Drael arranged for Marta and Timo to be accommodated at the inn until such time as The Grapes could arrange for their transport home. Adala, at Drael's suggestion, wrote the letter that would outline this request and further explain the reasons for her flight. This could then be entrusted to a courier, said to operate from Ilkenfold, the next town along the road. Adala, having set down her pen, reflected bleakly on the reception it might receive. She wondered whether Corasto would eventually set out in vengeful pursuit of her. In this next town there was a constabulary office, at which Adala might report the crimes that she and Marta had suffered. Having taken a further day to recover, and to see to her sister's recovery, she professed herself well enough to travel and set out after breakfast, after many tears and embraces, with Drael riding at her side. In truth, she was far from recovered, either physically or in her spirit, but it seemed unfair to impose further delay on Drael's own journey. His offer to accompany her had been a generous one. It appeared that he had been a cavalry officer before his employment with the investigators. Certainly, his coal-black mare and the sword at his side presented a formidable deterrent to further potential thieves or brigands on the road ahead. The stern impassivity of his features in repose suggested a resolute and determined character that none would readily trifle with or oppose. It appeared that Drael was not given to smiling. What Adala had supposed was the bleak and unyielding mask of officialdom proved to be the face he habitually presented to the world. Still, there was nothing to suggest he lacked for compassion. He was most attentive to her needs, extending every courtesy that convention demanded. Nor did he importune her with his views about the futility of her mission, and for this she was profoundly grateful.

She felt as though she had been changed by her traumatic experience, that she would never be quite the same person again, that the burden of guilt for Marta's rape would forever trammel her being. The same sense of alteration had been the case after her vision, a growing closeness to the presence that she knew to be Tio, one that had given her a strange sense of the extension of her person and her senses. The violence visited upon her body, once the immediate sense of shock had passed, left her with a curious feeling of disassociation from this world but connection with another. In addition, a corrosive rage curdled within her breast, one that robbed her of her appetite and dulled her enjoyment of the world around her. The fields and the hedgerows at the roadside, the cottage gardens and the tumbling streams were grey to her, entirely stripped of their capacity to please.

'I am a stranger to myself', she mused. 'This mortal frame of mine seems as a vessel that my spirit fills like some ethereal fluid'.

'I suppose we shall easily reach Ilkenfold by dusk if we maintain this pace', observed Drael, whose place in the saddle obliged him to look down upon Adala as she sat managing the trap.

'I'm sure you are right', she replied.

Drael was not one to make small talk for conversation's sake, but even he must have noted the shortness of her replies, when communication was essential, the strange distance in her eyes as she held the pony's reins. It was not until they arrived in Ilkenfold that the reasons for this became apparent. It was late in a warm afternoon when they reached the Plough Inn, having first seen to their post and visited the constabulary. Here, they were told that the constable and his men were addressing disorder in a neighbouring village but were expected to return the next day. By sunset, they had stepped down at the inn, and a stable boy was tending to the needs of their horses.

In the entrance hall, Drael was negotiating for rooms with the proprietor, whilst Adala waited at his shoulder. From here she could see along a corridor past the kitchen into the main bar. The place was busy with cheerful conversation and a constant procession of servants bringing food or drink. Adala turned and took a few steps towards the corridor.

'Two rooms, if you please...' she heard from behind her, and 'No, not at all, the prospect does not signify...' as she found herself drawn towards the bar.

There was a voice amongst those voices, one that was odiously familiar, one that brought every fibre of her being to sudden tingling attention. Danno. It was Danno, he whose flesh had pierced her sister's, he whose ruin and damnation she had pictured hungrily in her thoughts ever since. She advanced along the corridor, conscious that every one of her senses was suddenly supernaturally alert, that a vague trembling had begun in her hands.

There he was, half-turned from her, seated at a table, playing cards, his head cast back with coarse laughter. In the kitchen, backs were turned. She reached in swiftly to seize up a knife from a bench close to the door and continued, step by resolute step, to approach the man who had so cruelly injured and humiliated her sister. People came and went along the corridor, talking amongst themselves, turning to ease past her, but no one remarked on the hard steel in her hand.

She was then at his side and she paused, regarding him grimly as he studied his cards. A strange power seemed to flood through her body. She felt light-headed, as though the incandescent rage that possessed her was pouring from her like a clear white radiance. There was no doubt in her mind, no consideration of past or future, no awareness of immediate circumstance or future consequence. The moment was complete unto itself, and

her world shrank to encompass only herself and the man she would destroy. He became aware that she was there, turned, lowered his cards and his eyes met hers. Recognition dawned, became alarm and his pupils widened. His jaw dropped and the first stiffening of violent movement seized his frame.
Too late.
Adala's left hand sprang forward to grasp Danno's chin. She pushed upwards with a firm smooth pressure that no muscular resistance could oppose.
'Burn in hell!' she said, jaw clenched.
In the same moment, she thrust her knife upward with brutal force, through the floor of the man's mouth, through his tongue, his palette and onward through bone into his brain. It was as though time slowed to a trickle. She was dimly aware of chaos erupting around her, of screams, chairs falling over, Danno's companions lurching jerkily to their feet, horror written in eyes and faces. Blood spurted around her knife, a lazy spatter of distorting globules that arced through the air to splash upon her clothes and face. Strong arms seized her, but it was too late, too late, and a fierce exultation leapt in her heart.

'Adala! Adala!' came Drael's voice in her ear. 'What have you done?!'
It was his arms who pinioned hers as the supernatural strength leached from her frame and a black rush rose up to extinguish her consciousness.

Chapter Twelve

Annagaar

When she awoke it was to find that she was secured to a bed by ropes wrapped tightly around her ankles and wrists. She wriggled and tugged experimentally but found herself immobilised. It was dark and a single candle burned on the table at her bedside.
Turning her head, she found that Drael was sitting at the other side of her, his face half lost in shadow.
'Well, there you are', he said. 'I trust you are recovered from your exertions'.
'I do not regret my actions', she said. 'I swore to myself that I would put him in the ground, given the chance, and so I have'.
'Indeed. And you may swing for it', observed Drael dryly. 'You are fortunate that I am an officer of the law and was able to intercede for you. Tomorrow, I shall need to convince the constable that he may trust me to convey you to Annagaar, where you will face justice at the next court session'.
'Justice is already served', murmured Adala, returning her gaze to the ceiling. I have delivered it with my own hand and spared the authorities the trouble. They should congratulate me'.
'They will not. I assure you they will not, as you know full well. It may be that you will be spared death', conceded Drael. 'I shall testify on your behalf, of course, and it was certainly one of your true assailants that you slew. I was able to satisfy myself of that, having interviewed a number of those present. He was not well-loved in these parts, far from it. Many will applaud you for your deed, but the law stands above the promptings of emotion. The

law is blind to such urgings, guided only by facts and circumstances. Your case may persuade a judge that you deserve to live, or it may not'.

'Why would you testify for me?' she asked.

'Because I am a servant of the law and I desire to see justice done', replied Drael.

'And is that all?' asked Adala, turning her head to him once more. 'Is that the only reason?'

For a long moment, Drael cast his eyes downward, and when he looked up once more there was a strange gleam in his eye.

'There is something about you, Adala Radagarion, that I find most fascinating', he said. 'How is it that a slender maid such as I see before me could wrench up a man's jaw as though it were of no consequential weight and thrust a knife with deadly precision through flesh and bone into his brain? It was a blow of singular destructive force, delivered with uncanny accuracy', he added. 'And I use that term advisedly'.

'Uncanny?' she laughed. 'Is that what I am?'

'I don't know how else to describe it. It was as if there was a glow around you. More than one of those present remarked upon it, and I overheard dark mutterings of witchcraft, I should add'.

'So, what is it?' scoffed Adala. 'Am I to be hanged or burnt? Let me ask you a question, Officer Trimestrion. Do you believe in God?'

'Of course', shrugged Drael. 'Why should you doubt it?'

'But in the abstract, no doubt, the notional inhabitant of prayerbook and legend, the theoretical sponsor of church and cathedral. But would you recognise Tio if he appeared in your dreams? He did to me. To me, also, he was once a vague theoretical notion, but now he is become concrete reality to me – and what you witnessed earlier was the work of his hand, I assure you. His hand guided mine and lent to me his superhuman strength. Believe it, Officer Trimestrion, for it is so'.

Drael sat back in his chair and considered her pale, earnest face whilst his mind picked over the evidence of eye and ear. Could it be so? Everyone knew that the luminaries were God's sacred vessels on earth, that they channelled a little of his divine power into this world, but was he to believe that Adala was similarly blessed? He was a hard-headed man, a man for whom logic was a lodestone, for whom rationality was a guiding star. He dismissed superstition as the folly of weak minds and dismissed subjection to emotion as frailty. Accordingly, it was deeply unsettling to gaze upon this young woman and trace with his eye the elegant line of her eyebrow and her nose, the contours of lip and chin, still marred by the bruises of the assault upon her. She was very beautiful, and it was not hard to conceive that a prince might have been captivated by her. What was this flutter in his heart, what this curious fixation of his vision? He assured himself that chivalry and simple fellow feeling had been his motivations when he had offered to accompany her to The City, but that assurance was built on foundations of sand and now he felt the slow erosion of that platform, the slow erosion of all that he had once held dear.

'And so, Officer Trimestrion, will you deliver me unto the authorities in Annagaar?' asked Adala, breaking into this reverie.

'That is what the law demands', answered Drael.

'And that is no answer at all', observed Adala with a wry smile.

Many curious observers were on hand the next day to see Adala's departure from the inn. It was not often that the town witnessed a murder, and the culprit was said to be a rare beauty. On this occasion, Drael drove the trap with Adala sitting at his side, her hands bound. Drael's own horse trotted behind on a tether. The constable of the town, returning to find that a serious breach of the peace had occurred in his absence, had required a detailed account from Drael and attention to various official forms. He also offered to send a couple of his men to accompany them on their journey to Annagaar. An imperial investigator far outranked a humble town constable, however, so there was no difficulty in declining this offer. There were some mutterings in the crowd about irregularity, but there were few who would miss Danno, and so there was little in the way of hostility as they turned the corner out of the inn yard and out onto the highway.

Once they were a mile or so from the last outlying house of the settlement, Drael untied Adala's wrists.

'I don't suppose you will run from me', he said, the corners of his mouth twitching momentarily upward.

The trap carried them onward throughout a day that brought heavy rain towards midday, so that they must necessarily huddle beneath cloaks. The trap rattled and splashed through puddles in potholes. Adala glanced sideward to observe the face of her companion, feeling the gentle intermittent pressure of his shoulder against hers as they swayed with the motion. A dewy drop was poised on the end of his nose, wiped away with a gloved hand as he turned to meet her eye. She saw uncertainty there and discontent, a perfect misery of indecision. For her part, she felt content. She felt entranced, freed from the anxiety for the immediate future that the typical charged murderer must endure. Her heart contained a vision of her prince, and her heart likewise assured her that she would never swing on a gibbet.

Adala had correctly judged Drael's mood. As an agent of the law it was his inflexible duty to convey her to the proper authorities in Annagaar. He must certainly seek out the Duchy Chief Constable's office and consign her to justice there. These things he knew. These things oppressed his mind with a bitter persistence as the miles unrolled beneath them. Drael was unused to listening to the voice of his heart, had previously dismissed it completely from the rational structure of his reasoning. But now it importuned him ceaselessly. It told him that he must abandon duty and professional responsibility in order to set this girl free, in defiance of all logic. He must, in fact, engage in behaviour that would certainly bring disgrace and dismissal upon him were word of it ever to reach the ears of his superiors.

And so, at last, they reached a fork in the road, literally and figuratively so far as Drael was concerned. Traffic passed them by in both directions as Drael brought the trap to a halt. Ahead, beyond trees and market gardens, the higher towers of Annagaar could be seen along the main road, as well as the first semaphore station on the line to Garabdor. The other arm of the fork, a lesser way, turned leftwards amongst cottages and orchards, a way that would skirt the city and join eventually with the main road south to the queen of cities, Callisto, that which was called simply *The City*.

'Why have we stopped?' asked Adala after a minute or so during which Drael sat with his eyes cast down, his shoulders hunched.

'Hush a moment, I must think!' he said peevishly.

I must think whilst I decide whether to abandon my career and my prospects in favour of attaching my fortunes to this extraordinary girl, he observed to himself. *And now at last I must take that leap or see her condemned.*

Adala, who had some inkling of the nature of his thoughts, folded her hands in her lap and regarded him calmly.

'Oi, are you moving on, or what?' enquired the driver of a large haycart that had come up behind them and was unable to pass unless Drael turned off the paved surface.

With a sigh, Drael raised a hand and pulled on the reins to urge the pony leftward along the suburban lane. His decision was made, the die was cast and his future was no longer his own to command.

'Am I not to face the court, then?' asked Adala when the trap was under way once more.

'You are not', grunted Drael. 'At least not under my auspices. I shall conduct you to The City'.

'I thank you', she said, placing a hand on his arm, looking into his face. 'You have been truly good to me'.

'I have indeed', agreed Drael, meeting her eyes now. 'You have overturned everything I thought I knew, and I set out on this road a different man'.

'Not too different, I hope', said Adala. 'I should certainly regret that'.

Drael found himself smiling, the unfamiliar configuration of muscles somehow spreading a warmth that permeated his being.

Callisto

Jory, although initially somewhat wary of their hostess, found himself oddly fascinated by her. He had heard her story, of course, as most of the court had heard it, but Cortesia had faded from the public consciousness and the public mind during the past twelve years. She was said to be impoverished and embittered, which was hardly to be wondered at, given the gravity of her wounds. Even so, Jory found himself wondering at the manner in which she had imposed herself on their enterprise since the prince had appeared in her cellar.

'We approach this issue from different directions', she had explained, when Rayo and Jory had spoken of departing with the prince. 'You are motivated by a laudable loyalty to your friend, and I by a desire to see that bitch brought low. You have awakened me, my friends. Year after year, I hid myself away in this house and wallowed in self-pity, but now those days are done. Your arrival here has been the vital catalyst, the tinder that has sparked the fire of vengeance in my heart. I will see her ruined – and I shall do all in my power to help you to raise up the rightful prince once more. I shall ride with you'.

This was no request; it was a simple declaration of intent. It seemed unlikely that Cortesia herself represented any access of strength to their desperate enterprise, but her man Ohk was a formidable presence and might prove useful if there was fighting to be done. Bardo, perhaps rather less useful in a fight, but evidently valued by Cortesia, also insisted on joining them. Accordingly, it was as a party of five that they set out westward, bearing the stricken prince with them in a covered wagon. Cortesia travelled within, as did Ohk, who was no horseman and would have seriously inconvenienced any but the largest of beasts. So Bardo took the reins of the wagon and the two noblemen rode on either side, mounted uneasily on the two ill-tempered and flatulent nags that had been available at short notice. Both men wore cloaks with deep hoods, and both had suffered an agony of anxiety as they urged their beasts through the west gate and out into the suburbs beneath the gaze of the guards stationed there. It was a huge relief to emerge onto the open road and set their faces towards the first vague foothills of the Vertebraean Alps that loomed beyond the western horizon.

'It seems odd to be turning our backs on The City', observed Jory as they passed through one of the great ancient cemeteries that lined the road.

'I suppose you'd rather march up to the palace and demand justice', laughed Rayo. 'No doubt your silver tongue would convince them of the error of their ways'.

'Not I', said Jory, regarding him sidelong as a party of mourners emerged in front of them from a side road. 'I'm in no hurry to place my head on the block. It's just that everyone we know, all our friends, family and acquaintances, are there...'

'And all our enemies', interjected Rayo with a grin.

'Indeed', agreed Jory, but where we are bound, we have no connections at all. We are on our own'.

'Then we shall make *new* friends', insisted Rayo cheerfully. 'Soon we shall communicate with others, convince them of the righteousness of our cause and tread this road once more with an army at our back'.

'What a soaring spirit you are', declared Jory, slapping him on the shoulder. 'In the heart of Hell, you would wonder what ails everyone, no doubt, why such long faces and lamentations?'

'Is it my fault that my soul is of feathers and yours is of lead?'

'Well perhaps we may agree that this errand of ours is a fool's one?' continued Jory. 'That this Balian fellow is no more likely to restore our prince to his proper self than he is to turn him into a statue of gold'.

'We shall see', said Rayo with infinite complacence. 'We shall see what each new day has to offer. We must certainly go *somewhere*, and this direction seems as good as any'.

Balian Drumarion looked up from his book as a soft knock on the door of his chamber immediately preceded the entry of his steward, Grae.

'Hmm?' enquired Balian mildly, looking over his glasses. 'I suppose you are going to tell me that luncheon is ready'.

Grae, tall and gangling with a meagrely fleshed frame, regarded his employer with the supercilious air of those who secretly deprecate the fat. As ever, his disapproving eye fell upon Balian's fleshy jowls and the generous paunch that, in Grae's opinion, disclosed a weak and self-indulgent devotion to food. His head, having of necessity dipped to avoid the door frame, now bobbed upwards.

'It is, sir', he agreed. 'But in addition, I should say that we have visitors'.

'Oh!' exclaimed Balian, his brow creasing. 'How very inconvenient. I suppose it is not that Kerkuoas fellow, complaining about his wretched partridges again?'

'It is not, sir', said Grae, regarding the disorder of Balian's desk with another twinge of disgust. He was a person for whom order was his guiding star, who worshipped at the altar of organisation, indeed, and the chaos of piled books bread crusts and forgotten plates to be seen there filled him with gloom.

'Rather, it is a party from The City', he continued. 'Although one of them shares that illustrious name'.

Balian groaned.

'They'd better not be another delegation of monks and bishops and other religious busybodies. Tell them I am indisposed...'

'I believe the lady amongst them was called Cortesia Tyverios', continued Grae, his eye travelling to the gravy stain that disfigured the front of his master's shirt and lingered there with grim fascination.

'I see', Balian noted, his eyes widening.

He took off his glasses and placed them in the open book, absently smoothing down the leaves on either side.

'Well, that *is* a surprise. Cortesia, eh?! Hmm. Well, I suppose you had better show them in. Put them in the west drawing room, would you, Grae? And tell them I shall be down presently'.

Grae inclined his narrow head gracefully.

'May I suggest that you change your attire first?' he said with the vaguest twitch of that head in the direction of Balian's shirt front.

'What? Oh yes. Of course', muttered Balian, flicking ineffectually at it with his fingers. 'Do send in Medoes'.

Whilst Medoes fussed about him with various clean shirts and combed at his thin brown hair, Balian mused on the strange unpredictability of life that had brought a ghost of the past to his door. His existence was entirely bound up with the small, quiet world of his books and his research. Fulfilling though this was, his life was one of untroubled regularity. Consequently, he found that his interest was sparked by this unlooked-for event, this unforeseen reminder of The City and the past.

When he descended to the drawing room it was to find Cortesia standing with two young men, all dressed in mud-spattered travelling clothes. Grae, at Balian's, shoulder, looked aghast at the crumbled, dried mud which disfigured the Samarang rug.

'Cortesia, what a pleasure', Balian began, his voice oddly affected by the sight of her head swathed in black silk.

Nor did his own eyes rest easily on *her* one eye. The pleasure he spoke of was leavened with dismay. He had heard of her humiliation, her disfiguration, along with half of the world, but to be brought face to face with it was still very shocking.

'I have so few visitors in this far-flung corner of the realm. You do me great honour, as you always did. How fondly do I recall those blissful, blissful hours spent in your library, all those years ago'.

He raised a questioning eyebrow at her companions.

'And these gentlemen. To whom do I have the honour...?'

Jory and Rayo introduced themselves with a courtly bow, begging Balian's pardon for this unannounced trespass upon his hospitality. Balian, for his part, muttered a few words about having the honour to be acquainted with Rayo's uncle, was his neighbour, in fact, as he supposed they knew.

'How well informed are you of events in The City?' asked Cortesia when all were seated and drinks had been called for.

'Tolerably well, I suppose', answered Balian. 'We have the news courier in the village every week or so, and my servants convey what they hear to my ears. I am well aware that we have a new emperor, of course', he said, tilting his head to one side. 'May I ask what has drawn you here? It seems improbable that this is merely a social call. My understanding was that you had entirely withdrawn from society after... after...'

'After the destruction of my face, you mean', supplied Cortesia dispassionately. 'And your understanding was correct. But I have awoken from my long sleep now and have committed myself to addressing a grave injustice'.

'Injustice?' murmured Balian, feeling uneasy. 'The world is full of injustice. How may...?'

'I suppose you would consider the murder of Gelon's second son an injustice', interrupted Cortesia, leaning forward in her seat.

'Prince Taian?' asked Balian. 'I *had* heard that he had died, under unusual circumstances. But murder...? He had been ill, had he not?'

'He was being poisoned', supplied Jory, provoking an impatient glance from Cortesia.

'And he is *not* dead', added Rayo, causing Balian to sink back into his own chair, eyebrows raised.

'He is not?'

'He is very much alive', continued Rayo grimly. 'And he lies this instant in the wagon in your courtyard'.

'Oh, my word!' gasped Balian, pressing the back of his hand to his mouth. 'What trouble have you brought here?'

'We do not mean to importune you', asserted Cortesia improbably. 'We do not mean to draw you into any form of palace intrigue'.

'I see', said Balian peevishly, 'but you have nevertheless presumed to introduce a fugitive prince into my property, in defiance of all custom and, er... decency. I don't doubt that you are all fugitives from the law and that my hospitality may be viewed as complicity if...'

'Please, dear sir', interjected Cortesia, raising a gloved hand. 'Do not imagine for a moment that we wish to enmesh you in any conspiracy'.

'Conspiracy!' Balian declared, his face registering a very significant degree of alarm now and his eyebrows edging even further upwards. 'Conspiracy! I think you should leave, right now. I shall summon Grae to see you out'.

He rose from his seat with a speed surprising for one of his corpulence and made to ring the bell pull.

'Please!' implored Jory, who had anticipated this, placing his own hand on top of Balian's. 'Do hear us out'.

Between the three of them, Balian's unwelcome guests told the story of the prince's slow poisoning, of their desperate escape from the palace and of the palace's convincing attempt to erase Taian from the public consciousness.

'Triado Melanthros is a competent general but a thorough-going villain', observed Jory at the conclusion of this. 'As everyone knows. And now he is teamed with an equally unscrupulous and amoral empress. The ship of state sails in turbulent waters, would you not agree?'

'I would', conceded Balian, running an anxious hand through his hair. 'They both have an evil reputation, of course, and I imagine they will deal harshly with those who oppose them... oh dear. I am not a brave man, not at all, and here you are bringing doom and suspicion to my doorstep.

'Anyway, what would you have of me?' he finished querulously. 'And neither am I a rich man nor a military one, for that matter', he added for good measure.

There was a long silence, during which a flight of doves flew past the tall window, the susurrus of their progress and their soft shadow traversing the wall swiftly behind Balian.

'You are known to be a leading authority on drugs, on chemistry in general', observed Cortesia. 'Perhaps we could induce you to examine the prince'.

'Oh very well, bring him in', conceded Balian plaintively after a few moments in which his face betrayed the evidence of some internal struggle. 'Although, I warn you, if I am subject to any investigation, I shall certainly claim this was under duress. Duress, I say! I shall send my servants to assist you'.

Before long, Prince Taian exchanged a thin straw mattress laid on bare boards for a soft feather bed in Balian's house, not that he appeared aware of this improvement in his circumstances. His face remained pale, his limbs as flaccid as ever.

'Completely unresponsive, you see', said Rayo, letting down his friend's eyelid. 'Great wide staring pools of nothingness'.

'And yet his pulse seems strong enough, his breathing unlaboured', mused Balian, having investigated these. 'Did you say you had the spoon with which this physician administered his medicine?'

'I did', grunted Rayo, unwrapping the item in question. 'Although I fear it has lost the strong smell it once had'.

'Hmm', said Balian, sniffing at it cautiously when Rayo had described its original smell to him. 'Well, I can detect little of that now. Cherries could be an indicator of Eutorpomine, of course, which allegedly induces similar symptoms, but the drug has an evil reputation and is

associated with dark magic, I'm afraid. I have never come across any in this realm, and I only know of it through legend, in fact. Crytopios mentions it in his Euspathiad, and there are various other allusions in less distinguished works. I must consult my books. Perhaps I could borrow this?' he asked, brandishing the spoon.
'Of course', agreed Rayo with a brisk nod.
'I shall not be long, I should think', said Balian with a glint of interest in his eye, which seemed to have driven out anxiety. 'Do bring in those other fellows from the yard. I shall speak to Grae. He will certainly provide you with food and drink in the interim'.

'I think we have him', declared Cortesia triumphantly, when Balian had withdrawn. 'We have piqued his interest, and now he is like a bloodhound on a scent, do you see?'
'It is one thing to establish what drug was used to poison him, quite another to propose a remedy', observed Jory, causing Rayo to cast his eyes up in exasperation.
'And yet it is progress, friend', said the latter wryly. 'Real progress. How skilled you are in concealing your exultation'.

It was more than an hour before Balian returned. By this time, Ohk and Bardo had joined the others in the drawing room and tea had been provided, together with small cakes that Rayo attacked with enthusiasm. He looked up and wiped his hands on his breeches as Balian entered, an expression of contained triumph on his round face. He handed the spoon back to Rayo and beamed about him at the eager faces of his guests.
'Yes, as I thought. It is almost certainly Eutorpomine. I have subjected it to immersion in a number of agents to check the resultant surface changes and flame-tested it to observe the colour of the flame. Really, quite remarkable.

I almost felt in awe of handling it. Whoever administered this has some rather sinister connections, I would say. Did you mention Mordanios?

'Doctor Mordanios? Yes', answered Cortesia. 'He is the empress's private physician and so was engaged to attend to the prince'.

'And he has been in the East, no doubt. The drug almost certainly originated there'.

'Excellent!' cried Rayo. 'And doubtless you will be able to propose a remedy that will undo the damage this drug has wrought, a man of your wisdom and experience'.

'You flatter me', said Balian with a bow. 'But I fear you also overestimate my capabilities. So far as I am aware, the alterations wrought by this drug are not susceptible to reversal. I'm afraid to say that Prince Taian is permanently... er... indisposed. Hmm? Why are you all looking at me like that?'

The momentary optimism that had seized Taian's friends was suddenly dispelled, like the snuffing out of a candle, and all regarded Balian with varying degrees of dismay or disappointment.

'But you must...' began Jory.

'Please!' Balian raised a pudgy hand. 'I believe I have done what I can. I have entertained you here, at no small risk to my person and my reputation, and now I must ask that you carry the prince away. I can do no more'.

'Wait', said Cortesia, her eye settling on Balian and subjecting him to a fierce glare. 'I do not believe that you are as incapable as you claim'.

'I see, and on what grounds do you make that assertion?' demanded Balian, bristling now. 'I suppose you are going to bore me with that ridiculous luminary nonsense. My reason for moving to this region was to evade the superstitious importunings of the ignorant, and here we are again, another party of the credulous ready to invest me with godlike powers'.

He nodded, placed his hands on his hips and returned Cortesia's glare with one that was equally ferocious.

'You were identified by the revered Perico Aspenthios', persisted Cortesia. 'He named you as his successor. That much is certain'.

'I never met the man', complained Balian, striding about distractedly now. 'Nor did I invite this *distinction*. I have absolutely no wish to be revered or prayed to, and I have absolutely no power or desire to overturn the iron rules of nature in order to oblige the church. I am demonstrably not a *holy* man. I speak plainly now in saying that my attendance at church is entirely governed by necessity and that I don't believe a word of what I hear there. I believe what I can see and prove with my own eye, hand and brain. I believe in the power of the human mind to unlock the secrets of the universe and to incrementally subject to reason what was once attributed to the divine'.

'You are an atheist, then?' suggested Bardo.

'Not at all', retorted Balian. 'Because if I were to declare as much I would soon incur the wrath of church and state, would I not?'

'I do not believe you', laughed Cortesia. 'And you evidently don't believe in God, which is ironic enough for one of his chosen earthly vessels. However, it doesn't necessarily follow that because you don't believe in God, God doesn't believe in you. Because, as yet, you have not glimpsed the divine does not mean that such a revelation may not await you'.

'Well, if it does in the next few minutes', sniffed Balian, 'I shall certainly let you know. Now, there is a perfectly good tavern in the village, and I suggest that you seek accommodation there'.

'Please, sir', begged Jory. 'It is growing late now. May we not stay just this one night and leave on the morrow? You may argue that we held you at knifepoint, if you wish'.

There was a tense silence during which all fixed Balian with an earnest gaze and Balian shook his head, folding his arms across his ample bosom.
'Oh, very well', conceded Balian at last, frowning deeply. 'But I have assisted you as best I can, and tomorrow you must be away'.

Balian's sleep was troubled. He argued to himself that the presence of such fugitives beneath his roof would be sufficient to disturb the peace of mind of many an honest citizen, but there was something else besides. He felt oddly light-headed, oddly restless, and at length he pulled on his slippers, turned up an oil lamp and made his way along the corridor to the chamber where the prince lay sleeping. It was impossible to tell what the hour was, although a glimpse through his window had shown Mother Moon riding high in the cirrus-barred heavens. There was no compelling reason for stealth in his own house, but nevertheless he trod lightly, anxious not to disturb his guests in the adjacent rooms. Balian found the prince much as he had left him, the lamp's warm glow disclosing those wan, impassive features, a sheet pulled up beneath the chin. For long moments, he stood regarding that figure, wondering what impulse had drawn him there. There was a vague prickle across his brow and a strange flutter in his breast, which caused him to take a sharp intake of breath. He had the oddest sensation that there was someone else in the room, other than the prince, but swinging his lamp around revealed only emptiness. He transferred the lamp to his left hand, and with no clear motive in mind stepped forward to place his right hand on the prince's brow. It felt cool and then suddenly hot beneath his fingers. Alarmed, he drew back, muttering under his breath, flexing tingling fingers.
'What are you doing?' asked a voice from behind him.

He swung round to find Cortesia standing at his shoulder. She placed her gloved hand on his upper arm, causing another unexpected prickling sensation. With an almost inaudible gasp, Cortesia twitched that hand away.

'It is a pitiful sight, is it not?' she asked after a moment of apparent distraction, turning her attention to the prince.

'It is', agreed Balian, grateful for this intervention. 'It is indeed. I was just checking to see that he... er...' he trailed off, a vague nod of his head perhaps intending to supply the conclusion to this train of thought.

'I thought I heard someone in here', murmured Cortesia when Balian turned his wondering frown upon her. 'No matter. We should sleep now'.

'We should', agreed Balian, stepping past her into the corridor.

Balian slept extraordinary well thereafter, a deep, restorative and dreamless sleep that was only brought to a close by the sound of excited voices from the corridor outside his chamber. When he emerged, having drawn a fur-trimmed gown hastily around him, it was to find his visitors in urgent conference in the prince's room.

'He moved! I swear I saw him move', said Rayo, his eyes wide. 'I just walked in to wish him good day, and his hand moved on the coverlet.

'He's not moving now, sir', muttered Bardo, stroking his beard.

'No indeed, but he was just a moment ago. Watch him. All of you. Watch him now'.

In truth, there was no need for this injunction, since all of Taian's friends were subjecting him to a penetrating stare. Balian came up behind them, feeling oddly excited.

'There! His eyeballs moved', gasped Jory. 'Observe.'

He leant over the prince and drew back an eyelid. The pupil instantly contracted upon exposure to the morning light.

'Did you see that?' he cried, staring about him at the intense, amazed faces of his companions. 'That reaction did not previously occur, did it? Hmm? I ask you...'

'It did not', agreed Cortesia. 'Something has changed'.

She turned her eye upon Balian, who found himself blushing.

'I came in during the night to find you standing next to him, sir', she said accusatively. 'Which rather begs the question, what have you done to him?'

'Why nothing! Nothing at all', protested Balian, throwing his arms wide. 'I only placed this hand of mine upon his brow – and then only for a moment. That was all. I am not a physician. I administered no...'

'And yet his condition is improved', interjected Cortesia.

Suddenly, Balian found that he was the sole object of his visitors' attention, all eyes directed towards him.

'It could easily be a coincidence', stammered Balian, conscious that the sturdy edifice of his simple orderly life was suddenly imperilled.

'And will you turn us away now?' asked Jory.

Balian swallowed hard.

'I will not', he said. 'I am obliged, under threats of violence, to allow you to remain here a little longer'.

Chapter Thirteen

Callisto

Adala had not set foot in Callisto since she was a small child, so it was interesting to see how her first impressions of the greatest city in the world matched with her recollections. It was almost inconceivably vast, of course, the white walls of its outer circuit encompassing a space that accommodated more than a quarter of a million busy citizens. It was for this reason, and because of its huge and noble secular and sacred buildings, that all Erenori referred to it simply as The City.

There was nowhere in the world to compare with it. The low buildings and market gardens of the surrounding suburbs served only to accentuate the towering scale of the great limewashed walls that loomed over them.

'Never been taken', grunted Drael as the trap clattered over the bridge of Argentios that spanned the mighty Canto and led to the east gate. 'Never in a thousand years'.

'So I am told', answered Adala. 'Although I understand that base treachery has admitted enemies on a number of occasions'.

'Very true', nodded Drael with one of his rare and momentary smiles. 'More than cannonballs and scaling ladders, gold is the true vanquisher of walls'.

It was mid-afternoon on the eighth day of Adala's journey from her home village, and the road was thronged with traffic of all kinds as they approached the famous Sun Gate. The doors themselves, fifty feet tall, were sheathed in polished bronze, moulded and inlaid with gold to represent scenes from Erenori history. A great gilded lion, as large as an elephant, stood proudly above the lintel, nestled amongst intricate inscriptions and ornaments. At dawn, and before noon, the rising sun blazed brilliantly from skilfully wrought gold and bronze, dazzling visitors approaching from that direction and visible from the heights of Malavant, more than twenty miles distant.

They passed through the portal dedicated to incoming traffic and made their way up the winding road that hugged the shoulder of Mount Silpion, the riverside eminence that their ancestors had first identified as a defensible site for their settlement nearly four thousand years previously. In the broad space between the outer and the middle wall there were inns and places of entertainment to suit all tastes and budgets. Drael secured rooms and stabling for them in a tavern where the great broad road, known as the Torospina, made its junction with the street of the lamp-makers.

'I have secured you a corner room on the second floor', said Drael, 'and explained that you are my niece, an invention that I hope you will excuse. You will have a good view over the rooftops of the lower ward to the river, I should think. I must go to call at my mother's house now, but I should be back before nightfall. I pray that you will be patient and remain here until then. The staff will certainly bring you dinner presently'.
'I should anyway feel ashamed to set foot in the street wearing these rags', said Adala with a gesture that encompassed her roughly repaired dress, torn in several places during the assault on her. 'Even the humblest folk here are arrayed as princesses with ribbons and laces at cuffs and hems. And so many wear their hair uncovered, too! My father would purse his lips and raise his

eyebrows and wonder at their virtue, no doubt. I shall hope to buy a little cloth and run up something more fitting, if I can learn where to acquire the necessary items'.

'All shall be possible with the new day, no doubt', Drael assured her. 'And doubtless you will wish to assure yourself that the object of your affections lives and breathes. However, I would urge you to be patient until then'.

Privately, Drael had no doubt that the reports he had received from the city of the prince's death were correct, although he said nothing to challenge Adala's settled view to the contrary. The investigators were most unlikely to be mistaken about such a momentous occurrence, and official news of it had reached Garabdor along the semaphore signal towers within a day of it happening. Still, Adala would need to assure herself of the true circumstances and learn to adapt herself to them in due course. The inhabitants of The City, once questioned, would surely acquaint her with the truth, relate details of the immediate aftermath, of the imperial pomp of the funeral, even. His greatest concern was that Adala might abscond in his absence, but she showed no sign of concealing such intention as he bade her farewell. When he arrived at his mother's house in the middle ward, it was to find that he was too late, that his mother had died within a few days of his departure from Garabdor. He found the house garlanded with black and with black drapes drawn across the windows. It was strange to revisit the house he had grown up in, after so many years, strange to find the little fountain in the inner courtyard just as he remembered. The house steward met him in the lobby and extended his condolences in sombre tones. His younger brother Sanda was only recently departed and had made all necessary arrangements, leaving a note to say that he would return the next day at noon. Drael, removing his hat, made his way through to his mother's chamber, where she was laid out in her casket. For a while he sat at her side and gazed upon her grey, waxen features. Convention demanded sad reflection and tears, but in truth she had been a harsh and unyielding woman, one from whom her children expected imprecations and the swung rod more than soft words and caresses. After a time consistent with his filial duty, but no more, Drael withdrew, making his way back through streets where the lamps were already being lit and shopkeepers were drawing down their shutters.

The next morning, an excursion into the surrounding streets furnished Adala with the necessary tools and material to fashion a new frock for herself and writing materials to assure Marta of her safe arrival. There was also opportunity to question various people and for Adala to be assured that the prince was indeed dead and had been conveyed likewise to his tomb in plain view of thousands. Drael had expected that she would be downcast, tearful even, as her fond hopes were dashed, but it seemed that her sure knowledge of the prince's continued existence was impervious to mere established fact. She listened attentively, made appropriate noises of regret, but she did not contradict those she heard from, nor did she show any evident sign of dismay.

'I shall take you to St. Mardonios when you have arrayed yourself to your own satisfaction', he said after luncheon the next day, when she had printed patterns, fabrics and threads strewn about her room.
'I'm sure that is very kind of you', she replied, a needle clamped between her lips whilst she drew an expanse of smooth fabric into place. 'And I shall enjoy stepping into such an exalted place, but if you seek to convince me that

Taian is dead, you will be disappointed. Unless you prise open his tomb and show me his dead face, which I doubt you may accomplish'.

'Your doubt is well-founded', laughed Drael, rubbing the back of his head ruefully. 'You will look well in that', he continued, referring to the work in progress. 'The colour will suit your complexion'.

'Do you think?' she asked with real pleasure, holding a length of the beautiful teal-coloured fabric to her face. 'I never saw anything so lovely in Garabdor'.

Drael found that he was regarding her fondly, her evident delight kindling an unfamiliar warmth around his heart. His mouth twitched upwards at the corners in response.

'He smiles, I do declare!' she said, her eyes sparkling mischievously. 'I wonder that your jaw does not suffer injury!'

In truth, her beauty would have been perfectly plain to see in any colour, but Drael had paid for this fabric himself upon seeing her empty her slender purse and her brow furrow at the dowdy selection its contents might secure her. She protested vehemently at first but was reluctantly persuaded to accept this loan when he assured her that he expected prompt remuneration with interest, when she was safely established as a princess. It was money well spent, he declared at the time, and nothing had since occurred to change his mind.

Adala watched him withdraw, blushing and awkward, to his own room and picked up her needle once more. She thanked the fates, thanked Tio, that their paths had crossed in that fortunate manner. Had they not, she doubted she would yet be alive, of course, but he had proven to be a most useful companion since that fateful night. Who else but an imperial investigator could have plucked her from the hand of justice in Ilkenfold in such a manner? It seemed strange that the stony-faced and brusque individual who had interrogated her at The

Grapes should now have become her saviour and her companion. She wondered why he had taken such risks on her behalf. Surely, he had imperilled his own career through his failure to deliver her to the Chief Constable in Annagaar. Her eye caught her own reflection in a mirror above the fireplace, showed her that the livid bruise on the left side of her face was almost gone now. Was he besotted with her in some way, despite the difference in their years? He must be approaching forty, she judged, and she was barely seventeen.

Do not even consider such a thing, she told herself, plying the needle once more. *Investigator Drael is a most honourable man, if I am any judge. Besides, he knows that I am devoted to my prince, wherever he may be. And I shall find him. Of course I shall. And then we shall be together.*

So she argued to herself. Thoughts of this nature, and they came often, caused her to reflect grimly on how close she had come to losing her maidenhead to that brute on the road to Annagaar. Although she doubted her prince would condemn her for it, as some might, the world generally conspiring to blame women for their own misfortunes as it did. She felt quite sure of him, quite sure of his mind, a circumstance that she often wondered at, given the brief nature of their acquaintance.

Drael decided that he wished to investigate the circumstances of the prince's death, since he found his young protégé's inflexible certainty of his survival a challenge to his own intellect. The death of an emperor and both of his sons in so short a space of time was indeed an extraordinary event, on which historians of the future would surely remark. If reports were to be believed, Gelon and Cato's demises had come about through simple accident and enemy action, respectively, but the destruction of the dynasty was made complete by the subsequent death of Prince Taian. With *his* demise, the

Starcorid bloodline ran thinly in elderly or infirm distant relatives, and Triado Melanthros' claim was as good as any. The fact that it was backed by the soldiers of the empire's seven professional legions made it irresistible. But to what extent had Prince Taian's death come about through misadventure? It was said that he was mortally ill and that conspirators, seeking to establish a rival claim to Triado's, had sought to spirit him away, in order to employ him as a figurehead for their own ambitions. Unfortunately, the prince had died during the rescue attempt, bringing about the ruination of their own plans as well as conveniently clearing the way for Triado. Having taken a day to attend his mother's funeral and to deal with family affairs, Drael set out to find out more about the death of Prince Taian. He pondered what he knew about this story as he sat in the officers' club across the road from the Directorate of the Investigators, awaiting the arrival of Peric Gandelion, a former friend from his army days and now a senior officer in the Directorate. Drael was an abstemious man, sober in every aspect of his life, and sipped his beer thoughtfully whilst he subjected the known facts to the rigours of logical deduction. It seemed altogether too convenient for the new emperor that fate had swept away the Starcorids with such brusque efficiency, and it was impossible not to suspect that foul play might be at work. Triado's conscience was known to be a hardy organ, and the empress's reputation for duplicity was long established. Nor did he consider that he would be the only one to suspect foul play.

Gandelion, who might be expected to have come to a similar conclusion, came in from the rain shower that was presently lashing the streets outside, brushing ineffectually at his hat and staring around him owlishly.

'Here!' cried Drael, raising a hand.

Peric beamed, crossing the intervening space with hand outstretched. They shook, exchanged cheerful greetings and were soon enjoying steaming mulled wine whilst a servant took Peric's coat. It had been several years since last they had met. Peric had been a ruthlessly efficient cavalry officer, whose propensity for growing fat had been held at bay by the rigours of military life. Now, stationed at a desk all day and wielding nothing more deadly than a paper knife, he had amply indulged that propensity.

After conventional enquiries after the health of family and mutual friends had been dealt with, conversation moved to the business of the bureau.

'I'm afraid my station out in Garabdor left me scandalously ill-informed as to events in The City', declared Drael, having judged for himself that Peric knew nothing of his recent dereliction of duty at Annagaar. 'I suppose the identity of Prince Taian's abductors is generally known?'

'Very generally', agreed Peric, setting down his mug and wiping his mouth with the back of his hand.

'It was two of his best friends, one Rayo Kerkuoas and one Jory Marinaris. We are told that the prince perished during the course of their abduction'.

'So I understand', nodded Drael. 'And I understand also that these young lions intended to advance Prince Taian's claim to the throne'.

'I have it on good authority', said Peric cautiously. 'No lesser authority than the Director himself'.

The look in Peric's eyes, the years of service between them and the trust established there enabled Drael to draw his own conclusions. The Director was no servant of the truth. He served only his own interests – and these with a close attention that had won him vast wealth and influence. He would certainly cheerfully promulgate whatever falsehoods the emperor required of him.

'So, I suppose these two young noblemen were the tip of a spear consisting of a considerable faction, in the senate and the military, opposing the new regime', suggested Drael.

Peric looked around surreptitiously, took off his eye-glasses and polished them carefully before replying.

'I shall speak plainly, since we are old comrades, and I trust no disclosures I may make today will go any further'.

Drael nodded, and after a pause, Peric continued, leaning closer to his friend.

'I can assure you that no such conspiracy has come to light, no such commonality of purpose, and you may be certain that there have been thorough investigations. Besides, Prince Taian had previously shown no interest in politics, no interests other than the hedonistic pursuit of pleasure. He could have mustered no support, even had his friends desired it'.

'Then why would his friends seek to spirit him away?'

'Need you ask?'

'Because they feared that the new regime would find his existence *inconvenient*?' suggested Drael. 'Would that be it?'

Peric inclined his head.

'And where are they now?' asked Drael.

'Nobody knows, so far as I am aware, although of course their dwellings and their families have been placed under surveillance'.

'But the prince is certainly dead,' pressed Drael, more than ever conscious that Adala's interests prompted his own enquires.

'Certainly he is. I have seen him with my own eyes', agreed Peric. 'Lying in a casket with a shroud pulled back to reveal his face'.

'And how close were you?'

'Within a few paces. Naturally, I was not admitted as close as his step-mother or senior members of the court.

None of them seemed in any doubt as to the identity of the deceased, however. May I ask what prompts your enquiry?'

Peric had his head tilted to one side now and was regarding him shrewdly.

'I like to be sure of things', answered Drael, gesturing with his mug. 'I am a slave to certainty. Mere trivialities trouble me, leave me agog with anxiety. May I enquire as to the address of the prince's nurse, for example? I understand she was amongst the last to see him alive'.

'You really are a devoted seeker after knowledge, aren't you, Trimestrion?' observed Peric with a grin.

'And a servant of the truth', said Drael, breaking one of his own. 'And a very old friend, to boot, a friend who saved your sorry hide on more than one occasion, as I recall'.

'Indeed. Meet me here at the same time tomorrow and I shall see what I can do',

grunted Peric, reaching into his pocket for a few coins for the pot boy.

The next day dawned bright, and Adala went to call upon her aunt and mother. She continued to wear her roughly mended dress, but consciousness of her good progress with the new one gave her a new spring in her step, and she wore ribbons in her hair. It was highly unlikely her mother would even recognise her, but her Aunt Anditi certainly would, and she could assure her of her good health in case any enquiry should reach her from The Grapes.

It proved to be a strange and formal conversation. Adala did not wish to lie, but neither could she truthfully explain the reasons for her journey. The fact that she was accompanied and protected by a stranger, and an older man, only added to her discomfiture. Fortunately, Anditi was an oddly incurious creature, long estranged from the residents of The Grapes, and so she accepted Adala's exceedingly thin story with little sign of interest or curiosity. Nevertheless, it was with relief that she made her way back to their residence, throwing herself down on her bed and letting out her breath with a great sigh. Drael proved to be out, and he had left a message with the bar staff to say that he did not expect to return before nightfall of the following day and that she should see to her own meals. Accordingly, after another stroll around the closest market, which was still wonderfully exotic and entertaining to her, she returned to her room and turned her hand once more to the engaging task of cutting and sewing.

As their third full day in The City drew to a close, Drael returned to the lodgings he shared with Adala to find her already at the top of stairs, waiting for him, arrayed in her new dress and wreathed in smiles besides.
'Do I not look fine?' she asked, twirling round so that her hair rose from her shoulders around her.
'I cannot deny it', said Drael with a nod and another warm surge of affection in his breast. 'You ply a needle with rare skill, and those ribbons at the bodice, they are a masterly touch, I declare'.
'I cannot claim it was all my own work, as the mistress of the house and her daughter kindly assisted me', she said cheerfully, drawing up the hem to show the ribbon sewn into it there, too.
Looking upon the simple, unaffected pleasure in her face, Drael was faced with a strange dichotomy in his feelings for her. His body wore all the evidence of the passage of thirty-seven years, and yet the person that looked out through his eyes remained the same twenty-year old who had taken a bride to the altar all those years previously. The same animal urges motivated him, a shameful but

irrepressible desire to possess her smooth soft flesh, to arouse her to a height of passion that matched his own, in joyous union. These feelings had inflamed and engorged his own flesh and held sleep long at bay, and when that blessed sleep did come at last, it was accompanied by haunted, humid dreams. Hand-in-hand with this primordial beast walked his rational being, a creature that stood appalled by slavish submission to the urgings of the flesh. This being wagged a stern finger and argued that only princes and plutocrats might set aside such disparity in years when taking the objects of their desire to the marriage bed, that lesser mortals faced censure or even ridicule for so doing. This side of Drael argued that the sensations he felt growing within him might mutate to become the simple wholesome affection of father for daughter, that all might applaud and admire. And yet to allow his thoughts to stray in that direction invited unbearable pain.

'Are you not married, then?' she had asked on the road between Annagaar and The City, when that road had led them past field after field of ripening wheat. 'I suppose you are of marriageable age', she had added with a wry chuckle and a sidelong glance.

'I *was* married', he had answered, his eyes remaining fixed on the road ahead and his lips set in a firm line.

Something in his voice, and in the set of his features, had caused her to bite her own lip and to return her gaze slowly to her hands, where she had been plaiting strands of grass. Nor had she asked again, and for this he was grateful.

And yet, now, looking at her slight figure as she babbled about the challenges to be found with button holes, his thoughts moved inexorably in that direction and a shadow fell across his face.

He had been posted to command a troop in a mounted constabulary unit on the far south-western border with

Zanyawe, in the Duchy of Acra. His wife, Marli, and his daughter, Ari, had accompanied him, taking up residence in the settlement outside the fort. For a year they had been happy there, enjoying the rugged, hilly landscape, so different from the flowery gardens of Vannistar, where Drael's legion was stationed. Ari was just four years old and Marli twenty-six when the unit had ridden out to intercept a strong party of cattle raiders that had crossed the border and was hurrying to return to their own country before they were caught. Unfortunately, this proved to be a feint, a diversion to draw the imperial troops away from the fort that was the objective of a much stronger raiding force. Drael's troopers returned in triumph, having killed a score or so of the thieves, driving the liberated cattle before them, only to find the fort smoke-blackened and the settlement at its gate razed to the ground. The raid had been at dawn and taken everyone by surprise. The sentries on the walls had sounded the alarm in time for the administrative staff, the cooks and servants, the smith and the sick in the infirmary to rush to the walls and fend off the scaling ladders of the enemy. It was too late for the hapless villagers in the settlement, however, and the frustrated tribesmen had exacted a fierce vengeance on them when thwarted by those high walls. Drael had found his wife and daughter, what remained of them, in the street. Evidently, they had been found cowering in their house and had been put to death in the most brutal, sadistic manner; mother and daughter raped, mutilated and finally eviscerated in a way that he could not unsee, in a way that rose up through the layers of self-control he had imposed upon memory, in a way that caused him to cry out in his sleep or gnaw savagely at his fists. Ten years had buried the past, and days on days had laid down the slow silt of peace upon his spirit, but there were chambers of his mind where he still dared not to tread.

'Truly you are become a princess', he continued now as she led him into her room, where scissors, threads and scraps of fabric were strewn across every horizontal surface.

He realised immediately that his momentary distraction had prompted indiscretion, as Adala's delight faded from her face. There was nothing he could say to undo this, and the strangely abstracted look that came into her eyes brought no immediate response from her.

'Well', he said, rubbing his hands together, 'perhaps we shall dine downstairs tonight. I have much to tell you', Drael added, peering over his shoulder before closing the door quietly behind him. 'And it has been a most stimulating day'.

Peric had proved as good as his word and provided other valuable information as well. Accordingly, having been provided with her address, Drael had visited Prince Taian's nurse, finding her at home and happy to answer his questions, once it appeared that Drael was working in a private rather than an official capacity. From here, a walk of twenty minutes or so had taken him to the north side of the middle ward, where Taian's tailor had his residence in the smart street named Tindersgate. Finally, his enquiries led him to the opposite side of the city, to a street beneath the great grey shoulder of St Trichinos. Here, in a fine stone-built house that reflected his status as official undertaker to the palace, Dunister Marcusio plied his trade with offices, courtyards and workshops behind. Here, Drael was obliged to draw out his official investigator's amulet of the lion surmounting an eye and employ as much bluster and guile as was necessary in order to be admitted into Dunister's presence.

'I do apologise for troubling you, Master Marcusio', said Drael as he was shown into the man's office. 'And I quite understand that you have already received visitations from the bureau. However, you must understand that our enquiries are ongoing and that new information – information that I regrettably may not share with you – has led to the need for further investigation'.

'I see', said the man who had committed two generations of the illustrious imperial family to the silence of the tomb and to the anonymity of dust in time to come. He was a small, round man with a round head and an expression of wary intelligence in his eyes. *I know the secrets of the dead*, they seemed to say. *And I know that even the greatest are no more than mute, cold meat when they come to my slab, whatever their pretensions in life.*

'I shall not detain you long', said Drael. 'I have a few simple questions relating to the late-lamented Prince Taian and the condition of his body upon his committal to you'.

'I am not a medical man, nor an anatomist', retorted Dunister, taking up his glasses and reaching for a file. 'I leave that to those more qualified, but I shall assist you as I can'.

'Thank you, sir, you oblige me. May I begin by asking you the length of the prince's body? I trust measurements are generally taken in order to make the casket'.

'Five feet and ten inches', said Dunister, having consulted a file.

'You are sure of this?'

'I applied the tape to him myself, Officer Trimestrion, and I am no novice in this business', answered Dunister with a wry smile.

'Indeed', nodded Drael pensively, his gaze momentarily distant. 'And were there any distinguishing marks upon the corpse, birthmarks, large moles or blemishes of any kind?'

'There were not, sir'.

'And finally, the condition of the body struck you as consistent with one who had died of a fever – malaria, shall we say?'

'There was a degree of emaciation, yes, and you may be sure that we took precautions against infection when preparing the body'.

'Of course, of course', murmured Drael, having asked a few other questions of lesser consequence and made small talk about the fine ceramics with which various shelves were adorned. 'Well, that is all, for now. I must detain you no further. I thank you for your cooperation'.

'No trouble at all', smiled Dunister, getting to his feet. 'Glad to be of assistance, I'm sure'.

Drael was out of the office and well along the corridor beyond when Dunister called out to him.

'Oh, and there was one other thing that puzzled me, officer, which perhaps I should mention'.

'Hmm?' Drael turned on his heel, eyebrows raised.

'The hands were rather calloused, as though their owner was accustomed to hard manual labour of some kind. It struck me as odd. That is all'.

'I have made some enquiries relating to the prince', Drael told Adala now. 'And I think you will be interested to hear what I have discovered'.

'Do go on', said Adala, eyes wide, placing her hand on his.

'How tall would you say the prince is?'

'Perhaps six feet', she tried, her heart leaping within her at Drael's employment of the present tense.

'You are correct', nodded Drael. 'And the prince's tailor confirmed your judgement. He should know, after all. And yet the undertaker measured the same prince at a mere five feet and ten inches. Do you suppose his death occasioned such a singular shrinkage?'

'No, I do not', said Adala, her grip on Drael's hand tightening, her eyes remaining fixed on his with unbreakable intensity.

'And in addition, his nurse, she who had raised him since a child and knows every inch of his body, reported that he had a birthmark, shaped like a claw, upon the inner thigh of his left leg. The undertaker reported finding no such distinguishing mark, no marks at all, in fact'.

'Extraordinary!' gasped Adala, finding it hard to keep her feet still now.

'And finally, the undertaker reported that the corpse's hands were calloused as though by a life of manual labour. I trust the prince was not accustomed to such a life'.

'Most definitely not!' confirmed Adala, shaking her head vehemently.

'And from this evidence', continued Drael, 'I conclude that whoever lies in that great marble tomb up yonder, they are not the prince. There', he said, his eyes gleaming now and his mouth approaching the shape of a smile, 'have I told you what you wish to hear?'

'Oh, you have! You have!' cried Adala, throwing herself into his arms. 'Thank you so much for your endeavours!'

'It was my pleasure', said Drael, stroking her hair abstractedly, realising that Adala's reaction was the only reward he sought, or needed, for his labours on her behalf.

'There are many questions that remain unanswered, however', he said as Adala released her grip on him and they drew apart. 'We might legitimately wonder how the corpse in that tomb came to possess a face so similar to the prince's, so much so that a large proportion of the court was wholly taken in by the substitution. How likely is it that an identical twin came conveniently to hand at the moment of the prince's supposed death? I place great reliance on logic in my work, but I have pondered this

strange substitution for much of the afternoon and I find that logic is at a loss to explain it'.
Adala folded her arms.
'I can explain it', she said firmly. 'It must be sorcery'.
'When all other explanations are found wanting, what remains must be the truth', conceded Drael. 'But dark magic is wholly antipathetic to logic, and it pains me extremely to recognise it'.
'Well, you must', urged Adala. 'And if I may beg you to turn your investigative powers in another direction...'
'I know', nodded Drael. 'Where is the true prince?'

Chapter Fourteen

Callisto

'My lady, I have brought you breakfast: yoghurt and some berries', said Tyverios Ohk, having entered Cortesia's chamber in his usual self-effacing manner.
'And about time. I thought you would never come', snapped Cortesia. 'What hour is it? I suppose it must be...'
The hour remained unspoken and Cortesia's single visible eyebrow darted upward as she swung to face Ohk. For a moment, she stared at his dark, impassive features.
'Ohk', she said at last, in a smaller voice altogether. 'You spoke to me. I heard your voice'.
Ohk stared back at her.
'You could not have done', he said. 'I am...'
'Stop!' Cortesia cried, holding up a hand, shaking her head and placing her hands to her head-covering. She had heard the voice *inside* her head.
'Ohk, you are speaking to me inside my head. I can hear you. Not with my ears. In here!' Cortesia explained, tapping her forehead for emphasis. 'Go on, say something else'.
Ohk's face registered only confusion and his lips moved silently.
'Not with your mouth, you fool', she snapped, approaching him now. 'We both know that doesn't work. Think it!'
'But how?' he asked inside her head once more, his voice the bass rumble she had always anticipated it would be, disclosing the accent of those islands in the far north-west beyond the Cyrrhenic Sea that were said to be his origin.
'That's it! You're doing it again!' she said, clapping her hands. 'How are you doing that?'

'I don't know, my lady', came Ohk's voice, his eyes clouded with anxiety now. 'Does this mean...?'
'Does this mean I can read your thoughts and see when you're damning me to Hell? Is that what you mean?'
Ohk cast his head down and shuffled awkwardly.
'Well, you're not saying anything now, if that's any comfort', replied Cortesia, placing a finger beneath his chin and lifting it. 'So perhaps your private thoughts remain just that'.
'Yes, Ma'am', agreed Ohk, brightening. 'Perhaps it is only when I think of addressing you'.
'I hope so, too', laughed Cortesia, her giggle causing Ohk's heart to flutter, since it was to be heard so infrequently. 'I hate to think what manner of disgust must come my way if I could hear all of your private thoughts. But this is remarkable. We must tell the others. First, the improvement in the prince's condition and now this. What is happening?'
'Perhaps it is Master Drumarion, Ma'am', said Ohk, his voice sending a strange shiver along Cortesia's spine. 'We came here in search of miracles, did we not? I believe he has begun to work one with the prince, although he will not admit it. These are your own thoughts, are they not? Perhaps he has worked one also on you and on me?'
'I touched his arm', mused Cortesia, 'when I found him in the prince's chamber, and I felt a strange sensation. Perhaps that was the genesis of it'.

It soon became apparent that Ohk's voice could only be heard inside Cortesia's head and that this strange mental communication was confined to them alone. It was also apparent that the prince's condition continued to improve as the days went by. On the fourth day after the improvement had begun, he gained consciousness.
'Where am I?' he enquired in the faintest of voices, once his friends had been summoned.

'You are safe, in the house of Balian Drumarion', Jory told him, squeezing the prince's hand.

'We carried you away', informed Rayo. 'The empress and her doctor were practising to reduce you to a state of permanent insensibility, which would probably have resulted in your death in due course'.

Jory shot him a critical glance, occasioned by the blank look in the prince's eyes upon hearing this assessment.

'We might be able to get some solid food into him now', murmured Bardo.

'Very true', agreed Cortesia. 'And very urgent. You are very wasted by your illness, Prince Taian', she added. 'It is important that you eat. Do go and get Master Drumarion, Ohk. He will wish to see this'.

Balian was delighted to see the prince awake, and he had called in on him on many occasions since that first day, but at the same time he was somewhat disturbed by events. His guests appeared to regard him with superstitious awe, and they were inflexibly committed to the view that it was he, Balian, who had channelled Tio's power into curing the prince. The same reverence was now extended to him by his own servants. Even Grae, whose settled disapproval of his ways he had been vaguely aware of, had taken to murmuring prayers upon entering his presence.

It is all coincidence, Balian told himself. *The prince has recovered. I have laid my hand upon his brow, as have many others, and the two events are not necessarily connected.*

Nevertheless, the awkward fact that the last High Luminary had officially designated Balian as his successor was hard to ignore. Balian had done his best to set the divine at a distance but faced the inconvenient prospect that, regardless of this, Tio was all too ready to engage him in His work. Balian, who was unaccustomed to prayer, moved his lips wordlessly when custom required his presence in church and occupied his mind

with more important matters. It was extremely troubling to consider that he might now be required to function as a channel for Tio's power – and rather ironic that Tio had chosen an atheist as his earthly vessel. What did it mean? Balian had no sense of consciously wielding that power. Certainly, he had wished the prince well, but in what way could he have caused him to enter the path to recovery?
And then there was Cortesia. She had approached Balian to say that she was now able to hear her servant's voice in her head, this fellow having been mute for many years since the removal of his tongue. She attributed this, likewise, to a miraculous intervention on his part. More than that, in a deeply shocking disclosure, she had invited him to her chamber and unveiled herself, to reveal the truly pitiful nature of the injuries to her face and scalp. One of her eyes was no more than a red-raw depression, her nose a ruin, her mouth an irregular, distorted hole and her right ear almost destroyed. He had felt the bile rise in his throat even to gaze upon her. How well he recalled the beautiful young woman she had been, and tears rimmed his eyes as she stood before him.
'There are places and there are people where the wall between the worlds is thin', she said. 'Whether you like it or not, you are one such person and Tio acts through you. I can see this, if you cannot. Accordingly, I address Tio through your ears and ask him to look upon me and take pity. I have entreated his ears a thousand, thousand times in my own home, wetting my pillow or raising up my prayers before his altar, much good it has done me. But now, perhaps, he will have mercy upon me and restore my face to me. I do not require that it should be as fair as it once was. I do not require that it should win me the admiration of men and the envy of women. I only ask that I should be able to look upon the world without swathing this horror, for fear of inspiring shock, pity or revulsion'.

She approached Balian, who found that he was trembling, and lifted his hand in hers.
'Please', she said, her one eye filled with tears. 'Please'.
What was almost as shocking as the appearance of her face was the tone of her voice. He had come to know this as imperious and harsh, but now it was as though he heard a small child. He allowed his hand to be lifted and placed to that dreadful red flesh, held it there for a long moment whilst she closed her eye and sighed deep. 'Dear Tio, have mercy on me', she said in that small voice.

But Tio withheld his mercy, at least so far as his servant Cortesia was concerned, and although she devoted hours to fervent prayer, there was nothing to suggest that he had heard her voice. Ohk and Bardo became concerned for her.
'She has not eaten these last two days', said Bardo as Ohk emerged from her chamber with a tray that remained untouched, 'has she?'
Ohk shook his head regretfully, lamenting also that Balian's speech miracle had applied only to his conversation with his mistress.
'You must speak to her', Balian continued. 'Now that you *can* speak to her. She cannot continue in this way. She is not physically strong, I think, and this, this unhealthy focus on...' *miraculous intervention*, he wanted to say, but the words lodged in his throat.
The truth was that she had grown to accept the destruction of her beauty, and although bitterness and resentfulness were the walls she threw up around herself, those barricades had enabled her to continue from day to day. Now all that was threatened, not by a fresh plunge into despair but by the existence of hope, a hope that obliged her to confront once more the horror of her injuries and imagine a world in which they were healed.

'The prince's condition continues to improve', Ohk told Cortesia, when he took the same tray in to her a few hours later. 'He begins to take solid food and his strength grows from day to day. You must eat, too', he added when she continued to stare out of the window, her back to him.

'And who are you to command your mistress, Tyverios Ohk?' she demanded, turning upon him now. 'Is your station so greatly improved now that you may make your voice heard?'

Ohk only bowed his head, placed the tray on a table and withdrew without further comment, leaving Cortesia to stare after him, brow knitted.

'Damn you, Ohk', she muttered, albeit without conviction. With a sigh, she sat down at the table and regarded the cheese and salad without enthusiasm. At length, she picked up a piece of celery and took a bite.

'See, I obey', she murmured.

A week later, the prince was sitting up in bed and evidently much recovered. With Jory and Rayo supporting him on either side, he had even taken a few halting steps around his chamber, which reminded both of them of the last time they had carried him between them. It was time to discuss the future, if such a circumstance existed for them, and all were gathered on chairs brought about his bed.

'I have thanked you already, Balian, but let me do so again now that this whole enterprise is brought together', said Taian with a nod in the direction of the reluctant luminary. The prince remained pale and thin, but there was a lively glint in his eye now, and Balian inclined his head gracefully in response.

'I reject attempts to portray me as the author of your glad recovery', Balian answered. 'But naturally, I rejoice in it and I suppose it is futile to deny what all of you here maintain. As I have said, Tio may conceivably have acted through my flesh, but he has certainly not had the decency to introduce himself in any formal manner, nor has he made his intentions plain'.

He looked up to find that his audience was regarding him with various degrees of disapproval or amusement, depending on the depth of their religious convictions. Cortesia made the sign of Tio before her, and Bardo shuffled his feet awkwardly.

'Well, it does appear that Tio has spared me', said Taian after a moment. 'And support from the heavens can only be to our advantage'.

Various countenances in the room reflected the thought that this was very likely the only support they could count on, at least for the foreseeable future.

'We must ask ourselves what outcome we desire', continued Balian, causing a perceptible warming of the atmosphere. All noted the luminary's use of the word *we*, his attachment to their cause now evident.

'The blessed Balian is correct', nodded Cortesia, causing the latter to knit his brows at this honorific. She turned to Taian.

'Do you desire a guarantee of your personal safety under this new regime? Or do you seek to overturn it?'

'I have never sought power or responsibility', said Taian, glancing around. 'As you well know'.

'Of course we do', agreed Jory. 'But you must ask yourself whether any guarantee of your safety, that we might potentially secure from the emperor, can be trusted'.

'Or from the empress, for that matter', added Cortesia. 'I think the pair of them have already made it quite clear that they would rather have you dead. I would certainly not advise you to trust any undertaking they might make'. She looked around, taking note of the nods and grunts of assent signifying approval of this stance.

'And besides', added Rayo. 'Sometimes greatness is thrust upon one, as the proverb says'.

'Well, yes', conceded Taian, lips pursed. 'But I am not sure I have it in me to be an emperor'.

'If I may speak, my lord', said Bardo, raising a finger. 'If *you* do not believe that you may command the nation's loyalty and obedience, I don't suppose there will be many who will contradict you'.

'He's right', grunted Cortesia. 'Hear him. This is the simple choice that fate has made for you. You must embrace it or be destroyed by it'.

An uneasy silence settled in the room.

'You are right, my lady', said Ohk, inside Cortesia's head, causing her to spare him an approving glance.

Taian settled back on his pillows and his eyes shifted to the stone tracery of the ceiling above him. At last, he sighed and his mouth set itself in a line suggestive of fierce determination. It was as though that instant had seen his transition from one state of being to another.

'And you will all follow and support me?' he asked, raising himself up once more, sitting as straight as his bedding would allow. 'I may count on your loyalty?'

'With all my heart!' said Rayo, clasping his hand amongst a chorus of similar declarations.

'Well', said Taian with a smile. 'That foul Triado and my cursed step-mother Cresara may have the support of the senate and the populace, and seven legions at their backs, but I have these six friends around me here, and that is worth as many legions. With your help I promise you that I shall take back the throne that is my birth-right, or die in the attempt'.

It came into Rayo's mind to say *Behold! See how our prince has become an emperor!* but the words died in his throat, quashed by a warning glance from Jory, who always knew his mind.

'So how should we proceed?' he asked instead.

'The prince was ill, we are told', said Drael, wiping his mouth with a napkin, having set down a pheasant's leg.

'Indeed', agreed Adala, regarding him expectantly from the other side of the table at which they sat, eating a dinner of various roasted fowl with peas and parsnips. 'Everyone maintains as much'.

It had been a week since their arrival in The City now, and their rooms above the inn had become a familiar and secure residence to Adala. There were many times when her thoughts turned to The Grapes and its inhabitants, particularly when she passed through the bar downstairs and saw the staff engaged in the familiar activities that had once been her own preoccupation. On occasion, a cloying chill of home-sickness oppressed her, but this could always be dispelled by summoning into her mind that glorious vision of her prince's face. She knew that she must be patient, that Tio would guide her in her quest and that Drael, in his turn, would facilitate that outcome. She had already come to recognise that he was a man of rare intelligence, that she was fortunate indeed to have him at her side, and she had reminded herself of this on countless occasions, in fact.

'And so', he continued, 'having made good their escape, our two noblemen must have stood in need of a physician, or certainly of medical advice of some kind, would you not agree?'

Adala swirled a small amount of thin red wine around in the bottom of her glass and nodded as Drael mused on.

'But those two noblemen must surely have known that to approach any reputable physician might have invited suspicion. If I had been in the Director's position, I should certainly have had such people watched. Which makes me wonder if they might have sought assistance from less conventional sources'.

'I'm not sure if I take your meaning', admitted Adala.

'Well, there are many charitable institutions in the city that provide simple medical care to the poor', continued Drael, rubbing his chin thoughtfully. If I had been our young noble friends, I should have concealed my identity and that of the prince, passing him off as a humble citizen. Perhaps tomorrow we should enquire of such places, to see if any provided care to a party answering their description in the day following from the abduction'.

'But, as you admit, there must be many such abbeys and priories in the city and its surroundings. Such enquiries might take weeks', objected Adala, eyebrows raised.

'They might, but would you rather that we abandoned our search?'

'Certainly I wouldn't', exclaimed Adala, a flush rising in her cheeks.

'Well, I must acquire a plan of the city, mark out on it all such institutions and evolve a plan for calling upon them, beginning with those closest to the palace', said Drael, putting aside the napkin and pushing back his chair.

There were three such institutions close to the palace itself. The first and closest was the hospital attached to St Serdinos. Here, the infirmarian recalled no visitation that matched the description provided by Drael. The same was true in the second, the priory of St Andrian. At the third, the convent of the Blessed Birch, the sister in charge also shook her head. However, as Drael and Adala thanked her and took their leave, she called them back, casting a glance over her shoulder, as though she feared being overheard.

'I shouldn't really tell you this', she said, in a low voice. 'But a lot of the local people place their trust in Sister Mora, not that she really deserves that title'.

The woman's medical reputation far outstripped her virtue, she explained, but those seeking help with broken bones, difficult childbirths and fevers seemed to find it in them to forgive any deficiencies in her moral character.

'Thank you kindly, Sister', said Adala when they had been told where they might find Sister Mora. A significant glance from Drael showed that instinct told him this might be important.

Sister Mora proved to be out, but a neighbour indicated a house further along the narrow street of humble dwellings, where she was said to be attending at a childbirth. This proved to be correct, and after an hour or so of observing from the other side of the street, the sister emerged, wiping her hands on her robe and exchanging cheerful remarks with a grateful householder.

'Sister Mora?' asked Adala, catching up with her as the door closed and she turned along the street.

'Yes, dear?' replied Sister Mora mildly, eyebrows raised. 'How may I assist? What ails you or yours? This is a busy day, indeed!'

'It is not for ourselves that we enquire, good sister', said Drael, arriving at Adala's side and taking off his hat. 'We are trying to trace my son, who recently disappeared'.

He mentioned the night of the prince's abduction, at which the sister's eyes momentarily clouded, causing Drael a leap of exultation in his heart. She knew!

'May I ask if this is an official enquiry?' she asked, rather than address his question. 'You have the look of an investigator about you, if I may say so'.

'Not at all', answered both Adala and Drael together, in a manner so earnest and sincere as to deny the possibility of deceit.

'I *am* a member of that profession, but I must assure you that my enquiry is made in a private capacity', added Drael beneath her narrow-eyed scrutiny.

She glanced about at the streams of citizens passing them by, going about their business: the tinkers, the hucksters, the lavender sellers and the like.

'Perhaps here is not the place', she said. 'Perhaps you would come home with me, it lies only a little way yonder'.

Once the door was shut and they found themselves in her simply appointed parlour, Sister Mora shrugged off her cloak and bade them sit down on some of the plain, hard chairs with which the place was furnished. A small fire burned in the grate, which she stirred up with a poker, adding a few sticks for good measure.

'Now', she said, rubbing her hands together, 'I think we must be honest with each other, because I do not think for one moment that you come in search of your son, sir, and I shall not answer your questions unless I am satisfied of your sincerity. So, do please tell me the truth of your motivations, and if I am convinced, I may be able to assist you'.

Adala directed a wondering gaze at Drael, who cleared his throat and looked uncharacteristically awkward, toying with his hat on his knees.

'Very well', began Drael. 'Although I think it only fair to warn you that our story may seem far-fetched...'

'Let me be the judge of that', said Sister Mora with a vague wave of her hand. 'Do go on'.

'Prince Taian is said to have died during an attempt to abduct him from the palace', said Adala impulsively, before Drael could continue. 'We believe this not to be the case. We believe that the friends who sought to carry him away from imminent danger tried to carry him to a place of safety and may have looked for medical help for him'.

'He was said to be very ill', added Drael. 'We wondered if they may have approached you'.

Sister Mora stared from face to face, the colour draining from her cheeks, making the sign of Tio before her.

'Well', she said. 'That is certainly not a story many would choose to present as a plausible one, if they sought to dissemble'.

'Indeed', said Adala, leaning forward in her chair, brow creased with the ferocity of her sincerity. 'Because it is the truth, implausible or not'.

Sister Mora's gaze moved to the fire, which she regarded fixedly for some moments.

'The prince', she murmured at length. 'Could it really be true?'

'Could what be true?' urged Drael, struggling to conceal his impatience.

'I was called upon that night to attend to a young man', said Sister Mora, looking back to her guests once more. 'He appeared to be quite insensible, quite close to death, I judged, and there were injuries to his feet consistent with being dragged through the streets for some distance, now that I consider. Perhaps *he* is whom you seek'.

'Perhaps indeed!' cried Drael, leaping from his seat, held back by Adala's restraining hand on his arm.

'Pray, will you tell us where he lay?' she asked, eyes wide.

'I will', said Sister Mora.

Ohk awoke to find The City lashed with summer rain and with thunder rumbling in the west. It was the second day since their return from Balian's house, leaving the reluctant luminary with Taian, Rayo and Jory for company. It was agreed that it would be folly for them to return to the centre of things just now. With no support, no nascent foundation of discontent within the empire to build upon, their position would be hopeless, and it would only be a matter of time before their arrest and their necessary elimination from the great game of imperial politics. It would be necessary to lie low, perhaps for years, until events could be turned to their advantage. Predictably, Rayo saw such circumstances coming rapidly to pass. Equally predictably, Jory took the view that long-term exile in obscurity was the best that might be hoped for. Cortesia's role, and by extension that of her tiny household, was to monitor events in the city and send word of developments to the prince. Nothing of note had occurred in the interval between the party's journey into the west and Cortesia's return, but the project seemed to have sparked her interest and given her a renewed focus in life. There was a new lightness in her step and a glint in her eye that spoke of a resolute determination to bring about the downfall of the empress and her spouse.

'Are you ever going to bring me luncheon?' she asked now, peevishly. 'I heard you come back an hour since'.

It was no longer a surprise to hear his mistress's voice *inside* his head. In a further development, it had become apparent that Cortesia was able to communicate with her servant without the necessity for opening her mouth or spending her breath.

'I shall certainly be with you presently, my lady', answered Ohk, looking up from cutting bread.

His journey to and from the market had resulted in a soaking. The cloak he had worn hung dripping from a hook now, on the back of the kitchen door, a dark puddle growing slowly beneath it on the uneven tiles of the floor. Rain pattered on the glass of the windows, little fingers of it driven hither and thither by a gusty wind.

'And I believe there is another leak in the ballroom', continued Cortesia. 'I trust you will not permit us to drown'.

'I shall take a bucket to it in due course', said Ohk evenly. 'It is always when the wind is in the west'.

He could have added that mending the roof might be the best long-term solution, if Ma'am would countenance selling the harpsichord she never played or one or two of the better paintings in the library. One was a Marcutio, which would certainly fund the restoration of the whole building, if Ma'am could be persuaded to part with it. However, it had been dear to her late father – and so indispensable to her. Besides, her library, the inner sanctum of her soul, was not to be touched, the many hundreds of volumes it contained, her faithful companions from day to day. She was there now, poring over a copy of Doranthios' "The Dream of the Raven," so ancient it was held together only by tape and glue.

Ohk was adding cheese and a little dried sausage to her plate when he heard the jangle of the bell at the front door. Frowning, he wiped his hands on his apron, straightened his shirt and made his way along the passage to the entrance hall.

When opened with the type of groaning creak traditional in ancient and neglected mansions, Ohk saw that a young woman was standing on the step, hunched beneath a cloak, water dripping from a hood that revealed pale features of extraordinary beauty. Damp black curls framed her face and her eyes, and great grey pools of earnest enquiry looked up into his own so that his heart fluttered within him.

'Good morning, sir. Are you Ohk?'

Ohk inclined his head, continuing to regard her curiously.

'I should like to speak to your mistress, if I may', she continued. 'Perhaps you would tell her that a Miss Radagarion desires the pleasure of her company. May I step inside a moment? It is hellish wet out here'.

With a grunt, Ohk moved aside so that the girl could edge past him and then stand dripping in the hallway, looking about her with interest.

'A Miss Radagarion to see you, my lady', he said internally.

'Who? Who? Do send her away. Ask her what she wants. Oh dear. Of course. Ohk, Your want of a tongue is really very inconvenient at times. Is Bardo on the premises?'

Ohk raised his eyebrows at this conflicting set of instructions.

'I am aware that you are unable to speak, Mr Ohk', said Adala, wringing out the hem of her skirt and momentarily exposing a white petticoat and a slender ankle. 'How very galling that must be'.

By use of signs, Ohk attempted to enquire as to the nature of his visitor's business. Adala cocked her head on one side and observed his motions with interest.

'My business is of a confidential nature', she said after a moment. 'And it is essential that I speak to your mistress. I assure you she will consider it to be of the most pressing urgency'.

'She claims it is very important, Ma'am'.

'They always do, do they not? I'm never going to get my lunch before supper time, am I, Ohk, damn you? Oh, very well. Send her up, I'm in the library'.

'As you wish, Ma'am', answered Ohk with a nod, his face wearing an expression that could only be interpreted by his visitor as evidence of some form of internal dialogue. With a nod and a motion of his hand, Ohk took her soaking cloak and hung it on the pegs beside the door. Then he gestured towards the broad sweep of stairs in the gloom at the end of the hall and set off in that direction with Adala in pursuit.

Chapter Fifteen

Callisto

Cortesia rose as Adala was admitted and made her curtsey.

'I was reading', she said, indicating the open volume on the low table next to her leather-padded armchair, 'and propose to continue doing so without delay. So perhaps you could tell me on what basis you importune me so?'

'I have never seen so many books', breathed Adala, glancing about at the bookshelves that lined every wall on two levels, dimly lit by the pair of tall windows behind her reluctant host. 'I did not imagine there were so many in the world. Have you read all of them?' she asked, turning suddenly upon Cortesia.

Her eyes widened still more, as though noticing Cortesia's black-swathed head for the first time, and she cast them down awkwardly.

'I have not', replied the other, her voice softening.

'You have sent me a rare beauty', she said in her internal dialogue. 'Extraordinary!'

'Indeed, Ma'am', came Ohk's sonorous tones, causing Cortesia to picture in her head the dip of his own, the knowing glint in his eye.

'She reminds me of me', she added before she could stop herself, the instinct that had prompted that declaration finding answer in an immediate spasm of pain.

'But perhaps I shall live long enough to do so', she added out loud, once she had composed herself. 'But you are leading me astray. Do tell me your business here. I understand that your name is Radagarion'.

'It is, my lady', agreed Adala, wondering how her hostess came to know this.

'And your business?' insisted Cortesia, tilting her head on one side and placing her hands on her hips.

'I beg that you will be patient with me, because a bare sentence or two will never suffice to encompass it. Rather, I must tell you a tale that may seem strange to your ear and, may I venture, stretch your credulity'.

Cortesia sighed, but the tide of irritability that might ordinarily have risen in her upon this intrusion was quite absent, and she found herself strangely fascinated by this lovely stranger, even as her stomach grumbled within her.

'Well, perhaps I shall be the judge of that', she said. 'Draw up that chair. You had best be seated if I must endure a lengthy and improbable yarn'.

Adala began, telling of her home and her background, her first serendipitous meeting with the prince. She told of their secret meetings, the shocking news she had received of his illness, her visitation from Officer Trimestrion and her journey to The City. Tears came into her eyes as she related the story of her encounter with the highwaymen on the road to Annagaar, causing Cortesia to draw her own conclusion about her use of the term "ill-used by them." Adala's description of her activities, and those of Drael, in The City since their arrival brought a slow nod of approval from Cortesia and a drumming of her fingers on her knee.

'Your birth name is Adala, is it not?' asked Cortesia at length, when the story was complete.

'It is, Ma'am', agreed Adala, surprised. 'May I ask how you know it?'

'Well, I judge that I may trust you', said Cortesia. 'And that we may be open with each other. It will please you to know that your surmisings are entirely correct and that the prince yet lives. I was with him only a few days ago, and his recovery continues apace. It will also please you to hear that your name was on the prince's lips', said

Cortesia with a wry smile beneath her swathings. 'Which is how it is familiar to me. It was amongst the first words upon those lips as he recovered, and he has spoken of you on many occasions since then. I must confess, I begin to see justification for his preoccupation', she added, causing Adala to blush furiously.

'But he lives. He lives and breathes', she cried, rising from her chair, her face a picture of radiant joy, pressing her hands together. 'Do tell me how he fares. How did he come to be cured? How was he spirited away from this place? Is he far away?'

'Please, give me respite!' laughed Cortesia, raising a hand and feeling a curious warmth in her heart. 'I shall answer all your questions presently, but perhaps you will share luncheon with me. The hour is late, and although my ears have been your eager servants, my stomach rebels against me'.

Ohk brought food without apparently having been summoned, and the two of them talked for hours whilst the rain gradually ceased outside and the low clouds cleared away into the east. Adala had been warned that the mistress of this house was a proud and imperious woman with a rapier tongue and a vast reservoir of scorn to pour out upon the world. She found that the woman before her listened attentively, spoke softly and asked penetrating questions.

'And where is Officer Trimestrion now?' she asked at last. 'I trust you came here alone, for fear that we would be suspicious of him'.

'Indeed', agreed Adala. 'He readily admits that the mark of the investigator is forever upon him, and although he is a thoroughly decent man, as you have heard, even his most loyal friends would agree he has a forbidding aspect'.

'You must certainly bring him here upon the morrow', said Cortesia. 'He sounds a most useful acquaintance'.

Discussion moved onto books, and Cortesia's heart opened still more to one whom so evidently shared her passion.

'Every book contains a whole world to be explored, does it not?' suggested Adala 'And a window into the minds of those who lived long ago'.

'Far have I travelled in these last twelve years', laughed Cortesia bitterly. 'Although my body has remained huddled within these walls, surely I have journeyed to the dawn of history itself and peered into the brains of prophets, bards and dreamers. You read Cantrophene, I gather? A rare accomplishment in one of your age, and... station, if I may venture to suggest'.

'I do', agreed Adala. 'And much pleasure has it given me over the years'.

She went on to discuss her uncle's books and his nurturing of her interest, until those regrettable frailties of the flesh had overcome him and sundered her from him forever. Together, they passed along the shelves of Cortesia's library, drawing out this volume and that, talking like excited schoolgirls about Adala's old friends Viridon, Cantanoro and Miron and finally standing in front of the large painting that hung above the great fireplace at the furthest end of the room.

'How odd', exclaimed Adala after a few moments gazing upon it. 'It depicts the legend of Arcteaon and Cataria, does it not? The wandering sculptor chances upon the saint bathing in a pool in the woods, and she turns him into a pillar of marble'.

'You are quite correct', agreed Cortesia. 'Various episodes are depicted together, and here in the corner we see the approach of his son, bearing his sculptor's tools. But why should it seem strange to you?'

'It is a very fine painting', said Adala, turning to her. 'I never saw a finer, I declare. I only say strange, because

Prince Taian referred to this very legend when first we met'.

'He did? A strange coincidence, indeed'.

Cortesia's eye narrowed as she ran a finger along the ornate gilded frame, holding it up to reveal dust. For a moment, she considered drawing Ohk's attention to this, but instead she merely nodded slowly, lips pursed beneath those folds of dark cloth.

'It is a Marcutio', she said. 'One of his best, and one that is worth more than the whole of this house, if I am any judge. My father bought it, many years ago, but now I am minded to sell it'.

'You are?'

'I am. This house is falling to pieces, as you may have noticed, and I stand in need of ready monies if I am to advance the cause of our prince'.

She crossed to the table and picked up the book she had set down there, passing it to Adala.

'"The Dream of the Raven," the collected works of Doranthios', she said. 'Or perhaps of various ancient authors collectively encompassed in that name. Scholarship is divided, as you may know. Anyway, I was reading this passage in the Book of Ohbrid when you came to my door. I have read this volume almost to destruction, as you see'.

Adala looked down at the yellowed, frayed page and at the familiar lines that described the occasion when Ria, the earth mother, rejected the wooing of Tamarin, lord of the underworld'.

'It is beautiful, I...'

'Do you believe in omens, Adala Radagarion?' interrupted Cortesia.

'I did not, could not, at one time... but now I find I do', admitted Adala, looking into the intense gaze of her host's single eye.

Cortesia placed her black-gloved hand on Adala's forearm, a hand that trembled with sincerity now.
'In recent days and weeks, I have trodden the slow path from the halls of darkness, step by faltering step, my friend. But now I am awake'.

Bardo came in later that afternoon, sporting a black eye and a painfully swollen nose. Ohk, looking up from washing pots, set aside his towel and approached to turn Bardo's face, tenderly examining his injuries. A raised eyebrow enquired as to how Bardo had come to acquire these.
'I was in the Candlemaker's Arms last night', Bardo explained, his voice curiously nasal. 'And these two fellows, rough-looking types, I should say, asked as to the nature of my employment. I mentioned that I worked for Mistress Tyverios and they ventured to suggest that she was an evil-hearted, black-swathed witch, so they did. Naturally, I suggested to them that they should keep a civil tongue in their ignorant bleedin' heads, whereupon one of them desired me to go fuck myself'.
Bardo paused, tipping his head here and there as he revisited the next few moments.
'You may imagine that I resented this extremely, and so I endeavoured to punch the bastard's lights out. Yes...', he said, touching his head cautiously. 'I did not escape retaliation. Still, her ladyship's honour demanded it, did it not? A small price, I should think', he added, moving to examine his reflection in the big mirror at the foot of the stairs.
'What's this doing back up in its proper place?' he asked after a moment. 'I haven't seen a mirror in here for years. This one was out in the shed back yonder, last time I saw it. And another thing... the windows are undraped all of a sudden. What's going on, Ohk?'

No gestures would be sufficient to tell the story of the day's events, or to tell of Ohk's own suspicions regarding the evolution in his mistress's state of mind. Instead, he merely pointed up the stairs and then traced on his own face the arc of a stylised smile.

That evening, Ohk attended to his mistress's hair and applied ointments to skin and scalp in the manner that was his daily duty. No lady's maid had undertaken this task for many years. None but Ohk were permitted to see what lay beneath the silks and soft chiffons that concealed the horrors of her face. Ohk was quite used to it, and he saw past this angry red flesh to the beauty that had once dwelt there.

'How did you come to be here, Ohk?' she asked abruptly, causing him to pause in his work with the soothing ointment that he was applying to her ear.

So unexpected was this that he almost let the jar slip from his hand. The salves and ointments were expensive, and the upkeep of the house left little spare for such luxuries. Even the pittance Ohk received for his labours was largely spent by him on their purchase, not that he would ever disclose it.

'I was a slave, Ma'am', he said, resuming his work. 'And your late father purchased me in the slave markets of Tazman. Set me free, he did, blessèd be his memory'.

'I know this', she answered, her brow knitting. 'Of course I do. But where did you come from before that?'

Setting down the jar, Ohk picked up a hairbrush, and a distracted look, redolent of distant times and places, came into his eye.

'I lived in a land where the eye of sun was near', he began. 'And where the beaches were whiter and the trees greener and the sky bluer than here. There were birds of colours such as painters never dreamed of, and butterflies the size of dinner plates bejewelled the forest glades. The flowers grew in such profusion and with such rich scents there that I can close my eyes and smell them still'.

He then told of growing up in a small village, of hunting with his brothers, tilling the rich earth around his family's home and fishing in deep pools beneath forest peaks.

'It sounds a simple, wholesome existence', mused Cortesia.

'It was good', agreed Ohk. 'And life was easy for those of us who were free men. The more arduous labour was undertaken by the slaves my tribe had taken from amongst our neighbours'.

'So you were a slave-owner yourself?'

'Not I, but it is the way of the world since time immemorial, and the principal men in my village had many. They were treated in the usual way, very often with the same contempt and cruelty that I was later to endure'.

'So how did you sink to that station yourself?' asked Cortesia, turning her head so that Ohk was obliged to cease his brushing.

'There was a battle, I suppose your great nation would call it a skirmish, and I was carried away by the warriors of that neighbouring tribe, together with some of their own fellows liberated from my village. We were marched for days through the jungle. Those who had behaved most harshly to our slaves were put to death in a manner so cruel that I hesitate to describe it. My own conduct was found less reprehensible. I was spared, to become a slave myself'.

'But your tongue, Ohk, how did you come to lose your tongue?'

Ohk toyed abstractedly with the bristles of the brush as he relived the pain and terror of that moment.

'Ohk', insisted Cortesia, when his voice remained mute in her head.

'I was a bard singer', he said at last. 'Trained from childhood to sing the songs of my people, to recount the stories and the legends that made us what we were. We did not write, you see, Ma'am. We had no books, no skills to record such things. They were passed along the generations from memory to memory, a precious gift from the past to the present, and from there to the uncharted future. My master was taught by his master, and my master was teaching me. They captured him, too, and a morbidity set in when they severed his own tongue. He died, taking his songs with him to the grave. He was old. The shock was too great, perhaps. They cut and tore my own tongue from my mouth, but I survived. They sought, you see, to destroy my people's past and so to diminish them in the present and the future, to still their songs, for what is a people without its past? And now they are scattered in the woods and they will perhaps forget who they are, who they once were. Such is the price of defeat'.

'I am sorry to hear that', said Cortesia with a tenderness that he had never heard in her voice before, one that provoked a curious heat behind his eyes. He blinked away tears. 'And tell me, do you yet recall any of those songs?'

'Only the barest outlines', he admitted. 'It is many years since I was able to voice them, and the patterns and the cadences of them have faded in my mind'.

'That is really very sad', said Cortesia, her voice continuing in that unfamiliar softness. 'I am sorry to have asked you to relive such things. I can see it is painful to you'.

'And then I was taken to the coast and sold to a Eudoran slaver', continued Ohk, having mastered himself. 'Along with a dozen or so of my fellows. A vessel out of Tazman, it was, and the sweating fever came on during the voyage south, and half of the human cargo perished and was pitched over the side. Barely half of us were alive when we docked. When I had recovered, only three of us remained. The other two I never saw again, sold to the galleys, perhaps, or the mills. I found myself in the docks with many others of my race, loading and unloading the ships. There are many, many slaves in Eudora, Ma'am. I had been there for more than a year when your father descended upon Tazman with his raiding fleet and razed the wharfs and the warehouses. In the confusion and the fighting, I rose up and beat down a soldier who might have slain him. My reward was my freedom and a place at his side when the fleet returned'.

'And you have served my family ever since', concluded Cortesia. 'Served me'.

'I have', nodded Ohk. 'It has been my privilege'.

'And don't you ever wish to go away?' she asked. 'Have you not exchanged one form of servitude for another, since we do not keep slaves in Erenor'.

'Indeed not', agreed Ohk, 'although there are many share-cropping peasants in the fields of your country, tied to their land, who would scratch their heads to see the distinction. And there are many forms of servitude'.

'There are?'

'There are. And to answer your question, I would never leave you, Ma'am. Never, so long as I live and breathe'.

It felt strange indeed to pull up in the courtyard of Balian Drumarian's house and step down from the trap as servants issued forth to take care of her pony. Drael, who had been a little ahead of Adala, was already conversing with a steward, one that spared a surreptitious glance for her, before turning and hurrying off towards the house. It was dusk on the second day of their journey from The

City, and the sun had already dipped beneath the ornate façade of what was evidently a building of some antiquity, albeit perhaps a little decayed. Such considerations, namely the broad sweep of cobbles in geometric patterns and the tall, plane trees around the verges of the courtyard, barely touched upon her sensations, so replete was her being with the consciousness of having finally arrived at the conclusion of her long journey. Her mouth was dry, and her heart beat furiously within her chest as she handed hat and cloak to another servant with a vague murmur of thanks. Her eyes were directed to the front door, where it stood at the head of a short flight of steps, and presently people began to issue forth, Rayo and Jory amongst them. Her mind barely registered their presence. Her eyes sought only Taian, and within a moment they were rewarded, sprang wide, indeed.

There he was, leaning on a stick, emerging at Rayo's shoulder. For days, she had rehearsed this moment in her mind; how she would make a low curtsey and advance in dignified fashion to receive his courteous greetings. How shocking, then, the impulse of the moment, which caused her simply to burst into tears and fly across the intervening cobbles to throw herself into his arms with a great cry of delight.

In retrospect, she deplored this shameful want of self-control. How she despised emotional incontinence. However, those wild and joyful impulses that fought for mastery of her body readily beat down the dictates of caution and of convention. It may easily have been that Taian had recoiled from her, his affection for her quite diminished by time and circumstance. How then would she be humiliated! But he did not. He received her trembling embrace with every indication of reciprocated delight, kissing her brow and stroking her hair in a manner that brought inexpressible joy to her heart and caused Drael's to lie within him like a stone as he watched from the lowest step.

Later, they walked together in the garden behind the house. It was a warm evening and the scent of roses unfolded in the quiet air. Gravel crunched softly beneath their feet and cicadas chirruped vaguely in the orchards beyond, but no sensory manifestation of their environment could pierce through the intensity of their absorption in each other. They held hands. They wandered amongst the arbours and the bowers and they talked, as though words themselves could entwine them into a single, united entity.

'I must sit', said Taian at last, drawing her towards the pergola where Balian was accustomed to sit reading of an afternoon. 'My head outlasts my legs, I find, although I grow stronger every day. Soon, I may sit on a horse once more, I think'.

'I knew that you were not dead. I always knew it', declared Adala, picking a moonflower from amongst those growing about the pergola and toying with it absently. 'I had a vision, you know'.

'A vision?' Taian asked, turning curious eyes upon her. 'Like a saint?'

'I am no saint, I judge', laughed Adala. 'But certainly, I had a vision'.

'You were in my dreams, too', mused Taian when she had described Tio's manifestation to her. 'For a time longer than I know how to describe, I felt that I was entombed within my own body, unable to stir a muscle, unable even to open my eyes, and I knew that I mouldered in that tomb and there would come a time when it would be destroyed – and me with it. Your name would not come to my lips, but it dwelt in the forefront of my mind, and it was like a shining light in the darkness'.

She gripped his hand more tightly and leaned in to his shoulder.

'You know, it is strange how matters have evolved', he mused, abstractedly stroking her hair. 'Naturally, I regret the reduction in my circumstances, the passing of my brother and my father... and yet...'

'And yet?' she prompted, gazing up into his eyes, now almost lost in the gloom. For a moment there was silence, in which the trickle of water into a fishpond could be heard, and then...

'And yet', he continued, '... there are advantages in being cast down from the highest height and being obliged to dwell incommunicado, when none shall rebuke me for my connections or my conduct'.

'There are?'

'There are, because an emperor and a tavern girl may never wed. My friends sought to remind me of this, as they did you. We were both of us living in an impossible dream, and though we were loath to admit it, at some point we must have confronted that implacable reality and been crushed by it. We do not inhabit a nursery tale; the senate and the court would deplore it. I would be the object of ridicule and scorn and the crown endangered by it. But I am not an emperor now, and perhaps I never shall be. Perhaps that is the best thing that could have happened. Perhaps Tio has smiled upon us. Besides, there is nothing to prevent an ordinary citizen married to another ordinary citizen from ascending to the throne. History can show many examples'.

'So what are you saying?' asked Adala, the flower falling disregarded to the ground.

'It is not so much what I say as what I ask', continued Taian, drawing her close. 'And I ask that you would agree to be my wife'.

The song of Ohbrid (part 2)

Beyond gull-haunted headlands, cliffs and strands
    Where bold Tetheos, Lord of Waters, dwells
    Full forty fathom-deep his palace stands
    Bejewelled all with oyster pearls and shells
    And here he rests his trident on his knees
    Imperious on the corals of his throne
    Majestic king of ocean, gulf and sea
    Commands and rules his briny realm alone
    He gazes now upon his ranks of lords
    The tritons and their dolphins all about
    The nereids and mermen with their swords
    Defenders of this watery redoubt
    The king calls out to all who gather there
    In rumbling tones within this hall serene
    'Will none amongst you find a maiden fair
    Fit to enthrone beside me as my queen?'
    On craggy rocks in moonlight-silvered bays
    Where mermaids sit and comb their oozy hair
    Reflecting constellations in their gaze
    They raise their star song in pellucid air
    But when they see the Mother tread that shore
    Resplendent in her beauty and her grace
    They hasten to recount all that they saw
    Regale their king of noble form and face
    He turns his head and hears, on their descent
    The tale of the fair maiden they have spied
    He rises from his throne with bold intent
    To woo her and to take her for his bride
    The Mother pacing lone upon the strand
    Looks up to see the sea approach the earth

White horses at the ocean king's command
Draw his bright chariot splashing through the surf
The foamy billows part as he steps down
And bows before the maiden where she stands
He offers to her brow a royal crown
All wrought with pearls by artful triton hands
'Behold my realm,' he says with regal pride,
'Adjoining yours it circles all the globe
My oceans deep, my empire reaches wide
If you were mine, my seas should be your robe.
My subjects, be they great, or be they mean
Beg that I take a wife to be my own
The throne there at my side demands a queen
And wretched are my days to rule alone
My people now are troubled and they weep
Partaking in my anguish and my care
Leviathan is stirring in the deep
Uneasy is the realm without an heir
The song of whales groans low in the abyss
And mermaids raise sad voices to the land
To dwell with you would be eternal bliss
I beg that I may take your noble hand.'
The Mother shakes the spindrift from her hair
And gazes on his noble countenance
She places there a hand with gentle care
And spares his briny realm a wistful glance
'I cannot be your bride, I fear to say,'
She says in tones regretful but unmoved,
'For though my heart would gladly see that day
My head warns me that I should be reproved
The creatures and the spirits of the glen
The denizens of mountain top and heath
The dwellers in the field and in the fen
The sightless earthy burrowers beneath
Would damn my name if I should so consent
To let you tread my green and pleasant hills

For where you place your feet I shall lament
A salt-cursed wilderness that no man tills
Where poisoned all is barley, spelt and wheat
Your hand upon my shores is judged a theft.
Though pleasure may be found where they do meet,
Forever shall the land and sea be cleft.'

Interlude

Prata - December 3993an

It was a quiet morning, although deathly chill, as Adala and Ureni paced the firm sand of the shore beneath the tideline, the sharp salt air in their nostrils. The susurrus of surf on sand was in their ears, as well as the lament of the gulls and the low pounding of the sea upon the headland far ahead. Behind, atop the dunes, a pair of heavily wrapped soldiers clutched their spears with numb fingers and watched, in case their captive should dive into the sea like a dolphin and make good her escape. Perhaps she would. Perhaps she would slip out from her room one night and walk out into the shallows, step deeper beyond until the ocean closed over her head and swallowed her up. She had considered it. Only death drew open the door from this place, and death paced beside her now, his implacable hand unseen upon her shoulder. She would embrace him gladly in due course. But not yet.

'And so you were married?' asked Ureni. 'There, out in those western hills?'

'I was', agreed Adala, pausing now and drawing her cloak more tightly around her as shore birds wheeled and settled in the sparkling shallows.

She gazed out to sea now, to the vague horizon where the sun shone pale amongst low, barred clouds.

'And it was all I ever hoped it would be,' she continued. 'But it seems a thousand years ago now, and at the same time like yesterday. How strange time is, how strange our recollections of it'.

A silence fell between them as Ureni nodded, but with a blankness in her eyes that spoke of the difference in their years.

'Do you ever yearn for home?' asked Adala, turning her pale face upon her, strands of hair raised about her face by a sudden vesper.

'I think about it often, my lady', admitted the other. 'Every day, and it pleases me to know that I shall return there when...'

The sentence admitted of no completion, although the thought continued to its logical conclusion and Ureni cast her eyes down.

'When I am dead', supplied Adala with a wry twitch of the lips that approached a smile. 'Do not fear to say it. We both know my days are numbered and I shall not leave here alive'.

'When my duties here are complete', said Ureni at length, poking at an upturned crab carapace with her toe.

'Indeed. And what is *your* home like?'

Ureni glanced up sharply, having never previously been asked to furnish such information.

'Well', she said, running her hand through what hair showed beneath her scarf. 'It lies in the Duchy of Arken, away northward, more than a hundred miles distant, I should think, as the crow flies'.

They continued to pace whilst Ureni told of the home she shared with her sisters, her mother and her brother, whose business as a carpenter sustained them now that her father was gone. She described the house and the workshop behind it, the big walnut tree in the yard and the hill beyond, where her sisters and she had once rolled in the grass when children, laughing and chasing their big black dog. Days of summer, when the shadows never lengthened. She found that her eyes were moist, wiping away a tear with the back of her hand.

'And what of you, my lady?' asked Ureni when she had supplied every detail that her mistress had required of her. 'Do you miss The Grapes, that you have told me of, or is it more the elegance and the luxury of the palace that you regret?'

'Do you know, I rarely think of them', said Adala, her grey eyes suddenly seeming as wide and as deep as the vast grey ocean before them.

'I do not think of home as a place, you see'.

Chapter Sixteen

Callisto - February 3975an

'I do not trust that man', said Cresara Rhovanion, turning from the window that looked out over the east wing of the palace.

The emperor Triado, lounged in a chair within a pool of sunlight, was eating an apple.

'Why, my dear?' he asked mildly.

'Because he is powerful, ambitious and well-connected, that is why', said his wife.

'As are most in my council', shrugged Triado. 'That is why they are in my council. A few of them are able, too, although naturally I must retain a large number whose only qualifications are the attributes you mention. These men are bound to us by ties of gratitude and mutual interest'.

'And for every man you have elevated to reward loyalty, you have spawned an enemy in those you have cast down. How many of the Melanthrodoi, or those otherwise connected to your clan, now occupy the highest offices of state?'

Triado cast his eyes upward, appearing to calculate.

'Why many', he replied, 'but they occupy those positions because I know that they are loyal to me, that my downfall would compass their own destruction, too'.

'And what of Vollangor? The infernal Duke of Vollangor? It is to him that I refer'.

'Of course you do. The Duke of Vollangor cordially dislikes me, and you as well, if we are to be honest. He also plots with the Dukes of Vannistar and Taal, if the Director is to be believed, not to mention a half dozen or so counts and other persons too trivial to mention. It is for that reason that I retain him. Were I to dismiss him, the plot might fire and all manner of unpleasantness might ensue. You see danger everywhere'.

'There *is* danger everywhere', snapped Cresara. 'As only a fool could fail to see'.

'The army is mine', said Triado, eyes narrowed, which caused his thin, bony face to look yet more gaunt. 'And power grows from the tip of a spear or the mouth of a cannon, does it not?'

'I wish I felt your confidence', sighed Cresara in more conciliatory tones, conscious of having overreached herself. 'I look upon the faces of council and I see a nest of vipers there'.

'You are overwrought', said Triado with an indulgent glance directed at Cresara's belly, pregnant now with a six-month child. 'It is no more than your condition provokes in you, especially given the difficulties...'

It was not necessary to bring this statement to its natural conclusion, nor had Cresara proved able to conduct any of her three previous pregnancies to such a conclusion. There had been two miscarriages and a stillbirth. He knew that she blamed him for this. His dead wife had likewise failed to bring forth live offspring, nor had he got any bastards that anyone was aware of, despite notorious promiscuity in the act of getting them. His endeavours in the marital bed had been dutiful and regular, if not conducive to any particular heights of passion on either part. He considered her to be incapable of unrestrained enjoyment, and she, for her part, deemed his male essence to be flawed, his very maleness, by extension, impaired.

She sighed and sat down on the chair before the window that had earlier been her resting place, stroking her belly absently.

'Do you not feel, husband, that the cup of power is poisoned, that the whole world conspires against us?'

'I do not', answered Triado, thinking it ironic that his wife should mention poison in this context, given her notorious propensity for administering such toxins to her enemies. Even her stepson had fallen victim.

'And besides, the crown is the burden as well as the prize, is it not? And if our enemies should one day overcome us; well, the purple makes a fair winding sheet, as I believe it is said. Let us enjoy what each day sends and set aside such gloomy maunderings'.

Cresara shot him a glance of weary resignation.

'I wish I could enjoy your peace of mind', she said, 'when the world is filled with our enemies'.

'And what of the prince?' she added when Triado only tossed his apple core out of the window.

'The prince is dead', he said with a thin smile. 'As everyone agrees'.

'We both know he is not', she grunted. 'He is out there somewhere, and I know in my bones that he remains a threat. The investigators pursue him'.

'A wastrel and a hedonist, in love with the wine cup and the chase', observed Triado. 'A significant threat, do you think? Could he ever command support?'

'I do not know', confessed Cresara, looking out across the rooftops of the palace once more. 'And the not-knowing of it oppresses me'.

The party could not stay forever in Balian Drumarion's house, since it was well known that the Directorate continued to search for them. Fortunately, both Rayo and Jory had family throughout the empire, and so it was never necessary to stay long in one place. Cortesia provided their connection to the beating heart of the empire. It was she who entertained the discreet couriers from the provinces, she who encoded messages and sent them away with intelligence of the developing situation at court. Drael had taught her the codes, and Drael dwelt with her now, his investigator's brain a crucial element in combating the Directorate's attempts to infiltrate their movement. For a movement it had become. In court and country there was a growing resentment at the capricious cruelty of the young regime, the ruthless ejection of long-serving lords, in order to accommodate Triado's blood relatives or the empress's favourites. There were rumours of poison, of extra-judicial killings of those too outspoken in their opposition.

'Is that from Vollangor?' asked Drael, walking into Cortesia's library one day.
Cortesia looked up from the letter that she had been reading.
'From Dradigorn', she said, naming the Duke of Vollangor's private secretary. 'But essentially, yes'.
"And what does he have to say?' grunted Drael, settling into a battered armchair. 'I suppose the noble lord continues to prevaricate'.
'He does', agreed Cortesia, eyeing Drael's muddy boots disapprovingly. 'He will not commit himself. I take it you have not encountered Ohk on your way here. I suppose he would have frowned upon you, if he had'.
'He has a frown that could put those of a nervous disposition in the ground', observed Drael wryly, looking at his boots. 'And a size and stature that could handily deal with anyone else, should he choose to exert himself. Has he ever been called upon to use his fists in anger, do you know?'
'He is a gentle fellow', observed Cortesia, having shaken her head, her gaze momentarily distant. 'A lamb within a bull. And do you propose to ride down to the others once more this month?'
'I do not', said Drael, his face impassive.
The remainder of their party was presently staying with Jory's second cousin in a town outside Vannistar, in the

far south of the empire. Taian and Adala were well into the third year of their marriage by this time, but still Drael found it hard to see her with him. They both treated him with cordial respect, both frequently expressed their gratitude for his expertise and his hard work on their behalf, but the fierce and shameful love he nurtured for Adala caused him to regret her tender glances for her husband, the touches and the gestures that he secretly coveted for himself. Such considerations welled up within him at such times, like a dark tide that would not be stemmed, no matter how much stern discipline he applied to his inner mind and to the ordering of his thoughts. How often that mind dwelt on those days he had spent with Adala in The City before their removal to the West and her reunion with the prince. Such days! Every fibre of his being knew that the extraordinary beauty of her person must forever be denied to him – and every fibre mourned for it accordingly. To be with her occasioned such tender sorrow, yet to be away from her was a sundering that oppressed his mind and soul. And yet absence was preferable. To be absent meant that he need not fear that his eyes or his countenance might betray him, and it meant that no fresh pain was heaped on pain. He sought distraction through complete immersion in his work. And that work was no longer the Directorate's. He had resigned his commission with that body at the end of his period of leave, in order to devote himself entirely to Prince Taian's cause, to Adala's cause, in fact. In addition, he was well aware that questions might have been asked about his dereliction of duty at Annagaar, and that to have remained in post would eventually have resulted in his investigation and censure. Now he turned his very considerable skills to the penetration of the Directorate itself. He had held no senior position there but had a number of close friends who had risen amongst its higher ranks. Some, who were hostile to Triado's regime, could be relied upon to supply intelligence of any operations that might compromise the prince's security. There were also rumours regarding the unorthodox manner of Triado's ascent to the throne. As yet, Drael's enquiries had yielded no concrete information, but he lived in hope that this might change.

'I'm sure Adala would be glad to see you', said Cortesia, who had a shrewd understanding of Drael's private mind. 'She values you extremely, you know?'

'She honours me', he grunted with a nod. 'Do you suppose Vollangor will oppose the emperor's new tax proposals?'

'I know he attempts to rally support against them', answered Cortesia, content to accede to this abrupt change of topic, having added more evidence to her private understanding of Drael's hopeless devotion to the girl. *There are many forms of servitude*, Ohk had once told her, and here was one of the cruellest.

'But Vollangor knows that the bulk of the council is in Triado's thrall', noted Drael, 'and the senate is too cowed to move. I am far from familiar with the court, as you know, but I am told that there is a growing atmosphere of fear and suspicion there'.

'The emperor's thirst for gold is truly wondrous to behold', observed Cortesia. 'And the preposterous luxury of the court is roundly condemned by those whose taxes must sustain it, so we are told'.

'So we are told', agreed Drael. 'But we remain far from an open break, a general insurrection amongst the people or the lords which might be turned to our advantage. And all the time I fear that the net is closing in, that the Directorate, with all its resources, all its many eyes, must eventually run the prince to ground'.

Drael's fears were realised very soon. The prince and his entourage were enjoying luncheon in a riverside inn to the east of Vannistar, entertaining a local nobleman and some of his leading retainers. Such a liaison was highly treasonable, but Vannistar was far from The City, and the Count of Linfeld was not one to be cowed by such circumstances. His younger brother, once a minister in government, had been executed on trumped up charges of conspiracy and his estates seized. Accordingly, the count was sympathetic to the approaches made to him by the prince and his agents.

'The regime is rotten to the core', said Linfeld, leaning across the table towards Taian. 'But the emperor, curse his name, has his foot placed firmly on the neck of the nation. The army is his through and through, and the senate lives in mortal fear of him'.

'But will the South rise against him?' asked Taian. 'I do not ask you to follow me, or to commit yourself in any formal sense at this time. It is too early. I seek only to judge the mood of the regions. But there may come a time...'

Linfeld regarded Taian steadily. His face was fleshy and round, greasy now from eating, but his eyes were cool and sober despite the great quantity of wine and mead he had consumed. He wiped his mouth on a napkin and set it firmly on the empty pewter plate before him.

'My Lord Vannistar will never move', he said. 'And without his example, the counts of this duchy will be loath to make such a bold move. His inaction will seal *their* loyalty, or at least their mute compliance, and give them the excuse they need to favour caution over action. It would be a brave man to be the first to raise the banner of revolt. The spectre of finding oneself alone beneath it haunts every nobleman's dreams'.

'But he is an old, sick man, notoriously timid and indecisive', objected Taian.

'Could we not approach him?' asked Adala, sitting at the prince's side.

'He would not countenance it, Ma'am', snorted Linfeld. 'Whether you come to him incognito or announce yourself in your own name, he will surely have you arrested – and there will be the end to your enterprise'.

He took a great swig from his wine goblet and glanced along the table to a scene of considerable noise and merriment. Rayo was laughing uproariously with one of Linfeld's sons. Jory was looking on with amused detachment. Adala's eye fell upon her husband, whose brow was creased now. Her hand moved to her belly. Her blood was late. Could it be that she carried his child at last? How fervently she hoped so, although an itinerant life, such as theirs, was far from ideal for either confinement or for child-rearing. Perhaps she would retire to one of the more remote cities in the West, live in obscurity for a while. Almost three years they had now been married. Their lovemaking had been every bit as passionate and as satisfying as she had hoped it would be, and yet she had not fallen pregnant. She knew he worried himself about it. Of course he did, poor dear. She worried, too, had worried that there might be some fault in her body that rendered her barren. But her blood was late. Perhaps the unfolding of the days would bring her the confirmation she yearned for. Certainly, she felt different today. There was a strange, acrid taste on the edge of her palette, a vague shimmer on the fringe of her vision and a sense of gathering agitation that increased with every passing minute. Was this it? Was this what it was like to feel a new life quicken within one? Or was it something else entirely? She frowned, glanced about her and stretched her fingers out pale on the table before her.

Further along the table, Balian Drumarion toyed listlessly with the food on his plate. As a man for whom food represented the sensual pleasure most congenial to his spirit, this was a rare and strange phenomenon. He had no appetite. He sipped at his wine without enthusiasm and made little effort to engage with his neighbours in conversation. They spoke enthusiastically of horses, he noted dully, a subject of little interest to him other than simple utility. Was this strange diminution of appetite occasioned by regret that he had become enmeshed in this dangerous enterprise? Regardless of his initial reticence, he had found himself drawn to Taian's cause within days of the prince's awakening. He was a rational man, so he told himself, but the faith his visitors had placed in him, their evident reverence for him, had made it easy to attach himself to that cause. Perhaps vanity was a strand in this, but perhaps also there was a gathering sense that their trust in him may not be misplaced. His instinct to equate faith with superstition, his suspicion of organised religion, had taken a severe knock, and there were times when he almost believed what his new friends insisted, that he had indeed been an unwitting vessel of divinity. It would have been easier to have embraced this notion had he had any sense of having gained supernatural powers. But he had not. His private attempts to levitate objects or to conjure fire from the air had resulted only in disappointment. If he truly channelled Tio's power, then it was done so in a manner that he seemed quite unable to prompt or control. No further "miracles" had occurred after the extraordinary gift of thought speech that he appeared to have bestowed on Cortesia and her servant. It was all very perplexing. And what was this sudden clutch at his heart?

From the corner of his eye, Jory saw Balian lurch abruptly to his feet.
'Quickly!' the luminary cried. 'There is danger approaching'.

Instantly, the hubbub died away. Chairs were thrust back and men rose up, reaching for swords, glancing uncertainly about.

'Where away?' demanded Taian, crossing to the door amongst the jostling throng as servant girls scattered and the proprietor looked on aghast.

'There!' gasped Rayo on the threshold, pointing away northward where the sun sparkled on the spearpoints of a troop of constabulary cavalry, riding along the main road. Already the thunder of hoofs could dimly be heard. They would be upon them within minutes.

'Horses! Get the horses!' went up the cry, and there was chaos as grooms and riders hurried to saddle and harness panicked, whinnying beasts.

'It's too late,' muttered Balian as his wide-eyed servant impelled his mount towards him. 'We'll never make it.'

Nevertheless, most were mounted in short time and urging their horses away along lanes and tracks or open fields. Taian and his party must remain together or be scattered across territory largely unknown to them. There were eight of them, including servants, and they had barely emerged from the tavern yard and out into the high road when their pursuers were upon them.

The troopers, twenty or so, slowed, brought down their spearpoints and spread across the road from ditch to ditch so that no living creature could pass. The four dark-clad investigators at their head rode boldly forward, crying out for Taian and his party to halt or be slain, their broad-hatted leader raising aloft the warrant for their arrest. Taian's men looked uncertainly to the prince for their prompt – whether to flee, to surrender or to fight – although their would-be captors surely outnumbered them three to one. A wild exuberance gripped Taian, a momentary sense that this was it, the end of all things, and it would be better to die in glory than at the end of a rope or on the executioner's block. Without hesitation, he drew his sword.

'At them, boys!' he roared, and set spurs to his black mare, urging her forward across the clattering cobbles of the road. After momentary glances of puzzlement, exhilaration or resignation, depending on the individual, his party surged after him. Adala urged her grey palfrey in pursuit, gripping the reins tightly and gasping with anxiety.

Within moments, there was the usual chaos and cacophony of cavalry combat: rearing, lurching horses, hooves flying and steel clashing as the two parties collided. Taian's blade parried a blow that would have decapitated him, had it connected, and he stabbed at the unshielded side of a rider on his other side. A man tumbled, shrieking. An ill-directed spear slid past him, but another struck his mare before the saddle and she screamed, lurching downwards, so that he lost his balance, gasped and tumbled, dropping his sword, clawing at the air.

Adala, wheeling on the edge of the fray, screamed also, a wavering wail of despair as she saw her prince fall. Something changed in her during that moment. A supernatural power seized her in its fist. It was as though the world slowed around her, blurred at the periphery of her vision and became intensely clear at its forefront. A cold rage gripped her, and a measureless energy flooded through every atom of her being. Her mare surged forward, possessed of the same heedless elemental power, and she plunged into the fray, snatching a raised sword from a swinging arm, as a man might pluck a trinket from a baby, and swinging it about her with a force no flesh or forged steel could resist. So slow, so slow, those futile blades came questing, so easy to flick them aside and follow the path of blade and arm to armpit or throat. Moments trickled past, in which a man fell away from her, mouth stretched in a rictus of pain. She rose in her saddle, stabbed and slashed with heedless abandon, her palfrey rising and falling beneath her with the violence of its motions. Impressions crowded in on her: terror-wide eyes, heads and throats that erupted blood in great vivid flying gouts, rearing, lurching horses, a shattered sword, a screaming man with an arm severed at the elbow, regarding it horror-struck, the rumps of galloping horses, backs turned, many backs turned, cloaks flying, hooves pounding, a man's pale face that spared a shocked glance over his shoulder. It was over. It was over, and Adala steadied her mount, lowered her bloody blade and looked around her. Already the power was leaching from her and an icy chill seized her veins. She shuddered, gasped and darkness rose up to engulf her.

'Is she alright? Is she alright? She must be alright!' stammered Taian, leaning over her whilst Jory placed a cloak beneath her head and shoulders.
'I caught her before she hit the ground', he said. 'It's only a faint, I think'.
'She's mortal pale', observed Balian, having dismounted and knelt at her side.
'What did I just see?' gasped Rayo, gripping Balian's arm. 'What in Hell's name did I just see?'
'Tio's work, I think', answered Balian, lifting her wrist to take her pulse.
'And that from an atheist', laughed Jory, glancing about him.
'Ex-atheist', grunted Balian. 'I don't know how to explain it, else'.
'Are you alright, my lord?' asked Rayo, turning to Taian, who was crouched at his young wife's side now, gently stroking her brow.

'Just bruises', he murmured. 'Nothing of consequence. It'll mend'.

'Did you see that?' demanded Ardani, one of Balian's two servants, to his brother, Gadoc. 'She put a whole troop of cavalry to flight. Just her. On her own!'

'Wasn't natural', breathed Gadoc, holding his horse's bridle whilst soothing it with quiet words. 'I never saw anything like it. There was a light, was there not? Did you see it? Uncanny, I call it'.

It was true. Into the hectic melee a white thunderbolt had ridden. It was as though Adala had moved with unnatural speed, her body and her sword a glinting whirl of movement, such as to baffle and amaze the eye. And a strange light had shone from her, one that sparked and shimmered like sunlight on breeze-stirred dew. But now it was gone and her party spoke amongst themselves in low voices whilst a physician was summoned from the nearby priory. Abandoned horses were rounded up. Adala's own was found standing in the corner of an orchard, wild-eyed and trembling. Four troopers and two men garbed in the black uniform of the investigators lay dead in the road. Another trooper lay in a roadside ditch and expired quietly of his injuries within a short time. None of Taian's party was injured beyond bruises and the occasional superficial cut. Jory became conscious of a slash to his upper arm, but it was not deep and should heal well when bound. He grimaced, though, as the shock faded and pain crept in to assail him.

'They'll be back, you know', said Balian in a low voice. 'That unit commander's going to send forth his whole force, and I daresay he'll be sending despatches back to Vannistar and The City, too'.

Various voices hushed him, since concern remained focused on the stricken girl, but at length her eyes sprang open and she sighed, and concern gave way to relief.

'Is all well?' she asked drowsily.

'All is very well, my dear', replied Taian, kissing her brow. 'Very well, indeed. How do you fare?'

Adala was about to say that she was quite well, although perhaps a little dazed, but upon trying to sit up she found that every muscle in her body felt as if it had been torn. She cried out and slumped back into Taian's arms, tears streaking her cheeks.

'Her body has been cruelly abused by the unnatural force that possessed it', muttered Jory in an aside to Rayo. 'Imagine if your frame were obliged to move with such speed and violence'.

'I'm sure you're right, but Balian speaks truly. We must be away', advised Rayo, looking along the empty highway in the direction from which the troopers had arrived. 'How far is the border?'

'Twenty miles, perhaps', shrugged Jory.

'Then I think we should seek refuge there', continued Rayo, his cheerful face uncharacteristically grave. 'I doubt we will find a place of safety in this province now. It will be crawling with our foes'.

'You are right', agreed Taian, having helped Adala carefully to her feet. 'Can you sit a horse, my dear?'

'It seems that I must', she groaned, clutching at her side. 'But I don't know that I can'.

'There must be a light gig or some such contrivance in the tavern stables', suggested Balian. 'Gadoc, Dani, go and see what you can find'.

The two young men pushed through the press of chattering village folk that had gathered, muttering amongst themselves variously of miracles and sorcery, witchcraft or saints, according to their suspicions or inclinations, whilst Taian's party urgently checked saddlebags and tack, sending to the kitchens for dry provisions and drink. A long ride lay ahead.

Chapter Seventeen

Perdannor

Sleep that night was, of necessity, taken at the roadside in a sheltered hollow that gave some respite from the wind that had arisen. It was bitter cold, and it was deemed impractical to start a fire, given their proximity to their enemy. In truth, there were enemies on all sides. To follow the main road south to the border would entail crossing territory patrolled from the constabulary forts that guarded this region. Instead, it was necessary to travel on one of the lesser ways, a road that became little more than a rutted track in places, winding through rough country, where the use of wheeled vehicles soon became wholly impractical. After no more than four leagues, it had been found necessary to abandon the light cart that Adala lay in and oblige her to mount a horse. She slept uneasily now, but all well remembered her stifled cries, the agony in her face as she endured the first few hours. The journey had been a torment to her. Huddled in blankets, putting this from their minds, the company leaned against each other for warmth, their breath silver in the moonlight.

'I hope you are right', muttered Balian to Jory. 'Who is to say that the King of Zanyawe won't simply bring us back to the frontier and turn us over to the emperor's tender mercies?'

'The king's writ barely runs in these northern parts', said Jory. 'My brother was here as part of the diplomatic mission at the end of the last war. The Earl of Perdannor offers compliments and tribute to the king, but the king is far away in the South, and the earl does as he pleases. He will surely ride to war with the king, if the king demands it, but until then he is more interested in squabbling with his neighbour, the Earl of Boronor'.

'And he will receive us well, do you suppose?' asked Taian, cradling Adala's head upon his lap.

'I do not know', admitted Jory. 'He is said to be ambitious to encroach on the emperor's domain. He may offer us support and succour'.

'At a price', grunted Taian. 'You can be sure his support would command a hefty price in gold or in land'.

'On the other hand, he may simply present you to the emperor', observed Balian. 'Doubtless, your grace's head would likewise command a high price'.

'Why, thank you for that observation', cried Rayo ironically. 'I usually rely on Jory, here, for my daily encounter with doom'.

'He's right', said Taian soberly. 'Of course he is. In these lands our fate is not in our hands. But what is the alternative? I doubt that we can find safety in Vannistar for now. Perhaps we may cross these borderlands and the mountains in the West out yonder, cross back into imperial territory in Acra'.

'Perhaps, my lord', murmured Jory. 'Although that also would be a long and perilous road. We are not equipped, and...'

His dimly seen gesture towards Adala caused all them to fall silent as they contemplated the fact that she seemed unfit to undertake any arduous journey at present. An owl hooted in the woods, and far away a fox barked. The party drew their cloaks more tightly around them and set jaws against chests to stop their teeth from chattering.

'They will call it witchcraft, you know', observed Balian. 'They will say she is a witch or a sorcerer, and if they catch her, she will burn for it. The emperor controls the newssheets, and the High Patriarch is his cousin now. The church will support him'.

'Well, those who support us will not believe it', said Rayo tetchily. 'They will acclaim her a saint. Besides, how do we know that what we saw derived from Adala at all? It may have been a manifestation of *your* power once more, Balian. We know you are the chosen one, singled out by your predecessor, regardless of your inclinations. We know that you can channel the will of Tio, whether you choose to admit it or not'.

'I do not deny it', admitted Balian. 'I have come to accept it, although it is an inconvenient power that cannot be wielded at will'.

'But you knew before anyone that those troops were on their way. How so?' demanded Jory. 'How could you have known unless through your connection to the divine?'

'Yes. Of course. I have considered that, but I do not think that it was I who wrought that extraordinary transformation upon Adala'.

'Nor do I', said Taian, looking up from gazing upon his wife's sleeping face. 'You are aware that she slew the brigand who assaulted her on the road to Annagaar?'

'Certainly', agreed Rayo amongst the general awkwardness and disquiet that attended any discussion of Adala's travails. All had heard of the assault upon her and her sister – and of her reaction to it.

'Drael saw her kill him', continued Taian. 'And he tells me that the knife she used was directed with uncommon skill and force. It was not a blow such as a slight young woman could have struck, penetrating six inches of flesh and bone as it did. No, Tio moves through Adala. He did then and he did earlier today. I am sure of it. Like Balian, she is a conduit for his power. Like Balian, she may not independently direct that power. Unlike Balian, the power is directly channelled through her body... and I fear it may destroy her'.

The anguish in his voice caused all of them to cast their eyes down. Silence fell once more, broken only by the soughing of the wind through the gaunt, black branches of the trees.

'But Tio is with us', observed Taian at last, in more measured tones. 'So, we must believe. And it seems our cause is his'.

'Interesting news on the semaphore line from Vannistar', said Triado the next morning, striding into the empress's dressing room, where her maids were laying out clothes and combing her hair. A clap of the emperor's hands sufficed to dismiss them, hurrying them out in the self-effacing manner essential to their role.

'News?' asked Cresara, raising an elegant eyebrow whilst turning in her chair.

'Indeed', said Triado, seating himself on the edge of her dressing table and looking down upon her complacently. 'It appears that the local investigators tracked your reinvigorated stepson down and came close to bringing him in, he and his confederates'.

'They came close, you say?' asked Cresara.

The news of Taian's survival, first a rumour, then an increasingly uncontested fact, was one of the few disappointments of the first years of the new reign. Mordanios assured her that his own attentions should have ensured the prince's neutralisation as a threat, regardless or not of his abduction. The accumulation of toxins in his body should have rendered him permanently insensible, relying on the regular administration of fluids and liquid foods simply to maintain his vital functions. If it were true that he had recovered, and the evidence of this was increasingly hard to ignore, then the nature of that cure was beyond the doctor's knowledge or experience, beyond his power to explain.

Not that it mattered. So Cresara assured herself. Everyone of significance had gazed upon the prince's dead face three years previously and seen him pass into his tomb. The person inconveniently at large in the remoter parts of the realm could safely be dismissed as an imposter and a deceiver, one that would struggle to gather support and would live perpetually with the fear of the investigators at his heel. It was a threat that could be managed. At least this was what she assured herself.

'Close', agreed Triado. 'They slipped through the net on this occasion, but the region is on high alert now. Every road, every byway is under observation. They must surely be run to ground now. Where can they run?'

'I believe you are about to tell me', observed Cresara, studying her elegant nails, most of which remained unpainted.

'I am', grinned Triado. 'We have flushed them out and now they must run in the only direction they *can* run'.

'South?'

'South, and thereby into the arms of the Earl of Perdannor, a particular friend of mine, although the world must remain forever ignorant of that circumstance'.

'I'm sure', nodded Cresara. 'Or the world would surely censure you'.

'And there was talk of witchcraft', added Triado, moving things hurriedly on.

'Witchcraft?'

'There was a skirmish; our troops were bested against inferior numbers, it appears. I suppose it is natural enough that they should ascribe it to supernatural forces, to spare their embarrassment. There was a young woman, I am told, who fought with demonic strength. Nonsense, of course'.

'Of course. Peasant superstition. I'm surprised that you should mention it'.

'Yes', Triado's eyes seemed momentarily distant. 'Still', he continued, 'the trap closes, I believe. It will be good to be rid of this... irritation'.

'And how go the preparations for the games?' asked Cresara, seeing that the emperor sought respite from this topic.

'Oh very well!' said Triado, brightening. 'Very well indeed! You must wait to see my costume, but I am convinced you will be surprised and delighted'.

Cresara smiled. The games, with their attendant masques, balls, banquets and theatrical productions, were in honour of the emperor's birthday, although in truth barely a month went by without some elaborate celebration. Last month it had been Ternate, the midwinter festival, when days began to lengthen once more. Before that it had been their glad duty to celebrate the anniversary of the foundation of The City with parades, history plays and fireworks, all accompanied by the usual amusements for the court and for foreign dignitaries.

'The empire must be splendid in the eyes of the world', the empress had once declared, when her husband had uncharacteristically baulked at the cost and elaboration of the jewelled headdress she had commissioned. 'Prestige, glory and self-confident display are the currencies of power, are they not, husband? And we shall want for none of them'.

Triado, then at the outset of his reign, might have reflected that arms, and the hard men to manage them, were the most convertible currency of all, but he rarely contradicted his formidable wife unless the issue was a vital one. Besides, he soon came to embrace such frivolities with a passion that matched her own.

'I am intrigued', she cooed, narrowing her eyes in a conspiratorial manner and giving his thigh a nudge. 'And what of the Count of Drumnestro? I trust your strutting peacock will make a spectacular display'.

The Count of Drumnestro, one Danilo Mellisantos, was a rising star at court, having come to the emperor's attention at one such festival. A graduate of the military academy, he had shoulder-length blonde locks and looks that won him the admiration of male and female alike. In addition to these attributes, his languid wit and his skill in the martial arts of sword and lance soon saw him singled out for Triado's devotion. He became a master-at-arms, a gentleman of the bedchamber, trusted informal advisor and the emperor's lover within months, such was the dizzying trajectory of his rise at court. With this place in the emperor's affections, and his bed, came wealth undreamed of by his humble Northern clan. In addition to a succession of rich presents and honorific titles, the young man was elevated to the title of Count of Drumnestro within the duchy of Arken, and he was rumoured to have his sights set on the supreme prize of a ducal title at last. Naturally, this excited jealously and suspicion. Those who coveted Drumnestro's influence, or envied his good looks and his good fortune, grumbled amongst themselves and murmured darkly of those legendary birds that approached too nearly to the sun, only to be scorched and destroyed.

The brilliant young count was sure to participate in the coming tournament, was sure to compete in the jousting against the emperor himself, in fact. The Count of Drumnestro had often been pierced by the emperor's lance, according to wags of all sexual inclinations. Nor did the emperor deny this dalliance despite the dignified and tight-lipped disapproval of his wife. His tastes were famously diverse. His eye fell on male and female alike with equal approval. On more than one occasion, the emperor had quipped that the doe and the stag made equally good chase and was apt to apply the same standards with regard to sexual pursuit. For her part, Cresara made no complaint and ventured no criticism of him even amongst her closest confidantes. She was content to allow the emperor his amusements, so long as he was attentive to his duties in her own bed. The last pregnancy had come to its baleful conclusion at twenty-eight weeks, precipitating a period of deep gloom and introspection in which the empress had barely shown her face in public. But now she had set that pain and disappointment behind her, at least so far as she was prepared to admit.

'He is to be arrayed as the Swan Knight', said the emperor. 'All in dazzling white with great wings upon his back and silver inlaid armour. For my part, I shall be the Sun King. My shield... well, you shall see in due course. I should not spoil your anticipated pleasure and the delight thereof. I trust the weather will comply'.

'We must hope so', agreed the empress, sharing her husband's recollection of the expensively bedraggled spectacle that last year's thunderous cloudburst had wrought. 'Truly we must hope so'.

The rain coursed down at that moment upon a castle in the border country, a region that had once been a core province of the empire but now belonged to the Zanyari Earl of Perdannor, having belonged to his father and his grandfather for a hundred years or so. The castle itself was owned by a petty baron by the name of Raykob, whose obedience to the earl was of the same kind as the earl's obedience to their king. From his strong tower, perched high on a spur above a narrow valley, Raykob looked out upon a land that looked to him – and him alone – for its protection. He exercised no such vigilance now. Instead, he stood in a high stone chamber with Taian and his party, pondering whether to declare that they were guests or indeed captives, but leaving that vital status undeclared for now. If they should stir themselves to leave, a decision would be forced upon him, but so long as they were content to drink his drink and eat his food, the die need not yet be cast.

Adala slept peacefully in a room upstairs with Raykob's womenfolk to attend to her. Balian's servants idled in the kitchens, flirting with the servant girls and trying their tongues with the rough Zanyari and corrupted Erenori that was the patois in these parts.

'You are a prince, I am told', said Raykob, crossing to the fire and rubbing his hands in front of it.

He had just returned from one of the more distant villages that owed him allegiance and had shrugged off his sodden rain cloak in the passage downstairs, before mounting the steps to his hall, two at a time. His steward had told him that a patrol had brought in a party of strangers from the northern lands. They had been looked after and accommodated until the baron's return. Now, once the steward had introduced his master, that lord turned to face the party with an expectant air.

'Your information is correct', said Taian, standing now, having risen from the table at which they had eaten their meal. The others were standing, too, wearing variously wary or anxious expressions. 'I am Prince Taian Starcorides, son of the late emperor Gelon'.

Taian had been about to list the various honorifics attendant on that imperial title, but standing as a supplicant in a foreign baron's hall and claiming to rule the whole continent of Toxandria, as was traditional, seemed pretentious at best. Instead, he merely held his head high and looked Raykob in the eye, in what he hoped was a proud and dignified manner.

'I had heard that you were dead', grunted Raykob, warming his rump at the fire.

'Then you were misinformed', said Taian with a grim smile. 'Although there are many that would wish to make that fiction fact'.

'And these, fellows...?' asked Raykob, having silently considered Taian's statement for some moments.

Taian made his introductions, whilst Raykob drew up his own chair and bade them all be seated once more. He was not tall, but he was barrel-chested and strong as an ox, his bald head gleaming but his chin furnished with a huge black beard that spread across his broad chest. His Erenori was fluent but strongly accented.

'I see', he said, reaching for a jug and pouring himself a mug of beer. 'Am I to regard this incursion as an invasion? Yours is a small expedition, is it not? The last invasion ended in grief and ignominy, as I recall, with your late father dashing out his brains on a rock not twenty leagues away. Very tragic. If you wish to subdue us, perhaps you should have thought to bring legions with you, perhaps some of your famous cannons that speak thunder and shit fire. No, I fear this is a very paltry invasion – and one that can result in no conquest, no glory, no accession of territory to your imperial realm. Zanyawe does not tremble before your reputation and your name alone, and you may be sure that you will receive no abasement or submission in this hall'.

Raykob made this statement with a wry smile, punctuated here and there by pensive swigs of ale. At the end, he threw his head back and laughed, thumping the table in a manner that caused his visitors a collective twitch of anxiety.

'So why have you come here?' he asked now, head cocked to one side, mug embraced to his breast. 'Do you wish to enrich me? I wager a considerable chest of gold will come my way from the grateful Emperor Triado if I hand you over to his officials. But I cannot believe you would be so magnanimous, so altruistic as to bestow such riches upon a simple border chief'.

'I come simply to make an offer of future favour, should I recover the throne that is rightfully mine', said Taian awkwardly, all too conscious of the precarious position their flight had placed them in. 'If we may beg to be favoured with your hospitality for a while'.

He explained the circumstances of their skirmish with the investigators and their troops, making much of the support for his cause that was growing in every corner of the empire. Raykob listened attentively, gesturing with a hand to require further detail where necessary.

'And this young woman upstairs? She is your wife, I gather. I trust she brings no sickness with her'.

'Not at all', insisted Taian. 'She is merely exhausted by the rigours of our journey'.

'Is she now? Hmm', murmured Raykob whilst regarding Taian with interest and swilling beer around his mouth.

An elderly woman came into the room, sparing the briefest of glances for the prince's party before advancing to the baron and speaking softly in his ear. He nodded thoughtfully. The woman turned to gaze upon the faces of the party now, regarding each of them with solemn intensity. When her eye fell upon Balian, she gasped and her eyes sprang open. She hurriedly made a sign in the air before her, cast her eyes upward and returned to mutter once more into the baron's ear.

'My mother is a seer', explained the baron. 'A holy woman in our faith and a priestess of Maia. I am a practical man, and I give little thought to what I may not see or confidently expect to see, so you may be sure I stand in no fear of wholly notional powers. She tells me that the young woman upstairs possesses an aura, however, and the same is true of this fellow here. An aura, of all things! The mark of divinity, it is said, or at least of the touch of it. Hmm. Why might this be? I suspect that you have not been as forthcoming with me as you might have been. Which is unwise of you, given that I can easily deliver unto the grateful emperor a sack of your severed heads. I expect you will wish to tell me more'.

Motivated by this grim prospect, Taian told him more, describing the various occurrences that some might think showed evidence of divine favour.

'You are a lucky man, you know, a lucky princeling. Had you fallen in with my neighbour in yonder vale, you would certainly soon be on your way to endure your emperor's tender mercies'.

'He is not my emperor', grunted Taian. 'But why so?'

His spirits had risen remarkably at this disclosure and he felt emboldened to meet his host's gaze once more.

'Because, because, because', began the baron, refilling his mug, gesturing with the jug in case anyone else should desire a drop, and then setting it down once more. 'Because Maygar is a creature of Triado's', he continued. 'Because his castle is glazed with Callistene coloured glass and his rough walls hung with Vannistari silks, because his bed rides high on chests of Erenori gold lions and Garabdori wine flows in the Ericannan crystal goblets on his table. How do you suppose he came by such uncommon wealth?'

'I do not know', answered Taian cautiously.

'Well, perhaps you should hear it from a countryman', laughed Raykob, gesturing to one of the armed guards at the door. 'You! Go fetch the Erenori'.

Presently, the sound of footsteps and low conversation outside preceded the limping entry of a tall but stooping man into the room. He was perhaps thirty years old but already greying at the temples and with a great livid scar traversing one side of his face from temple to jaw.

'This gentleman looks after my falcons', said Raykob as the man regarded the party dispassionately, pursing his

lips and looking sidelong to his master for guidance.
'Perhaps you would care to introduce yourself', he added.
'My name is Gendrian Curopelantes', said the man.
'And perhaps you might explain how you came to be here', prompted Raykob mildly, drawing out a chair for him.

February 3975

It had snowed a little during the night, and the roof tops of The City were dusted with it like pastries under the new day's light that spilled out from the east. It would be another fine day but a cold one, and that orange glow brought with it little warmth as the shepherds blew swirling silvery clouds on chilled hands on their distant hills, or the mariners cursed icy ropes down on the city wharves. The poor stirred in their garrets, tormented by the smell of the bread rising in the streets, the bread that they may not eat. Merchants yawned and scratched their bellies as a new day of commercial enterprise dawned. As the sun ascended further in the heavens, these same golden rays slanted down to stream through the fine glass windows of the emperor's chambers, painting his walls with a soft geometry of coloured light. They picked out the fine and noble profile of Danilo Mellisantos, Count of Drumnestro, where he lay next to the emperor, his lithe, athletic body disclosed amongst silken sheets. The emperor, who had been awake for some moments, was content to lie and to watch the slow passage of the sun trace a golden path through the wisps and curls of fair hair that framed the young man's face. Triado, very much a creature of the flesh, was not much given to abstract thought, but on this beautiful morning and in this beautiful moment, the notion of eternity came into his mind. Together with this came the connected concept of impermanence, of the ephemeral nature of beauty and the inexorable onward march of time. "Seize the day" had forever been his motto, an axiom that had guided him to this pinnacle of worldly success, but days and hours and instants trickled through his fingers like sand through a glass, and the grave yawned always in the back of his mind. Death stood always at his shoulder, ready to still his beating heart. But not yet, not yet, and every day must throw in death's dark face the dazzling glory of a life well lived.

'Uhhhhh', moaned the love of Triado's life, lifting an arm to shade his eyes. 'What hour is it?'

'Past seven', said the emperor, having glanced at the clock above the mantel. 'Do not stir yourself yet. Let us enjoy the moment. Let us live in the instant'.

Danilo turned his head, his tanned face contrasting splendidly with the clear bright blue of his eyes and the even whiter teeth as he smiled.

'There can never be too many moments with you, my lord', he said.

He might have mentioned that his head ached furiously with last night's wine, and his bladder importuned him with its own needs, but he was nothing if not a calculating observer of the emperor's moods, and so he lay back on his pillow and submitted to the man's caresses, his gentle stroking of that smooth chest, with the appearance of ease.

'We are such a brief time on this earth', observed the lord of a goodly share of it. 'And it behoves us to pile up riches while we can, does it not?'

'Surely, it does', agreed Danilo with every particle of his being. 'For we are a long time dead, as I believe it is said. You are troubled, dear', he continued, placing his own hand on the emperor's. 'What ails you?'

'Only the sense that we must exult in the moment', replied the emperor. 'And this is a golden one with you at my side'.
'Is there nothing more that you could want?' asked Danilo.
'Nothing. I am content. This moment is entire unto itself', sighed the emperor. 'I have everything that I could want. And what of you?' he added, meeting his lover's eyes.
'I have piled up the envy of the court', laughed Danilo. 'And the gold and honours that you have lavished upon this humble servant. I am rich beyond my dreams, but the richest jewel that I possess is the love that you have declared for me, the love that I reciprocate with all my heart. That is the wealth that I celebrate with every beat of my heart. To be admitted to your company, to stand at your side as your companion, ranked almost as highly as your noblest peers'.
'Almost', said the emperor after a moment, provoking a little thrill of satisfaction in his companion, and then again. 'Almost'.
'Not that it matters to me', said Danilo, squeezing the emperor's hand. 'What does rank signify, after all? It must surely satisfy those lords to see that the emperor's pleasure knows some limits at last, that some mere mortals may never be admitted to their illustrious company'.
Triado threw back his head and laughed.
'Really! Your ambition truly knows no bounds, Danilo! You are quite, quite immoral, I do declare!'
'It is why you love me', said Danilo in a small, coy voice.
'I do', nodded Triado. 'And I have already made you a count, but that is not enough, it seems. Only a duchy would satisfy your craving for rank and glory. Is that it?'
'The robes are so pretty', mused Danilo, tickling the emperor's chin. 'And my mother would be so proud. It would give her such great pleasure to crow amongst her

friends. Besides, you are the emperor. You can do as you please. You are truly the only free man in the empire. And we are living in this glorious moment, as I recall'.

'And the next moment will see a furious muttering amongst my noble dukes if you are admitted to their ranks, my dear. You must see that. It is always inconvenient to dispose of those who overstep the mark with their objections, and I fear that some of them would make those objections broadly known'.

'Of course', said Danilo, sliding his hand beneath the sheet, his lip curling lasciviously. 'It is folly even to aspire to such a thing when there are more glorious moments to be made'.

'I shall consider it', murmured the emperor as they embraced.

Chapter Eighteen

Callisto

The Duke of Vollangor was too old for the joust; too old, in fact, for any of the competitions of martial skill that the tournament encompassed. Nor was his temperament suited to the absurd and fanciful displays of costume that the court was required to engage with, once the fading light brought a close to the games. Those ambitious to rise in the emperor's favour put forth their wealth in furs, feathers, velvets and taffetas, in the hope that they might catch the approving eye of the imperial couple. The Duke of Vollangor, a grizzled veteran of a dozen wars, was a simple man, so he told himself, the enemy of pretension and of ostentation. The animal world was the theme of this event, and all manner of elaborate costumes were to be seen, ranging from butterflies to fish. The duke's face, behind its scowling wolf mask, wore a scowl of its own, and his eye darted frequently to the big clock at the end of the vast ballroom. Convention required that he attend this masked ball in celebration of the emperor's birthday, but he attended it with ill grace, and the costume that he wore, at his wife's insistence, was hot and uncomfortable. 'A wolf, of all things', he had objected, when it was brought forth. 'Do you think I should wish to drape myself with furs when that hall is always infernally overheated'.
'Well, if you had wished to commission an alternative, you should have done so weeks ago', she told him in that familiar tone of voice that made him feel like a small child. 'Besides, it looked very well on you last year, and with the new embellishments no one will remember that you have worn it before'.

But they would. Vollangor knew that they would, and they would say that he valued economy above wholehearted commitment to the common enjoyment of the court and the celebration of the reign. Which he did, of course, but it was damned inconvenient to have foppish young creatures looking askance at him, giggling foolishly and whispering behind their fans.

Reaching for a drink, from a tray borne by a passing servant, Vollangor's eye fell on the Duke of Vannistar, a man of similar age and disposition. It was likely that Vannistar's discomfiture approached his own, although his costume, that of a woodpecker, appeared to offer more respite from the heat. Certainly, although the upper part of his face was concealed by a colourful beaked mask, the lower part allowed peevishly pursed lips to be displayed to the world.

'How do you do, Vannistar?' called Vollangor, gesturing with his drink.

'Huh?' Vannistar enquired, cocking his head on one side, giving him a genuinely bird-like appearance, but despite insistent repetition, Vollangor was unable to make himself heard over the music and the hubbub of conversation. Instead, despairing of further attempts at communication in this context, the wolf drew the woodpecker aside into an ante-chamber, where there were seats amongst large potted plants and ferns, and where ices were being served at the further end. Here it was quieter; here both men's retinues could be required to maintain a discreet distance whilst their lords conversed. Vollangor tilted up his mask to reveal his fleshy, sweating face, an unhealthy shade of red.

'Too old for this damned nonsense', he grunted.

'And too corpulent', observed Vannistar, who was stick thin himself. 'It appears that you approach apoplexy. You must surely set aside that coat, sir, at least for a while, unless you resign yourself to inviting imminent stroke or to...'

'I thank you for your concern, sir', interrupted Vollangor, undoing a number of buttons and fanning ineffectually at himself. 'I swear I have not set eyes on you at court in recent times. I trust you have not been indisposed'.

'My health is a delicate flower, as you know', admitted Vannistar, having tilted back his own mask, in order to better sip at his wine.

Vollangor was very much aware that his companion's absence from court had derived more from a reluctance to be drawn into the disloyal gossip or critical conversation that had permeated the court during the course of the last year. There had been a palpable atmosphere of fear, an atmosphere where even the most innocent of conversations took place under conditions of severe self-censorship. The empress's spies were everywhere, it was said. Those whose rank placed them at the top of the social pyramid were largely immune from the immediate enquiries of the investigators, unlikely to face summary arrest and interrogation, but they could readily be drawn into the circle of suspicion, if those whose rank was less exalted than their own were too free with their tongues.

'I have heard', agreed Vollangor. 'Although I have also heard that our presence at court pleases the emperor, that he likes his friends to be in close attendance. There are those around him, persons of a base and mischievous nature, who may whisper that such persistent lurking in the provinces stems not from frailty of health but from an inclination to engage in treasonable activity beyond the immediate scrutiny of the authorities'.

'So I gather', said Vannistar, glancing about him anxiously, as though spies might be concealed amongst the ferns. 'What are you suggesting, Vollangor? Do you accuse me of sedition, of plotting against the emperor?'

'I do not', laughed Vollangor, 'because I know you to be an exceptionally cautious man'.

'A loyal, steady man, I should hope', protested Vannistar, eyes narrowing. 'I take it that is what you mean'.

'I'm sure that's how you regard yourself', observed Vollangor. 'And yet I fancy your good opinion of the emperor and his regime faces assault from his actions on a daily basis, is daily undermined by his greed and his perfidy'.

Vannistar stiffened, as if he had been slapped, and his face assumed an unhealthy pallor.

'You presume too much, sir!' he stuttered.

'Do I? Do I indeed? Well, I do know that every man's loyalty to his sovereign has a breaking point, when he may endure no more capricious injustice, and honour must rise above expediency'.

'Your speech is most injudicious, Vollangor', grumbled to his companion. 'I tire of this conversation. You must exc...'

Vannistar attempted to rise from his seat but found himself restrained by Vollangor's firm pressure on his arm.

'That gentleman', nodded Vollangor, as the Count of Drumnestro hove briefly into view beyond the ferns and palms, surrounded by a group of fawning toadies and admirers, 'that gentleman has risen high in the esteem of the emperor, and he is said to be most talented, most deserving of elevation even to the highest ranks'.

'Pah! A preening peacock!' scoffed Vannistar, now apparently setting aside the discretion that was his habit.

'Indeed, and one that has set his eyes on a duchy, I am reliably informed', said Vollangor, leaning close.

'A duchy! Absurd! The man is a parvenu. His blood is of the most undistinguished kind, his qualifications...'

'And yet his ambition knows no bounds, and the emperor values him highly. Very highly indeed. Should a title become vacant, I believe he may be minded to accommodate him'.

'Which title?' asked Vannistar, eyes wide, now.

'Your own title, sir', said Vollangor with a satisfied grin. 'Your own, should you relinquish it'.

'What do you mean, relinquish it? Why would I relinquish my title?'

'You are of relatively advanced years, you will forgive me for observing', continued Vollangor, toying absently with his wolf mask. 'And your health is not of the best, as you are happy to admit. Who knows when the Lord may choose to gather you to his embrace?'

'Or when others might hasten it', said Vannistar suspiciously. 'I trust that is your implication'.

'I do not assert it as fact, but I do allow it as a very real possibility. Or alternatively, should it be found that you have entered into treasonable relations with those who would wish to cast down the emperor, in a manner offensive in the eyes of God and injurious to the good of the realm...'

'None shall accuse me of such infamy', interjected Vannistar in outraged tones. 'I am guilty of no such...'

'Tell me, old friend, do you think that the mere absence of such evidence should constitute an effectual bar to the making of that accusation? How long have you dwelt on this imperfect earth, amongst these imperfect creatures, fallen so far from the throne of heaven?'

Vollangor's broad gesture encompassed the great hall beyond, the raucous revellers of the imperial court.

'You accuse me of naivety'.

'You have a son that you dote on, a fine young man'.

'What are you saying?'

'A son that you would wish to do well in the world but might be cast down, might he not, if his illustrious father were to be stripped of his title, might ascend to the executioner's block at last'.

'I do not recognise this picture that you paint', said Vannistar after a few moments in which his lips worked silently.

'I think you do'.

'The emperor faces no evident threats. The army is entirely his. There is no obvious alternative'.

'Oh, but there is', insisted Vollangor, looking full into the old duke's face. 'There is Prince Taian'.

Vannistar blinked.

'Prince Taian? He is dead. Everyone knows he is dead'.

'He is *not* dead, as you would know if you had not shut yourself up in your castle for so long. He is at large out there in the provinces. He is very much alive and his name is on the lips of many who murmur at the outrages perpetrated by the emperor and his creatures'.

'This talk is treason. You know this', said Vannistar slowly.

'I am not a prisoner to fear, Vannistar, and once, long ago, you had a reputation for courage, too'.

For a long time, Vannistar's face remained impassive, although his eyes appeared fixed inflexibly on a spot beyond his companion's shoulder.

'Tell me more', he said at last.

'I am... was... a retainer of General Triado Melanthros', began Gendrian hesitantly, glancing about his audience. 'He that is now emperor of the Erenori. I served with him in the most recent campaign. I was with him, at his side, when your father died, my lord, blessèd be his name'.

His eyes met Taian's now, and the prince's posture stiffened.

'Aye, I saw him fall that day and the black rock... take his life', he finished judging it indelicate to speak of spilt brains in this context.

'Go on', urged Raykob when Gendrian's voice faltered.

'And, having secured the scene and arranged for camp to be established, my lord rode away with us to bring tidings of the emperor's death, taking with him only myself and my friend, Tustin. We rode eastward along a stream towards the secondary column, led by your brother, sir', he said, casting a respectful nod in Taian's direction. 'But he halted and had us draw aside in the cover of some woods, saying that he wished to wait until nightfall, when the prince would be encamped, before conveying the ill-tidings to him. Then he went off to scout about, so he said, bidding us remain in our places. When he returned, after more than an hour, we continued to deliver our news, and the prince, as you may expect, was keen to confer with his generals as quickly as may be expedient. We rode out with a troop of his guard but fell into an ambush on our road back. All were slain except my general, so it was said, and even he was knocked on the head and injured in the leg when found. But I survived, too'.

A nod and a deferential gesture for Raykob prompted their host to take up the story.

'I was riding with a party of my men, meaning to keep a close watch on Baron Maygar's band, since they absented themselves so suddenly from the earl's camp that night, and since Maygar's actions are rarely to my benefit. We came upon the scene of a battle, where scores of dead Erenori lay about in their fine armour. Guardsmen, by the looks of them, I judged. It was too late to go down amongst them and check the bodies for loot, and it was likely enough that Maygar's men would already have stripped them of what they could quickly take. Besides, the light was growing and we could see Erenori troops were coming up in force, so we thought it best to retire. We came upon this here fellow lying half-dead, where he had dragged himself into a gully above the stream, thereby saving his throat from being cut by my good friend Maygars' lads. Now, the armour and fittings made me think this is a hostage that might be worth the ransom in time, so we spirited him away and patched him up. I'm glad we did. He had a very interesting story to tell, as you have heard'.

'So what are you saying?' asked Jory of the Erenori. 'Are you saying Triado crept off to communicate with this Maygar fellow and arrange for him to ambush Cato's column?'

'I am', agreed Gendrian with a slow nod. 'Why else would he go off privately in the night? Tustin and I wondered about it, but it was not for us to question our lord. He had dealings with Maygar in the campaign down here back in 3969, so he knew him well enough. He must have promised him fabulous reward if he brought his men and fell upon the column as it rode west. Of course, there was the risk that Cato would escape or he, Triado, would be killed, but I imagine care was taken to ensure he was looked out for and spared from any but the most superficial harm'.

'And it worked', said Taian grimly. 'Fortune smiled upon him and my brother rode to his death, a victim of the most base treachery'.

'This could change everything', cried Rayo, eyes gleaming, 'if the lords and the senate come to hear of how Triado seized his blood-stained throne'.

'*If* is a big word in this context', said Raykob with a broad grin, causing Taian and his party to shut their mouths and curb their own smiles.

'What do you want?' asked Jory bluntly.

'Well', said Raykob, studying his fingernails. 'I have always wished to be a truly wealthy man'.

In his attic room, Tyverios Ohk sighed and set aside the inky quill that he had been plying inexpertly upon the papers before him. These held line after line of wobbly characters, intended to secure mastery of the fine control necessary for writing. Ohk now flexed the aching muscles of his right hand and looked upon his work with some satisfaction. His mistress had resolved that he should learn to read and write, had taken his education upon herself and set aside an hour each day to instruct him in her library. How Ohk's spirit soared that she should have devoted her time to him in this manner! She listened attentively when he read to her, when he learned to release the secrets of the printed page and his finger crept hesitantly along the lines, his voice in her inner ear. When his daily duties were complete, he spent long hours labouring beneath the lamp in this room, bringing the rebellious quill under the spell of his great hand. At last, he was succeeding, and his mistress's approval brought joy to his heart.

'You have no tongue to sing the songs of your people', she had told him as she announced her commitment to him. 'As you told me, once. But there are more ways than one of conveying them to the future, and I shall teach you to read and to write, should you will it. Do you will it, Ohk?'

'With all of my heart!' he had answered.

She was a harsh critic of his failings, of course, quick to condemn his faulty draughtsmanship or his stumbling over the more challenging combinations of vowels and consonants. And yet she persevered, and Ohk devoted himself to his labours with a determined and sustained commitment that many a schoolmaster, faced with a recalcitrant class of boys, would have envied. Ohk made progress, and as the months passed by, he began to see that the closed world of books might one day admit him to their secrets and that he might, himself, contribute there in time.

'Drael is here', she said inside his head. 'Would you come down?'

'Yes Ma'am', said Ohk, pushing back his chair.

Once, Ohk would have been required to attend to the door to admit their visitor, but now Bardo was employed for this and for other purposes besides. Likewise, a cook had been engaged and a maid to assist in the cleaning of the house. As Cortesia had predicted, the sale of her Marcutio had raised a princely sum, and the house had benefited accordingly. The roof no longer admitted water, regardless of the vagaries of the wind, and painters had been at work to brighten some of the more frequented rooms. The windows were undraped now during daylight hours, and the house seemed to have shrugged off gloom and torpor in the same manner as the chief amongst its residents.

She looked up now as Ohk made his entry, seeing that Drael and she were poring over a paper laid out on the big table before the windows.

'Refreshments, please, Ohk, but you may care to hear what Officer Drael has to tell us, first'.

'My contacts at the Directorate inform me that the prince and our friends have been obliged to seek exile in Zanyawe', informed Drael, stroking his chin pensively, having offered his greeting. 'Naturally they are sparing no effort to see to it that the Zanyari Earl of Perdannor may be induced to hand him over. So far without success, I might add, since the earl is unable to surrender what he does not have'.

Ohk's raised eyebrow, the slight tilt of his head, induced Drael to continue.

'As is made plain in this letter', he said with a gesture for the table. 'Received and decoded in the early hours of this morning. It is from Jory. He says that they have been kindly received and entertained by a Zanyari border baron and have since re-entered imperial territory, bringing with them another exile from that place. His name is Gendrian and he was once a retainer of the emperor. He has a most extraordinary story to tell. He tells us that he was left for dead on the battlefield when Prince Cato was slain. He tells us that he was carried away from that place by this same baron's men, thinking that a hostage might prove useful. He also tells us that the emperor treasonably colluded with the enemy to arrange the ambush of Prince Cato's party to his own advantage. The emperor's reign is built on treason, Ohk. He may not be guilty of Gelon's death, but he is certainly complicit in Cato's. What do you think of that?' he finished with one of his momentary tight smiles.

'Ohk wishes to know how this knowledge may be to our advantage', observed Cortesia, after listening to her servant's internal voice.

'Well, it certainly undermines the emperor's legitimacy', replied Drael. 'And anything that plucks at the sand beneath the foundations of his reign strengthens our own cause, does it not? Any lords seeking a banner of legal outrage to unite beneath, before venturing their revolt, may find it to their liking'.

'We must hope so', said Cortesia vehemently, taking the letter and crossing to the fire. 'But now such an incendiary document must itself be condemned to flames. If what you tell me is correct, Drael, the eye of suspicion may also have fallen upon this house'.

Once Raykob had accepted Taian's promise of future gold to recompense him for his troubles, life settled down into a comfortable pattern in the baron's castle, whilst winter assailed the walls and the lands beyond. Deep snow carpeted the land for week after week, and even had they desired to return to imperial territory, the incessant snowstorms, the impassibility of roads and tracks, must surely have prevented it. It was a time for recovery, relatively secure from the emperor's reach, and for the evolution of a plan by which they might proceed, once winter released its icy grip. Their journeys over the course of the previous months and years had assured them that they might command some support in the provinces, but sympathy and kind words were not enough. Something more radical needed to be attempted, unless they should accept permanent exile or the life of outlaws, forever looking over their shoulders and starting at shadows.

'The Duke of Acra could undoubtedly muster well over a thousand armed retainers, if he summons his counts and Margraves', Jory observed, studying the list laid out on the council table. And then there are the constabulary units, perhaps another thousand if they could be induced to stir'.

'*Could* be', laughed Rayo. 'A fine notional army takes shape before us, does it not? What have we by now? More than thirty thousand spears, is it? I swear that this is hopeless and we have marshalled these paper armies too many times before. It gets us nowhere'.

Rayo had sat silently, apparently absorbed with his own thoughts, whilst the others gauged the potential strength of an entirely notional revolt, as they had on so many occasions. Now he found all eyes directed at him.

'Well? What alternative do you suggest?' asked Jory wryly. 'We eagerly await the introduction of your proposal, the masterstroke that shall sweep our enemies aside'.

'Listen, then', instructed Rayo, standing up and stretching himself before the fire, turning his back on the table for a moment.

'We listen', said Taian quietly, toying with his goblet.

'We well know that many amongst the great in our land have promised their support, should a rebellion occur. We also know, or suspect, that no duke is eager to be the first to show his hand. If he does so, the full weight of the imperial might will descend upon him with the swiftness of a hawk upon a vole, and if his peers and his neighbours do not immediately stir, he is doomed. That is the quandary they face, even if they do not love the emperor, even if they cordially dislike him, in fact. I fear that it is all or none, when we consider the duchies, and until *all* can be guaranteed at a stroke, there will forever be *none*'.

'So what do you propose?' asked Adala, leaning close to her husband, having quite recovered her strength in recent weeks. 'I take it you would not weary us with this reiteration of our predicament unless you had conceived of a remedy'.

'Which of the dukes do you consider most amenable to our advances, should we propose taking arms?' asked Jory. 'Caneloon, behind all those marshes might...'

'No combination of ducal levies would be enough to take on the legions, should they march against us. Besides, we would have barely any artillery', retorted Rayo.

'Well what, then?' asked Taian, his brow now furrowed.

'We need to take The City', announced Rayo, his eyes blazing now. 'At the centre of all, and we need to secure the immediate support of the dukes, foremost amongst the nobility. Their counts and lesser lords will largely follow. The support of the senate would also be to our advantage'.

'So... what... do... you... propose?' demanded Jory irritably, as though interrogating a child.

'Simple', answered Rayo, beaming about him. 'We must go to The City and address our potential allies there'.

For a long moment, there was stunned silence, and then, at last, Taian laughed.

'The City', he said. 'Under Triado's nose with his bodyguard, the City Watch and the investigators all in attendance, and the First Legion standing by outside the walls? That would certainly be a bold stroke'.

'A final stroke', scoffed Jory. 'Have you taken leave of your senses?'

'Listen to him', urged Adala, pressing her husband's arm. 'Go on, Rayo'.

'When do we find the dukes all gathered together in The City?' asked Rayo, looking from face to face. 'Whenever there is a great festival, if I may answer my own question, and Triado dearly loves a great festival, does he not? The dukes and the greater counts dare not stay away, for fear that their absence may be mistaken for disloyalty. This we know. This we have gleaned from years of correspondence with them or their agents. So, should we address them altogether in The City, we can be sure that they may agree to rebel all as one'.

'So simple!' cried Jory ironically. 'We have only to hire a commodious hall and send out invitations to the noble lords, and we shall surely achieve the unanimity of thought and of action we desire in due course, as surely as night follows day. What a noble scheme. What could possibly hinder its inevitable success?'

'The tournament', continued Rayo with a pained expression. 'All the lords will be gathered there to watch beneath the emperor's gaze, and the emperor himself will compete. He is puffed up with pride at his skill in the joust and has never yet been unseated, because all fear the consequences of so doing, of course. Whoever is bold enough and skilful enough to knock him from his saddle shall take the prize and then, in accordance with tradition, be permitted to address the lords and the gathered masses there, a hundred thousand of them or more. The acoustics are beyond compare, of course, as we all know'.

'So', said Jory, 'as I understand it, you are proposing that Prince Taian enters the contest without first giving away his identity, defeat the undefeated jousting champion of the realm and, without restraint from the emperor and his men, successfully appeal to the gathered masses to depose Triado in his favour?'

'Yes', admitted Rayo, swallowing hard. 'I am'.
'Then you have clearly lost your mind', said Jory into the resultant heavy silence, regarding him incredulously.
Up to this point, Balian had kept his counsel, but now he raised a finger.
'If I may interject...' he began.

Chapter Nineteen

Perdannor

Balian had barely slept the previous night, or if he had slept, it had been a sleep of extraordinary intensity, extraordinary meaning. Tio came to him during those hours. He found himself pacing side by side with Tio on a vast and empty beach. Before him the white sand curved away into a hazy distance. To his right the surf sucked at the pebbles as it advanced and receded with a distant sigh. To his left paced a golden lion with great easy strides, white wings folded upon his back and eyes like liquid honey.

'It appears that you do not believe in me', said Tio. 'That you consider me to be a construct of folklore and human imagination, a being that dwells on the verge of reality'.

'I did once', admitted Balian. 'Although recent events have obliged me to reconsider. This event, for example. However, if you think that I shall worship you and pray to you, then I'm afraid you will be disappointed in me'.

'Worship is the currency of godhead', said Tio. 'My power is increased by the faith of my followers, diminished by their neglect. It has always been the way of things, even since the Creation. However, you may be sure that my might can withstand the withholding of a single mortal's prayers'.

'I am glad to hear it', answered Balian, regarding Tio sidelong, admiring the smooth lines of his flanks and the tousled splendour of his mane.

It was strange to find himself talking to God, but the dream-state enabled him to view this with a serene equanimity.

'Dare I ask why you singled me out and honoured me with this visitation?' he asked. 'Because I believe it is traditional that mortals should take the initiative in that respect'.

'You are correct', stated Tio. 'Mortals are forever importuning me, largely in vain, I should say. But you must understand that the Great Game lies delicately poised, that some form of intervention on my part is absolutely essential at this stage'.

'The Great Game?' asked Balian, pausing for a moment, brow furrowed.

'The Great Game that my brother and I play for mastery of this world', explained Tio, his head tilted to one side. 'Had you attended more in church, had your mind not been full of geometry and anatomy, you might have become aware of it through listening to the sermons of the priest, or through the urgings of scripture'.

'Well, yes', conceded Balian. 'I am aware of the Forever War between good and evil, the war that you fight with your brother Yuzanid until the End of Days'.

'It is to that which I refer', agreed Tio. 'And our war is fought out in the hearts and in the actions of mortal men. When Yuzanid's adherents advance the borders of their realms, so do mine contract, so does my strength diminish. Conversely, when soldiers advance to victory with my name on their lips, so is my kingdom strengthened and enlarged'.

'Well, why do we not see you two leading your troops on the battlefield, then?' asked Balian.

'Even gods are bound by the laws of their creators', observed Tio, his head momentarily cast down. 'And our power to intervene directly in the world's affairs is strictly limited by inflexible statute. Rather, must we fight our battles in the minds of men, apply our influence to the thoughts and deeds of those best placed to advance our cause, whether they be philosophers or kings. The wall between the worlds stands between us – and that wall is almost impenetrable to us'.

'But not quite', suggested Balian.

'Not quite', agreed Tio. 'There are places and times and individuals where that wall is thin, and where we may project a fraction of our power. You are such an individual, your friend Adala Radagarion is another'.

'So the last High Luminary, he who designated me as his successor, was correct to do so, although I long sought to deny it'.

'He was', agreed Tio. 'However, the Radagarion girl falls into a curious category, one that I might call a "wild card," if I may borrow an earthly analogy. She does not fit neatly within the rules of our engagement, and I sense that my brother resents it. He may seek to retaliate with some creature of his own'.

'I see', mused Balian, stepping forward once more. 'And what do you desire from me, since I must presume that your presence here is more than a mere social call?'

Tio laughed a throaty chuckle and flexed his wings so that brilliant white light sparkled from them.

'Well, dear Balian, it appears that godhead has no power to awe you, nor fear of the abyss to seal your lips. You are right to ask. It will not surprise you to hear that the fate of your earthly Erenori empire is very dear to my heart and that its present situation is perilous indeed. The current emperor and his wife are powerful agents for chaos, unwitting though they are, and Yuzanid delights in their reign, a reign, I may add, that threatens to dissolve in civil conflict highly injurious to my interests. Such unrest can only embolden the empire's foes and those who nurture Yuzanid in their dark hearts. I see along the path of years, and I see peril. I see the triumph of Yuzanid and my own enfeeblement written there'.

'I am sorry to hear it', said Balian, shaking his head.

'But such a disaster may yet be averted', replied Tio, earnestly now. 'Prince Taian is my shining hope, unfitted though he is to sit on a throne. However, he may yet serve to overthrow the odious Triado Melanthros and his wicked empress, and that would certainly advance my cause'.

'Why do you not simply strike them with a bolt of lightning or cause them to choke on their food or suffer a heart attack or apoplexy, or some such traditional divine contrivance', demanded Balian. 'Surely your powers would be sufficient unto it?'

'Oh dear', said Tio sadly, shaking his huge head. 'Have you not been listening at all? The wall between the worlds prevents me from intervening in so direct a manner, as it does my brother, or the world would be a sea of fire by now. Each of us has advantages to play, like pieces upon a games board. You are one such advantage that I propose to bring into play'.

'I'm not sure that I don't resent being a pawn in your chess game', muttered Balian.

'Resent it as you wish. However, you are too modest in your assessment of your role on the board', laughed Tio. 'You undervalue yourself to a remarkable degree. Besides, surely your own interests align very closely with my own. I know that you desire to see Prince Taian supplant Triado on the throne. I propose to give you the means to improve his chances in that enterprise'.

'I see', said Balian', eyebrows raised in interest. 'And to what *means* do you refer?'

'I think you understand that my power is channelled through you', said Tio. 'Your complaint has been that you lack the ability to bend that power to your will. I shall unlock that power and give you a mastery over the physical world that will surprise and astound your companions'.

'You will?'

'I will. I have studied your physiology and the structures of your mind, to see how my power might be most effectively deployed there. All mortals are constructed differently in that respect, and it is a matter of weighing the potency of the potential effect against the likelihood of material failure. Your body and mind, the mortal vessel, if you like, are now configured in the manner I judge to be most effectual. It may be that you now have some ability to create illusions in the minds of others. I leave that for you to explore. However, my chief endowment upon you is the power to freeze men into immobility, at will, so that they cannot move a muscle. They may still hear and see, but their tongues will be stilled in their mouths, and they will be as statues until you release them from that spell'.

'I can see that might be useful', conceded Balian. 'But I sense reservation. I sense that there may be a catch'.

'You are correct', sighed Tio. 'The mortal frame is ill-suited to the containment and deployment of such vast supernatural force. Your own life-force will be depleted when you use it. You will share in a little part of my divinity, but your flesh will be too frail to contain it for long'.

'So, you have given me a power that will kill me if I use it?' demanded Balian, frowning. 'Is that what you mean? How will I know how seriously it will affect me, or how many times I might deploy it without bringing about my own destruction?'

'You will know', said Tio, solemnly.

'And how will I know when these powers are available to me?'

'You already do', said Tio.

Balian awoke, sweating, twitching, to stare at the dark ceiling above his bed. Was it a dream or was it a vision? He wished more than anything that it had been a dream, but as the new day unfolded, it became more than ever certain that it had been a true vision of the divine. Now, finger raised, the attention of all his comrades upon him, the time had come to put that vision to the test.

'There is something that I have been meaning to tell you', he continued. 'I believe that I am now fully functional as a luminary. I believe that I may now contribute materially to our enterprise'.

'I see', said Taian, glancing around. 'Well, I'm sure that is good news. In what manner?'

'In this manner', said Balian simply, raising a hand and exerting the newly available force of his mind upon his companions. 'Perhaps any of you would care to move or to stand up or to raise your voices?'

But they did not. Balian had feared that the vision had been unreal, that his attempt to deploy this power would result merely in his friends looking at him with blank faces, quite unaffected. Instead, his companions remained frozen in place like a display of waxworks. It was as though he had closed a lock on them. Balian counted to twenty in the ensuing silence, conscious of a vague fatigue growing at the back of his mind, conscious that his own life force was very slowly ebbing away through the efficacy of this demonstration. At twenty, he waved his hand and the lock snapped open. There was a collective gasp. Rayo thrust back his chair and leapt to his feet. Suddenly everyone else was staring at him, wide-eyed.

'That was you! You did that!' cried Jory, amongst various expressions of dismay from the little group.

'I did', admitted Balian. 'I am sorry if I alarmed you, but it was necessary to convince you of the truth. The truth of what I am about to tell you'.

He told them of his dream, of his visitation from Tio and of the power now bestowed upon him, although in truth, none needed any further demonstration of his sincerity.

At the end of this, the room became silent as each of them pondered the nearness of God and the fortunate conjunction of His will with their own.

'He is beautiful, is he not?' said Adala at length.

'He is', agreed Balian.

'And you think this... ability may be turned to our advantage?' asked Taian, when thoughts began to turn to practical matters once more.

'Tio gave me no direction as to how I might use this power. I imagine he left that for me to explore. And my insight led me to make my intervention just now'.

'Go on...' prompted Jory when Balian hesitated.

'Should Taian be able to make the appeal that we have envisaged, addressing the highest powers in the realm, I believe I may be able to prevent intervention from those around him, whether they be members of Triado's own entourage or of the guard. I believe I can hold them at bay until Taian's call to action is complete'.

'How many can you hold at once?' asked Rayo, after a few moments of thoughtful silence. 'And at what distance?'

'I don't know', admitted Balian with a shrug. 'And I fear to put it to the test until I must, because, as I have explained, it may lead to my destruction'.

'Well, I think this is the best chance that we have', said Rayo, glancing about.

'I agree', said Taian with furrowed brow. 'A slight chance indeed, but I hear no better suggestion. I thank you for your... commitment, Balian. No one could ask more of a friend'.

'If it succeeds, it will be worthwhile', murmured Balian with a curious sinking feeling in his stomach.

It would be a bold stroke, perhaps amongst the boldest in history, but as time passed, it began to seem that it was their best – and only – chance. Triado was simply entrenched too firmly in power, and it seemed that the dry tinder of rebellion may never otherwise be induced to take flame. In the distant city, Drael and Cortesia were written to and asked to investigate the circumstances of the jousting competition that would be part of the Midsummer Festival, this one traditionally dedicated to Niall and the foundation of the empire.

A further obstacle in the path of this fanciful scheme was the necessity of Prince Taian demonstrating exceptional prowess in the joust. Even competing required that he should be able to successfully enter the competition under a pseudonym and escape detection by the authorities. Taian was highly competent as a horseman, had competed successfully at polo, in fact, and he could handle a hunting spear as well as any man. However, managing a heavy destrier and a twelve-foot lance whilst wearing all-encompassing armour from head to foot represented a very different challenge. It was not merely necessary that he should be competent in these respects; it was essential that he should excel. In order to face the emperor in the tilt-yard he would undoubtedly first need to unseat a number of lesser opponents. At first, these obstacles seemed insuperable.

'Unless...', said Adala, thinking aloud the next day. 'Unless you were to take the place of the Count of Drumnestro. He excels in the joust, and the likelihood is that he will face the emperor in the final contest, as he has on several occasions, we are told. With Balian to help us, we may then succeed'.

'Why yes', cried Taian with a broad grin. He reserved this for her, and her only, now that he tried to maintain some of the more dignified demeanour he judged necessary for an aspirant to the throne. 'That would certainly bring us closer to our objective'.

It was a day in March, and spring was beginning to loosen its icy grip of winter on the valley beneath the castle.

Snowmelt engorged the streams that came hurrying down the stony hillsides to tumble into a swollen river already verged with a tentative scatter of the first wild flowers. The two Erenori walked along the path that led through woods into the valley, glad to feel the pale warmth of a watery sun on their backs.

'How easy you make it sound, my dear!' Taian continued, grasping her hand in his and swinging it easily. 'Caught in this remote wilderness it is possible to imagine that even the most improbable of contingencies might readily be brought to pass in that far-distant city. Perhaps a host of singing angels might also descend from the heavens to assist us in the removal of the count's armour and its girding about my frame'.

'Perhaps', she smiled, without showing any obvious sign of resentment at being teased so. 'And perhaps also, Tio may wish to appear to you, as he has to me, to remind you of the importance of trust in him'.

In truth, Adala had been glad to spend these weeks under the baron's roof. The baron assured them that he had no intention of replying to the earl's peevish demands that he should surrender his guests into his custody, and until the snows in the high mountain passes melted, it was most unlikely that any armed body might arrive to enforce his writ. Besides, the baron had proved to be a generous and considerate host, apparently content to throw defiance in his lord's face and flaunt his disdain for Triado's ally in the neighbouring vale. However, it was certain that this time must draw to a close, and that the rising spring must find them moving secretly back once more into imperial territory.

For now, though, Adala was content to walk at her husband's side and to wonder at the days and the months and the years that had brought her from her small coastal village to her place here beside a prince, albeit a prince with no empire to call his own. He ruled her heart, however, would rule it forever, and the advent of this thought brought a new lightness of step.

'You skip, I declare', said Taian, regarding her with amusement. 'Sometimes the five-year old within you can barely be contained'.

As soon as these words were spoken, he regretted them, his eyes clouding and his own gait stiffening as the notion of the child that had thus far been denied to them came into his mind. It came into Adala's, too, and for a moment they paused, looking out over the grey-green valley with its scattered flocks of sheep and the stands of dark trees.

'If Tio wills it', she said.

Taian sighed and squeezed her hand.

'Rayo says that we may ride to Soangarten whenever we are ready. He has heard from Bradon', he added, naming Rayo's cousin. 'They have just the horse for me, he says, a fine and steady four-year old Turman, and Drael will come down from The City, too'.

'I shall be pleased to see him', said Adala, glad to acquiesce in this change of subject, and glad also to think fondly of the man to whom she owed so much.

As a former cavalryman, Drael was well suited to schooling Taian in the complexities of managing horse, armour and lance, although Bradon's father, a former champion of the joust, might be called upon to advise on the finer points of technique. But first they must reach Soangarten, an estate on the borders of the duchies of Acra and Capra, at least a week's journey away across the Vertebraean Alps.

Doctor Mordanios was dissecting a cadaver when Yuzanid came to him. He was investigating the blood supply to the spleen and making a detailed sketch in one of his many notebooks, comparing this with the disembodied organ, where it lay on a pewter plate. The doctor was well used to his master's caprices, so he was not wholly disconcerted when the cadaver suddenly sat bolt upright and began speaking to him. A raised eyebrow and a wry smile sufficed to illustrate Mordanios' surprise. It amused him to consider how other anatomists, less well-connected than himself, might react to such an occurrence.

'Good afternoon, Mordanios', said the cadaver in a strangely hoarse voice. 'I trust I find you well'.

'You do, my lord', replied Mordanios with a vague bow from the waist, wiping his hands on a towel. 'How may I serve you?'

'It appears that this time and place are unusually significant in the Forever War that I fight with my brother', continued Yuzanid through the cadaver's mouth. 'The wall between the worlds is thin in a number of places, and it may be that Tio seeks to take advantage of it. I rely upon you to be my eyes and ears, in order that I may respond to any sudden challenge that emerges. The empire has entered upon a significant crisis that may hasten its demise. It is vital that my unwitting agents, the imperial couple, should continue to steer the course that leads to civil war and disintegration. I sense that Prince Taian and his agents represent a threat, and this threat may take more tangible shape during the course of the coming months. I cannot see him – and that troubles me. I believe that Tio has aligned himself with that cause and that we must be exceptionally vigilant'.

'Of course', agreed Mordanios, sensing that there was something more to be disclosed.

'The emperor seems incapable of putting a child in the empress', continued Yuzanid after a pause, during which the cadaver appeared to lose something of the rigidity that had seized it.

This was restored now as the cadaver's eyes sprang open and appeared to regard Mordanios balefully.

'This appears to be a deficiency in the emperor's seed. The empress desires a child above all else and, in desperation, considers taking a lover in order to facilitate this. There are some who may be bold enough to brave the wrath of the emperor'.

'The emperor is far from continent in his own sexual relations', observed Mordanios.

'Indeed', agreed Yuzanid, 'but jealousy readily shares a breast with hypocrisy, and I have heard that their relationship is less than cordial in recent times. I believe that she has respected her marriage vow until now'.

'Until now...' prompted Mordanios with a sinking sensation in the pit of his stomach.

'Until now, repeated Yuzanid. 'But all that is about to change, Mordanios, because *you* are about to put a child in her. More to the point, you are about to put *my* child in her'.

Mordanios' mouth was suddenly dry. Objections crowded in on him in such profusion that none could reach utterance for some moments. He raised a finger, at last, having made some progress in ordering his thoughts.

'So, you seek to express some of your divinity through mortal form?' he began. 'I cannot believe that such a course does not violate the rules under which your "game" is played'.

'As I have said', said Yuzanid. 'The wall between the worlds is exceptionally thin here. The opportunity has not previously occurred. A child growing to a man, and in possession of even a fraction of my powers, would be a powerful asset indeed, you must surely understand, and would be hard for Tio to oppose'.

'I see', said Mordanios with a dread sense of inevitability gathering in his breast. 'And how might this... pregnancy... be brought about?'

'It will be brought about by you, Mordanios, in the traditional manner, although you may be sure that I shall be present at the conception'.

'My relationship with the empress does not approach the level of intimacy that might facilitate such a coupling', objected Mordanios. 'She respects my professional competence, has made the most obliging comments, but I doubt that she will readily take me to her bed. She has come to me on several occasions to seek guidance relating to fertility, but such a direct intervention on my part... well...'

'The introduction of your virile member will most assuredly cure her of her complaint', croaked the cadaver in something approaching laughter. 'And you *must* accomplish it, Mordanios. I require it of you'.

'I shall do what I can', conceded the doctor gloomily with a bow.

'And I shall reward you', said Yuzanid. 'More years...'

'No more years, I beg you', groaned Mordanios. 'Years have no more capacity to please me, nor have months, nor weeks nor days. I have lived too many of them and I tire of living forever. To live forever without a true friend or companion that I must not one day wave farewell to, or see grow old and die, that is a hard thing, one that gnaws at my soul. I am lonely, Master, that is what it amounts to'.

'Mortals are weak, Mordanios, and you were once amongst the strongest. But perhaps I may offer you hope. This child that shall be incarnate in the empress's womb', said Yuzanid, 'he shall be your companion and his days shall be numberless. On earth you will have the satisfaction of a father, although the emperor must acknowledge him as his own and necessarily remain ignorant of the circumstances of his conception. You will doubtless attend him as physician, tutor and companion,

although only we shall know the truth of it. Does that thought not please you?'
'It does', agreed Mordanios after some moments in which he contemplated the prospect. 'It really does. And you are sure that this notional child will be a boy?'
'I am', said Yuzanid. 'And I am sure you will do your utmost to plant our seed within the empress. For my part, I shall do what I can to exert a favourable influence on your behalf. You must succeed in this'.
'I will. I shall bring new life into this world', smiled Mordanios as the cadaver collapsed back onto the table with a dull thud.

'You are unwell, I perceive', said Mordanios that same night as he attended upon the empress.
Indeed, Cresara Rhovanion's face was pale and her posture lacking some of its usual taut self-discipline as she sat in her chair before her mirror. Her maids had been dismissed now, and she could regard her reflection in that mirror with complete freedom, stretching the skin around her eyes to momentarily dispel wrinkles and crows' feet. Her body was ageing, and the fierce spirit that inhabited that flesh was powerless to prevent it. She had spent a long afternoon with her agents, attending to the security of her reign, while the emperor looked at horses. She resented it, resented also the notion that he was likely enough to be bedding the Count of Drumnestro further along that corridor, even now. There were times when a great weariness crept upon her, a weariness of spirit as much as of body.
'May I take your pulse?' asked Mordanios, reaching for her limp wrist.
'You may, Mordanios', she answered, offering him a faint smile.

There was a silence whilst he counted under his breath and the warm pressure of his fingers was upon her flesh, an agreeable sensation.

'You seem a little agitated, if I may say so', he observed, having released his grip and pronounced himself satisfied. 'My care is for your health. Nothing is dearer to my heart, as I trust you are aware, and the mind and body are an inseparable whole, are they not? One cannot thrive unless the other is likewise free of malady'.

'That is very true, Mordanios', admitted Cresara. 'And your diagnosis is correct. There is a sickness in my soul'.

'A sickness, Ma'am?' asked Mordanios, inclining his head.

'Don't patronise me', sighed Cresara with a glint of irritation in her eye. 'You know exactly what ails me'.

'You are without child', he said in a carefully neutral tone, observing the empress closely.

'I am, as you say, with*out child*', she agreed, that flash of annoyance ebbing now, to be replaced by a fresh loosening in her posture. 'And I must begin to grow used to the notion that it will always be the case'.

'You are not yet too old', said Mordanios, moving on hastily to acquaint her with cases of women of her age, and older, who had successfully conceived and delivered children.

'I'm sure you are right', agreed the empress, inviting the doctor to draw up a chair next to her. 'But I think we both know that the fault is not mine, if fault it can be called'.

'The emperor...'

'Yes. The emperor. None has been more prolific in the sowing of their seed, but that seed has not taken root. Nowhere has it taken root, whether in the bellies of servant girls or in my own. There is something amiss with his seed. I must accept it. We must all accept it'.

Mordanios nodded slowly, wondering that this conversation should have come about so soon after his own with Yuzanid, wondering at that being's power to bring his influence to bear on mortal minds.

'Or must I?' she enquired.

'Hmm?'

Mordanios judged that the direction of this conversation must be managed with the greatest of care, that any proposition of his own must seem to come in response to her own urgings.

'Must I make a cuckold of the emperor and invite his lusty young squires to my bed?' demanded the empress, raising an elegant eyebrow.

Mordanios knitted his brows, declining to venture an opinion on this suggestion. Privately, it occurred to him that it would be a bold courtier who would couple with the formidable empress. How many would seek in vain for tumescence in Cresara's bed, when her evil reputation and the potential vengeance of her imperial spouse weighed upon their minds.

'No. Do not answer that, Mordanios. I shall seek no counsel from you'.

She pursed her lips and stared into the mirror for a while as Mordanios sat patiently beside her, wondering as to the direction of her thoughts. His suspicions were confirmed when she turned to him at last.

'You can do extraordinary things, can you not, Doctor Mordanios? I have seen the evidence of that with my own eyes. I do not enquire as to your connections. To make such enquiries may be injurious to my peace of mind, perhaps. But you can make things happen that defy earthly explanation. Tell me if I am wrong'.

'My only desire is to serve', said Mordanios cautiously. 'And I do indeed have capabilities that some would wonder at. May I beg to enquire where this conversation tends?'

'Oh, Mordanios', laughed Cresara bitterly, casting back her head, revealing her even white teeth. 'Must I spell it out for you?'
'I believe you must'.
'I wish you to make me pregnant'.
Mordanios blinked, giving a passable impression of shock.
'You are an intelligent man. You are not unattractive, and your appearance is not so far removed from that of the emperor that people shall wonder if a child of yours were to be born to me'.
'I am of suitable stock, then?'
'Let us not reduce this to the level of the farmyard, Mordanios. You know exactly what I mean', said the empress with a wry smile. 'This is not a proposal I make lightly, as I'm sure you must appreciate, and I make it only on the understanding that you can put a child in me at the first attempt. Am I correct to make that assumption, given your undoubted powers'.
'I believe you are, Ma'am, although I warn you that my *intervention* must necessarily be through the usual channels, there will be no...'
'Fine. Let us have no more shillyshallying about *interventions*. I am not an abbess to be tiptoed around and to have my tender sensibilities soothed. You must fuck me, Mordanios. That is what you assure me of, and that is all I need to know', she snapped, waving a hand airily, her posture resuming its usual proud rigour once more, now that this decision was made. 'You will do this, then?'
'As your doctor it is incumbent on me to address your mental and physical needs, although some would propose that this exceeds the usual bounds of the doctor/patient relationship'.
'Yes or no?'
'Yes', agreed Mordanios with a nervous cough that concealed his quiet exultation.

Cresara narrowed her eyes and regarded the doctor considal"ingly.
'Well, come on then'.
So saying, she stood, took Mordanios' hand in hers and led him to her bed.

Mordanios had undertaken many tasks on behalf of his master over the years, some of which had bought him revulsion or disquiet. This, on the other hand, was amongst the most congenial of the duties imposed on him. Nor did he attend to the task fearing detection or retribution, given that his powerful master protected him. Accordingly, he was free to take enjoyment from the act. Nevertheless, conscious of the role he was ostensibly required to play, he provided his inseminatory service in a manner that he hoped gave the impression of dutiful exertion rather than mere absorption in selfish pleasure. Cresara, for her part, had intended to lie back and endure Mordanios' attentions as she might any medical procedure, but she soon found herself warming to the task and taking real pleasure from their union. At the moment of climax, a strange sense of unearthly heat flowed through her as well as the sense that Mordanios' body had been briefly possessed by another, a more powerful being by far. She cried out, clasped Mordanios in a fierce grip that encompassed all four of her limbs and trembled briefly in a hot palsy of pleasure.
'It is done, then', she said at last, when her breathing was hers to control once more and the two of them had rolled apart.
'Time will tell', murmured the doctor. 'But yes, I believe it is'.
'The genesis of a child is within me', sighed the empress ecstatically, placing her hand to her belly.
'A child indeed', agreed Mordanios, privately adding the rider *or something.*

Chapter Twenty

Capra

At Soangarten, Bradon's father's estate in Capra, Taian learned to joust, under the critical eye of Drael and a number of Bradon's aged male relatives, said to be skilled in this field. Taian was used to riding sturdy hunters, the kind with limitless stamina that could bear their master from dawn to dusk, over any manner of country, and loved the chase with a passion that matched their riders'. Glanymo, the fine black Turman, was a different beast altogether – proud, deep-chested and almost twice the weight of anything Taian had ever ridden before. Bred over many generations to bear an armoured warrior into battle, Glanymo's ancestors had ridden down the empire's foes the length and breadth of Toxandria. Now Taian must learn to manage this imposing mass of muscled flesh, bending her to his will with knees, reins and the slightest of subtle bodily movements. The two should ride as one great inseparable whole, a perfect union of man and beast, directed by a single mind.

'I think I could come to love this creature', admitted Taian, one day in late April, having dismounted and handed the reins to a groom.

'Now you make me jealous', laughed Adala, standing with the group of interested bystanders that had been observing Taian's practice.

'You may be sure that I shall do nothing to merit it', smiled Taian amongst ribald laughter from his friends.

'It seems that you and she approach an understanding', said Bradon, Rayo's cousin, patting Glanymo's nose.

'I feel it', agreed Taian, and then in a lower voice, 'but I fear that riding Drumnestro's mount will be quite different. She will be alarmed by the substitution. That understanding will be absent, and we shall ride as Glanymo and I did three weeks ago when first I sat astride her, strangers to each other'.

'We can only do what we can do', observed Rayo. 'The rest is Tio's will'.

'Or Yuzanid's', murmured Taian, so that only Adala could hear. She squeezed his arm sympathetically.

'I have seen Drumnestro's mount, Canfel', said Bradon's elderly father, 'when I was invited to his stable by the old count, two years since. The two are very similar in temperament, if I am any judge. They are both steady, quiet souls, unmoved by novelty. If she were some flighty, nervous creature, I would share your concern, but things could be much worse'.

'I suppose we shall try the full panoply after luncheon', deduced Taian, glancing down at the armour that clad him from waist to shoulder.

Military men were accustomed to being burdened with the various encumbrances of mail and plate, but for Taian the experience had been a novel one and he still found the weight of it trying, quite apart from the various limitations to his movement. Now he was to have the cuisses, poleyns and greaves applied to his legs and a visored sallet helm placed over his head. He had already practised riding with the sallet on many occasions, in order that he may become accustomed to observing the world through a narrow slit in the steel. Nevertheless, it would be a novelty to wear the entire array.

'Indeed', agreed Bradon approvingly. 'And perhaps we shall also bring out the lance again'.

'I should hope so', agreed Rayo with a grin. 'You must certainly do better with it than you did yesterday'.

'An old woman with a bargepole could have done better', laughed Taian, slapping him on the shoulder.

Drael watched from his place on the grassy slope that led down to the tilt-field, having earlier adjusted the straps and fittings on Taian's armour to achieve the most comfortable fit. He had watched the prince's exercises with professional interest, noting that he was a thoroughly competent horseman, growing more used to the war saddle, more used to the ears of the raised cantle embracing his hips. Taian might come to be similarly competent in the use of the lance in time.

His eye fell upon Adala now as the party turned towards the manor house behind him. She was arm in arm with her husband, laughing, joshing, her face wreathed in smiles. Drael's own dour features twitched in response, and he cast his eyes down as they approached, twisting a strand of grass between his fingers. It was truly a joy to see her happy but one that made the bitter void within him yawn still wider.

'I think we should bring out Milwin this afternoon', he said, naming another of the estate's great horses, and having approved the prince's performance. 'I shall ride against you from the other side of the tilt-rail at the full gallop. I shall bear no lance, but it will accustom you to the sight and sound of a rider approaching you at speed'.

'We are truly lucky to have you', said Adala, placing a hand on his forearm and causing a thrill of pleasure to traverse his body.

She had some inkling of her friend's difficulty in her presence, some notion of the awkward emotions he must struggle with, although she must never disclose as much. Nevertheless, it was impossible not to betray some hint of this in the glint of her eye, and Drael found a flush rising in his sallow cheeks as they stepped out onto the path.

'The pleasure is all mine', he heard himself saying. 'And we shall make a paladin of the prince in due course, I declare'.

And yet time was against them. The risk of detection by the agents of the crown remained a constant creeping anxiety, but the more urgent concern was the passage of the weeks. May advanced to its glorious conclusion amidst some of the finest weather anyone could remember, and the fields and orchards around Soangarten were rich with wild flowers or heavy with blossom. Taian's skills blossomed likewise, until he could sit his mount with confidence and place his lance tip reliably through one of the coloured target hoops that swung above the tilt-rail. There had been actual contests, too, in which Taian had ridden against Drael and Bradon. On more than one occasion he had found himself lying bruised and winded on the hard earth, having been toppled from the saddle, but he gave as good as he got, and as June approached, Drael declared himself satisfied. It was time to return to The City, to place their heads within the noose or to hold them high in triumph at last.

Ohk had known that Cortesia's harpsichord had been renovated and tuned, had commissioned the tradesman, indeed, on his mistress's instruction. Nevertheless, it was a delight to his soul to approach the ballroom and to hear the sound of music from along the corridor. Her playing was distinctly hesitant, halting, the same phrase attempted, abandoned and repeated until she had remastered what once had been second nature to her. Ohk stood outside the door and listened as her fingers caressed the keys, as the notes fell once more into familiar patterns unfamiliar to his ears for more than a decade. He smiled. He tilted his head back and closed his eyes, the better to focus his being on a sound so redolent of a carefree soul. He was transported then to a time before her beauty had been stolen from her, a time still longer ago when he walked a forest where birdsong and flowers had uplifted his spirit on a summer's day.

'Is that you there, Ohk?' came Cortesia's voice after a while, recalling him to the moment, to a dim corridor on an afternoon in early June.

'It is, Ma'am', responded Ohk, clutching to his chest the sheaf of papers he had brought. 'I wondered if I might show you my latest poor attempt? But I can see that you are... busy'.

He entered the sunlit vastness of the ballroom, where great slanting shafts of light came down through high windows, glinting on the polished parquet floor and on chandeliers likewise freed from the decade-long accretion of dust that had dulled them. She turned from the harpsichord, and he saw that her face was unswathed once more. This was often the case within the house now, although she continued to conceal her injuries for the sake of visitors or when abroad in The City. Her poor face had no power to shock him, of course, but its appearance nevertheless stirred the vast well of pity in his heart whenever he saw it anew, and a constriction came into his throat as he placed the papers into her open hand. She turned in her seat, held them to the light and her eye traversed the uneven lines of spidery script that he had written there.

'It is the story of Bran-to-Tiss, the bird thief, and Jan-co-Cass, the child of waters', said Ohk.

'I can see that, Ohk', said Cortesia, her eyebrow arched. 'I am reading it, am I not? Your hand remains execrable, but you convey the sense of it very well. You may wish to attend to this word, and this', she added when she had finished, indicating a few misspellings. 'And this. How long did this take you?'

'A little while', he admitted, a term that encompassed a whole week, the better part of his waking hours when not engaged in his official duties.

'Well', she said brightly, handing him the papers, at last. 'You have done very well. You have learned a great deal'.

'I have had a good teacher', he said, a glow of pride and pleasure suffusing his being.

Her mouth formed itself into the approximation of a smile, and her eye smiled, too. Cortesia looked upon her servant as he turned to withdraw, and a curious sensation entered her heart. It was as though a scale fell from her eye and she saw him for the first time, his great dark frame in its shabby clothes, his perpetually bowed head and his soft, careful step, so much at variance with his ponderous bulk. And so familiar, so much a part of this house... and of her. His eyes, too. There was a gentleness and a reverence there, was there not? She was suddenly a blank page, naked to the pen of novelty and sensation, a wide-eyed wanderer on a dawn-lit hill.

'Ohk', she said, standing now, causing him to pause and turn.

'Yes, Ma'am?'

For a long moment she could say nothing as various jostling thoughts came crowding in on her.

'Do you remember... that day?' she asked at last, the merest twitch of hand and head sufficient to make her meaning amply clear.

'I do, Ma'am', intoned Ohk solemnly. 'I remember it only too well. I remember it every day'.

He now also sailed in uncharted waters, for the attack on her had not been mentioned for many years, not since the abandonment of the official investigation, in fact. Now she nodded slowly, and her lips moved, but no sound emerged. Her eye filled with tears and the great and powerful woman he had revered was suddenly shrunken and diminished before him. He looked upon her, and it was as though a spear was thrust through his heart.

'Ohk...' she said, bringing the back of her hand to her mouth. 'Ohk...'

In his mind, Ohk advanced towards her and enfolded her in a gentle embrace, murmuring soft words, the while, and stroking her hair, feeling the dampness of her tears on his breast and the trembling of her small body against him, like the little birds in his hand when he found them trapped in the scullery.

'Thank you, Ohk, that will be all', she heard herself say in a voice that was barely hers to command.

Later, as she ate the evening meal that Ohk had brought to her in the library, she reflected upon those few moments in the ballroom. She admonished herself for a woeful lack of self-control. To permit herself to approach tears before a servant demonstrated an unseemly relaxation in the mental fortitude that she prized in herself. This mental strength had held despair at bay when every atom of her being had longed for that entity's destruction. On how many occasions during those first years had she prayed for Tio to snuff out her unquiet spirit as she slept, or considered how she might hang herself or open her veins in the bath? But she had found the strength to carry on, to greet each new day with equanimity and to turn her back on a past that was such a bitter treasure to contemplate. She dared not revisit it, dared not recall to mind the joy that she had once known, the beauty of the world that her face had reflected in such full measure.

A book lay open before her on the table, and yet the printed page swam before her eye, refusing to yield up its meaning to a mind that turned now inward. Was it the music that had provoked this? Was it the unfamiliar unison of mind and eye and sinew, which brought forth that succession of notes and chords to reverberate within her heart? It had been so long. So long. And she could look at last with a quiet soul upon the day her beauty died. Her mind's eye disclosed to her the splash of acid in the morning air, and her mind did not recoil from it. Not anymore. It was as though she had read that moment in the pages of a book long ago, in the life of a fictional character. It made her sad and her heart embraced the pity of it, but the event had lost the power to shock and to wound. Perhaps she had at last recovered and could now step confidently into the future.

'I am awake once more', she said to herself. 'Observe how I am engaged with the world. I have set darkness at a distance, have I not?'

She had done so, as recent months had shown, but her awakening had encompassed only her response to immediate events, to the challenges that each new day placed before her. For a deeper reckoning with the past, a slower tide of healing had been building, but now, at last, it washed over her and she clenched her fists, swaying her head slowly from side to side.

'I have been a monster', she said. 'I have driven away those who loved me and have immersed myself in hatred and bitterness. How I regret these wasted years'.

She sighed, enumerating for herself the friends and the relatives whose sympathies and whose kind words she had spurned, repaying gentleness with unrelenting spite until she was entirely alone in the world. But not entirely. Her eye fell upon one of Ohk's attempts at writing where it lay, having served her as a bookmark, traversed by the clumsy lines of his childish hand. Ohk had always been there for her, impervious to the rapier of her tongue or her unfeeling and imperious scorn. A warm congestion gripped her heart and rose once more into her throat. A hot tear splashed upon the page so that the ink of his words eddied and clouded like smoke within it.

The Midsummer Festival was to be the greatest of Triado's reign, so he assured himself. Assured of this fact also were the great legion of functionaries and officials, whose professional duties were to bring this into being or else face potential disgrace or dismissal. Foodstuff and materials were sourced from the furthest corners of the empire: exotic silks from Vannistar, shellfish in iron tanks from Garabdor, furs and feathers from the trading wharves of distant Caneloon in the far North. No expense was to be spared to celebrate the glory of the empire and of Triado's realm. As the palace storehouses piled up a treasure of readily expendable fripperies, so did the treasury officials ponder over the ledgers that recorded the emperor's debts, and so did the exchequer consider new measures to squeeze more tax from the realm. The greater nobles in their palaces might grumble at these exactions, might instruct their agents to exert their influence to minimise their commitments, but the poorer folk, the tradesmen and the guildsmen, the peasants in the fields had no power to resist the rapacious state, and a vast tide of resentment was growing, from Arken to Vollangor. There had been riots in provincial towns and peasant revolts in remote provinces, but as yet The City itself remained untouched, although even there the spectre of insurrection was abroad in the streets, the timber and tinder of rebellion awaiting only a spark to ignite it. The murmur in the taverns was contained – for now. All feared the ever-vigilant ear of the informer, the tap on the shoulder from a dark-clad investigator, should an injudicious word be let slip. And yet there was a sense that this could not last, that the simmering broth of rage would soon boil over and that chaos would ensue.

It was into this tense city that Taian's party rode, a few days before Midsummer, arriving singly or in pairs when the streets were busiest and the gate guards necessarily less vigilant. Bright bunting already flew bravely in the streets, but the atmosphere of impending doom was palpable. It was like a flock of white doves glittering bright before a dark, portentous storm head.

Their first place of reassembly was at Cortesia's house, and there they would stay for three days, but on the day before the festival, Taian's party would relocate to Jory's friend Hosto's house, which lay adjacent to the jousting grounds. For now, though, there were glad reunions to be celebrated and pressing business to be transacted. Suitable clothing and supplies must be acquired, movement routes reconnoitred and intelligence gathered and shared as necessary with all those party to the plot. For a plot it had become – no longer merely a vague and formless aspiration to challenge for power at some indeterminable point in the future. Over weeks, the practical requirements of the tournament itself had been pored over and addressed in every detail. And yet still it remained an enterprise so hazardous, so beset with uncertainty, as to be condemned as folly whenever a rational mind should pause to consider it. The minds that now considered it had become increasingly rational with every passing mile of their long ride to The City. The bold stroke that they had conceived gradually unrobed itself before their eyes to reveal a fragile contrivance of naive folly, one that must certainly dissolve in ruin upon its first exposure to the real world. And yet still they continued, because there was no alternative, and because they knew in their less rational beings that Tio was with them, paced at their side, indeed, His indomitable will underpinning their own.

'I take it the Count of Drumnestro is well?' asked Taian on the night of their first arrival in The City, when they had taken dinner. 'It would be insufferably grim if he were to retire with a head cold on the eve of the tournament'.
'Certainly, we must all pray for his good health', observed Cortesia, who, as ever, had taken her own food and drink privately but sat with her guests as they ate.

Her dining room, furnished only with table and chairs, was as clean and as neat as Ohk and Bardo could make it, smelling of beeswax polish and enlivened with flowers from the garden.

'There are a great many things that we should pray for', said Jory, looking pensively through the red wine in his glass. 'And if we were to pray for them all with sufficient fervency, we should certainly put out the knees of our breeches in the next few days'.

'What do you hear from the Directorate?' asked Adala of Drael as various nods and expressions of solemn agreement greeted Jory's assertion.

He glanced up from his own empty plate and his eye met hers for a moment, disclosing an unfamiliar emotion to her. Was that yearning she saw there?

'They have us in the South still', he said in his low, measured tones. 'I see no reason to fear that they suspect we are here within the bosom of their power'.

'We are so lucky to have you, Drael', said Taian, to general agreement, a thumping of the table and a raising of glasses.

'I have some fortunate connections', Drael admitted with one of those rare momentary smiles, like the sun breaking through cloud. 'And you may be sure I have drawn freely from the well of friendship. I pray that my pail may not come up empty before this week is out'.

'If your past friendship with your contacts has been as your friendship to us, that well will never run dry', said Adala with feeling, causing a flush to rise in the investigator's cheeks.

'And Prince Taian, you are become a champion jouster, I learn', suggested Cortesia into the awkward silence that ensued from this briefest exchange.

'I believe that I can sit a saddle and direct a lance as well as the next man', agreed Taian. 'Although only Tio knows how I shall fare against Triado'.

'He will fare very well, I'm sure', said Drael, brightening now. 'Besides, Balian will help him, or at least interfere with Triado in a manner beneficial to his opponent. Isn't that so, Balian?'

All eyes turned to Balian, who had been a far from convivial table companion, who had eaten sparingly and whose glass remained full.

'I will do what I can', he conceded, looking around him owlishly.

Amongst various vital roles, Balian had undertaken to attempt to freeze the emperor into immobility as he rode towards Taian, should such a contingency ever be brought to pass. It was hoped that this would give Taian the necessary advantage to place his own lance securely and topple the emperor from his horse. This was all very well in theory, but in practice Balian found it hard to direct his will at a rapidly moving object. He had succeeded in three out of four trial attempts, but that single failure weighed heavily on his mind.

Cresara Rhovanion sat at the head of a long table and regarded Mandoro Kyrenion steadily until the door closed upon the last of his subordinates and the two of them were alone. In his place at the far end of that table, the head of the Directorate of Investigators fussed nervously with the papers before him. He was a powerful and irascible man, made all the more irascible by consciousness that the empress had the ability to overawe him. Besides, it was after midnight. The empress appeared indifferent to the need for sleep, but the same could not be said of her subject. Kyrenion's eyes were gritty with fatigue.

'Well', she said. 'I have listened to a great many words that tell me nothing'.

'I'm not sure I take your meaning', ventured the Director. 'We have just heard of three plots detected and a further seven under investigation. Twelve individuals are subject to torture of the most persuasive kind, even as we speak, and two are to approach the scaffold within days. Surely, you must accept that the Directorate is most assiduous in its duties, most attentive to the security of the realm...'

'I think you know what I mean, Kyrenion'.

'Seedlan gave you a full report on Prince Taian and his confederates', objected the Director.

'Which told me nothing, other than the trail has gone entirely cold'.

She placed her hand to her belly, where the child was growing, and stroked it in the manner she had when faced with anxiety or frustration.

'We do what we can', sighed the Director. 'But our resources are stretched, and as you well know, threats crowd in upon us from all directions, given the... er...'

An uncharacteristic disclosure of his private mind came close to utterance, a peevish objection to the imperial couple's insufferable pride, greed, arrogance and spite. Such deplorable conduct, and the realm's growing resentment of it, inevitably burdened the Directorate with a workload far beyond its capacity to manage. He had a very real sense that disaster approached.

'Be careful, lest you permit an unguarded tongue to offer criticism in place of counsel', warned the empress, eyes narrowed, having apparently perceived his thoughts with her usual terrifying perspicacity.

He cast his eyes down, composed himself and looked up once more.

'If I may be candid with you', he began. 'Your *excessive* concern with regard to Prince Taian and his tiny entourage leads you to take an unbalanced view of the undoubted threats and challenges that we face. He has no significant support, so far as we can tell, and the vast majority of those who count in this realm have looked upon his dead face as it was committed to the tomb. He can only be regarded as a charlatan and an imposter. Unless you know better...'

Now it was Cresara's turn to disclose a momentary flicker of doubt in her eye. Kyrenion, a most astute observer of his fellows, noted this with interest.

'Which you would surely disclose to me', he added.

'Of course', she said smoothly. 'However, I sense that a crisis approaches and I would be glad if you would focus your efforts on this particular threat, regardless of your own assessment of it. I trust that I may rely upon you to make this so?'

'Of course, Ma'am', agreed the Director with the closest approximation to a bow that was practical while seated. 'Will that be all now?'

'It will', said the empress. 'Thank you, Kyrenion'.

When the Director had withdrawn, Cresara frowned and drummed the fingers of one hand on the table in front of her. Regardless of his assurances to the contrary, she knew that Taian was now close and that he plotted her downfall.

No more than half a mile away, that same prince lay abed with Adala. The next day, they must relocate to an address in the outer ward of The City, and so this was their last night under Cortesia's roof. The hour was late, but Taian was restless where he lay with Adala nestled against his back, her arm around his middle. She knew he was afraid. Of course he was afraid, she told herself, although he would never admit to it. They were all afraid. The plan that they must soon attempt to put into action must inevitably result in their destruction, should it fail. Adala could feel his heartbeat beneath her hand.

'It beats for me', she told herself. 'And I shall always have that. No one shall ever take that away from me'.

Her restless mind maundered over the years since their first chance encounter in The Grapes, so long ago. It had seemed like a dream even then, and it still it did when she set her rational mind to consider it. She lay beside a prince! A tavern girl! How could such an astonishing event have come to pass? And perhaps in a few days he would be an emperor and she an empress. Perhaps. Anxiety gnawed at her when her mind turned to the complex set of circumstances that must brought into existence for such an eventuality to occur.

'Are you awake?' he asked softly, an enquiry that always made her smile.

'No', she answered in the usual way, prompting his gentle squeeze of her hand.

'What are you thinking about?' he asked.

'I was thinking about how we came to be together, you and I', she answered.

It was not necessary to rehearse the strange circumstances of their chance meeting, so many times had they done so. It was sufficient merely to know that it lay in the other's mind.

'So unreal it seems now', murmured Taian, when each had given this some thought. 'So distant. In another world'.

'A world that led to this one', said Adala, giving him a nudge. 'And so a world I love'.

'I do not fear to fail, you know', he said after a period of companionable silence, whilst a breeze stirred the black branches of the dead tree beyond their window.

'Of course, you don't', she affirmed. 'You are the bravest man I know'.

'Rather, I fear to succeed', he added, turning over to her now, his face a lighter patch in the darkness. 'I was never made to rule men'.

'Tio will guide you', said the one whose lips that name had been a stranger to for so long.

But now Tio came often enough to her thoughts. She longed to see him once more in her dreams, and so she would drift to sleep, praying that he might come to her, or wander from the halls of Morpheus in search of him as she awoke. But he did not come, and the consciousness that he might nevertheless take possession of her body in time of need was small consolation to her. Gods were creatures of whims and caprices, of course, whose attendance to the prayers of mere mortals was governed by no evident logic or justice. And yet hope remained in her heart. That one glorious vision was more than millions were privileged to witness in a lifetime, and she nurtured it in her soul, like an amulet at her throat that she could bring out on its chain and caress in times of need.

'He will need to', sighed Taian.

The week before the festivities saw the usual frantic round of activity in The City. The emperor's love of ostentation and conspicuous consumption meant that this was far from being an unusual burden upon the citizenry. Those many citizens whose shoulders bore the weight of the emperor's exactions grumbled and frowned. Those whose livelihoods depended upon furnishing the material needs of the festivities rubbed their hands together and exulted in it all. As ever, the taverns and inns filled up with the middling people and the merchants from the provinces. As ever, the dukes and their entourages, the hundreds of the lesser nobility, began to arrive from their country seats, unless The City was already their primary place of residence. The weather seemed set fine as Midsummer Day approached, and there was an atmosphere of gathering excitement as preparations moved towards their climax. In the tournament ground outside the city's walls, the temporary wooden grandstands had been erected, the field sufficient to accommodate as many as a hundred thousand spectators, and the surrounding open spaces were given over to paddocks, stables and storehouses for the equipment the competitors would require. There were to be contests of all kinds, ranging from dance, through archery and musketry, culminating in the final jousting match towards the end of the afternoon. Each of the twelve duchies provided a champion for this and each of the three wards of The City. The emperor himself took the final place of the sixteen and always competed in the final. The emperor was a genuinely formidable competitor, and his succession of victories owed nothing to reluctance amongst his opponents to unseat him. It was said that the Count of Drumnestro, competing beneath the banner of the Duke of Arken, was most likely to advance to this final contest, but each of the competitors had a fair claim, and the sport was notoriously open to the fickle interventions of fate. An ill-timed lurch on uneven ground, a momentary involuntary twitch of muscle or wavering of attention, could make all the difference between success and failure.

Taian was all too conscious of these concerns as he stood with his companions and watched the preparations amongst the gaudy pavilions of the competitors, each decorated in the livery of the ward or province they represented. It was necessary to be discreet, of course. There was to be no crowding into the stands for them with the wealthier citizens. Instead, once the events began, they were to join the mass of common people who watched from the rising ground on the open side of the enclosure, with allotments and the great curve of the Canto at their backs. From here they would be able to observe the outcome of the jousting matches and trace the progress of the competition. When the time came, they would be able to make their way to the pavilion of the champion, who would face the emperor in the final contest. The likelihood was that this would be

Drumnestro, and so the pavilion and its environs had already been thoroughly reconnoitred in terms of access and egress, should escape become necessary. However, because Drumnestro's success was far from absolute, the same had been necessary with all the other pavilions – a process that had taken the better part of the morning. It was a weary group that stood taking refreshment from one of the many food stalls that the usual entrepreneurs had set up amongst the throng.

'Well, I think we have done all that *can* be done', observed Rayo, swerving to avoid a drunk who came reeling hilariously through the crowd, pursued by an angry, red-faced woman clutching a goose. 'Now we must watch the competition and pray for the good count, that Tio might guide his lance'.

Chapter Twenty-One

Callisto

The sun had yet to rise that same day, when one of the empress's ladies-in-waiting knocked softly on her door to announce that the Director of Investigators awaited her pleasure in the vestibule. Cresara, recognising that only an event of considerable significance could have prompted such an untimely visitation, pulled on a gown, stood impatiently while the same anxious girl brushed some order into her hair and then made her way through to meet her visitor. She found him rather more self-possessed than he had been on the occasion of their last meeting, making his formal bow and the necessary enquiries after her health, before her raised hand cut him short.

'Do get on with it, Kyrenion. I trust you have something important to tell me'.

'I believe I have, Ma'am', said the Director smoothly. 'Intelligence has reached me regarding the imposter who wishes to be known as Prince Taian'.

'It has?' said Cortesia, folding her arms and feeling a quickening in her pulse.

'Indeed. A person answering his description, accompanied by a number of others, was seen entering the property of one Cortesia Tyverios, several days ago'.

'I suppose you have placed it under observation', said Cresara, stroking her chin now.

The name Cortesia Tyverios was not one she had heard for many years, and hearing it now caused her a sudden stab of anxiety. If anyone had cause to hate and resent her, it was Cortesia. If anyone would gladly conspire with her enemies, it was her. The years rolled back, and the envy that had gripped her then was upon her once more, together with a ripple of the rage that had brought about the destruction of her rival's power. That challenge had been neutralised, her threat and her influence crushed. How did she now dare to renew that challenge?

'I have', agreed Kyrenion. 'Ever since that intelligence reached me, an hour or so ago. Since that time, no one has been observed entering or leaving'.

'Excellent. Then what are you waiting for? Gain entry to the property and place them under arrest'.

'As you wish, Ma'am. Shall I convey them to the Directorate?'

'You shall, and I shall wish to join you in your interrogation'.

'This morning, Ma'am?'

'Of course!' she affirmed, eyes blazing.

Drael was awakened by the sound of voices – harsh voices, barked commands and a woman's scream, abruptly curtailed. It was still dark. Doors slammed, timber splintered and there came the urgent tramp of footsteps on the stairs outside his room. Already, even as these alarming sounds assailed his ears, he was rolling out of bed, reaching for his sword belt, drawing out his sword. There was no finesse amongst these intruders. No one tried the handle of his door. Instead, with a mighty crash, some large man's boot burst it asunder and three came striding in. The lamp that still burnt at Drael's bedside and the dim light of coming dawn was sufficient to disclose two members of The Watch and an investigator turn towards him, the latter's own lamp in one hand, a sword in the other. The lamp came up, flooding the room with light.

'Hey!' said the investigator, bringing up his sword, too. 'Stand just where you are. Drop that now, sir, easy now', he added, tapping his own sword point against Drael's, whose mind was racing.

Could he successfully take on these three and make it past them? The calculation took mere fractions of a second. Distantly, he heard Cortesia's voice, raised in protest as she was urged down the main staircase. One of the maids was shrieking in a room upstairs, and there now was Ohk's voice, an inchoate roaring further along the corridor, together with the sound of cursing and that of large bodies being cast about. Ohk was not submitting easily, it appeared.

Drael laughed, having made his decision, and lowered his sword.

'It sounds like one of them's not going quietly', he said.

'Them...' said the investigator with a glance over his shoulder, a note of uncertainty in his voice. 'You say, *them...*',

Drael reached beneath his shirt and brought out his official investigator's amulet on its chain.

'Agent Trimestrion', he said. 'I'm with Gandelion's office, embedded in this damned nest of vipers. I see the word finally came through, then'.

'Lower your swords', grunted the investigator to his companions, raising the lantern high in his other hand and bending to scrutinise the amulet.

At length, he sniffed and appeared satisfied.

'Beroes, of Dantones' division', he said, looking up into Drael's eyes now. 'Have you been here long?'

'Too long', laughed Drael easily as Ohk, still struggling and roaring, was impelled past the door and down the stairs after his mistress and two of the weeping housemaids.

'What's going on?' asked one of the watchmen with a sigh, re-sheathing his sword.

'Trimestrion here has been undercover with these people, it appears', Beroes said, and then, glancing out of the open door, 'Tio's breath, will you look at the size of that one. You'll be wanting to speak to Chief Investigator Mailoc, then', he added. 'He'll be waiting out front with the wagons'.

'I hope you got them all', said Drael, pulling on breeches and coat, groping for his shoes. 'I sent precise intelligence'.

'You two go on', said Beroes to the guardsmen. 'I'd better take care of the introductions with Trimestrion here and Mailoc'.

'Two female servants, a male servant, a large male servant, I should say, and the lady of the house. That's what you should have by now', said Drael, buckling on his sword belt as the two watchmen nodded and left.

There was another commotion downstairs, together with the sound of breaking furniture. Beroes' head swung round towards the sound. Drael, with an intake of breath and a silent invocation to Tio, punched the side of that head with all his strength, knocking the hat that covered it flying. The blow connected with a satisfying, knuckle-bruising thud. Seizing Beroes' startled, stunned face under the jaw, Drael thrust the back of his head hard against the door frame, once, twice, three times, until he was quite certain that the man must be insensible. Then, leaving the investigator slumped in the threshold, he turned the corner into the corridor and took the stairs three at a time.

'That took you a damnable long time', he called to the group of watchmen who had Ohk face down on the floor by now, swearing, panting and rubbing bruised parts of themselves.

Drael had his amulet out once more, holding it up as he approached. The two guards Beroes had just dismissed were with them.

'Undercover', he snapped with a nod at his amulet. 'You two', he ordered. 'Beroes wants you upstairs. You missed one'.

They nodded.

Good, Drael smiled inwardly. His bogus authority was already recognised, taking root. There was another, more junior investigator with this group, nursing a tender jaw and regarding Drael's amulet with suspicion. Drael would need to add bluster to this heady mix.

'And you', he said, 'I suppose you're going to introduce yourself. I'm guessing there's precious little communication between your office and mine'.

'Carnio', grunted the man, succumbing readily to this ploy. 'When is there ever?!'

'Desk warriors', laughed Drael, a wary exultation gripping him now. 'You'd better go tell Mailoc there's another one at large up there', he instructed while directing a nod up the stairs. 'I'll take care of this one'.

Carnio, with a grim nod in return for Drael, hurried off through the hall towards the front of the house.

'You three', barked Drael now. 'Top floor. Get yourselves up there. Room at the end of the corridor. Investigator Beroes is waiting for you there... Go on! What are you waiting for?!'

There were advantages, Drael reflected, in possessing a countenance so well-suited to the expression of stern authority. With barely a twitch, barely a hint of reluctance, the three guards thus designated pounded off up the stairs, leaving only two, both of whom were lying across Ohk's recumbent form.

'I know this one', grunted Drael. 'You can leave him be. Ohk, are you going to come quietly now? It'll go ill for you if you don't'.

Ohk, whose face showed evidence of confusion, giving way to relief, nodded and his captors rolled off him, brushing themselves down, regarding the big man warily as he climbed to his feet to loom over them.

'*We're* going this way', snapped Drael as the two guards moved in the direction of the hall. 'My own men are at the rear. You two go after the others'.

Drael had his sword point at Ohk's back now as he impelled him along the passage that led towards the kitchen. The two guards glanced at each other and made mental calculations involving the relative sizes of Ohk and Drael. They concluded that it was Drael's funeral if he wanted to get himself thumped, and anyway, he was evidently in charge of things. Having processed these thoughts, they shrugged and withdrew, picking up a hat each and enroute laughing loudly on a theme of "rather him than me."

Ohk and Drael kept moving. As soon as the two guards were out of sight, they ran, passing quickly through the kitchen and out into the garden. There were no longer any watchers here. Presumably they had all been engaged in the incursion, so it was easy to slip through the garden gate and out into the same dark passage that Jory and Rayo had come hurrying along, three years previously. Once there, they both took a minute to recover their composure, breathing deep, bent over, hands resting on thighs.

'You had better conduct me to Bardo's house', croaked Drael when he had mastery of his breathing, although it still seemed that his heart must burst from his chest.

Bardo, an early riser, was already dressed, already readying himself for his short journey to work when Drael and Ohk arrived at his door. It was immediately apparent that something was amiss, a circumstance made even more certain as Drael pushed past him, muttering about getting *that damn door shut, quick as you like!* Ohk's own face bore an expression that mingled fear with apology.

'They've taken Cortesia, damn them!' cried Drael, waving aside an invitation to sit down, striding from side to side of the small room in agitation and slapping one fist repeatedly into an open palm. 'They'll have her at the Directorate by now'.

'They'll torture her', gasped Bardo, eyes wide.

'Of course they will', snapped Drael, running a hand through his hair distractedly whilst his two companions regarded him anxiously. 'We have to get her out of there'.

'What of the others?' asked Bardo. 'We should tell the others. She may spill the plan'.

'She may, she may!' admitted Drael, demonstrating a degree of agitation quite shocking to the others, accustomed as they were to his calm, steady demeanour. 'But it may already be too late to contact them. They will be joining the throng at sun up, and then we may never find them, unless by chance. No, we must focus our attention on freeing Cortesia'.

He turned to Bardo.

'Get you to Lando's house', he said, mentioning Rayo's cousin. 'See if he may not gather a body of his staff or young friends that might make a demonstration in front of the Directorate. If we can distract their attention at that point, we may be able to gain access through the side entrance. This amulet still seems to work, thank Tio', he added, patting his breast.

Chief Investigator Mailoc had greeted his underling, Carnio, with surprise and irritation, although it had taken some moments to determine what had happened.

'What do you mean, *infiltrated*?' he demanded. 'We had no one on the inside in there. We have only just learned of it'.

'He said he was with Gandelion's office', stammered Carnio, alarmed by his superior's incredulous expression.

'Did he now?' enquired Mailoc acidly as he stepped into his carriage. 'Did he really?'

'He did', said Carnio, clutching his hat.

'Then I gather you don't know that Gandelion's office deals with Directorate administration, office supplies and filing, you fool! They're no more likely to be running embedded agents than sprouting wings and flying to the moon. And now you've let two of them go! What did you say the fellow's name was? Trimestrion, you say? I'm sure I've heard that name somewhere'.

The carriage door shut, but before Carnio could recover his composure, the window flew down and his superior's angry face appeared once more.

'Tidy up here, and do it now!', it barked. 'If you can be trusted to do even that, expect to be doing a great deal of routine paperwork from now on'.

The window slammed closed once more and the carriage trundled off, leaving a disconsolate officer regarding his ruined career prospects with dismay.

'Damn!' he uttered. 'Yuzanid's teeth!' he cursed, and then, turning to survey the group of attendant guards, showing every indication of amusement, 'and what are you all staring at?!'

Cortesia, having been ejected from her bed and led to the door of her room without ceremony, had time only to snatch up the silk cloth with which she habitually hid her injuries. The dismay upon the faces of the young men, whose lamps had disclosed her features to them, had caused her a new twinge of shame amongst the fear and confusion that had gripped her. Now she had only this and her nightgown as she sat in a cold cell in the basement of the Directorate, awaiting the pleasure of her interrogators. She knew very well what that might entail, had considered it every day since first she had set out to oppose the imperial regime. That vague, abstract notion had nevertheless given her no means of comparison with the actual terror of captivity, the discomfort and the sense of being entirely helpless in the arbitrary power of others – others who might oppress her mind or torment her flesh according to their whim. The cell was quite dark, except for what little dim radiance crept around the door, and contained nothing at all except herself. It was a bleak, stone cube that stank of urine, excrement and sheer naked terror. Cortesia made her own contribution to the last mentioned,sitting hugging her knees with her back pressed into a corner.

Her only consolation was that she could speak to Ohk. His voice, in her head, was infinitely comforting to her. For a while, during the chaos and confusion of her capture, there had been nothing, but even as her captors bore her away in that carriage, his voice had found her.

'Are you there, my lady?'

'Yes. Yes, I am', gasped Cortesia, the twitch in her body causing the investigators who shared the carriage with her to regard her warily.

'I am with Trimestrion', he said. 'We have made good our escape. He tells me that you must take careful note of where they conduct you. We must know where to find you'.

'I will', she replied, a glow of hope in her soul, a renewed surge of affection for her servant.

'I am with you', he had assured her. 'I will release you, or I shall die trying'.

She knew that this was the simple truth. And in truth, the relationship between them could no longer be described as mistress and servant, except in as it pleased Ohk to maintain that convention. When all the restrictions of convention placed upon them by society were set aside, they were simply man and woman. When Cortesia sat to listen to him read, watched his finger move haltingly across the page and heard his soft voice in her head, her heart filled with a curious warmth that rimmed her eye with unshed tears and brought a joyful congestion to her throat. There was a real sense, after all these years, that they were like an old married couple, infinitely familiar to each other. It was as if those years were a trellis upon which the creeping tendrils of their lives had become entwined and grown inextricably together, flowering at last. At last. Cortesia had never known love, not in her years before the crime and certainly not since. She assured herself that she would have known, had it been there, having read so extensively on that theme as a teenager, having immersed herself in thrilling tales of romance. Certainly, her famous beauty had attracted a multitude of handsome suitors, who brought that promise with them, in whose eyes and whose faces she had seen the glimmer of its potential, like the rainbow in a raindrop. She had wondered what it would be like. Would it burn within her like a sudden flame and drive out all other considerations so that she lived to cherish that flame alone? But now she must consider that her love for Ohk had always been there, growing quietly beneath the dark surface of her mind, ready to set forth its green shoots to greet the sun at last. Perhaps it was too late – already too late – and she would perish there in that cell, alone, having never acknowledged it, having never spoken the words that were in her heart.

She closed her eyes against the darkness without and dwelt in the soft darkness within, summoning into her mind images of Ohk – the softness of his great hands, the tight curls of his hair. How she regretted her harsh words and her cold indifference to him over those lost years, years that existed only to oppress her mind with regret now. That mind turned to the bitter, bitter day with which it had begun... and to Cresara Rhovanion.

Cresara Rhovanion's arrival at the Directorate threw the place into a tumult. There had been no notice, no time to sweep corridors or to make all ready, all flawlessly neat and tidy for a formal inspection. Fortunately, the empress spared barely a glance for the ranks of curious officers, sweeping through the halls and corridors with the Director at her side and a crowd of anxious underlings in her train. An interview room had been prepared and provided with a more than typically comfortable chair for the empress. She sat now with the Director and Nailac Pontopheles, one of his leading subordinates, in the soft yellow light cast by a number of hanging lamps. There were no windows, nothing to suggest that anything at all existed beyond the confines of this bare, uncluttered room. On the opposite side of the table stood a single hard chair, and it was to this that the chief amongst the prisoners was presently led.

'The prisoner has a number of severe facial injuries', explained Pontopheles as Cortesia was shown into the room, between two uniformed guards. 'And for that reason, she has been permitted to retain her head covering'.
He did not mention that his own encounter with that face, an hour or so earlier, had caused him some disquiet, and this from a man who had seen many things that a settled mind should forget.
'However, it can certainly be removed, if you desire it'.
'It may remain', said Cresara with a shudder. She had heard much of her victim's injuries but had no desire to set eyes upon them.
Cortesia, wearing a nightgown already soiled by the brief sojourn in her cell, seated herself and regarded her

captors steadily with her one eye. Her back was straight and her carriage proud, despite the indignities of her circumstances.

'Her imperial majesty has graced us with her presence today', began the Director. 'So you would be wise to conduct yourself in a manner...'

'We are here to establish truth', interrupted the empress, raising a hand that enforced immediate silence upon the Director. 'And the prisoner will face the consequences if she does not offer the most fulsome cooperation with my Director's investigation. We know each other of old, do we not, Cortesia Tyverios? So, I do not expect deference'.

'Nor shall you receive it', scoffed Cortesia.

'You blame me for your injuries. I know this...', began Cresara.

'I blame you because you caused them', interrupted Cortesia, her eye blazing fiercely.

'Then you lie', snapped Cresara. 'Besides, I believe it is you who stands accused of a crime here, and should your answers to our questions not be to our satisfaction, you must surely suffer the consequence of your crimes'.

'What crimes?' said Cortesia with a harsh laugh.

'You stand accused of harbouring and offering succour to criminals and traitors', said Pontopheles upon a nod from the empress. 'Namely, the notorious imposter who presents himself as Prince Taian Starcorides'.

'I know nothing of this', said Cortesia, continuing to regard the empress steadily with a gaze that would have caused a less formidable person to quail.

'So you say. And yet we have it on good authority that persons connected to that imposter have been visitors to your house. We believe that a plot injurious to the security of the realm has been fomented beneath your roof and that you are party to it. How do you answer this charge?'

'I deny it', said Cortesia. 'And I look forward to facing my accusers in court'.

'Oh dear', said the empress with a humorous glance for the Director. 'She thinks she will appear in court'.

Now Cortesia's demeanour disclosed the faintest hint of dismay, a twitch of the headcloth perhaps suggesting that she had swallowed hard.

'As you well know, Cortesia Tyverios, the Directorate is not bound by the ordinary constraints of law', continued the empress. 'Its work is too important. No, we judge that the plot we suspect is far advanced and that its detection is a matter of the greatest urgency. Accordingly, you will answer the questions that are put to you until those answers are to our satisfaction. The flesh is a frail vessel for the spirit, is it not? And we shall torment that flesh with every implacable cruelty that human ingenuity can supply until that spirit yields up its truth, or the flesh can no longer sustain it. Consider that prospect, Tyverios. Consider it well'.

So saying, the empress rose from her seat, prompting her companions to rise with her, and swept from the room, leaving Cortesia to stare at the empty walls.

'I want the truth out of her, and I want it soon', observed the empress to her companions as she made her way back to the front of the building, where her guards and ladies-in-waiting had stationed themselves. 'I have a sense that this is very urgent'.

'You may be sure that we shall attend to it', said the Director with a bow as she mounted the steps to her carriage.

As the carriage bore her away towards the palace, through streets already thronged in preparations for the day's coming events, Cresara had cause to reflect upon her motivations for making that visit. Of course, she had been keen to keep her pulse on an investigation she instinctively felt represented a genuine threat to her position. But there was more than that. She had been genuinely drawn to see what had become of her erstwhile rival at court. After her commissioning of the assault upon her, all those years ago, it had been necessary to tidy up a number of loose ends. The immediate death of the assassin she had set upon her rival was a pressing need and then a period of carefully presented regret, in which she had withdrawn from public life to some limited extent, ostensibly to show respect for the unwitting victim of her spite. And then, certainly, there were the accusations to be borne, her own innocence to be established and her reputation secured. All these things had taken time, and during this lengthy period, her exultation at her triumph must necessarily be shut up within her, like the embers of a damped-down fire. In time, as days followed days and years, years, those embers had grown cold, and in time the person who had once dwelt in the forefront of an envious mind was banished to the furthest dark corner of her memory. Cortesia had withdrawn from society and entered upon a decade of obscurity in which her name, once on the lips of all, was all but forgotten. It had been strange to find the fire of that fierce memory rekindled, strange to look upon the person she had so roundly defeated after all these years. It was hard not to exult once more that her own rise had been encompassed at least in part by her rival's fall, and yet that exultation was strangely tainted by a sensation unfamiliar to Cresara, one that caused her to bite her lip and look upon the streets with a wholly unfocused gaze. She had never felt a moment's regret, in all that time, that her actions had brought about Cortesia's utter ruin. Why now, then, was she assailed by this cloying coldness in her breast? She wished that she had never come, now regretted that mere curiosity had distracted her from more important tasks, cursed her own weakness in so doing. But it was too late. That tardy seed of guilt was sown.

Several hours passed by whilst Drael set in place his plan to release Cortesia. The Director, conscious of the empress's pressing concern, had already set in place the process by which the prisoner might be obliged to give up her secrets. There was no lengthy preliminary verbal enquiry that might progress gradually to a more physically exacting method. Instead, once the necessary staff had been located and brought in to the Directorate, Cortesia was stripped naked and her hands shackled behind her back. Then, a rope was tied to the shackles and passed up through a ring bolt in the ceiling. By hauling on this rope, Cortesia could be drawn upwards until the whole of her weight hung upon her tormented joints and ligaments. Her face was revealed in all its horror now, but such things held no power to dismay the men who plied their brutal trade in this place.

'I would urge you to share what you know with us', said Pontopheles, who had supervised these preparations.

His men stood by now, applying sufficient tension to the rope to pull Cortesia's arms up behind her so that she must thrust her head forward to seek relief from the sudden agony in her joints.

'It hurts, does it not?' observed Pontopheles as Cortesia gasped. 'But these sensations are a tiny foretaste of what is to come. My men are experts in the infliction of pain. You will not step out of this cell alive. The empress has decreed it. Your transition to the blessèd relief of death may encompass a world of excruciating pain such as you never imagined could exist, or it can be mercifully short. The choice is yours, my dear. Choose wisely. Now, what have you to tell me?'

Chapter Twenty-Two

Callisto

Ohk, working quickly and listening to Cortesia's voice in his head, had drawn a crude sketch map that showed where she was held. Now Drael, Bardo, Lando and a number of that nobleman's leading retainers pored over it, laid out on a table.

'I know this place', grunted Drael. 'These are the west holding cells. There are six of them on the basement level'.

He pointed at the map.

'Fortunately, they are the ones placed closest to the side entrance. Entry at that point places us in a short corridor. We turn right at the end of that and descend the staircase, which appears at our left after thirty yards or so. That staircase brings us to the end of this corridor, which is closed with a locked iron gate. There are three cells on either side. It appears that Cortesia is confined within the last on the left-hand side'.

'I'm presuming there'll be a guard in there with the keys', observed Bardo, stroking his chin.

'Certainly there will, and any number of other staff on the stairs or in the corridors, depending on how our luck runs', said Drael grimly.

'And how shall we gain access in the first place?' asked Lando. 'I presume that even the side entrance will be guarded'.

'With this', said Drael, drawing out his amulet once more. 'Although I fear that its efficacy may be diminished by now. It may be that my name has already been circulated and that they await me there'.

The company exchanged uneasy glances whilst Drael picked up and folded the map, placing it in a pocket.
'So do we still go ahead, then?' asked Bardo. 'Is not the risk too great?'
'The risk is very great', said Drael, looking from face to face. 'But what other chance do we have? The sooner we act, the better. If Cortesia discloses the details of the plot, the emperor will be informed. The joust will be abandoned and with it all our hopes'.
He turned to Ohk.
'How does she fare, Ohk?'
The fact that Ohk's face was wet with tears told its own story. He shifted uneasily from foot to foot, shaking his great dark head.

It was past noon by now. The vast bulk of the populace had made their way down to the tournament fields by the river, so the streets were quiet. There were few to remark the passage of Lando's band of servants and retainers, armed with staves and baskets of stones. Drael marched with Lando, Ohk and Bardo at their head.
'We are coming, Ma'am', assured Ohk as they moved through familiar streets close to the spice market.
They passed the forge at the junction of Swinegate and the street of the candlemakers. Bardo and Ohk were friends with the blacksmith there, a man who had, together with the vast majority of The City's tradesmen, gone to observe the games and the festivities. His wife was there, though, and made no objection to Ohk borrowing his great hammer. This was a huge and massy block of iron, on a handle almost as long as Bardo was tall. With a nod and a bow of thanks, Ohk hefted it in his hands and hurried to catch up with Drael's group as they turned the corner into Aspenwall Square. Here, the Directorate stood at the west end, the dark mass of its walls and its steep pitched roofs looming over that

narrow space. Here, the group split, the majority, perhaps thirty young men, advancing towards the steps of the high-columned front entrance, whilst Drael and his small party made their way around the periphery of the square, to the narrow alley between the Directorate and the adjoining Justice Department offices. A private entrance allowed ready access for government officials going about their business, or for investigating officers or private agents to pass in and out without drawing attention to themselves.

'Ready?' asked Drael as his companions took their places on either side of the door.

Various nods and grunts of agreement indicated assent. Now they must wait. Soon, there came a commotion from the square. Lando's men could be heard shouting abuse, accompanied by the distant tinkle of breaking glass as stones were hurled. It was to be hoped that the Directorate would be thoroughly stirred up and that all attention would momentarily turn to the front of the building. The advantage would be a brief one. Most of The Watch would be stationed in the tournament field, but there would be enough to make short work of Lando's unarmed men. They would run, their task complete. Now was the time.

Drael strode to the door, knocked boldly and brandished his amulet at the face that appeared in the gap.

'Urgent!' he barked. 'I must speak with the Director immediately. Every moment counts!'

The ferocity of Drael's countenance and the mention of the Director's name, together with the word 'urgent', were sufficient to set aside official reluctance. The door opened wide to admit Drael and then, as he held the door ajar with his foot, the remainder of his party. The door warden, mouth wide, made to protest but was brushed aside.

The party hurried to the end of the corridor. There was a measure of chaos in the open space beyond, one occupied by the desks of various branches of the Directorate. Soldiers with muskets and smouldering match came rushing past to take up places at the windows, where various startled officials were staring out warily into the street beyond. Shattered glass lay on the floor, and the air was filled with urgent cries and barked commands.

Their timing was good, and Drael cast a glance over his shoulder at his grim-faced companions and indicated the direction of the stairs to the basement. Two more musketeers came charging past, and loud reports from the front of the building indicated that they were firing upon their assailants. Acrid smoke began eddying amongst the desks, the familiar smell of battle in Drael's nostrils as he strode along the corridor. A man stepped out of an office but was pushed roughly in the chest and withdrew, eyes wide.

'Make way!' snarled Drael with Ohk looming at his shoulder. 'Director's business!'

They turned into the staircase at the left, descended two flights and emerged into a lobby space lit feebly by oil lamps. Ohk and Drael stepped into this space while the others remained out of sight around the corner. Here, another guard sat behind a locked gate, whittling idly at a stick with his knife. He stood up, regarding the newcomers suspiciously as Drael approached, amulet held out in front of him.

'Note from the Director', he said brusquely, and then with a suggestive leer. 'He sent this fellow to liven up the lady prisoner'.

'Tio's breath', laughed the guard, squinting at the amulet in the dim light and then at Ohk. 'If that doesn't make her talk!'

He stepped forward to take the paper, at which point Ohk seized his arm in a vice-like grip and hauled him hard against the bars, stifling his cries with a huge hand pressed over his mouth. At the same time, Drael drew the knife from his belt and stabbed the guard in the chest and side until he was quite certain the man was dead. The man's dying whimpers echoed briefly around the space, mingling with those of Cortesia issuing from the end of that dark corridor beyond. The guard slumped to the ground, oozing blood from half a dozen wounds, whilst Drael groped for the keys at his belt. Within moments, the gate was open, admitting the party into the space beyond. There were more agonised screams from the cell on the left at the far end of the corridor, followed by a low moan and the sound of sadistic laughter.

Ohk was beside himself with anxiety and rage by this time, shifting his weight urgently from foot to foot, swinging the great hammer in his hand. Drael inspected the keys. It was impossible to know which one fitted which door. They would have to rely on trial and error. That would take valuable time and perhaps alert Cortesia's tormentors to their presence. Who knew what they might then do?

He and Ohk stared helplessly at one another for a moment, and then Ohk shrugged and stepped out purposefully towards the cell where his mistress was being tormented, waving aside Drael and Bardo's appeals for patience, knocking aside Drael's restraining arm as though it were a child's.

A moment later, as his companions stood well back, Ohk planted his feet squarely, flexed his powerful muscles and swung the hammer with every particle of his strength and will. The door, although sturdily constructed, was an old one, unused to violent attack from the outside. The first blow battered and bent the lock panel, splitting the wood on either side. The second, delivered with even greater force, split it asunder and the door burst open.

For a moment, Pontopheles and his two companions looked on, aghast as Ohk and Drael strode in, their four companions at their heels. In an instant, Cortesia's tormentors were dead, dispatched with a fury of avenging violence, Pontopheles' head smashed into a bloody ruin by a further mighty blow of Ohk's hammer. Dropping it, he rushed to support his mistress, throwing his arms around her and lifting her from the floor whilst Lando and Bardo cut the rope that held her arms.

'Mistress!' cried Ohk inside Cortesia's head. 'What have they done to you?'

Her face was wet with blood where Pontopheles had ripped and torn at her old injuries with his bare hands. Shockingly, her other ear lay discarded on the floor where he had severed and thrown it.

'Clothes', grunted Drael, reaching these from a table as Cortesia was lowered gently to the floor. 'Those animals can rot in Hell!' he added, giving one of the bodies a savage kick for good measure.

'Oh, Ohk', moaned Cortesia's voice behind his eyes. 'I thought I should die'.

'Can you dress?' he asked. 'We must be quick'.

With arms that shrieked their torment, Cortesia hesitantly drew her nightgown over her head, barely able to stand on legs that trembled with a palsy of shock.

'And can you walk?' asked Drael softly as Ohk wound the cloth around her head.

She nodded, but Ohk shook his head and picked her up like a child in his arms, where she nestled weeping into his breast.

In his office on the first floor, the Director and his secretary looked out of the window at the mob in the street. Musket shots continued to ring out from below and the mob were withdrawing, dragging with them a number of wounded and leaving one corpse slumped at the foot of the main steps. The attack had been deeply shocking. No intelligence had warned of it, and the Directorate was woefully understaffed on this of all days. What did it mean? What did they hope to achieve? Presently, as the noise and the chaos began to abate, a connection of ideas began to take shape in the Director's mind. It was a diversion of some kind, surely it was, but to what end?

He slapped his cheeks with both hands as realisation dawned.

It must be an attempt to rescue that woman, the woman the empress had seemed to regard as such a significant threat. The circumstances of her arrest came into his mind and with it the name of Trimestrion. Evidently, the man was a rogue officer, but events since then had evolved with such rapidity that the name and its significance had slipped from his grasp until that moment. All the pieces fell into place now, and he dashed from his office with a speed and agility that belied his fifty-two years.

'The cells!' he roared at the top of the stairs, leaning far out over the balustrade, causing various heads below to tilt upward. 'They're trying to free the new woman prisoner! Get down there!'

The Director's command rang out, even as the rescue party emerged from the staircase that led down to the cells and turned out into the corridor. Now there were cries as armed officers rushed to oppose them, jostling amongst the crowd of startled bureaucrats and officials. They were almost at the short corridor that was their destination, the one that gave access to the side entrance, by the time the guards were upon them. Drael, sword drawn, turned to Bardo and Ohk.

'Get her away, I'll cover!' he barked, before combat was joined.

There were screams and the clash of steel on steel as Lando and his two men came up at Drael's side, making a barrier behind which Ohk and Bardo might withdraw. A desk was overturned and a man toppled backward, clutching at his throat, and great gouts of smoke accompanied the sharp reports of musket shots. Ohk, with Cortesia whimpering in his arms, felt a tremendous blow to his back, staggered, grunted with pain and recovered as they approached the exit door, where the same guard that had admitted them now raised a quivering sword point. A vast pain began to grow like a searing hot flower within Ohk's massive frame, so that he clenched his jaw and shook his head. The guard blenched. His sword arm wavered. The sight of Ohk bearing down upon him like a vast, dark tide of fury unnerved him, and he dropped his weapon, darting aside into his cubbyhole beside the door.

Moments later, they were free, pelting along streets and alleys, desperate to place distance between themselves and the Directorate. Bardo became conscious that Ohk was lagging behind, becoming slower and slower. At last, he sank to his knees in a narrow alley between the houses of merchants, setting Cortesia down gently before him. Then he groaned and slumped sideward to the hard earth.

'Ohk!' cried Cortesia and Bardo with one voice.

Cortesia scrambled painfully to her haunches, leaned over Ohk and found the back of his shirt wet with blood, where the musket ball had penetrated.

'You are free', came Ohk's voice in her head. 'As you have freed me'.

'No, Ohk', moaned Cortesia, embracing his head tenderly now, pressing what remained of her torn lips through that blood-soaked fabric to his brow. 'No! Don't go. Don't leave me now!'

A great surge of hot grief swept through her, and another emotion that held her now in a grip so powerful that she could barely breathe. She was suddenly dizzy. Her pulse raced and the pain that had gripped her arms and shoulders relented. What was this, this overwhelming sensation that pervaded every fibre of her being and robbed her of her power to speak or even think? And then, in a glorious epiphany of joyous heart-rending pain, she recognised it for what it was.

'Ohk, I love you. I love you; do you hear me?' she moaned, rocking to and fro, cradling his head in her arms.

But it was perhaps already too late. His staring eyes were empty. He was gone, and the songs of his people were stilled.

'We must get us to the tournament field', she said at last, when she had wet Ohk's face with her tears.

'But mistress!' protested Bardo, anxiously. 'Your injuries...'

'Never mind my injuries', snapped Cortesia, struggling to her feet.

Her limbs were on fire with the pain that her captors had inflicted on her, but her mind shone with a determination that amazed her, and it was as though a glow of warmth and renewed vitality seized her frame. She was reminded of what Adala had told her about her vision. Was this what it was like to be divinely inspired?

'Help me', she said, nevertheless, when it seemed for a moment that her legs might betray her. 'Here. Let me put my arm around your shoulder. Hurry! There is not a moment to be lost!'

In the Directorate, Drael spent the last moments of his own life in buying time for Cortesia and for his friends. He fought with a fierce exultation, and Adala's name was in his heart. He took a sword-cut to the shoulder and a musket ball to the side, but still he fought with Lando at his side, once the others were cut down. They wove an impenetrable mesh of steel before them as moment succeeded frantic moment and they were driven slowly back along the passage. Drael found that the thought of death did not oppress him. It never had, not since that day he had witnessed her fall into Taian's embrace and she had passed from his own orbit into that of the prince's. His own love for her, a wholly unexpected love that had sprung upon him in defiance of all decency or convention, had doomed his days perpetually to regret and to disappointment. Sure, he had told himself that to witness her joy must console him, to see her happy must be a comfort to his own soul, but such assurances were like ash in his mouth, like feeble sparks in the vast coldness of his heart. In this world he may never possess that which he most desired, and each day was a torment to him. Now was a good time to die indeed, and the searing blade that entered his throat at last brought a blissful darkness rushing upon him. Adala's name breathed on his twitching lips as they fell still with that last breath.

The spectre of death loomed over the tournament field, too, as did the high white walls of the city. The broad acres of grassy fields were muddied and trampled with the passage of hundreds of thousands of human and equine feet, quite apart from the wheels of wagons, carts and carriages of all kinds. A vast crowd of humanity milled beneath the bright banners, stages and pavilions as the events of the day played out. There were wrestling matches, boxing bouts, contests of martial skill of all kinds, and the air was heavy with the smells of sweat, cheap scent, horseflesh, woodsmoke and cookery amongst the many food stalls that plied their wares. Men of The Watch maintained a rather variable vigil, to ensure that the law was observed, and small children ran laughing amongst the legs of their elders as they watched the competitions or simply exulted in the freedom of the day. And yet there was an uneasiness, too. The pride, the arbitrary abuse of power and the rapacious financial exactions of the emperor were in the thoughts of many, and on the tongues of many, too, whenever wary glances showed that conversations might not be overheard by the agents of that state. There was much quiet talk of rebellion, of a gathering storm of retribution that loomed beyond those high white walls, like an approaching thundercloud. There was a brittle quality to the festivity, and the bright good humour seemed as fragile as a glass lamp that might topple and shatter, a lake of spilt oil taking instant flame.

Death likewise occupied the forefront of Prince Taian's mind, for it seemed certain to him that the emperor's death was the only contingency that might secure the continuance of his own life.

The plan, long in gestation, required that the defeated emperor should mount the victor's podium at his side and that only then should Taian sweep off his helm to reveal his true identity and address the crowd. How simple that sounded, but when turned over in the mind, as it had been for months, more and more objections came flooding in. Would he even be permitted to speak to the assembled lords and the legates of the legions, if the emperor still stood there beside him? In his darker thoughts he envisaged the rushing of bodyguards to arrest him, heard the barked commands that must condemn him to prison and the inevitable scaffold that must follow. All depended on Balian.

'I do not know quite how much I may achieve, nor do I wish to put it to the test', Balian had said with a shudder when questioned about the parameters of his God-given powers.

Nor was he pressed too hard to answer. All knew that the exercise of those powers came at the cost of the expenditure of his life-force. The demonstration he had made at Soangarten had been more than enough to convince his friends of his capacity to assist their cause, but only Balian knew, or sensed, what toll it had taken of him.

'I shall try to freeze the emperor as he approaches at full tilt', Balian had proposed, 'in order that you may have the best chance of unseating him. Then, once you have ascended the address platform, I shall freeze him once more, so that you may make your speech unhindered'.

Perhaps, but a darker, more ominous contingency required that Taian should slay him where he stood, if Balian proved unable to prevent the onrush of bodyguards, for example. How that might be received was anybody's guess. Perhaps he would be cut down within instants by Triado's vengeful defenders. Nevertheless, Taian was determined that he should avenge the death of his brother by his own hand, since legal process was denied to him.

'You can only do your best', Adala told him, reading those thoughts upon his countenance with the ease of those who are truly in love.

They strolled arm in arm amongst the crowds, dressed in the inconspicuous garb of the common citizen, although wearing the flowered wreaths that so many were wearing in celebration of this auspicious day. Their objective was to blend with the crowd and to assume the relaxed ease of their movement, but Taian's awkward gait spoke eloquently of the uneasy mind within.

'No empress wore a finer diadem', said Taian with a smile, looking upon her with a glint of fierce, undaunted love in his eye.

She laughed and embraced him, sharing a moment that must perhaps be treasured in time to come. How she longed to be able to say, *relax, everything will be well,* but to say so would be to spit in the eye of reality, to bring down upon them the ponderous hand of fate to crush them, like so many insects. Instead, she squeezed his arm and reached up to kiss him, feeling warm tears sting her eyes.

'There he is', observed Taian after a moment, looking up to where the Count of Drumnestro rode through the crowd, above a sea of cheering citizens.

There were more than a few whose loud catcalls and ribald observations provoked laughter or the disapproving looks of their peers. The warm June sun reflected from armour burnished to a mirror-like finish, and his long blonde locks flowed upon his shoulders as he joked with the companions and retainers who rode with him.

'We must wish him well', said Taian. 'Or else infiltrate another champion's tent'.

All of the pavilions of the competitors in the joust had been reconnoitred since first light, the positions of entries located and a judgement made about the numbers or vigilance of the servants and retainers on duty there. If form were to believed, however, it would be the Count of Drumnestro's pavilion that would be their target as the contest drew to its conclusion.

The afternoon advanced and the competition began. The various members of the conspiracy had separated during the greater part of the day, but now they came together on the grassy bank that overlooked one side of the tilt-yard, to watch the competition with a hundred thousand of their fellows. The other side was occupied by the imperial box and the high wooden stands where the lords and nobles had their seats, the dukes and their subsidiary counts occupying the places of honour in the immediate vicinity of the emperor's throne. Next to this, on a throne of similar magnificence but lesser scale, sat the empress, and at her side sat Doctor Mordanios and various of her ladies-in-waiting.

From his position near to the top of the bank, Taian scanned those faces grimly, even as the first rounds of the competition began on the sanded tilt-yard below. In the past, he had shared the exultation of the crowd at the pageantry and the colour of the spectacle, the sparkle of polished steel and the thunder of the great horses as two armoured warriors hurtled towards collision. There were great cheers or great groans as lances shattered or competitors toppled from their saddles to thud to the ground. Fortunes were made or lost as bookmakers calculated odds and accepted the coin of those anxious to put their predictions to the test. Each contest was decided over three passes. In the centre of the tilt-yard stood the tilt-rail, a sturdy wooden barrier that prevented any accidental collision between horses. Upon the referee's command, the competitors urged their horses at full pelt towards each other, directing their lances over the barrier and seeking to land a blow on their opponent's shield or body that would throw them from their saddles. It was a dangerous sport. Many such contests ended in injury, occasionally in death, and many had urged the emperor that he would be wise to step back from his involvement in it. To no avail. Huge pride was attached to prowess in this sport, and great fame came to those who excelled. The emperor had competed regularly before his elevation to the throne, and his martial skills contributed to his reputation for power and for strength. Only the empress dared press him on this matter, and even her admonitions went unheeded. The emperor would have his way.

Taian and his companions found it easy to cheer for the emperor and for the Count of Drumnestro in the earlier rounds. Nor were they disappointed. If any warrior plied his lance with less than usual determination when faced with his emperor, this was not apparent to a crowd well-versed in the technicalities of the sport. Each competitor was required to ride in an initial pool of four, with the two best placed advancing to the next round, once each had faced their three opponents, unless withdrawal was necessary through injury. The remaining eight then competed in similar pools with a winnowing down process until only two riders remained.

The sun descended through the cirrus-streaked sky of a perfect June day as the culmination of the contest drew near, and only the emperor and his lover remained. The Count had ridden magnificently, toppling rider after rider into the clattering ignominy of flying sand and bruised bones. After his victory in the semi-final, he swept off his helm, let his golden locks fly and saluted all sides of the tournament grounds with raised lance, to cheers that reverberated from the walls behind. At this point there was to be an interval of half an hour or so whilst the emperor and his final opponent refreshed and readied themselves for the culmination of the day's events. The emperor, beaming about him indulgently amongst his servants and retainers, rode to the magnificent cloth of gold pavilion at one end of the field, embroidered with rich colours, heraldic symbols and Tio's great lion. Drumnestro, for his part, rode to his own scarlet pavilion at the opposite end of the field, where Taian and his companions awaited him.

Balian had dreaded this day, had felt its coming upon him in the way that a mariner senses the loom of a lee shore beyond the dim horizon. Perhaps all those years spent secluded from the world had been the result of a subconscious shrinking from the fate marked out for him in this coming moment. He must die. He must die so that Tio's will should be enacted in a manner all those long days ago when he had walked at his god's side along that beach. He would never live to see another dawn. He knew it, and he had always sensed that his day would be his last, as soon as the plan had fallen into place. But now it was here, and his body must perform the duties that he had long rehearsed, regardless of a directing mind almost paralysed with fear.

Whilst all eyes and minds had been preoccupied with the count's most recent victory, Taian and his companions had slipped beneath the canvas at the rear of his pavilion, finding this space quite empty except for two bored and frustrated guards assigned to watch over its contents. Turning from their places at the open front flap, they had seen Balian scrambling to his feet, made to draw their swords and opened their mouths to voice a challenge. It was into these positions that they were frozen as Balian exerted his will over them, hugely relieved to find that power remained at his fingertips. Within an instant, they had been toppled by Rayo and Jory, expertly gagged and bound by one of Jory's servants, whose previous service had been in the navy. They had only just been dragged roughly aside when the Count of Drumnestro strode in, laughing and joking with his friends and retainers. Their surprise at finding the pavilion already occupied lasted only as long as it took for Balian to render them immobile. Adala pulled the entrance flap across and peered through a narrow gap, to warn of any further approach. From here she could see the backs of three guards whose duty was to bar access to the pavilion, and beyond them stood Drumnestro's fine caparisoned charger with her grooms. There was no time to waste. Trumpets would announce the call to arms for the final contest, but before that the count must be stripped of his armour and Taian arrayed in it.

Twenty-Three

Callisto

Even as Drael and Ohk breathed their last in the high city, Mordanios was oppressed by a sense that something was amiss. Bardo and Cortesia hurried through streets almost deserted now, as Mordanios distractedly looked out over the early rounds of the jousting, barely aware of the dramas enacted before him.

'Are you alright, Mordanios?' asked Cresara, sitting down once more after rising to applaud one of her husband's victories. 'You look uncommon pale'.

'Very well, Ma'am', he said without conviction as a gathering tension developed in his frame.

His throat was dry and his palms moist as the contest drew towards its conclusion, and there was a curious yellow tinge at the periphery of his vision.

'I sense a challenge', said Yuzanid's voice within him, not wholly unexpected now. 'We must be alert'.

'I'm sure we must', murmured Mordanios aloud, blushing as the empress turned her wondering face towards him.

A huge cheer rose up, and there was a great drumming of feet that reverberated through the wooden stands beneath them as spectators thumped their feet in unison. Trumpets blew, banners waved bravely in the afternoon sun and the emperor and his opponent rode out into the lists, attendants around them in their gaudy livery. The emperor removed his helm to salute the crowd whilst the heralds read out the formal terms of the contest, disregarded by all, and a hush settled upon the great gathering of attentive citizens. Some were surprised to note that the Count of Drumnestro only raised his visor as he brought his lance up in the traditional gesture of respect, but the distance was too great for any to observe that the shaded features beneath that visor were not those of the count.

Taian felt that his body was not his own command, that every motion he made must fight against a paralysing reluctance of muscle and bone. Perhaps he had never felt true terror before, but now it rose up within him to drain his spirit and his strength. He felt that the weight of the lance in his right hand must drag him from his horse, and the ornate armour must surely soon crush him beneath it. Only success in this contest could offer the prospect of a broader victory, but even that notional triumph was shrouded in a vast uncertainty that no human eye could pierce.

At least Drumnestro's horse was quiet enough beneath him, having apparently seen no difficulty in the substitution of her rider. She responded readily to the urgings of rein and knees, apparently sensing nothing of the anxiety of the man who rode astride her. At the far end of the lists, the emperor awaited him, his gilded armour gleaming. A finely wrought effigy of Tio's golden winged lion glinted atop his helm, wings half-spread.

The people Taian would make his subjects were silent now as he urged his mount to the starting position, couched his lance in a way that had become automatic to him now and awaited the fall of the imperial banner that would signal the first pass. His pulse thudded in his throat, his bladder importuned him peevishly and his tongue lay dry in his mouth. Setting aside his vivid recollection of Adala's lips on his a few moments previously, the fear and the hope that mingled in her eye, he focused his mind on that banner beneath the imperial box, on the herald that brandished it. The man's liveried companion blew his trumpet, his cheeks inflating like purple veined balloons. The banner dropped, and a hundred thousand voices roared in unison. Taian's eye fell upon his opponent once more, whose lance dipped and who spurred his mount forward now with gathering speed, closing the distance with bewildering speed – as Taian did likewise.

'Come on now', he found himself murmuring, half to himself, half to the horse.

On so many occasions he had practised this art at Soangarten, so his body fell into a smooth pattern of familiar action and instinct supplied what conscious thought could not.

The emperor's form rose and grew alarmingly before him, swaying and lurching with the movement of his horse. The lance point that grew suddenly in his vision struck the edge of his shield and glanced off. Taian's found only air. He was past, unharmed, empty space before him, and he reined in his mount and swung her round panting for the second pass as the crowd's great cries and howls found their way to his ears, muffled by steel and by the padding inside his helm. Turning, bringing Canfel around the end of the tilt-rail, ready for the next pass, he spared a glance for his friends, picking them out at the far end of the tilt-yard. There was Adala, there Rayo, Jory and Balian, the latter's pale, round face turned towards the emperor as Triado readied himself.

'You're supposed to freeze him', muttered Taian under his breath. 'You said that you could freeze him'.

There was little time to reflect on the limitations of Balian's God-given powers. Another trumpet blast, another falling standard, and he was away once more, the sandy earth rushing beneath him as the two armoured warriors, as one with their mounts, hurtled towards each other. Once more, the emperor's lance found its mark, this time more securely, and Taian's glanced from his opponent's shoulder.

The tremendous, bone-jarring impact almost unseated him.

He gasped, cried out and somehow regained his balance during several precarious strides. The far end of the tiltyard loomed before him, and he brought Canfel to the walk, shifting his weight in the saddle and glancing about him at the anxious upturned faces of his friends through the steel slits of his visor.

'This time!' called Rayo, raising a clenched fist as Taian moved past to take up his starting position for the final attempt.

It was essential that he should unseat his opponent on this final pass. If he did not, the panel of judges would award the bout to he who had scored the most hits and whose technical performance was deemed to be superior. That was most unlikely to be Taian. He must prevail or be doomed.

There was Adala, dressed as a ludicrously beautiful page, her head pulled up beneath a cap, the ill-fitting clothes she had taken from Drumnestro's servant hanging loosely about her. The sight of her – her steady, serious eyes and the expression of earnest devotion on her face – filled him with an iron determination that had been absent before. A hard knot of intense ferocity came into his throat as Canfel approached the starting post once more, and he brought his lance down to the couch. He was almost oblivious to the noise now, the whole of his being focused on the lance point and those actions that must contribute to its guidance to the mark.

The banner came down, the trumpet blew and Taian surged forward with Adala's name upon his lips. Hoofs pounded beneath him, and the emperor surged huge into the field of his vision. Did that lance point waver? Was there a momentary lapse in control? The emperor's lance slid past. Taian's struck the emperor's shield full in the centre with a tremendous impact that almost unseated the prince.

In that glorious moment, as the horses passed each other, the emperor toppled from his saddle, his lance falling aside. The huge cheer of the crowd dinned in his ears as he brought Canfel to the walk once more and turned to survey the scene of victory. The emperor lay sprawled in the sand, struggling to sit up as servants and retainers hurried towards him.

Taian felt a hot surge of triumph in his veins as his friends rushed towards him, their faces wreathed in smiles.

'The victor!' roared the marshal of the games, raising his arms towards Taian, who dismounted with trembling legs that threatened to betray him.

There was only a moment to receive the congratulations of his friends, before they were urging him towards the victory podium beneath the imperial box. The emperor, helm removed, was already limping in that direction, waving at the crowd and doing his best to appear magnanimous in defeat, albeit a glint of fury raged in his eyes.

What do you think you're doing, Drumnestro, damn you?! was the question that resonated there.

More questions would soon be jostling that aside as Taian mounted the podium, his helm still in place, contrary to all practice and custom. A hush fell over the crowd in recognition of this strange circumstance. The emperor and the prince stood side by side now, heads tilted up to the imperial box and to the ranks of seats occupied by the leading nobles of the realm. There were the dukes, the counts, the dignitaries of the church, and there the commanders of the legions, all looking down expectantly as the two competitors stood before the marshal.

'Take off your helm, damn you', muttered the emperor, sotto voce. 'What on earth's the matter with you?'

The marshal was making the brief declaration of victory, his strident voice ringing out around the field, raising the wreath of gold leaves that most soon settle upon the victor's brow.

'You must take off your helm, sir', said the marshal in conclusion, and in an ordinary voice.

The time had come.

Taian felt surprisingly calm now. The adrenalin of action continued to course through his veins, but he felt fully in command of mind and body, and the speech that he had long rehearsed was there within reach of tongue and voice. Dimly, as his hands came up to lift away his helm, he was aware of his friends drawing up beneath the podium behind him, together with the emperor's own retainers. The helm rose up, as did a great gasp of dismay from those in the crowd close enough to remark the face thus exposed to view.

'It is the prince', called a few startled voices, piercing the resultant shocked silence.

The colour drained from the emperor's face.

'What?!' he cried. 'Arrest this man!'

No sooner had these words left his mouth than he was rendered as still as a statue. Guards and retainers, galvanised into sudden action, likewise found themselves frozen in the act of drawing swords and stepping forward. More importantly, a wave of supernatural power surged from the epicentre of Balian's form and rippled out through the crowd so that all were immediately stilled. Now was the time. Taian stepped forward.

'People of Erenor!' he roared, his voice echoing from the city walls beyond. 'I stand before you today as victor in this contest. But that is not all. I stand before you to embody the voice of justice and to cast down those who have unjustly and impiously raised themselves up to dominate this realm, those whose reign is built on the sand of treachery and lies. This is not your emperor', he cried, extending an accusative arm in Triado's direction. 'And she, she who sits enthroned there in all her avarice and pride, she has no right to call herself your empress'.

Balian felt as though he were entranced, barely aware of his immediate surroundings. A tiny part of him marvelled that his will and Tio's borrowed power had rendered such a vast crowd of his fellows utterly immobile. Another part, the greater part, strained to exert his will against the wills of all those who fought to cry out, or step forward, or lurch upwards from their seats. His will was prevailing, but for how long could he sustain it? His first attempts at deploying this power had left him conscious of the toll it took on him. This vast and profligate expenditure of his life-force must soon end in exhaustion and oblivion. It was as though he watched the sand of his existence falling through an hour-glass, faster and faster. He barely felt Adala brush past him as she hurried to her position beneath the podium.

Mordanios, his frame inhabited by the presence of his dark lord, was alone impervious to Balian's will. The doctor leapt up from his seat, eyes staring, as Taian's voice rang out.
'What?!'
'Everyone is frozen', cried Yuzanid's voice within him. 'Tio channels his power through someone'.
Mordanios, with Yuzanid peering through his own eyes, glared down at the podium, from where Taian was making his impassioned address.
A vibration ran through Mordanios, a sense that Yuzanid was exerting his own power to silence the prince.
'Damn!' cried Yuzanid in frustration. 'I may not affect him'.

'Can you free the empress?' asked Mordanios, glancing to where Cresara had her hand placed on her pregnant belly. 'There may be danger to her, to the child'.

'There may', agreed Yuzanid, causing Mordanios to feel another vibration of prickly heat traverse his frame.

This time, his power prevailed. The empress, jerked into sudden movement, gasped and glared about her in confusion.

'What?!' she began, her eyes wild. 'What is happening?'

'Make your way to the back of the stand and out into the way beneath the walls', urged Mordanios, placing his hand to her shoulder. 'You will be safer there'.

The empress looked into her doctor's eyes, made to speak, saw the red glint of Yuzanid there and fled, drawing up her skirts around her.

Mordanios was right. Beyond the sea of frozen faces there must be others still at liberty to move – guards and soldiers must even now be on their way to investigate this strange disturbance.

Taian's voice continued, raised in passion, describing how his own brother, heir to the throne, had been cut down through Triado's treachery, how a witness would come forward to confirm it in due course.

Mordanios, having watched for a moment as the empress made her way along an aisle and through a corridor out of sight, turned once more to the podium beneath. The prince must be silenced.

Yuzanid extended the doctor's hand in the emperor's direction and focused all available power on unfreezing him. It was hard. Mordanios was a narrow vessel to control, and he found the emperor's body clutched in an iron grip. He became conscious of another, a mortal, and beyond that mortal frame the divine power that controlled it. Tio. The hated brother. Now, more than ever, their contest was direct. Mordanios might be a

constricted vessel, but Tio's must exert his will against the combined resistance of a hundred thousand.
He pushed, he squeezed and set forth every particle of his strength... and began to prevail. There began a low murmur as a few in the more distant crowd started to regain their powers of speech and movement, although shock and fascination with the spectacle before them was sufficient to hold them in their places for now. The emperor, invisible to the prince, began to inch his hand towards the deadly poignard that hung at his belt, a slender shard of tapering steel designed to penetrate mail and the tender flesh beneath.

Adala, with two frozen musketeers in close attendance, looked up in horror towards where Mordanios stood at the rail of the imperial box. He could move! How could he move? Somehow, he was immune to Balian's power. More than that, he had his hand directed at the emperor. What was she seeing? Her eye darted to the target of that hand. Balian's power relented under Yuzanid's focused assault. The bonds that held the emperor snapped and he lurched into sudden motion.
'Taian!' cried Adala.
He stopped, mid-sentence, and swung round to thwart the emperor's thrust, even as the poignard darted towards the vulnerable spot beneath his left arm. Suddenly, they were wrestling awkwardly in their armour, each trying to push the other off balance. Taian, grunting and cursing, had his own poignard out, and each was jabbing and stabbing as opportunity dictated. Taian was strong and supple but lightly built. The emperor, although older, was thickset and powerfully muscled. Now there was a true contest of divinity. Rayo, Jory and their servants found themselves suddenly as immobile as the crowd, powerless to intervene.

'Two can play at that game, brother', laughed Yuzanid in Mordanios' throat.

A momentary stiffening in Taian's frame warned that Yuzanid sought to freeze him, too. Taking advantage, the emperor toppled his opponent, rolled over on top of him and laughed as he stabbed down at Taian's naked throat. Adala remained unfrozen, although a frisson of that attempt had passed along her spine. Rather, a sensation of delicious warmth came over her and a sudden calmness of mind.

Tio had entered her.

She turned quickly to the soldier who stood closest to her and reached for his musket. The match was already burning in the serpentine and there was priming in the pan. Easily, as though in slow motion, she found her muscles bringing the weapon up to her shoulder and her head moving so that her eye squinted along the barrel. That barrel swayed upward until the torso of Mordanios swam within her vision. Then she squeezed the trigger. There was a tremendous report, a gust of billowing smoke and Mordanios dropped backward, quite dead. Yuzanid's spell was instantly broken, his window on the world abruptly slammed shut. Taian gasped as the poignard approached his throat, twitched aside and thrust upward with his own weapon, taking the emperor in the armpit even as Balian's lock snapped back into place. The emperor's cry was abruptly cut off, and a dullness came into his eyes as Taian rolled his corpse aside.

Rayo and Jory rushed forward now, as did Adala, once she had tossed the heavy musket aside. Joy flooded through her as the power of Tio receded.

A few yards away, Balian was insensible to those emotions of relief. A darkness was closing on the periphery of his vision and he knew that his life force was almost exhausted, that death reached up to embrace him.

Within moments, he must release his grip on this great crowd, and then events would necessarily take their course. The emperor was dead. Perhaps his bodyguards would rush in to exact swift vengeance. Perhaps the victory he had contributed to was of the most transient and futile kind. And then, as the flame of his life dwindled, a notion came upon his diminishing spirit, a recollection of what Tio had said to him, almost as an afterthought. *It may be that you now have some ability to create illusions in the minds of others*, he had said. Tio came into his mind then and through that fading consciousness into the world beyond.

'The false emperor is dead and I shall take his place', declared Taian, rising to his feet and gazing up into the faces of the powers in the land. 'I demand your obedience. Tio wills it!'

Balian's diminishing strength let slip the bodies of the vast crowd then, but all eyes were immediately drawn to the centre of the tilt-yard. There, a hundred feet tall, stood Tio himself, in all his leonine glory, shaking out his mane and flexing his great wings, glittering, translucent but utterly magnificent – a sight that none who witnessed it would ever forget.

Cresara Rhovanion, she whose imperial husband was very shortly to breathe his last, hurried down the wooden stairs at the rear of the stand, holding in her hand the small knife that she habitually carried in case of adversity. And here was adversity. A great sorcery was at work and she must quickly seek the security of The Watch or of the emperor's guard. Everyone she had passed in the last hundred yards or so had been immobile, although others could be seen moving urgently beyond the rear of the stand, running, calling out, standing perplexed in small groups beneath the city wall. Her heart leapt as a file of watchmen came in sight.

As she swung round the corner of the staircase to the next flight, she found herself face to face with Bardo and Cortesia. She gasped, as did these sudden obstacles in her path, and then everything depended upon speed of reaction. Bardo, mouth half-open, moved instinctively to intercept the empress, having seen the glint of steel in her hand. Too late. Her recovery was more rapid, and the knife sunk into Bardo's flesh. Crying out, he slumped sideways, rebounded from the hand rail and tumbled down the stairs. Now she and Cortesia stood panting, eye to eye.

'You venomous bitch!' spat Cortesia, eye narrowed.

'Out of my way!' snapped Cresara, gesturing with her bloodied knife. 'Or you may feel this, too'.

'Never!' cried Cortesia, hurling herself at the empress in a frenzy of heedless rage.

Cortesia's hand seized Cresara's wrist, so that the knife, contested between them, swung wildly to and fro. With her other hand she clawed at the empress' face as the two of them lurched, stumbling down the stairs towards the narrow space of the landing. Cresara, somewhat taller, had the physical advantage, but Cortesia, whose mind was filled with the image of the dying Ohk, fought with a desperation borne of grief and hatred, regardless of the searing pain that still gripped her arms and shoulders.

The knife came down between them, and each strove to drive it into the other's belly, grunting, cursing, grimacing. Cresara, upon an impulse, reached up and strove to pull Cortesia's head scarf over her eye, thus blinding her.

For an instant this worked, but Cortesia, twisting her head here and there, freed herself from this obstruction, and Cresara found herself suddenly looking upon the naked horror of her erstwhile rival's face. This grim vision was what Cortesia had lived with for all these long years, a haunting recollection of what she had seen in the mirror when her friends had reluctantly brought one to her in the days after the attack. For Cresara it was a brutal shock. Others had reported to her the destruction of her rival's beauty, but she had never, herself, set eyes upon the consequences of her spite and her malice. Now her mind reeled, and disgust clawed at her stomach. A strange and unwelcome sensation obtruded itself upon her mind, one that had troubled her existence so rarely it was almost unrecognisable to her. Almost. It was guilt – and that guilt oppressed her with a sudden chill of muscle and sinew that rendered her momentarily quite still. It was enough. With a great yell of triumph, Cortesia turned the knife and drove it into Cresara's belly, watching with grim ferocity as the empress sank to her knees. She slumped forward, blood pooling about her as Cortesia stood gasping above. The moment was sufficient unto itself, a moment in which Cortesia's mind exulted and dwelt grimly on the justice she had delivered.

Bardo, hauling himself painfully to a sitting position, in order to probe the wound in his side, called out to her.

'Listen, Ma'am', he said. 'Listen'.

A great roar had gone up from the crowd upon those stands and on the bank on the far side of the tilt-yard. The thunderous drumming of feet reverberated in the timbers above them. A hundred thousand voices raised in unison.

'What are they shouting?' asked Cortesia, recovering her composure.

Bardo coughed and stretched his face into a grin.

'Long live Emperor Taian, Ma'am! Long live Emperor Taian!'

Epilogue

Prata - January 3994an

It was dusk, and a winter gale whipped froth from the wavetops that battered the black crags of the headland beneath the monastery. The wind moaned beneath the roofs in a manner that set superstitious fear in the minds of the ignorant and scoured the bleak hills and the stunted brush inland. Even with the fires banked up it was cold as Ureni sat at Adala's bedside, looking upon her pale face. The flickering lamp set on the table disclosed hollow eyes and sunken features. It would not be long, so the doctor had said.

'And what of Balian?' she asked. 'You did not say what became of Balian'.

'He was embraced unto the Lord', Adala said, her voice seemingly weaker from day to day, and little more than a whisper now. 'Exhausted, like a match that is burnt from end to end. At last, when the flame dies, there is nothing left but the wizened stem. So it was with Balian. We found him quite dead but with a seraphic smile on his face and an expression in his eyes that I hesitate to describe'.

'And Cortesia? She had her vengeance at last, it seems'.

'Surely she did. And her house became once more a centre of culture and learning in subsequent years. There was life beneath that roof once more, although Cortesia never recovered from the death of Ohk. I think she felt she owed it to him to turn her face to the sun once more and to embrace the light. She was...'

Adala's voice faded and she swallowed hard, her eyes turned upward.

'So, you became empress at last?' continued Ureni, when the duration of that silence became tiresome to her. 'And Prince Taian, emperor. How you must have exulted!'

'Oh, we did', agreed Adala, a shadow of a smile traversing her face. 'Certainly we did. Those were golden days indeed'.

She turned her head a little to look at Ureni and squeezed the hand that held hers.

'I treasure them'.

'They did not last, I collect', ventured Ureni.

'You know they did not last', sighed Adala. 'Or I would not be here present. Taian was an excellent husband, and I love him still with all my heart, but he was not made to be an emperor. His brother, unimaginative and dull as he was, would have made a better one. Taian lived only to burst the sweet grape of life against his palette and to dwell only in the moment. The necessary business of government left him cold and depressed his spirits to a remarkable degree. Naturally, he appointed strong ministers to lift the burden of state from his shoulders'.

Adala paused and her eyes moved from Ureni's to the ceiling, where cobwebs stirred in the chill air. Ureni knew that Taian's appointments had been unwise, that he had listened to voices that set personal ambition above loyalty.

'But Taian could see only that his days were set free for feasting or the hunt. And for me, of course. We had wonderful times together. Such days...'

After a while, Adala turned her gaze upon Ureni once more.

'But it did not please Tio that I should be with child. It is not for us mortals to discern his great plan, of course, but it was hard for us. And with each passing year, it became harder. There were those who muttered that the security of the realm demanded that the emperor should have an heir. I was barren, they said, and so those same voices argued that I should be set aside and that he should take another to be his wife. I was only a tavern-girl, was the objection I saw in their eyes and that I heard in the whispers of the court. Tio required a nobler vessel in which to nurture an imperial child, it was said. My womb was judged unworthy, by earth and by heaven alike. So they murmured'.

Adala's eyes filled with tears, and Ureni squeezed her hand, like a bundle of warm, dry sticks by this late stage in her progress towards the grave.

'That must have been very hard, Ma'am', she said at last, when the silence became unbearable.

'You cannot imagine', sighed Adala. 'If Taian had had loyal friends to support him, he may have found the strength to resist, but Rayo was killed, of course, in that accident on the polo field, and Jory entered the church. He was greatly altered by the events of that wondrous day, those days, and I suppose he was of a naturally pious disposition. Still, we missed him, and his monastery was far distant from The City'.

'How did you feel? The divorce, I mean.'

'I was distraught, as you may imagine. The Duke of Vollangor, leader of council by this time, brought forward his own youngest daughter and proposed her as a match. The blood of the Starcorids barely tinged her veins, but it was enough, they deemed'.

'It is said that the Empress Serakis is a proud, unyielding woman', observed Ureni.

'Certainly she is', agreed Adala. 'Surpassingly meek until the lion ring was on her finger and thereafter a vain, imperious bitch, jealous of her status and her name. Taian assured me, all assured me, that this marriage would be one of convenience only, that he would spend only enough time with the girl to plant his seed within her'.

'But you were deceived?'

'No sooner had she settled her broad rump on the throne than she began to insist upon her prerogatives. It was intolerable that the emperor should devote himself to

this barren child of the humble masses, in neglect of her own needs and to the scandal of the court. They tried to prevent him from even seeing me'.
'You must calm yourself, Ma'am', said Ureni as Adala lifted herself in agitation from the pillow, cheeks flushed. 'I can see the recollection is painful to you'.
'Painful beyond my power to describe', retorted Adala, lapsing into silence, settling back onto the pillow once more, her breathing recovering its usual pattern now.
'A child was born, of course, the darling of the court', continued Adala at last. 'And then it became still more difficult for Taian and I to be together. Vollangor dominated the council, his position as grandfather to the heir to the throne underpinning his power now. Taian had become no more than a cipher, almost irrelevant to the governance of the state. At last, Taian was persuaded to abdicate, to step aside so that his formidable father-in-law could rule in the name of the infant prince'.
'And he accepted. All know this'.
'He did. And we thought that then we might live together in peace as we had always wished, as man and wife'.
'But that was not to be', prompted Ureni.
'It was not. An ex-emperor, whatever his calibre, whatever his inclinations, remains a threat. Vollangor feared that his enemies would seek to use Taian as a figurehead by which to advance their own cause'.
'That was nonsense, of course', said Ureni sadly. 'From what you have told me'.
'Taian never sought power', continued Adala. 'He was a child in the world. They seized him and they put out his eyes, his dear, dear eyes, so that...'
Adala could not continue, and her face reddened, crumpled and tears traversed her cheeks. She sobbed.
'Because only a whole man may be emperor', observed Ureni.

'Yes', agreed Adala between sobs, recalling how Taian had come to her, to tell her that his blinding would be the end of their travails, that at last they might be together undisturbed.

'I do not need my eyes to love you', he had said. 'And your image is emblazoned in my heart for all time'.

She could hear it now, the brave gloss he placed on cruel necessity.

'And the act was done with such savagery that he died of it', said Ureni. 'Curse their names'.

'So here we are', said Adala, eyes closed, when it seemed almost certain that she had lapsed into sleep once more. 'You and I, brought together by my exile, for Vollangor and the empress would not countenance my presence in The City. Guilt is best placed at a distance, it is said, and this bleak isle is the inevitable place of exile for those The City would forget'.

She squeezed Ureni's hand.

'And your exile is almost at an end, my dear'.

Ureni made regretful noises, noises of a denial that they both knew to be a lie. Only hours since, Adala's doctor had emerged to say that it would be soon. She floated on a sea of drugs, he said, but soon they would bear her down.

For a while, Adala seemed to stare at the ceiling and then she began to hum a song in a small voice, almost inaudible to her companion.

'I do not regret', she said. 'I'm sure there are many lives that never know even a moment of the joy I knew. I will always have that. Always. In this life and the next. It was never in Taian's nature to be an emperor and to rule over men, and it was never in mine to turn from the path that my heart showed to me'.

Adala was quiet then, murmuring only a few more words in the next hour that was her last. Finally, the lamp flickered and Ureni turned in alarm, sensing that another stood at her shoulder. There was nothing to be seen when she turned her head, although a sudden icy chill prompted her to gasp and to make the sign of Tio. When, after a moment, she returned her gaze to her friend, it was to find that those eyes were empty, almost staring beyond her. Her body was quite still now, lips curved in a gentle smile. Ureni murmured a prayer and leant forward to close those eyes.

When, after quiet reflection, she rose to leave the chamber, Adala's last words hung in her mind, murmured so quietly that her servant must lean close to her mouth in order to hear.

'It is not given unto man for each to be a giant', she had said. 'Whatever the urging of vanity or pride. Rather, the soul should see the clear truth; that which the deep heart knows'.

Interlude

Yuzanid and Tio regarded the slowly turning globe pensively as the bisecting light of a new day crept across the continents and oceans, leaving the darkness of night in its wake. Yuzanid stroked his chin and turned to his brother.

'I suppose I should offer congratulations'.

'I suppose you should'.

'I had not seen that coming. You played your pieces well'.

'Pieces, brother? You call them pieces, these mortals who are destined to embody our game, these mortals who are destined to give up the sparks of their souls, to shed their life's blood to encompass it?'

'Oh, come on! Am I supposed to join you in weeping for those whose little lights we snuff out to further our ends? Am I supposed to join them in their foolish credulity? Am I supposed to believe you care one jot for their little lives and passions? You move them hither and thither on the game board as ruthlessly as do I, and if they perish to advance your cause, then so be it. Am I not right, brother?'

'You are certainly correct to point out that I will take whatever measures are necessary to prevent your shadow from falling irreversibly across the souls of men like this one'.

He indicated the creeping terminator line on the globe before them.

'And if that means that the blood of my people must be shed, well that is what I must endure. But if you imagine that I share your own callous indifference, well you are mistaken. Surely, my adherents may wonder at the apparent perversity and capriciousness of the heavens, but then they are unable to perceive the bigger picture, aren't they, the full magnificence, the full spatial and temporal scope of this eternal game we play? A game in which I have gained an advantage, you will allow. My empire is strengthened, set more securely on its course'.

'For now', grunted Yuzanid. 'You raise up your darlings and you cast them down as it suits you. You mentioned *love at first sight* when last we met. I see its significance now. I should have been less obtuse. I should have taken the hint you offered there and looked more perspicaciously for your machinations. Hmm. I concede to you this slight victory, this present contest. But there will be others. Oh yes, there will be others'.

He smiled a grim smile and turned to look his brother in the eye.

The Song of Ohbrid-Part (trans. Eudokios)

The earth lies cold and dark beneath the night
And flowers hold their petals in repose,
To turn their questing faces to the light,
When dawn shall paint the lilies and the rose.
But now the Maiden dreams within a glade,
Her hair entwined with fragrant myrtletine,
Embracing every heavy-scented braid
That frames the slumb'ring countenance divine.
The coming dawn now tinges eastern sky
And treads the further shores of her domains,
Advancing to surmount the mountains high
And overspill to flood the darkling plains.
The Maiden stirs and looks towards the skies,
Where Zah comes rising brilliant in the east
And tilts her face and shades her peerless eyes
To see the surly grip of night released.
He steps down from his chariot with pride,
His warmth and glory shining all around,
To plump the wheat and warm the furrows wide,
His radiant brow with golden sun beams crowned.
The Maiden feels a heat within her breast
And says, 'How much I mourn when you are fled,
To see your chariot sink into the west,
Your ruddy immolation as you tread
The shining path that circles both our thrones.
I mourn to see the shadows growing long
And feel the chill night gather in my bones,
Lament your dismal passing in my song'.
Says he, 'It is my pleasure to ascend
The azure heavens that encircle all
To look upon your face is to transcend
The bounds of joy, and hold my heart in thrall
So do not take the lily for your wreath,
Despair not at the dying of the light,

Or set your face to anguish or to grief,
For surely does the day succeed the night'.

Printed in Great Britain
by Amazon